Wings of Madness

Wings of Madness

Gus Wheeler FBI Thriller

R. John Dingle

TULE
PUBLISHING

Dedication

For Mom. You would have loved all of this.

Today I felt pass over me a breath of wind from the wings of madness.

—Charles Baudelaire

Chapter One

MICHELLE TOWNSEND SLOWLY awoke, her mind foggy, sluggish. The smell of rotten eggs and the sour stench of ammonia hung in the air and she winced. Her teeth were chattering, and her outstretched arm had become wrapped in goosebumps. The side of her face was numb so she peeled her eyes open to find she was lying on a dirt floor. She tried to remember how she'd gotten there but her thoughts were fuzzy, disjointed. Low humming came to her from behind and she froze. Michelle recognized the melody but couldn't place it until a man's voice softly sang its signature line.

"Hmm, hmm, hmm … Panama!"

Her breathing quickened, and she blinked her eyes several times, struggling to clear the fog. She surveyed everything within her limited field of vision, careful to not move and alert him to being awake. The walls around her were made of large stones and were damp and mossy. The far corner was dark, as were the rafters above; the only light, dim and porous, arcing along the dirt in front of her.

She heard the man clear his throat followed by the sound of a mechanical click and a bright light spread into her field of vision. The faint sound of a woman moaning reached her ears and as the light flickered, she realized it was coming from a television or screen of some sort. The woman's screams rang out louder and louder until she began to cry for her life then it stopped and the light was gone.

Michelle's eyes strained upward and she saw a doorway several feet away. She desperately tried to see something beyond its threshold, anything to get a sense of where she was or what was out there, but only saw the pitch black of darkness. She knew she had one shot at escape, and only if she could move quickly. Her feet were bare so she stretched her toes slowly and they seemed to move normally. Bending her fingers on the hand by her side, she found they too moved normally. She would have to trust that she could get her legs moving well enough to make it to the door and out.

She heard the loud sticky sound of tape being pulled from its roll and fear gripped her. It was now or never, she knew it. She took a deep breath and pushed her chest from the dirt then pulled her knees and legs beneath her. Suddenly she was standing and wobbling toward the black doorway, her frantic, watery eyes struggling to take it all in. She barely made it to the door before her legs gave out and she fell against the wall beside it.

"Oh, good. You're awake," said the man from behind her.

Michelle turned to him and gasped at what she saw. He had odd-looking, telescopic night vision goggles pushed up on his forehead and a compact GoPro video camera taped to a strap around her head like a miner's lamp. He gestured toward the doorway.

"Go ahead. Run," he said, his voice light, breezy and he was smiling as if joking with a friend.

Michelle saw him sway slightly to the side and it gave her hope she could get away if her legs would just steady.

She leaned into the door frame and screamed as loud and long as she could. "*Helllllp*!!!!! Somebody *helllllllp*!" Her voice quickly became raspy, and she swallowed hard at what little saliva she had.

"Ch…" He chuckled. "No one's gonna hear ya."

She looked in his direction over a shoulder. "Why are you doing this to me?" she cried.

"Play stupid games. Win stupid prizes."

She turned back toward the dark doorway. "*Hellllp*!!!" she screamed again. "*He's got me! Help!*"

She heard the crunching of his footsteps in the dirt so turned back to him. He was now standing in the center of the room directly beneath a single lightbulb dangling from the rafters. He tipped his head toward the door.

"But go ahead. Run." He dared her, the light, playful tone in his voice replaced with a darker, more sinister version.

Michelle shuffled into the doorway and looked left, then right, but couldn't see a thing. Her cloudy mind tried to work out what to do but kept coming up short. She turned back to her captor and watched as he reached a hand up and pulled the tattered string dangling from the lightbulb. And all went black.

"I said … *run*."

Chapter Two

<u>Friday</u>

- ✓ Charge GoPro
- ✓ Zip ties
- ✓ New battery
- ✓ Duct tape
- ✓ Goggles
- ✓ Cables
- ✓ Lightbulb
- ✓ Smelling salts
- Leave prize
- Take out trash
- Get replacement
- TV dinners
- New movie

Chapter Three

TAYLOR PUSHED THROUGH the metal bar on the side
door to the club and stepped into the alley, his soda
water spilling onto his hand as he did so. Kicking over a
small rock, he propped the door open a crack and slid his
cup onto the rim of a dumpster. He wiped his hand on his
jeans then, brushing unruly bangs aside, fumbled a cigarette
from his pack and lit it.

He took a long, soothing pull and watched its end crackle a brilliant red as the smoke warmed his lungs. Bending a
leg, he pressed his foot against the tacky brick wall behind
him to steady himself. A familiar song of the headlining band
oozed through the crack in the door and its percussion felt
good against his shoulders and back.

Taylor's band was the opening act and had finished their
set a while ago, but his ears were still ringing from the amps.
He thought of the mistakes he'd made during the show like
he used to do when first starting out, and it felt good to do
so. He would dissect them more later, figuring out how to
correct each one and would be proud when he did. But for
now, he simply thought of the cheers. The crowd had been
into it like he'd not seen in a long time, roaring louder and
louder with each guitar riff. And Philip-the-Tip-Jar was full,

which was good. He needed to do better if he was going to make it back to the New Orleans jazz scene, but this was a start. Baby steps.

He thought of all those years and sessions with his jazz professors at Loyola and how they'd scowl at the slightest mistake and make him do it again. Not only was he now playing his electric bass almost exclusively—that alone would make his professors cringe—but he was in an '80s cover band. But at least he made charts for the set tonight, unlike in the past where he'd just play his way through, watching the guitar player and hoping he'd guess what the next chord was before it happened. He thought back to a time when he'd spent an entire year, transcribing Charlie Parker solos on his upright, and now he had to play "Once Bitten Twice Shy" for drunken lawyers reliving their glory days. *But not for long*, he vowed to himself. He would do better. It was time.

He heard the muffled chime of an alarm and pulled his phone from his back pocket. It was ten p.m., time for his meds. He fished the small orangish-brown bottle from his front pocket and read the label to be sure he'd grabbed the right one. THORAZINE TABLETS. 100 MG 3X PER DAY. He popped a pill into his mouth and washed it down with a gulp of his soda water. The music suddenly got louder and Taylor realized the side door had been pushed open. Leon—the guitar player in his band and Taylor's closest friend—stepped out.

"Hey, last call." Leon was a tall, sturdy man with dark features, light eyes, and the disjointed nose that could only come from years of playing ice hockey.

Taylor squinted at the medicine bottle cupped in his hand. A bright red sticker beside the label read AVOID ALCOHOL. He slid the bottle back into his pocket and pushed off the wall.

"I guess I can have one."

Leon slipped back inside as Taylor took his drink from its perch and downed it in one gulp. He tossed the plastic cup into the dumpster then stubbed out the cigarette and put it back in his pack for later. He put his hand around the door's edge when something farther down the alley caught his attention. He squinted into the darkness.

"Anyone there?" he yelled, his voice rising at the end and echoing back to him.

He concentrated hard, trying to make out the shape of the person he thought he'd seen. But after staring at the same dark spot for nearly a minute nothing moved and no one answered so Taylor slipped back inside.

The headlining band had taken its first break, so a familiar Poison song played loudly from the overhead speakers. Taylor found an open spot at the end of the bar and was met by the bartender, Marjorie Jacobsen. MJ was an older woman with bottle-bleached hair and kind eyes highlighted with heavy Elvira-like mascara. A girl from the '80s, MJ seemed to know the lyrics to every song played in the club and regularly sang along with them as she slung drinks.

She pointed a finger at Taylor. "T, last call." MJ's lips were outlined with the small wrinkles of a lifetime smoker. "Can I getcha anything, honey?"

"Think I'll have a draft."

"Comin' up."

She went to the taps at the far end of the bar as a beautiful blonde woman filled the open space beside Taylor. Catching MJ's attention, she waved her hand in the air as if writing something.

"You guys were really good." said the woman, resting her arms on the barstool next to his.

Taylor glanced her way, and once he realized she was speaking to him straightened his stance. "Ehhh." He smiled shyly. He recalled his girlfriend in college telling him that his lazy smile turned her into putty. "It's only '80s and '90s rock. Not that hard."

She smiled and her glassy eyes lit up. She had high, pronounced cheekbones, beautifully radiant skin, and a small mole just above her lip that reminded Taylor of Cindy Crawford.

"It may be easy for you but it looks pretty difficult for the rest of us. The crowd loved it."

"Thanks." he said, "I'm Taylor." He extended his hand and his smile.

She looked at his hand and her mouth opened slightly to expose perfect white teeth. "A true gentleman. I'm Sadie." Her hand was soft and warm.

Taylor struggled to read the situation. Was this woman flirting with him? It'd been a minute since he had to put any effort into … this.

He tipped his head in a thank-you. "Nice to meet you, Sadie." He pronounced her name slowly, stretching it out, as if concentrating to get it right.

"My dad was actually in a band in the '80s and they were good, but not as good as you guys." She picked up her phone from the bar. "You guys on Spotify?"

He hesitated, searching for a reply. He could feel they had a real connection and didn't want to stuff up.

"Not yet." he lied. "We're trying to figure out the best path for our original material." She nodded as if she understood. "Can I buy you a drink?" he asked.

Her smile remained but she eyed him for several moments, weighing her response, then went about signing her check. He took a sip of the beer MJ slid in front of him, carefully eyeing Sadie's soft cheeks, her beautiful jawline, her tender neck. He hadn't scratched that itch in a while; he was due. A tap on his shoulder pulled him from his thoughts and he turned to see Leon standing there.

"Hey," Leon said, before turning his attention to Sadie. "Hi, I'm Leon."

A loud guitar riff filled the air as the band started their next set. Leon and Sadie laughed at the interruption before the volume of the music was lowered by the techs at the control board.

"I'm Sadie."

The band's drummer, Mick Preston, stepped beside Leon. He was noticeably older than his bandmates and did everything imaginable in hopes of closing the age gap. He wore black skinny jeans, had an array of artsy-looking bracelets covering his wrist, and multiple rings on each hand. He flicked long fly-away hair from his face as he slid three shots of tequila onto the bar. He and Leon each took one and popped it down. Taylor hesitated, thinking of the early morning he'd planned for tomorrow to practice on his upright. But seeing Sadie smiling at the others, he quickly knocked his back and slid the shot glass beside the others.

Leon held up his hand. "That's it for me, Mick. I gotta make it home."

Mick then wiped the sides of his mouth with a finger and thumb and, turning his attention to Sadie, said, "Hi. I'm Mick … the drummer. You know"—he began to tap his hand on the bar—"the one that sets the tempo just right."

Sadie eyed Mick for a moment then her eyes widened as if she'd just recognized him. "Oh, I know you." she said, matching his smile. "You're the one that overplayed most of the songs and came in too early after Taylor here's one and only solo."

Mick's smile evaporated and his jaw tightened. He gulped the last of his beer and slid the plastic cup onto the bar.

"Bitch," he said just loud enough for the others to hear then turned to Leon. "You coming?"

Leon shook his head, "Nah, I'm good." Mick headed for the door and Leon looked back to Sadie. "Sorry. That's our older but much less mature friend."

Sadie mock pouted. "He's dusty." Leon and Taylor smiled and she continued. "Taylor was just telling me about your band. You really should get your original material on Spotify, get your name out there."

"Original material." Leon repeated with curiosity. "We're trying," he added then turned to Taylor. "I can drop the van and gear at your house if you want."

Taylor looked around the bar at all the women drinking and dancing and casually glanced over at Sadie. She was scrolling on her phone, its light illuminating her soft features, but hadn't made any attempt to leave.

"Nah, I got it."

"It was nice meeting you, Sadie." Leon said as he turned to leave.

"You as well," she replied then turned back to her phone.

Leon leaned in closer to Taylor. "You good?"

"Dunno." Taylor looked at Sadie with hungry eyes. "But I might be."

Chapter Four

Three Weeks Later

G US SET HIS upright bass carefully into the velvet slot of its case and wiped the strings down one last time before he tucked the hand rag beside it and closed the lid. He was backstage after his set at Scullers Jazz Club in Boston, lost in his thoughts as he replayed the set again and again in his mind. He thought he crushed it but still sought areas he could improve. Realizing the murmurs of the crowd milling around in the hall had grown louder, he looked up to see Mel standing in the open doorway. She wore a cream-colored silk blouse untucked over dark jeans and her well-worn Blundstone boots.

Mel placed her long leather jacket on the back of a chair and, stepping to him, raked her hair behind an ear. "Hon, you were fantastic." She beamed, draping an arm over his shoulder. She pushed a rebellious curl away from his eye with her fingers then rolled onto the balls of her feet and gave him a passionate kiss. The two embraced for a long moment before she leaned back and looked up at him with her dark sultry eyes. "That was your best show yet."

Gus had been asked to sub for Wynton Marsalis's long-time bass player, Carlos Henriquez, after he'd suffered appendicitis during a tour date in New Jersey a few weeks before. Mel had gone to each show since as the Marsalis tour wove its way through Maryland, DC, New York, and, finally, Boston. Tonight's performance was the last of the tour.

"Thanks, but I think you might be a bit biased." He smiled as he always did when Mel was in his arms.

She squinted an eye and her dimples melted his heart. "Maybe just a little."

Gus and Mel had been a couple for just over a year and there were days he still marveled she was with him. She had started a technology firm then sold it, traveled the world over, and had lived in Australia for many years. She had excelled at everything she'd done. Gus studied Jazz, lived below the poverty line as a musician for many years before getting adventurous and moving to Boston. If Gus's parents hadn't joined the Peace Corps and moved overseas, he might've found himself living in their basement.

At first, he chalked their relationship up to the two of them sharing a traumatic experience after Gus had saved her life from a psychotic mad woman Mel once thought to be a friend. But there was more to their relationship, much more, and Gus quickly found himself truly in love with Mel and had been elated to learn she felt the same.

"Hey, remember I won't be home tonight. I'm going to get Fred so I'll stay with Mr. T." she said, referring to her rambunctious yellow Labrador retriever and her adopted father, Mr. Turner.

Mel had built an apartment onto her house in her

hometown of Kendalton for Mr. T but with Gus living in Charlestown, she found herself rarely staying there these days. She felt guilty at times for not spending more time with Mr. T and still had a few childhood friends there, but given the events that led to Gus saving her life, she had slowly drifted apart from them.

"Okay, but hurry home tomorrow," he said, putting her down. "I've been on the road for weeks, and you and I need some chill time at home alone. I told Jeff I'd need the next few days off so we have no plans until you head to Geneva on Thursday."

Mel hadn't worked a traditional job since selling her company several years ago but she still remained on a few boards of directors which took her to some far off places.

"That sounds perfect." Her right hand moved to the side of Gus's face and with a finger she gently traced the thin, hairless line from the tip of his ear to the crown of his head; a scar left from a bullet graze courtesy of the killer he'd saved Mel from.

"Battle scars," he whispered.

Mel nodded slowly, her eyes drawing him in. "Battle scars."

They were about to kiss again when there was a knock on the door. The band's drummer leaned in the open doorway. He wore a tight, short-sleeved collared shirt exposing arms completely covered with tattoos.

"Sorry, guys. Gus there's some guy at the bar asking for you."

They'd each turned to the drummer, Gus with his arm

around Mel's waist. "What's his name?"

The drummer shook his head, "Dunno. Sorta chunky guy, hair cut short so no one can see it's thinning. He's talking like a fan, but he's got the vibe of a fed."

Gus sighed and he and Mel both spoke simultaneously, "Jeff."

"Thanks, brother," Gus said as the drummer slipped back into the club.

Mel tapped his chest with an open palm and raised an eyebrow, "Tell Jeff I said hi. I'll text you when I leave Mr. T's tomorrow morning. Love you."

"Love you back." he said as Mel too slipped back out the door.

Gus finished packing up his bass then made his way to the bar where he saw his friend and head of the FBI's Boston office, Jeff Cattagio, talking to a waitress waiting for her tray to fill with drinks from the bartender.

"Hey," Gus said, sliding his phone onto the bar and moving Jeff's coat from the empty stool next to him. "You see the show?" He draped the coat over the back of Jeff's stool and sat.

"I did. It was great. Those cats can play."

The drummer was sitting behind Jeff farther down the bar and Gus caught his raised eyebrow at Jeff's comment.

Jeff leaned back into his stool and slung his arm over its back. "How was the tour?"

Gus told him about some of the shows they did and of the crowds they played for. He talked of hanging with Wynton and the band and of some of the crazy and funny times they had on the road. And when Gus was done, Jeff was laughing with him at all the stories.

"Sounds like a great time."

"It was."

Gus's phone buzzed and they both looked at it. On its screen was a short text from Jessica below a picture of the cartoon character Jessica Rabbit from the movie *Who Framed Roger Rabbit*. Jeff slowly turned to Gus with a look of confusion.

"It's Vanessa," Gus said. "She keeps changing her contact name and photo in my phone." He turned his screen toward Jeff. "This is her latest. You shoulda seen some of the looks I got from Wynton and the band."

"Why don't you change it?"

"I did at first, but she keeps changing it anyway, so I gave up." Gus cleared the text and, putting his phone face down on the bar, looked back to Jeff.

He knew Jeff was up to something; he just didn't know what. Gus and Jeff had been friends since they were roommates at Loyola University in New Orleans over a decade ago. So Gus had a long history of knowing when Jeff was working him. Gus's smile faded and he caught his friend's eye.

"So, c'mon, fess. Why're you really here? Last time I checked you were either at a kids' ball game or home having movie night with the fam on a Sunday."

Jeff lost his smile and ran his fingers through his short, wispy hair; a tick he did when he was stressed.

"We caught a new case."

"I'm not back until Thursday. That was the deal."

Years ago, when Jeff became director of the FBI's Boston office, Gus was still struggling to make ends meet in New Orleans, pursuing his dream of becoming a professional jazz musician. So Jeff offered Gus a spot in the FBI's training program and a path to a steady and reliable income. Gus refused over and over until, finally, Jeff agreed to let him have the ability to take sabbaticals when important gigs came up that could propel his music career to the next level.

"Yeah, about that."

Gus put his hand up in a stop gesture. "Dude, we had a deal." he said, chewing slowly through each word. "Four weeks."

"I know that's what we said but…"

"But nothing," Gus interrupted.

He thought about Mel leaving for Geneva on Thursday and the idea of not spending time with her before she left soured his stomach.

Jeff leaned forward so that just the two of them could hear what he said next. "Gus, this one looks tough."

"Give it to V," Gus said, referring to his partner Vanessa. "She can catch me up when I'm back. And, hell, we both know she should be leading her own cases by now anyway."

Jeff let out a long, theatrical sigh. "This one's … different." When Gus didn't object again, Jeff continued. "Two women in Pawtucket Falls, murdered a few months apart. Both found in fields but only after weeks of weather and wildlife so no trace and nothing to go on. The second woman was missing for three weeks and just found this afternoon. We got the call earlier. They said a third woman's gone missing with the same MO; they think she might be vic number three."

"Horrible, for sure, but why me? What's so special about this one that someone else can't handle?" His voice was rich with disdain.

"Each of the women were last seen in the downtown live music area, Music Row. They think someone may be prowling it." He paused and looked around, "If that's true, no one can navigate that world like you."

Gus clenched his jaw and followed Jeff's eyes around the club. The place was still packed, and everywhere he looked he saw people laughing and reliving the live band they'd just experienced. He thought of the drummer making fun of Jeff trying to fit in with this crowd. *He's talking like a fan, but he's got the vibe of a fed.* Jeff was right; not everyone could navigate this world. He exhaled long and slow, mostly for Jeff's benefit.

"The case file on the server?"

Jeff nodded. "What there is of it, yeah."

"You fuckin' owe me for this, Cattagio."

Jeff donned a shitty grin that Gus wanted to slap off his face.

Irritated, he jutted his chin toward his boss. "What the fuck you smiling at?"

"That's exactly what Vanessa said you'd say."

Chapter Five

NIFTY THRIFTY WAS a used clothing store at the corner of School and Maple Streets in Pawtucket Falls. Just inside Memorial Square, one of the Falls' eight neighborhoods and arguably its most dangerous, the shop was fortified with an iron fence and gate, as well as bars on each of its doors and windows. Nifty's had been around as long as Taylor could remember; he had childhood memories of running through its racks of clothes with his older sister while his mother did their back-to-school shopping. Taylor lived on the corner of Bowers and Mt. Vernon Streets, further into the heart of Mem Square but just two blocks from the shop. So, when he had moved back home and was looking for work to get him by until he got established in the music scene, a part-time job at Nifty's was a logical solution. That was three years ago.

It was a Monday morning and the shop had yet to open. Taylor stood at one of the display tables, refolding stacks of sweaters and long-sleeved shirts rummaged through by harried crowds. Weekends at Nifty's were usually very busy, so Monday morning was often filled with restocking and organizing the shop, the type of mindless routine Taylor needed after this past weekend. He and Leon and Mick had hit the clubs hard, and Taylor wasn't used to that anymore.

He nursed a cup of burnt coffee from the old pot in the kitchen, listening mindlessly to a show on the television mounted to the wall by the register. His coworker, Luanne, had gotten in before him so had dibs on the remote and had chosen a reality fashion show. Luanne might've looked like a guy—with that short, cropped hair and the piercings and tats—and she might've acted like one of the guys, but her television preferences were straight-up female.

Taylor hadn't slept well at all last night, a trend that was quickly becoming the norm. So, as he went about his mundane tasks, his tired mind turned inward. He thought about the jazz gig he played last week—the first in the three years since he'd moved home—and how great it felt. He knew when he left New Orleans to come back and care of his ailing mother that jazz gigs around the Falls area would not be the norm, and that he'd have to supplement his income with other music. But Taylor had fallen back into some bad habits from his younger years. And before he realized it, he was drinking and smoking pot regularly again and playing almost exclusively in an '80s and '90s rock cover band. Not because he wanted to, but because it was easy. And he couldn't even remember the last time he'd picked up his upright bass, let alone played a gig with it.

But then, a few months ago, his mother's dementia be-came too much for him alone to care for her, so he'd gotten her into a facility for the care she needed. And, finally freed from providing twenty-four-seven care, Taylor decided it was time he climbed out of the rut he'd been in for years and made a plan to get back to New Orleans and the career he'd left behind. And, to him, that jazz gig was the first meaningful step toward realizing his dream again, and he was not going to blow it.

He finished folding a shirt then took another hit of coffee. His mind skipped to his conversation with his sister Susie the day before. Susie lived in California with her husband and two kids and hadn't seen their mother for nearly four years. She couldn't fathom how frail their mother had gotten, and Susie certainly couldn't comprehend the sacrifices Taylor had made to move home and care for her. So he wasn't surprised when she scoffed at the idea of loaning Taylor the money he needed to move back to New Orleans.

Susie was living in la-la land in Taylor's view; a nice house, a husband that made a great living as a partner at a law firm, her oldest daughter in a private school, her youngest looked after by a nanny for parts of the day. And, still, she complained about them not having the money to bring their children to Europe for the summer. So, when the conversation got around to how much Taylor had spent over the past several years maintaining their childhood home and caring for their mom, he knew the answer to his request for some financial help before he even asked it. And when he explained that he was living so close to the edge that he didn't even have Wi-Fi, she actually laughed and told him that was a first-world problem. She then began to rant about her neighbors still driving gasoline-powered cars and Taylor knew he'd lost her. He'd have to try again next time, maybe in the afternoon after she'd had her first glass of chardonnay.

Finished with the men's shirts, Taylor moved to the next table and began rearranging the women's. His mind drifted to the band and their practice tomorrow night. He was looking forward to it. He'd even thought of a few songs from the Goo Goo Dolls they could add to their set. Their bassist, Robby Takac, played his upright on a number of songs and Taylor had practiced each of them a few nights ago.

Taylor noticed that the show Luanne had chosen finally ended. *There is a god.* After a few commercials, the morning news came on with the lead story of a woman having been found murdered in a field in the nearby town of Dracut. And when they put a picture of the woman on the screen Taylor choked on his coffee.

"There's gotta be something better on than this," Luanne said as she picked up the remote.

"Wait!" Taylor held up a hand and stepped next to her to see the TV better. The murdered woman was a beautiful blond with high, pronounced cheekbones and a bright smile. He might not have immediately recognized her if it weren't for the small mole just above her lip. Staring back at him was Sadie, the woman he met at the bar after his gig a few weeks ago.

"Turn it up," he said, his eyes glued to the screen.

"You know her?"

He put up his hand so he could listen to the news report.

"… confirmed the victim as Sadie Hogan, age twenty-three, of Billerica. She was last seen with friends at a live music club in downtown Pawtucket Falls three weeks ago and was reported missing the following morning. Police have notified the victim's family and have confirmed this is being treated as a homicide. News Center Six has learned that this case is thought to be connected to the murder of Michelle Townsend whose body was found in a field in Tyngsboro several months ago. Ms. Townsend was also last seen with friends at a club in Pawtucket Falls downtown, spurring speculation that there's a predator preying on women in the Pawtucket Falls area known as Music Row. Ms. Townsend's murder remains unsolved. Police have set up a hotline..."

Taylor felt Luanne's glare and, suddenly feeling paranoid, he looked away from the TV. Countless specks of dust flickered in the shaft of sunshine slicing between them.

"*Phew*, no." He wiped his forehead and shook his head. "For a minute there, she looked like one of my sister's friends from high school."

Luanne brought up the guide and clicked through it for something to watch as Taylor shuffled his way back to the table he'd come from. He opened the calendar on his phone and tapped the date they said Sadie had gone missing. And, as he feared, it was the night the two of them met at The Mills, the club where Taylor and his band had a regular gig. Taylor felt a wave of heat spread throughout his chest.

He tried to remember what he'd done that night after the gig but struggled with the details. He remembered taking his medicine in the alley. He remembered getting his free drink from MJ, talking to Sadie and Leon and Mick coming over. The rest was a fog.

As he tried to piece together his movements that night,

Taylor became frustrated and flicked his phone onto a pile of shirts. It'd become so common for him to not recall some things from the night before that he realized he'd stopped bothering to try. He sensed these memory issues had begun when he started taking the Thorazine his therapist had prescribed, then found it ironic he couldn't remember how long ago that was. He recalled looking into the side effects of the medicine and his eyes bulging at some of them—dizziness, lightheadedness, blurred vision, trouble sleeping, uncontrollable movements among the long list of others. And while he'd experienced each of these to some degree, none had presented a problem. But the memory loss was becoming a real issue. Taylor would mention it to his therapist during their next session.

He forced his thoughts back to that night he'd spoken with Sadie. How had he gotten home? Did he leave with Leon? He remembered saying he'd take the van home but didn't remember doing so. He checked his Uber app but there was no record of him Ubering home that night. Maybe he did drive his van home. Everything was just so jumbled in his head.

He heard Luanne flip the closed sign over on the store's window and unlock its door.

"We're open," she called over a shoulder and Taylor silently raised a hand in response.

There was so much about that night that Taylor couldn't remember but the one thing he did remember was talking with Sadie and feeling a real connection. After that, everything was black.

A wave of nausea hit him and he needed some air so told Luanne he'd be right back. He scurried through the back room and burst into the alley behind the shop, the metal door snapping shut behind him like ravenous teeth.

His mind whirred round and round, trying to fit pieces of that night together but there was just too much missing time. But through all the haze, Taylor realized one thing for certain.

He was likely the last person to see Sadie Hogan alive.

Chapter Six

G US PULLED BACK hard on the stick to downshift as he exited Route 3 and turned onto Thorndike Street. He felt Vanessa's hand plant firmly on the bench seat between them and noticed the fingertips of her other hand had turned white from the cold metal dashboard. He knew that as much as she joked about how unsafe his late-sixties Land Rover was or how she struggled to see over the studded tire bolted to its hood, that her fingertips were not white from tension or fear but from the Raynaud's disease she refused to believe she had.

"Poppin' off to the safari this morning, are we?" Vanessa quipped.

Her jokes about Gus's old truck being right out of an African safari had grown old long ago but Gus knew that was exactly why she kept them up. Vanessa was like that. He shot her a look and smiled as her thin, wiry body vibrated in the seat as if she were on a pony.

She returned the look, her green catlike eyes boring into his. Her strawberry-blond hair was cropped on top and this month's highlights were a vibrant purple. One side of her head was shaved and its fuzz caught the late afternoon sun when she turned toward him. Gus straightened the lumbering truck out and the sound of its tires fell back into a bassy rumble.

He tipped his chin toward her phone. "Keep going."

Vanessa had just finished reading the case file for the first victim, Michelle Townsend, aloud for Gus. Amongst the details, they learned she had gone missing just over four months ago and that her body was found in a field in Tyngsboro a few weeks later. She was nude but there was no sign of sexual assault. She had been strangled with something wide like a strap or a belt and there were abrasions around her wrists and ankles from being tied up. But exposure to the elements and animals had taken their toll on the body so there was no trace evidence found at the scene.

"There's a note here that there was some confusion as to where she was actually abducted from but no details are given."

"Let's run that down with the detective."

"But that's really all on the first vic. There's a ton of photos you can look through after." Vanessa tapped her phone several times before continuing, "The second vic is a Sadie Hogan, she went missing from the same part of town about three weeks ago..." She read on before turning to Gus. "We only have her missing persons file here."

"Makes sense. She was just found last night."

Gus let the information about the women marinate in his thoughts as he navigated the old truck through tight city traffic. The street lights had come on in anticipation of the coming night, putting a shine to the black pavement in spots. He had only been to Pawtucket Falls once before;

years ago when he was thinking about buying a Shen bass. He went to a shop that had several in stock and played one for a few hours, trying to really get a feel for her. He remembered her sounding warm and liking how she spoke under the bow. Gus was six-four with the wingspan of an Olympic swimmer so not every bass was a fit. But he liked the Shen, how the size of the upper bouts made it easy to transition in and out of the thumb position.

He slowed to a stop at another red light and looked at the city around him. September was a fickle month in New England. Some years it served up an homage to August with hot, sunny days deserving of T-shirts and long walks. Yet other years it pummeled one with frigid cold that made them want to hibernate until May. The angry winds lugging black, pregnant clouds through the skies over them told Gus they were in for the latter.

"These two women sound very different," he said into the windshield, "One's early twenties and single, the other's in her forties, divorced, two kids. They're from different towns, have different careers. I mean, they were both taken from the same area in the Falls but it's a big city and a dangerous one at that."

"Consistently top five in crime in the state."

"So, is that enough to link these two cases?"

"Dunno. But these women look totally different from each other too." Vanessa stared at her phone. "The first vic, Michelle Townsend, is a brunette with short hair and dark features and sort of average-looking; definitely wouldn't stand out in a crowd. The second vic, Sadie Hogan, has long blonde hair and the photo posted of her missing looks like a model's head shot; she's gorgeous."

"What about the third woman, the one that just went missing?"

"Let's see … Rachel Connors, twenty-five, lives in Billerica with her parents. She's a little edgier than the others with a lot of makeup, brown hair, dark features. She's attractive but in a different sort of way."

"Does it say where she was last seen?"

After a few moments of silence Vanessa said, "Nothing specific, just at a bar downtown with friends."

Gus took a left onto Arcand Drive, bucking his truck hard for Vanessa's benefit as he grinded the gears into second. She side-eyed him, hip to his play.

"You're a child." She laughed and her face lit up like Times Square. And when V laughed, her eyes squinted and the freckles dusting her cheeks seemed to dance.

Laughing with her, Gus glanced out his side window at the city hall with its tall stone clock tower and verdigris green roof. It was great to be on tour but Gus would be lying to himself if he said he didn't miss Vanessa while away. He checked the rearview mirror and his eyes—so light blue it was like staring into an iceberg—caught the lights of the traffic behind them. A few moments later, he parked in front of the police department and his phone buzzed in his jacket pocket.

"I texted you the link to the case files so you have it," she said, unbuckling her seatbelt.

Gus pulled out his phone and, turning its screen toward

him, he startled. On it was a photo of Linda Blair as the possessed daughter in the movie *The Exorcist* and the text was from Regan, her character's name. Vanessa guffawed at his reaction then they both hopped from the truck and headed into the station.

A large, uniformed officer the size of a small shed named Anthony led Gus and Vanessa through a set of double doors, past the bullpen crammed tight with desks, to a conference room at the back. Rapping on the door with his fist, he opened it then stood aside for Gus and Vanessa to enter.

A tall, slender female detective with broad shoulders and confident demeanor stepped over to Gus. Her round eyes were clear and bright and separated by a distinctive-looking rocky nose. She nodded a thanks to Anthony then extended her hand toward Gus.

"You must be Agent Wheeler." Not waiting for confirmation, she shook his hand. "I'm Detective Boyd. Amy." She rocked the cool, calm, collected detective vibe.

Behind her, Gus could see stacks of papers on the conference room table and a whiteboard with photos of three women lining its top.

Amy shook Vanessa's hand then stepped to the side. "Please, come in. Sit."

The three of them sat and Amy slid each of them a manila folder. "That's the case file for the Hogan woman's crime scene. Sorry we couldn't get that to you sooner, they hadn't finished processing it until after midnight so I just finished it this afternoon." She gestured around the room, "We're a bit short-staffed around here."

"We went over the file on the first vic…" began Gus.

"Michelle Townsend," Amy finished.

"There was a note in the file about some confusion on where she was abducted from?"

Amy nodded an understanding. "I put that in there; it was just odd. So, she's at this club called The Loft with a few friends and the place is pretty crowded. She tells her friends she has to get up early so leaves. We have her on surveillance video going to the rest room and coming back out. Then nothing. She doesn't reenter the club and we can't find her on any of the exit feeds."

"You look into the staff?" Vanessa asked.

"That's where we started. Our thought was one of 'em grabbed her and hid her in the basement or somewhere then came back after hours to get her out. The security system went through a regular data backup process at three a.m. for about half an hour and was offline so we thought we were on the right path. But they all came back clean. And we searched the place inside and out. Nothing."

"How about security footage? You check that?" asked Gus.

Amy nodded. "Inside and out. Nothing. It's as if she just vanished."

Vanessa made a note in her pad then looked to Amy. "We've also gone through the missing person report for the second vic," she said. "The Hogan woman."

"Yeah, same drill," the detective said. "Except the surveillance video. She was last seen at a different club—The Mills—and they don't have cameras inside.

"How about external cameras?"

"Well, that's where we stuffed up. The detective on it got pulled onto a murder investigation and that fell through the cracks." Vanessa made a note of that as Amy continued, "But uniforms spoke to her friends and went to the club; no one recognized her there so that's when things hit a dead end." She jutted her chin out toward the case file. "Autopsy report's in there. Pretty standard except that they found traces of coal dust beneath a few of her fingernails."

"Coal dust?" Gus questioned. He thought a moment then asked, "Are there any coal power plants around here?"

Amy was shaking her head before he finished his question. "Nah, I checked this morning. There's only one remaining coal-fired power plant in New England and its way up in Bow, New Hampshire. I talked to the vic's family; they have no knowledge of Sadie leaving the immediate area and none of the employees at the club have any link to that power plant or that area in general."

Gus looked to the board with the photos of each woman on it. "Other than being taken in downtown Pawtucket Falls these women appear to have nothing in common. Different backgrounds, profiles, completely different appearances."

Amy eyed Gus for several silent moments before speaking. "So you're wondering how the murders of two women with absolutely nothing in common except that they were taken in a large city are connected. Because, of course, you've looked at the crime rate in the Falls and seen its amongst the highest in the region. So maybe these women were just in the wrong place at the wrong time in a dangerous city. Shit happens, right?"

Gus smiled at her directness. He liked that in a person; no beating around the bush or namby-pamby talk to avoid hurting someone's feelings. *Just say it like it is.*

"Something like that."

Amy returned his smile. "Yeah, that's what we thought too." She opened one of the manila folders in front of her and began flipping through a stack of photos. "We didn't connect them until we got to the Hogan scene."

She pulled a photo out and spun it into the middle of the table. It was a closeup shot of the side of Sadie Hogan's bluish bloated face and neck, the type of shot Gus had seen dozens of times before but had still not gotten immune to. He knew every picture told a story, but felt some shouldn't be allowed to, not even in a whisper.

Across Sadie Hogan's neck was a thick line of bruising and in one spot was a noticeable straight cut above and below the bruising. And just outside one of the edges of the bruising was a line of mottled red marks, its end a noticeably straight square imprint.

"We think he used a belt and this was where he tightened its buckle." She slid another photo on top of that. "This is an enlarged shot of that specific spot..." She placed a long finger on the side of one of the cuts. "Look closely here."

Gus leaned over and squinted at the line of mottled red marks and the longer he stared the clearer some of the marks stood out until they seemed to take a collective shape in its middle.

"Is that..."

"The letter *X*? We think so," Amy replied.

She then opened a different manila folder, rooted around in its pages until she took out a similar photo of the first victim, Michelle Townsend. She spun it next to the photo of Sadie and the same mark was on Michelle's neck except on hers the *X* was clearly visible.

"That's some clean shit," Vanessa said.

Amy smiled. "You think that's good…" She flipped through one of the folders again until she found the photo she was looking for.

Then, like the others, she spun it into the center of the table. Gus and Vanessa both leaned forward and saw a close up shot of Michelle Townsend's driver's license.

"A photo of the first vic's driver's license?" Vanessa asked, confused. "What's significant about that?"

Amy leaned back in her seat and slung a long arm over its back as she crossed her legs.

"Only that we found it lodged in the second vic's throat."

Chapter Seven

G US AND VANESSA went over the case files for both
victims—Michelle Townsend and Sadie Hogan—with
the detective to be sure they hadn't missed anything before
the case was handed off to them. But they hadn't. They both
had the same abrasions on their wrists, ankles, and necks and
Michelle Townsend's driver's license being found on Sadie
Hogan's body connected both murders without a doubt.
And given that they found no one else's driver's license in the
mouth of the Townsend woman, or anywhere at the scene,
strongly suggested she was the first victim. But the fact that
Sadie Hogan's driver's license was missing from her wallet
while ample cash and multiple credit cards remained also
told them their suspect was not done. That led them to
discuss the missing woman, Rachel Connors, and why the
detective believed her disappearance was connected.

"She really didn't hit our radar until the Hogan woman's
body was found last night. Then it all just fell in line like
dominoes. The first vic, Townsend, was murdered and now
we know Hogan was also murdered and by the same suspect.
Then one of our guys flags a missing person report from
earlier yesterday for the Connors woman who's also gone
missing from Music Row."

"Same club as either of the vics?"

The detective's eyes widened, and she tilted her head slightly. "No, but one close by."

They went over the file on Rachel Connors and all agreed that she was yet again different-looking from either of the prior two victims so, other than each of the women being Caucasian, they were becoming comfortable their suspect wasn't selecting his victims based on appearance. She lived with her parents whereas the other two lived in apartment buildings so that removed the victims' living arrangements as a likely causal factor. Each of the women worked in offices, but in very different geographic areas and types of businesses so that didn't provide any obvious link. And as they continued to knock various other factors off the list, they were left with just one common link. Each woman was abducted from Pawtucket Falls' Music Row area.

"So, you've not spoken with anyone at the club where the Connors woman was last seen." Vanessa clarified.

"Not yet, no."

"And she was reported missing last night but how long has she been gone?" asked Gus.

"Two days as of now, since late Saturday night."

"Have you spoken with her family or friends yet?"

Amy answered with a brisk shake of her head. "Haven't gotten to it. Only the uniform that took the info for the missing person report."

Gus pulled the Sadie Hogan file toward him and opened it. "What were the estimates of time of death for Townsend and Hogan? Did he keep them alive for any period of time?"

He leafed his way through the autopsy report.

"We think so, yes," the detective said. "Given the state of the Townsend body, the window was pretty wide so we can't be sure. But it looks like he did for Hogan. The time of death for her is estimated to be seven or eight days after she was taken."

Vanessa jotted a note in the tiny pad in front of her. "Okay, so for Hogan, the uniforms took a statement from her parents for the missing person report," she said, running her finger down the side of a page. "And it looks like they spoke with the friends she was with at the club."

"That's right," the detective confirmed. "They said they all left except for Sadie who was going to watch the end of the show."

"And they hit the club but got nothing, right?"

Amy nodded a confirmation.

Gus looked to Vanessa who was spinning her pen across her hand like an airplane propeller. "Let's focus on the Connors woman. We're only a couple days in, so with any luck, she's still alive. Let's hit the club where she was last seen." He looked to the clock on his phone, "Seven thirty on a Monday, maybe they're open. And maybe they even have surveillance footage for that night."

Vanessa's eyes widened. "A man can dream."

"Then we speak with family and friends tomorrow," Gus finished.

The room fell quiet and Gus thought a moment. Each of these women might be different in many ways, but they weren't living on the fringe of society like hookers or drug addicts or the homeless, working the streets, living on them, jabbing them in their veins. They had to be aware of the basic safety cautions most women were told their entire lives—*stay aware of your surroundings, stay in well-lit areas, trust your instincts. Watch your drink.*

"Did anything odd show up in the tox screens?"

"No, nothing," the detective replied.

"How's he able to get them to go with him?" Gus asked. "I mean, they're in crowded places with friends. Do they know him? Is he a familiar face, like a bouncer or a bartender? How's he make 'em feel comfortable enough to be alone with him?"

The room fell quiet again as they thought about Gus's questions. But his mind had already switched gears. Who was their suspect as a person? Was he old or young, outgoing or introverted? Were these murders his first or had he practiced before? There would be time later to delve into these questions and many, many more. They'd inspect and analyze the smallest speck of information for days, forming view after view to the traits and drivers of their suspect. But Gus knew they didn't have that kind of time now. Their suspect's activity was already accelerating. Fortunately for Gus, he had a secret weapon. Vanessa. Her combination of a doctorate in psychology from Notre Dame and innate street smarts made her extremely perceptive in reading people— what traits were they likely to have, how they viewed the world and themselves in it, what drove them.

Gus gestured to the case files spread out on the table. "V, any thoughts on this guy?"

She paused, her eyes flicking across the folders laid out in front of them. "Well, he's Caucasian for starters. Likely between twenty-five and forty years old."

"Why d'ya say that?" the detective asked.

"The women's ages mostly. Mid-twenties to early forties. It's far easier for a younger man to pick up an older woman than vice versa. And a woman in her mid-twenties is much more apt to be attracted to or comfortable with a man around her own age." She scanned a closeup photo of Sadie Hogan and her bruised neck. "His crimes are violent, brutal even, and he likes it that way. He likes to look them in the eye, watch the light go out. That suggests a hatred of women from being rejected or betrayed, not one born of mommy issues. And the licenses suggest an arrogance, a confidence that's only growing stronger. He wants the attention, craves it." Vanessa picked up the photograph and studied it closely. "He's feeling it now. And he likes it."

They discussed the cases for a few more minutes and when they were done Amy closed her folder and, checking the time on her phone, leaned back in her chair. "I think that's everything. Is there anything we can do here?"

"We'll take the Connors case from here," Gus answered. "And I think we're good on Hogan. With no surveillance video, we'll hit the club she was at last to take a look around." He then thought a moment. "On the Townsend case, you said you couldn't find her leaving the club on the surveillance tape. You get traffic cams around the club?"

"Yeah, and other businesses nearby. Nothing."

"What time frame did you watch it for?"

"The entire night up until the three-a.m. data backup when the system went down."

"Could you have someone go through it again, this time carefully looking for anyone wearing the same clothes or having the same body type? Maybe our guy disguised her somehow to get her out."

"Sure thing."

"Also have 'em watch the tape for the forty-eight hours following her disappearance. Maybe he stashed her somewhere inside and came back to get her later."

"Will do." Amy stood. "And let me know if you need anything else. My cell is written inside each folder." She looked around the room. "Do you guys need space to set up or are you going to do the commute each day from Boston?"

"Chelsea." Vanessa groaned.

Amy chuckled. "Right. Chelsea."

"We've got a room at the Pawtucket Falls office so we'll be staying around here for a bit."

"Where ya stayin'?"

"Dunno yet," Vanessa answered. "Any suggestions?"

"Any place not in the city."

"Got it." Vanessa thanked Amy, then she and Gus gathered their folders and followed the detective back past the bullpen toward the exit.

When they pushed their way through the double doors into the large marbled lobby, they were met by the blinding lights of a television news crew. An attractive young woman stepped up to Gus, her cameraman at their side to be sure he got both of them in the frame.

"Agent Wheeler, Christina Collins, News Center Six." She gestured to the camera. "Sources have told News Center Six the FBI is taking over the murder investigations of Michelle Townsend and Sadie Hogan and that it's believed the recent disappearance of Rachel Connors is connected." She thrust the microphone below Gus's chin. "Do you have any comment?"

Gus squinted at the woman and, surprised, paused briefly which provided her the opening for a second question.

"And, agent, can you confirm that it is now believed a serial killer is responsible for these murders?"

Before Gus could say anything, Amy stepped in front of him and stuffed an outstretched hand into the camera's lens. She looked down at the petite newswoman.

"Christina, this is out of bounds even for you. No comment. Now, please, you and your cameraman…" She looked over her shoulder. "Hey, Tommy."

The cameraman's eyes were couched in laughter lines as he lowered his lens. "Amy."

Amy looked back at Christina. "Now, please leave. If there's anything to say we'll do so through public relations."

Chapter Eight

TAYLOR HAD SPENT most of his shift at Nifty's on his phone searching online for information about Sadie Hogan and Michelle Townsend and their murders. The first thing he noted was that Townsend was last seen at a different club in the Falls' Music Row called The Loft. Taylor knew the place well, having played there with the band a few times. But they hadn't played there the night she went missing so was comfortable there was no connection to be made between her and him.

It was just after seven o'clock and he was on his walk home, having stayed late at Nifty's to pick up some extra hours. During his breaks, Taylor had put together a set list he could use to practice his upright. First, he would clean and oil her then, after tuning her just right, he'd play some of his favorite jazz tunes tonight to help get his mind off Sadie Hogan and Michelle Townsend. What was done was done; he had no way of changing any of it. So, what better way to move on than playing some of his favorites and revisiting his plan to move back to NOLA?

But as he approached his side porch, he heard noise coming from inside the garage. He stepped into the living room then leaned in the doorway to the garage and found the singer of his band, Chris, rummaging through some of the band's equipment.

"Hey," Taylor said. "What's up?"

"Hey," Chris replied, distracted by his search.

He picked up the side of a small amp on the floor then eased it back down before turning to Taylor. Chris had shoulder-length, dirty blond hair with subtle red highlights throughout that could only be seen when the light touched them just right. He wore black jeans with ankle-high Cole Haan leather boots and a long sleeve button-down, bright fuchsia shirt.

"You see my lyric sheets for the set tomorrow night? I can't find 'em anywhere."

Chris was a very talented singer that had joined their band a year ago when his former band replaced him after Chris told them he was gay. Taylor knew Chris could take their band to the next level and was amazed when he agreed to join.

"No, but we can print some more if you want."

Chris flicked a hand in the air. "Nah, I'll do it later. I just thought maybe I left them here when I couldn't find 'em at home."

Taylor felt a presence behind him and turned to see Mick, the drummer, leaning against the wall.

"Hey." Taylor nodded. "You see Chris's lyric sheets?"

Mick smiled and tipped his head toward the door to the garage. "No, I just helped him rip apart the practice room looking for 'em and just checked the living room. They're not here anywhere."

"You guys wanna hang out and jam a bit?" Taylor asked. "I've got a few new songs I thought we could add to the set."

"Dude, slow your roll," Mick said. "We're booked out solid for months; we've never made so much bank as we're making now. I think our set is good as is."

Chris stood and dusted off the front of his pants. "Sorry, can't anyway. I've got a fundraiser thing for work I have to go to tonight." He raked his fingers through his hair, still looking around the room.

"But, hey," Mick said. He gestured to one of the corners of the living room where Taylor's upright was. "What's with the upright? You moonlighting on us?"

Taylor followed his extended arm then looked back to the drummer. "Nah, just been feelin' it lately. A few of the songs I wanted to add to the set are from the *Goo Goo Dolls* and their bassist uses an upright for 'em."

Mick eyed Taylor wearily before turning his attention back to Chris and his missing lyric sheets. "Chris, I gotta blast."

"Yeah, me too," the singer replied.

Chris and Mick soon headed out, leaving Taylor once again alone with his thoughts and the dread percolating inside him. He cleaned and oiled his upright then, after tuning her, played her for a bit but couldn't get Sadie Hogan and Michelle Townsend out of his mind. He needed something more intense so decided to play some video games. But when he tried to go online, he realized he had no internet connection. He turned the Wi-Fi off in his gaming console then, waiting about thirty seconds, turned it back on and waited for the network options to populate. The three networks of his closest neighbors loaded into the menu. Two of them needed a password but thankfully the third, old Mrs. Givens's, still needed none. He chose it again but the little wheel just kept spinning and never connected.

Frustrated, he stood and looked around the small, dimly-lit living room. The table that held his gaming console and small monitor was filled with crumpled up napkins and tissues, an empty plate, and a half-eaten bowl of cereal. The brown cloth sofa had shirts and sweatshirts hanging from it and the coffee table in front of it held several empty soda bottles and an empty pizza box. He turned toward the kitchen to see the sink full of dishes surrounded by counters covered with cereal boxes, piles of mail, and a few empty mac and cheese boxes. He felt that the lack of Wi-Fi was the world's way of screaming at him to clean things up a bit. But as he moved to do so he heard the front door open and in stepped Leon, the guitarist, holding a plastic shopping bag.

"Hey," Taylor said as he picked up a pizza box. "What's up? I thought you'd be home by now."

"On my way." He held up the shopping bag. "Just dropping this off." Leon's eyes widened as he pulled a VHS box from the bag and tossed it to Taylor. "*Kiss the Girls*. Morgan Freeman, Ashley Judd. Classic."

Leon was a technician at a small family-owned company, The Memory Garden, that provided analogue to digital video and audio conversion and 35mm slide scanning services. Leon was constantly working with old, dusty photo albums, near-ruined projector reels, and out of date VHS material from people all across the country. And since Taylor had no cable or streaming services—luxuries he'd cut after taking over his childhood home—and the only equipment in the house was a VHS player, Leon had begun copying movies onto blank tapes for him.

"Nice." Taylor gestured to the stack of VHS tapes on his TV. "I was just getting tired of the last one so good timing."

"I gotta give you something for hosting band practices and letting us hang here whenever we want." Leon's eyes then fell on Taylor's upright bass on its stand in the corner and he smiled.

"*Heyyy*, you pulled Olive out." They both knew that Taylor had named his upright after Emma Stone's character in one of their favorite movies, *Easy A*. He caught Taylor's eye. "She looks great."

"Yeah, I've been feelin' 'er lately." Taylor went to her and took her from the stand. "I cleaned her up and she's all tuned."

Leon's head was nodding slowly. "Your mom'd be proud."

Both knew that Taylor's mom's greatest wish was for Taylor to follow his dreams of being a professional jazz player. And as she began to fail and her memory worsened, she would cycle on that notion, often repeating it over and over to herself like a mantra. And they knew of his mom's guilt for Taylor having moved home to care for her, leaving his dreams on the streets of New Orleans like a strand of discarded Mardi Gras beads.

"Yeah." Taylor sighed. "I think she would too." He took

one last look at the bass then gently placed her back on the stand. Looking to Leon, he smiled. "I actually played a jazz gig last week in Acton."

"No shit." Leon smiled wide. "Where?"

"That new club on Main Street; the place that used to be that boujee coffee house?"

"Dude, nice." Leon slapped his shoulder. "Why didn't you tell me?"

Taylor shrugged. "Eh, didn't wanna make a big deal out of it."

"But it is a big deal. It's a very big deal."

"Yeah, and I'm finally feelin' it again. And now with Mom in the home there's really nothin' keeping me from getting back to NOLA."

Taylor dropped the new video onto the desk and looked around the dingy room. Once he'd gotten his mother settled in the care facility, he'd begun planning his return to New Orleans. But that plan had him moving back in a year or so, once he'd saved enough money. Since learning of Sadie Hogan's murder, however, the idea of leaving the Falls much sooner had taken root. And, besides, what the hell had this city ever done for him anyway, except fuck him up?

"Wow, heading back to NOLA," Leon said.

"Just thinkin' it might be time."

"Says the guy who already made it out once but came back."

"Yeah, well, things are different now."

"Maybe for you," Leon said, his eyes bulging. "Things are still shitty for the rest of us."

Taylor thought of asking Leon if he remembered what happened that night they met Sadie but decided against it. "You wanna hang and put that on?" he asked instead, gesturing toward the new VHS tape.

"Nah, maybe tomorrow. Sheila's waiting for me at home."

Leon left Taylor alone with his new movie and the dread swirling around in his head. Taylor couldn't wrestle down his thoughts about Sadie and her murder so decided to clean up a bit while he thought it all through. The first thing he did was pick up all the dishes, bring them to the sink, and scrape their remnants into the trash. He filled the dishwasher and got that going then brought the smelly garbage outside and dropped it into the barrel against the side of the house. Next, he took his last trash bag and went room to room, dropping empty pizza boxes, soda bottles, and assorted other trash into it then deposited it on top of the other bag in the barrel outside. Next up. Laundry.

Taylor couldn't remember the last time he did some wash so his first attempt at filling a laundry basket lasted about a minute before it was overflowing and he had only cleared about a three-foot square space on his bedroom floor. He knew that to wash all of his dirty clothes would take days so took a more discerning eye to the pile in his basket. He had work the next few days and band practice tomorrow night which made jeans, underwear, and a few clean T-shirts a priority. He sorted those out and piled them into the basket, scraping the remaining dirty clothes into one of the corners of his bedroom. He would strip his bed and wash his sheets next week or maybe the week after.

He hauled the bulging laundry basket down the cellar stairs and dropped it onto the cement floor beside the last step. To his right were dusty wooden shelves filled with canned goods and empty mason jars and beside that a large metal oil tank with shiny stains on its side. To his left sat the washer and dryer, both resting on cement blocks to avoid the seasonal water that made it into the basement. Taylor slid the basket in front of them with a leg and pulled the dangling string to turn the lightbulb on.

He opened the top lid of the washer and poured in the last of his detergent. Then he went about the drill of pulling jeans from the basket, checking the pockets and adding them to the load. It wasn't until the fourth pair that Taylor found something other than loose change in his pockets when his fingers clasped something thin and smooth about the size of a credit card. He pulled his hand from the pocket and his heart dropped at what it held.

In the center of Taylor's open palm was the shiny white driver's license of Sadie Hogan.

Chapter Nine

MUSIC ROW ENCOMPASSED a four-block area in Pawtucket Falls of former mills and mill-related buildings that ran along the Merrimack River. The area began decades ago when a small Irish pub named Mac's allowed a local band to busk on the sidewalk in front of it during its happy hour. When patrons began taking their drinks outside for the live music, Mac's invited the band inside and it became a regular event. Mac's quickly became one of the busiest bars in Pawtucket Falls so naturally others in that area drafted on the idea and began hosting bands as well. And Music Row was born.

In the 1990s, the city blocked off several streets with granite pillars, paved those sections with cobblestones and planted trees along the sidewalks to make it into a sort of music enclave. But unlike Memphis with its Beale Street or the Quarter in New Orleans, Pawtucket Falls Massachusetts didn't have music in its genes. So instead of the music pavilion envisioned, they created a cordoned off area of the city where public drinking flourished unabated and drug dealers roamed free from the watchful eyes of passing police.

Vanessa took a look at her phone's GPS to get a sense of where they were going then slid it back into her pocket. Gus followed her as she confidently walked through the nighttime city streets as if she had lived in Pawtucket Falls her entire life. Having been raised in one of the more dangerous parts of Detroit, navigating concrete jungles safely had been stitched into Vanessa's DNA from a young age.

The missing woman, Rachel Connors, had been last seen at a bar called Blue Agave and it took only one look at the large gaudy neon montage over its door to realize it was named after the plant used to make tequila. And upon closer inspection, a chalkboard sign in its window boasted over 100 types of tequila on its shelves in swooping cursive script. Vanessa stopped beside the door then turned toward Gus with her hand open wide like Vanna White, directing his attention to its hours of operation. Gus squinted and hunched over slightly to read that the club was closed Mondays. Vanessa opened her mouth and widened her eyes in mock surprise.

It was nearly eight p.m. and they hadn't eaten anything since munch time; Vanessa's mid-afternoon Diet Coke and snack time. Gus could tell by her body language and clipped answers that she was treading into hangry territory. He looked around and two doors down on the other side of the street saw a sign for The Mills, the bar that the second victim, Sadie Hogan, was last seen at. Its full name was The Mills Bar & Grille. He gestured that way.

"Yes, chef!" she said.

Stepping into The Mills, Gus was immediately hit with the smell of stale beer and fried food, and it brought him back to his college years and the small jazz clubs he'd play at in the Quarter for twenty-five dollars and a hot meal. He heard the familiar melody of the Scorpions' "Rock You Like a Hurricane" playing from the speakers just loud enough to be heard over the ambient noise of the crowd. He noted the dark wood décor that shined from what he guessed was about a dozen coats of clear polyurethane and knew this was more function than some trendy fashion choice. It was much easier to wipe up spilled drinks and the occasional vomit from nonporous wood than virtually any other surface.

"Jesus, Darwin would have a field day in here," Vanessa said, scanning the room.

To their right was a large open area with lighting cans affixed to its ceiling directed at a stage along the side wall. Gus saw a few old battered guitar and bass amps pushed to one side of the stage and noticed the bass amp had a large hole in its speaker. There were a few empty beer bottles on the edge of the stage and behind them several mic stands drooping over at the elbow, missing mic clips the bands would need to bring themselves.

In front of the entrance where Gus and Vanessa stood was a half-wall extending away from them that separated the live music space from a large horseshoe-shaped bar and pub area to their left. Gus felt Vanessa push past him so followed her to two open seats at the bar.

"Hungry?" he asked as they sat.

Vanessa glared at him then leaned over the bar and grabbed two menus. And as she did so, her jacket and shirt pulled up, exposing parts of the intricate tattoos running along her side. Over the years as she and Gus's friendship grew, Vanessa had shared stories of growing up in the projects in Detroit and how choosing no gang allegiance was a death sentence. Switzerland did not survive in that world. So Gus knew the majority of V's body was covered in tattoos and that she had spent much of her adult life covering or altering those from her early years. Gus eyed her edgy haircut, the tat on her neck poking out from beneath her shirt, her black leather combat boots and, glancing past her, saw bits and pieces of that same vibe in the growing crowd. She wasn't a musician, but she fit right in with this scene.

The bartender swooped by and, seeing they already had menus, kept going without making eye contact like a pro. Gus side-eyed Vanessa who was glaring into the woman's back as she walked away from them. He leaned away and pulled a bowl of nuts over and put it between them.

"What're you insane?" she asked, scowling at the bowl.

He clawed a scoop from it and popped it into his mouth. "You need to allow yourself to experience joy."

"Death gives no refunds." she murmured, her eyes back on the menu.

Gus was scanning his when a gravelly woman's voice asked, "Okay, what can I getcha?"

He looked up and into the hardened eyes of a woman who'd been bartending for too long to give a shit. She had thick mascara and heavy makeup, crow's feet extending to her temples, and small wrinkles surrounding her mouth from a lifetime of smoking. Gus pulled his badge from the pocket of his leather jacket and flapped it open onto the bar.

"How 'bout a few minutes of your time?"

"Ah, shit." She looked around at the swelling crowd. "What, couldn't come during happy hour?" She sneered.

Her black retro 1984 Van Halen concert T-shirt was stretched tight across her large chest.

"We're investigating the death of a young woman who was last seen here a few weeks back." Gus placed a picture of Sadie Hogan on the bar and slid it toward her. "Recognize her?"

"Sure, I recognize her," MJ said, touching her own upper lip in the spot where Sadie's mole was. "She was in here, oh shit, must be three, maybe four, weeks ago now."

"Did you tell this to the police that came around a few weeks back?"

"What police? I just got back from vacation. I haven't seen any police."

Gus and Vanessa exchanged a look. "Was she with anyone or was anyone bothering her?" Gus continued.

"That's why I remember her. She was talking to a few guys in the Bowers Street Band. She gave it back to one of 'em and I could tell she pissed him off."

"How so?" She had Gus's complete attention now.

"Well, the drummer, Mick, he hits on any woman with a pulse. I saw him talking to her with that smarmy smile of his and she was havin' none of it. And whatever she said to him clearly bruised his fragile male ego 'cause he gave her a look of death then just walked away."

"What'd she do?" Vanessa asked.

MJ shrugged. "Didn't seem to faze her. She hung around talking with the other two—Leon and Taylor—for a bit then when Leon left, she hung with Taylor for a while after that."

"She leave with him?" Vanessa pressed.

"Not sure. The place was hoppin'. I know he showed her the green room just before last call though. So that woulda been around one thirty or so."

"You know how we can get in touch with this Taylor guy?" asked Gus.

MJ's lips jutted out and she nodded. "Ya T's the MD so…" She pulled her phone from her back pocket and began tapping on its screen.

"MD?" Vanessa whispered to the side of Gus's head.

"Musical Director," he whispered back, his eyes drifting around before settling on Vanessa. "Basically, the band leader." He continued, "But for a place like this it's really just the contact for the band."

"Let's see…" MJ said as she swiped at her phone's screen. "Okay, Taylor Franklin." She slid her phone onto the bar for Vanessa to copy down his phone number.

"Taylor Franklin," Gus repeated slowly. "Is he, like, early thirties, brown hair, thin, good-looking? Plays the bass?"

MJ nodded. "Yeah, all but the thin part. Why?"

He gestured to her phone now back in her hand. "You got a photo of him in there?"

"Don't need one." She pointed a finger to the wall beside Gus. "He's right there on their band's poster. They're one of our house bands for Thursdays and weekends."

Gus slid off the stool and walked to the poster. Across its top in large white letters read THE BOWERS STREET BAND and beneath it in smaller print it added, PLAYING THE BEST

OF THE '80S and beside that written in marker on a piece of tape was '90'S AND BEYOND. There were four small circles, each containing a photo of a band member with their name and instrument written beneath it. Gus's eyes were drawn to Taylor's photo and he recognized him immediately. Taylor's face was a bit rounder and scruffier, but it was the Taylor he remembered. He took a photo with his phone then stepped back to the bar.

"You know him?" Vanessa asked.

"He was a couple years behind me at Loyola. Kid was a savant on the upright."

"He and Leon—the guitarist—grew up around here," MJ said. "They actually worked here as bar hands in high school. Before Leon went away."

"College?" asked Gus.

MJ's lower lip jutted out again and she shook her head. "Big house. Did a dime for dealing." She tipped her head toward the poster. "But to your point, T could *always* play. He and Leon would busk outside as kids on their acoustics and you'd swear Taylor'd been born with that thing in his hands."

"Can we take a look at the green room?" Gus asked.

"Sure, it's back behind the stage. Follow me."

MJ told the other bartender she'd be right back then Gus and Vanessa followed her through the crowd and down a narrow corridor beside the stage until they got to a solid wooden door. MJ pushed it open then stepped aside for Gus and Vanessa to enter first. Gus stepped in and looked around the disheveled room and a familiar feeling washed over him from years of touring with bands on the road.

Beside the door was a small mini-fridge and an overflowing round barrel. The door to the fridge had paint chipped off it in several places and a thin green line of mold along its white rubber seal. Gus peeled it open with a finger, only to find a single Bud Light can lying on its side on the top shelf. The barrel beside it had empty beer cans and bottles in it and wedged into its top was the corner of a party platter from Subway with a few half-sandwiches still in their wrappers resting in the trash just beside it.

"Gaggy," Vanessa muttered as she walked past.

The walls were covered with graffiti and stickers of bands, many of which were crooked with turned-up corners. Gus walked farther into the room, careful to step around the bits of broken strings on the floor and the foldable plastic chairs. He stepped over to the small jail-size window on the back wall to see if it opened but it was painted shut. Its corners were covered with dead spiders and spider eggs and along its narrow bottom rim Gus found several cigarette butts and the roaches from smoked joints. He turned back to Vanessa and MJ who were still standing at the door.

"Well, don't think they could've gotten out this way."

"I coulda told you that," MJ said.

"And you didn't see her leave the club that night?" Gus asked again.

MJ shook her head. "Nope. Like I said, it gets nuts around last call."

"We understand you don't have surveillance cameras," Vanessa noted.

MJ sneered and shook her head. "Nah. We got cameras up all over the ceiling in there but they're just for show. Donny—the owner—is too cheap to put the system in."

Vanessa looked around the room slowly. "I'd say let's get a forensics team here but I'm afraid of what they might find. We could have a Mike Tyson situation here," she said, referring to Mike Tyson's rape conviction case years ago when a forensics team processed his hotel room only to find many other samples of semen in the room not attributed to that case or Mr. Tyson.

"Nah, there's no way she was done here. Too public a place." Gus walked back toward the door and stood beside Vanessa. "Let's see if Taylor Franklin is free for us to stop by."

"After food." Vanessa stressed.

"After food," Gus agreed.

He showed the photo of the missing woman, Rachel Connors, to MJ. "Recognize her?"

MJ held the photo up to the light and looked at it carefully before shaking her head. "No, sorry."

"How 'bout her?" Gus asked, handing her the photo of the first victim, Michelle Townsend.

MJ nodded immediately. "Yeah, that's Michelle. I saw the news; terrible what happened to her. She used to pick up shifts waitressing here now and then."

Chapter Ten

RACHEL CONNORS PRESSED her clammy forehead against the cold stone and began to pray. She wasn't a religious person; she couldn't even recall the last time she stepped foot inside a church other than maybe for a wedding or a funeral. And she hadn't been raised religious; in fact, the only person in her extended family she knew of that went to church was her nana, rest her soul. But Rachel did believe in karma and manifestation and cosmic balance in the universe. And during the past few days, she had experienced evil of an untold kind, so knew it existed. So, in her mind then, it stood to reason, so too did good.

When her captor had told her to run, Rachel had no idea where to go. They were in complete darkness, and she'd awoken in the room she'd been kept in so had no idea what was outside. But then he screamed it again. And again. And again. So she took off.

She felt her way around the door jamb then, with an open palm pressed against the wall, ran as fast and as long as her weakened legs would carry her, stopping only when the pain and burning became too much. She'd dared to look back once, but the terror of seeing the distant light from her captor's headlamp in the darkness moving her way drove her to focus on the path ahead. But eventually, she could run no more. So hiding became Rachel's only option, her only chance at survival. And that was when she found the small crevice in the stone and squeezed her way in as far as it would allow.

She strained to hear him approaching, for his footsteps on the hard dirt, but heard nothing over her heartbeat pounding in her ears. She tried to calm her frantic breathing but the image in her mind of his miner's lamp slowly trudging behind her lit her terror on fire like a match to kindle. So she simply stood as still as her shaky legs would allow, squeezed into the cold, wet stone, and prayed some more.

And when she was done reciting the only prayer she knew—The Lord's Prayer—Rachel opened her eyes and rolled her head to face the opening she'd squeezed through. She stared into the darkness, squinting to see anything; a light, a shadow, any movement at all. But she saw nothing, not even the hand in front of her face. So she focused harder, straining her watery eyes, staring at one spot in the darkness that she knew he'd pass by and she waited. And after a minute when her eyes adjusted to their new reality, she saw something; a swirl of darkness, a different shade of black.

A form.

Rachel would never remember which came first—the whirring mechanical sound or the white light blinding her. But she would remember him.

He made sure of it.

Chapter Eleven

T AYLOR WOKE TO the loud sound of birds squawking. He slowly opened his eyes and looked up to see two large crows standing on the hood of his van looking down at him through the windshield. One of them tilted its head left then right, as if it too was wondering what was happening. Taylor watched as they pecked at something on his hood— then at each other—before noisily flying off.

He squinted at the sunrise sky with its smudges of pink and purple announcing the coming day before the pounding in his head had him squeeze his eyes closed. He tried to understand what was happening. After a few deep, concentrated breaths, he peeled them open again and found he was looking straight at the small section of dashboard between the steering wheel and driver's door of his van. Confused, he wondered what the fuck was going on.

His eyes slid down his body to see that he was slumped in the driver's seat with the side of his face resting against its door. He raised his head from the cold window and pulled himself upright using the steering wheel. Clasping the wheel tightly with shaking hands, he took in his surroundings through the windshield.

The van was parked on the side of a narrow country

road, listing severely to the right. So much so, he wondered if he'd run off the road or got stuck in a gulley of some sort. The pavement stretched away from him for what seemed like miles and he thought he saw a house or building far off in the distance. Out the passenger side window were trees but he noticed they ended about thirty or forty feet up the road where it opened up into vast fields on both sides.

Taylor looked around the inside of the van for any clue for why he was there. He saw a few fast-food bags crumpled in the footwell of the passenger seat and behind him on the floor was an assortment of discarded beer and soda bottles. The rear seat was down but the back of the van was oddly empty of the band's equipment. He rummaged around in the glovebox until he found an old bottle of Tylenol and shook the last few tablets into his palm. Grabbing a Coke Zero bottle from the floor behind him, he washed down the pills with what was left of the soda and leaned back against the headrest.

Taylor sat there quietly for several minutes, waiting for the Tylenol to kick in so he could function enough to drive home. He watched the sun come up over the fields in the distance and saw a few deer and a fox scurry near the tree line. He tried repeatedly to remember what happened last night and how he got there but, despite how hard he tried, nothing came to him.

He zipped up his thin jacket tightly against his chin then opened the door and stepped out onto the side of the road. Hunching his shoulders at the cold, Taylor instinctively looked around but saw no one. Having lived in cities his entire life, he found the quiet of a country dawn eerie and unsettling. He slowly circled the van and the crunching of dirt beneath his boots echoed around him. There were plenty of dents and scratches on the old girl, but nothing he hadn't seen before. The shoulder of the road he'd parked on had tall grass and scrub that sloped sharply down toward the tree line. He looked around carefully for anything odd, but found nothing.

Taylor stood by the driver's door for a beat, taking in the trees, the fields, and the wildlife, then got back in the van. He tapped the screen of his phone and it lit up, telling him it was just after six a.m. He hoped he'd be able to grab another hour or so of sleep before work but then realized he had no idea where he was or how far away home was. He unlocked his phone and paused in confusion at what he saw.

The Google app was open and on a Reddit thread about crime scene forensics. He closed that page and immediately checked his search history and his heartrate jumped. He scrolled the list of searches he'd done during the night and saw *how long does DNA evidence last on a dead body* and *can you get fingerprints from skin* and *how long do clubs keep security tapes*.

Panic crashed down on him and he began to feel dizzy. Realizing he was going to be sick, he grabbed an Arby's bag from the floor and vomited in it several times. When he was done, he crumpled the bag closed as best he could and placed it back on the floor. He had to get out of there before someone saw him, so he tapped on his maps app and found that he was on a remote road in Pelham, New Hampshire.

Typing in his home address he learned it was just twenty-four minutes away.

Taylor twisted the ignition key on, then off, several times until the laboring cranks finally started the old van's engine. He pressed the gas pedal to rev the engine and heard the familiar whine of loose belts coming from beneath the hood. Taylor then yanked the lever on the steering column into drive, checked his side mirror to be sure there was no oncoming traffic, and rumbled off the shoulder headed for home.

Chapter Twelve

<u>Tuesday</u>

- ✓ Take out trash
- ✓ Get replacement
- ✓ New movie
- Clean van
- Tylenol
- Eye drops
- Garbage bags
- Laundry detergent
- List of places to live
- Side effects of meds
- Erase phone GPS
- Erase phone searches
- Water
- Protein bars

Chapter Thirteen

I T WAS AROUND eight thirty a.m. and Gus was carefully weaving his truck through the narrow Pawtucket Falls side streets toward Taylor Franklin's house. It rained overnight and the roads and sidewalks were shiny in spots, filled with oily puddles. He had called Taylor's number from the bar last night but got no answer and instead of leaving a message Gus thought the element of surprise would be best. After dinner, Vanessa found them a small inn in the neighboring town of Tyngsboro at a reasonable, FBI-friendly rate.

Gus found Taylor's house then slowly drove around the block to get a sense of the area. He noticed Vanessa was unusually quiet, focused on their surroundings out the window as they crept through the streets. He watched her eye the houses as they passed, each as rundown as the last, and inspect the cars parked along the street, some potentially drivable while others clearly not. She craned her neck to look into yards and down alleys as if she were mentally charting escape routes as they went. After circling the block Gus parked a few doors down from Taylor's house but kept the engine idling for what little heat the old truck had to offer.

Vanessa wedged her Dunks coffee into the rectangular metal opening in the dash Gus claimed was a glovebox so she could hold her egg sandwich with both hands while she ate. Gus stared out his side window at Taylor's house as he mentally played the bassline of Oscar Peterson's *Night Train*. He pictured his Giuseppe Marconcini Italian bass, its elegant, smooth lines, firmly beside him, his fingers moving through the changes. Gus had transcribed the song's bassline freshman year of college and remembered it well. It was the first bassline he'd transcribed by bassist Ray Brown and he'd gone on to spend years studying videos of the legendary bassist, zeroing in on his hand positions and technique. But for Gus, this particular song was special. He'd often recite it in his head as if it were a long-ago memorized motivational speech.

"Penny?" V asked.

Gus blinked into the frosted window as if turning the channel then turned to her. "Nothin'."

"You playing music in your head again?"

Gus tried to stare her down but knew V wouldn't buckle. "Before I was so rudely interrupted, yeah." He smiled.

She gestured to Taylor's house with her chin. "So, what's this guy's origin story?"

Gus followed her eyes to Taylor's house and thought a moment before speaking. He and Taylor had a shared history with the Loyola connection, and he knew he'd have to rake through it at some point.

He turned back to her. "He was the cockiest, most arrogant person I'd ever met. But he was also the best bassist I'd ever seen too."

Gus turned and looked back out his side window, his

thoughts trampling down old paths. "There are three types of musicians," he began. "There are those that glamorize it and dream of stadium tours and jets and being rich and famous. Those are the guys you see playing rock or country; they learn a few chords and can play almost every set and it's all about the flash. Then there are those that just have it in 'em and grind it out *every day* to get it out the best way they know how. Those are the cats you rarely hear of. They're working two jobs just to be able to play, and they're playing at no-name clubs in no-name towns. Or, if they do happen to hit it big, you know the name of the singer and maybe the guitarist." He shook his head. "But not the bassist."

"And Taylor?" V asked.

Gus turned to her. "And then there are those where music's like a second language imprinted at birth; it just flows from them naturally, as if they're born knowing how to do it. Like … breathing. That was Taylor."

"So, what happened to him?"

"Not sure. Everyone has their own story, and I'm sure he's no different. From what I'd heard, he was offered a full ride to all the big-name music schools—Berkley, NYU, North Texas—but chose Loyola to be in New Orleans, the birthplace of jazz. But I suspect the partying and sin of the city helped attract him."

"Sounds like he had a moment."

"And then some. Having that big fish in the program made the rest of us feel very small. As much as we all hated to admit it."

"You? Small?"

Gus raised an eyebrow. "There's typically thirteen to fifteen different levels of groups in the Loyola jazz program."

"Thirteen to fifteen? That's cray-cray."

Gus held his hands out flat, one above the other that he moved up and down. "Yeah, there's a lot of dark money in there." They both laughed, "The first thing you do in a music program, though, is an audition," he continued, "so they can assess and rank you then they organize the groups in each level. I started in the lowest level, thirteen, and by the time I was a junior and Taylor came, I had worked up to level two. As a freshman, he was first chair in the first group. He was *that* good."

Vanessa swallowed the last of her coffee and shook her head.

She raised her chin toward the ramshackle house. "So how'd he end up here?"

Gus wedged his empty coffee cup into the glovebox and shrugged. "Dunno. He was in the New Orleans scene for a couple years after graduation then was just gone. Let's go find out."

Chapter Fourteen

T HEY CROSSED THE narrow street, the bitter morning cold biting at Vanessa's neck until it was numb. Gus knocked several times on the front door but heard nothing from inside. There was an old, rusty Dodge Caravan listing badly to one side parked in the driveway and a few trash cans in front of it against the garage door.

After knocking again, the front door squealed open and leaning into the narrow space was a man Gus wouldn't have recognized if he didn't already know his name. Taylor Franklin wore baggy grey sweatpants and a stained burnt orange T-shirt that was tight around his midsection. His hair was greasy and sticking up in various spots from having just woken and it looked as if he hadn't shaved for a week. He rubbed a hand over his blotchy, round face and squinted at Vanessa's outstretched hand holding her FBI badge.

Gus stepped forward. "Taylor."

Taylor looked up at Gus and Gus could see the confusion in his eyes. "Wheeler?" he asked, his voice scratchy and uneven.

"That's right. Long time." Gus said.

Taylor blinked several times quickly then straightened and opened the door a little wider. "What ... what're you doing here?" he stuttered, confused.

Gus held out his badge. "Got a minute? We need to ask you a few questions."

Gus watched Taylor look from the badge and back but say nothing.

Seeing his confusion Gus added, "Yeah, my day job." He slapped his leather wallet closed and slid it back into the inside pocket of his leather jacket. "This is Vanessa," he said, keeping it casual.

Before Gus could continue, the ringing of a cell phone from inside the house stole Taylor's attention, and he looked over a shoulder then back to Gus.

"I gotta get that," he said, swinging the door to close it as he turned and left them.

Gus poked his toe into the opening just as the door was about to click shut and watched Taylor slog away with the labored shuffle of a wounded animal.

"Looks like an invitation to me," he said.

"Mat says *welcome*," replied V, stepping past him and into the house.

Gus followed her and once his eyes adjusted to the darkness, he realized they were standing in a living room where time had stopped decades ago. The shades on the windows—pulled tightly together—were bland, tan cloth right out of the '60s. There was a dark sofa along the far wall that looked like the one Gus's grandmother had when he was growing up and in front of it was a simple wooden coffee table. Gus's eyes were drawn to the corner of the room and Taylor's beautiful upright bass he remembered coveting while at Loyola.

"Boujee," V whispered.

Gus looked over a cluttered desk to his side which held a dusty monitor in its center and a gaming box beside it. He saw yellow Post-it notes stuck to the edges of the monitor with lists scrawled on them. Eggs, frozen dinners, bring Mom puzzles. Hearing Taylor wrapping up his call from somewhere toward the back of the house, Gus turned to see him stepping through a doorway into the far side of the room.

"Hey ... what?"

"Just thought it'd be easier to talk inside," Gus said, stepping away from the desk.

Gus watched Taylor rub his eyes with a finger and thumb then turn on a dingy ceiling light with a switch on the wall beside him and saw the small black spots of dead flies inside its hazy glass shade. There was clutter on the coffee table and in various spots around the room and beside the door was a rubber mat with a pair of worn sneakers and leather boots caked with grey dried mud.

Gus gestured to a scratched-up sunburst Fender P bass on the sofa. "I saw you're in a band."

"Yeah, mostly rock and some alternative."

Gus gestured to the upright in the corner. "You're keepin' her up, though. She looks just like I remember."

"Tryin'. Played a gig with her last week. Just not a big jazz scene up here."

"I hear ya," Gus agreed. "I'm down in Boston. Same."

Taylor looked to Vanessa then back. "So ... you're FBI?" he asked with an air of confusion.

Gus held his hands up, palms to the ceiling. "My day

job. Gotta pay the bills." Gus knew his six foot four-inch frame could be intimidating so he swiveled the plastic chair in front of the gaming equipment around and sat.

Taylor took his electric bass from the sofa and, as he put it on a stand to the side, Gus noticed a GoPro video camera attached to the end of its neck. A lot of musicians recorded their playing to drop online and Gus had been urged by several to do it himself. He just never felt like being that much in the spotlight but wasn't surprised to see Taylor with one.

Taylor sat on the edge of the sofa. "I got one of those too." He looked at the time on his phone and Gus noticed it was a very plain-looking model, the kind you prepaid minutes on. "I gotta head out in a minute so…"

"This won't take long. We're investigating the murders of a few local women that were last seen in Music Row." Gus paused, waiting for some reaction from Taylor.

But, instead, what he got was Taylor almost looking through him, as if counting the seconds until this conversation was over.

"We know your band plays there a lot so thought maybe you'd seen them."

"Don't know nothin' about no murders." Taylor ran his fingers through his hair, keeping eyes on Gus the entire time. "Just doin' my thing, keeping my head down."

Vanessa held up a photo of the missing woman, Rachel Connors. Taylor slowly leaned forward as if it was an inconvenience and looked at the photo.

"This woman went missing this past Saturday night,"

Gus said. "You seen her before?"

"Nope," Taylor said with a shake of his head.

His voice was clipped, as if he were bored.

Vanessa then handed Taylor a photo of the first victim, Michelle Townsend, as Gus continued, "This woman was found about two and a half months ago. Dead in a field. You recognize her at all?"

Taylor glanced at the photo then handed it back to Vanessa. "Nope."

"You sure?" Gus asked. "Take a closer look. MJ at The Mills said she picked up waitressing shifts there once in a while."

Taylor kept his eyes on Gus. "Dude, there are new waitresses in that joint every week."

Gus nodded once to Vanessa who handed Taylor a photo of Sadie Hogan. "How 'bout this woman? She went missing about three weeks ago and her body was just found Sunday night."

Even in the dim light, Gus could see Taylor flinch as he looked at the photo. He casually handed it back to Vanessa but Gus had seen it and he'd bet V did too.

"Nope." The boredom was back in his voice.

Gus tipped his chin to the photo. "Take another look," he suggested.

Vanessa held the photo up until Taylor looked at it again then shook his head. "Don't know her. But you know how gigs are. Strangers coming up to you afterward, talking about the show and stuff."

Gus tilted his head slightly. "We didn't say anything

about a gig." He leaned onto his knees.

Taylor licked his lips, and his eyes darted to the wall behind Gus then back. "I just meant, you know, if I had ever seen her, it'd be at a gig." He forced a smile and held his hands up, gesturing around the dark, grungy room. "I mean, where else would I see a woman like *that*?"

"See, now, MJ at the club said she saw you talking with her at the bar late, the night she went missing. Think again. We're just trying to put a timeline together for her."

Taylor's eyes widened, and his mouth opened into a smile. "God, that's embarrassing. If it was late, I musta been trashed by then. We get an open bar there when we play so…"

"So you didn't see her leave the club that night?"

Taylor's eyes scrunched together. "I don't even remember talking to her."

An alarm sounded, and Taylor turned his phone over and tapped it off.

He looked back to Gus and held up his phone. "I gotta bounce. Time for my day job."

Gus and Taylor both stood, and Gus put his hand on Taylor's shoulder. "Thanks, brother. Good seein' ya again."

They said their goodbyes and Gus and Vanessa left as Taylor closed the door behind them. Standing on the cement front steps, Gus raised an eyebrow to V. He let her go first down the cracked cement walkway toward the street and when she stepped by him, she side-eyed him and spoke in a deep voice similar to his.

"Thanks, brother."

Chapter Fifteen

"OKAY, VIBE CHECK," Vanessa said as she yanked the truck's door shut.

Gus turned to her, his forehead scrunched.

"What'd ya think?" she clarified impatiently, tipping her head toward Taylor's house. "Vibe check." She then snapped her fingers, "C'mon, old man, keep up."

"That was definitely sketch," he said, turning back to the house.

"So is your rizz," Vanessa observed.

She had told Gus once that when he tried to speak like her it made her brain hurt.

Gus paused, confused, then pushed through it. "He definitely flinched when we showed him Sadie Hogan's photo." He then looked at her, his eyes squinted in thought. "The detective said they had no idea how the first vic, the Townsend woman, left the club she was at. She wasn't on any exit videos or neighboring cams. Let's see what we find for the other two. Let's get the video footage for any traffic cams within a few blocks radius surrounding the club the Hogan woman was last seen at. And have someone canvas the surrounding businesses for any cameras that might've caught the entrance or the sidewalks in either direction. We need to see who, if anyone, followed her out. Maybe we catch Taylor leaving with her or following her."

"Got it," Vanessa said, spinning her phone around in her hand.

"And do the same for last Saturday night when the Connors woman went missing. These women are leaving these clubs sometime. We figure out how and when, good chance we'll figure out who."

Vanessa looked back to Taylor's house and Gus saw the suspicion in her eyes. But before he could prod at it his phone rang and, seeing it was a local number, he answered it. After listening for a few moments he said, "Okay, got it. Text me the address. We'll meet you there." He ended his call and, thrusting the stick shift into first gear, looked to Vanessa. "That was Detective Boyd. Rachel Connors's body was just found in a field up in Pelham."

Gus and Vanessa made the drive in twenty minutes and used the time to get the investigation amped up. The first call he had her make was to the FBI's head pathologist, Rob Pappas, to see if he could meet them at the scene. Gus had dealt with his share of local coroners and as a rule preferred Rob or someone from his office to process his scenes. After bitching through Vanessa to Gus for a minute, Rob agreed to postpone a scheduled autopsy and meet them. Vanessa then called another agent in the Boston office assigned to the case, TJ, and got him going on getting the surveillance footage Gus wanted.

Gus let the annoying mechanical voice on his phone lead him to the scene but turned it off when they got close enough to see flashing blue and red lights. He steered the truck around a large farm, down a narrow road along one of its fields, and pulled to a stop behind a Pelham police cruiser parked on the shoulder. He and Vanessa got out and stepped around to the front of the truck and took in the view.

The road was slightly higher than the field so they could see for what seemed like miles in every direction. Crime scene tape had been strung up along the road and into the field, creating a bright yellow square in the lush, green haying field. There was a white tent erected near its center and Gus saw a path of raised forensic platform steps leading into the flattened tall grass with Detective Boyd standing at its end. He and Vanessa signed into the scene with an officer wearing sunglasses that ate half his face, slipped on booties and latex gloves then made their way along the steps. The ground on either side of them was damp and slightly muddy from the recent rain and the platforms rocked precariously with each step. Gus was reminded of leaping from rock to rock as a kid crossing streams in the Colorado wilderness. He stopped beside the detective as one of the crime scene unit techs working the scene looked over at him.

"FBI?"

The tech had goggles for glasses and long, fuzzy side-burns running down his cheeks like out-of-control vines on a British castle. Gus nodded and remained on the last footstep awaiting instruction. He could see a trail of small yellow placards with numbers on them leading to the body. The tech waved a gloved hand through the air. "Stay clear of those." He pointed to the other side of the body. "If you approach from that side, you'll see only one spot to avoid. They said you have a pathologist on the way?"

"That's right." Gus stepped off the last footstep and his hiking boots squished into the mud, covering his bootie. Vanessa looked from Gus to her stylish black boots then back.

"Nope." She remained on the footstep next to the detective.

Gus stepped beside the CSU tech and took it all in. Rachel Connors's nude body was on its back, arms and legs splayed wide as if she were in the process of making a snow angel. Her skin looked white and rubbery like the belly of a frog and her cloudy eyes glared up at the sky. Gus knelt down to get a closer look at the bruising on her neck.

His thoughts went to the person that did this, and he had so many questions in his mind, but *why?* was not one of them. He knew they very rarely—if ever—understood why a serial killer killed. They knew most began their gruesome career before the age of thirty, the crescendo to the mounting violence in their lives to that point. There have been so many books, movies, and TV shows made about serial killers over the years that the causal factors for their behavior had been boiled down to a primetime-ready, soundbite-sized short list digestible to the casual viewer. Parental abuse—sexual or psychological or both—torturing animals, fascination with fire, and some type of sexual deviance. But this list has been gravely oversimplified, masking an all-too-true reality.

There were millions of psychopaths in the US alone walking amongst everyone. Probabilities suggested that the majority of people had come in contact with at least one at some point during their lives. But the reality was that most psychopaths never killed; they led ostensibly average lives, content in their existence as janitors or retail store managers or truck drivers. If they acted out, it was in small ways, never deserving of a movie or a book about them. And, unfortunately, those that were known about were learned of far too late, after death and destruction had been done on a painful scale. The sad reality was that science was at just the precipice of an infinite chasm that was the human mind and knew surprisingly little about serial killers and what drove them.

"Pathologist?" the CSU tech called, breaking Gus from his thoughts.

He looked up to see Rob Pappas standing on one of the footsteps. His lean frame was bundled up beneath a tight parka. Rob rubbed his firm jawline and adjusted thick, industrial-grade glasses as he looked around then instinctively took the same route to the body and knelt beside Gus. Feeling the peer pressure, Vanessa did the same, tiptoeing on clumps of flattened grass along the way.

Rob performed an initial assessment of the body; lifting and examining the extremities, checking the lividity of the body and the bruising on her neck then assessing each eye. He pointed to the clusters of small red dots beneath the eyes.

"All but certain COD is asphyxiation." He then pointed to her wrists. "Abrasions from restraints. Same on her ankles. And look here," he said, waving a finger over her cheek. "There's residue here, could be adhesive left from tape. We'll get it tested." He leaned back on his heels and took in the positioning and overall state of the body.

"Time of death?" Gus asked.

Rob rocked his head side to side. "Based on lividity … ten, eleven hours ago. I'll confirm once I take the temp."

Vanessa checked the time on her phone and caught Gus's eye. "So, about eleven p.m. or midnight."

"Can you check her throat?" Gus asked. "The other vic had a driver's license wedged in hers they found during the autopsy."

Rob forced Rachel Connors's stiff bottom jaw open, straining against the rigor mortis. He slid a small headlamp on then placed a hand beneath her neck and pulled up slightly to elongate the throat. He took a pair of silver tweezers from his medical bag and inserted them into her mouth until his fingers touched the front teeth. Concentrating for a few moments, he slowly retracted the tweezers. But as their tips emerged, Gus saw nothing in their grasp.

"I don't have my long tweezers here and I can't see past the molars."

Gus carefully felt around her hips then slipped two fingers into the front pocket of her slacks and slid out a thin leather billfold. He checked its content then looked up to Rob and Vanessa.

"No license." He stood and waved for a CSU tech to bring over an evidence baggie. "This is our guy." He dropped the billfold into the bag before turning back to Rob. "When can you confirm cause of death?"

"Tomorrow," Rob said, glancing toward Vanessa. "After,

you know, I do the autopsies already scheduled."

Vanessa smiled. Rob did not.

A Pelham police officer approached them along the footpath. "Agents, you wanna speak to the person that found the body before we let him go?"

"Yeah," Gus replied, taking one last look around the scene and Rachel Connors's body.

Back on the street, Gus and Vanessa and Detective Boyd removed their booties and gloves and joined the officer and a husky man leaning against the cruiser with a large dog at his feet. The sun had pierced the clouds, sending shoots of light toward the ground that looked like ropes to the heavens. Gus measured the distance with his eyes from where they stood, to the body at nearly thirty yards and, as if anticipating the question, the old man spoke up.

"Norman here saw a fox and took off." He shook his head. He had salt and pepper hair and kind eyes. "It was my fault. I had him off leash. And when he wouldn't come back, I went in after him. That's when I saw her."

"Did you touch the body at all?" Vanessa asked.

The man grimaced. "No, only got about halfway in when I saw what Norman was sniffing at and called him out."

"You see anyone else around here this morning?"

The man shook his head. "No, just me and him." His eyes flicked toward the field then back. "You need anything else?" He wiggled his shoulders. "I kinda wanna take a shower."

Gus looked to the officer. "You got his statement and

contact details?"

"Yessir."

"Alright, have the CSU guys take a mold of his boots so they can rule out those prints in the field." Gus turned back to the old man. "Once they do that, you're good to go."

The officer headed back into the scene while the old man stepped down the embankment to let Norman take a pee. And as he did so, Gus got a good look at the old man's boots for the first time. They were almost completely grey with dried mud caked over the toes and along the sides.

Seeing the odd look on Gus's face, Vanessa squinted. "What?"

Gus raised his chin toward the old man. "Check out his boots."

"What about 'em?" Vanessa questioned, looking back to the old man.

"That dried mud all over them? They look exactly like the boots on the mat beside Taylor Franklin's front door."

Chapter Sixteen

TAYLOR LEANED INTO the oversized door, opening it just enough to peer around. He remembered the tour guide telling him that standard interior doors are typically thirty-two inches in width but theirs were designed to be forty inches wide to accommodate easy access for wheelchairs and other equipment, if needed.

His mother was sitting in a chair with her back to him, looking out the window. Her thin, grey hair looked recently brushed and her shoulders rose and fell in a steady rhythm with her breathing. Standing there, the world fell away from Taylor as memories melted into his thoughts; his mother making dinner at the stove, him as a young boy playing with his matchbox cars on the linoleum floor in their kitchen, its spots worn through to the wood creating craters for his trucks to jump. The next moment, he was a middle schooler taking a bow with the rest of the cast of the musical *Bye Bye Birdie*, squinting past the bright lights to see his mom standing amongst the other parents, smiling and clapping excitedly. But before the memories could continue, Taylor pushed them—and the door—aside and entered the room.

He stepped around the bed, with its light-colored faux wood and matching nightstand, and noticed the photos his mother had brought with her were hung on the wall above its headboard. There was one of him in his Loyola cap and gown, one of his sister on her wedding day, and one black and white photo with all three of them from a Christmas when he was a child that he couldn't place. On the nightstand sat a small digital clock with large, striking red letters and beside it, Taylor saw a framed picture of Saint Michael the Archangel—the patronage saint for the sick and suffering—that had hung beside her bed at home. The room looked as homey as one could expect; the small chrome fixtures and ports in the wall beside the bed and the orange electrical outlets strategically placed around the room the only signs she was in a medical facility.

Pulling a chair from beside the small sofa, he placed it next to her and sat. His mother turned to him and before he could say anything a wide smile spread across her face.

"Hi there," she said, shifting sideways slightly to better see him. She gestured to the window. "The cardinal was just here but those nasty crows scared him off again. But the hummingbirds have been around all morning. They're not scared of those crows, no sirree."

Taylor looked to the large bird feeder just outside her window with several large black crows blustering around it. A hummingbird zipped past his vision and pulled up to hover over a flat red feeder hanging from a lower branch on the tree.

"Those crows are so smart, though," she continued. "They've figured out that if they sit on the metal bar it closes the door to the seed. So they hold onto the branch next to it and lean in to eat. Crafty little suckers." She chuckled to herself.

"Yes, they are," Taylor agreed.

Taylor's mom turned toward him and with a wide smile said, "I'm Evelyn. My friends call me Evie."

"I know, Mom. It's me. Taylor."

She stared blankly at him for a moment like the cyborg in the Terminator movies performing a risk assessment, then her face relaxed. "Oh, of course, honey. I'm sorry." She waved a hand through the air. "My head gets all scrambled sometimes. Of course, of course." She patted his knee with a hand. "And how are you?" she asked, looking back out the window.

Taylor's mind swirled with where to begin; so much had happened in the past few days since he'd seen her last.

"Well, not great. Some stuff's happened, and I'm not sure what to do."

"Go on. Tell me about it."

His mother had always been the calming presence in Taylor's life, which was exactly what he needed now. She was there—talking him off the ledge—when he was about to perform for the first time at his high school's open mic night as a freshman. And she was there—telling him to chase his dreams—when instead of buying a car like many of his friends were doing, he wanted to spend all of his savings on a crappy, old upright bass so he could learn how to play jazz. And she was there when Taylor stepped in front of the audition committee at Loyola to perform his original music as part of his application process. Taylor's mom had been his rock his entire life, never wavering no matter how frazzled he'd become.

He paused, wondering where to begin. He thought of waking in his van that morning parked on the side of the road, not remembering how he got there. And of the searches he'd done on his phone about crime scenes and fingerprints and other odd things. He thought of finding Sadie Hogan's license in his pants pocket and of the visit he'd gotten that morning from the FBI; Gus and his partner Vanessa. But he couldn't tell his mother about any of that; it'd crush her.

"It's just been hard, ya know? Moving back to the Falls; same old scene, same old grind…"

Same old urges.

"Things just don't feel right here anymore."

"You should always follow your dreams," she said, her nose raised slightly as she followed a hummingbird whizzing past the window.

"Thanks, but it's not that simple anymore, Mom."

"But sometimes it's exactly that simple. Sometimes you just need to look on the bright side. There must be good things in your life now too, right? There always are if you know where to look."

"Well, I played a jazz gig the other night and loved it."

"See? Now, that's something good. Do you have more planned?"

"I do, several."

She patted his thigh again. "Ya see? Ya just have to look."

"And I'm making plans to move back to New Orleans too … gonna get my jazz career back. Connected with some cats down there I used to play with; they're excited for me to get back. And I've been saving as much as I can; something out of every paycheck, no matter how little. Just like you taught me."

Taylor went on to tell her about what some of his friends in New Orleans were doing, about the gigs they'd been playing, and how he'd have work as soon as he got back. He told her how good it felt to polish and tune his upright bass again; how good it felt in his arms and of how he lost track of time and played for hours when he first pulled it out again. And through it all, his mom smiled and nodded. And when he finally stopped talking, a comfortable silence settled over the room and the two of them watched the crows do their high-wire act again and again. They watched hummingbirds zip this way and that and his mother pointed excitedly at one of the smaller ones and laughingly said his name was *Buzz*.

And after a while, Taylor felt his anxieties fade and his mind begin to settle. And some time later, his mother turned to him and her eyes widened and she smiled. And that made Taylor smile also. And then Taylor's mom leaned in closer, put her hand back on his knee, and spoke to him in a soft, conspiratorial whisper.

"My name's Evelyn," she said. "My friends call me Evie. What's your name?"

Chapter Seventeen

THE BAND HAD just finished rehearsal, so the guys were milling around in Taylor's garage and packing up. Mick rushed to load his cymbals into a case and snapped its cover closed. He ran a palm over his forehead and looked around for anything else to pack up.

"Somewhere to be Mick?" Leon asked. "I thought we'd hang a bit." He raised a joint in the air.

Mick wiped sweat from his brow. The sleeves of his untucked button-down shirt were rolled up, exposing toned, hairy forearms. He bent his right elbow, raising his hand upward, and wiggled his wrist until the cluster of bracelets slid down his forearm.

"Can't, dude. Got a date."

Mick had recently gone through a very messy divorce. And while most forty-year-old men twice divorced would tend to look inward, do some soul-searching about what had gone wrong, not Mick. He had persevered and pushed forward. He wasn't going to let a divorce, that small speedbump in life, jeopardize his dating schedule, much like he hadn't let his marriage do so.

Leon gestured with the joint to Chris.

"Sorry, man, I gotta blast too," the singer replied.

"Give him some," Mick said, pointing to Taylor with a wide smile. "He's been moody all night. You can teach him how."

"Ah, he don't need no lessons, do ya, T?" Leon swiped his arm through the air. "T was quite the stoner back in the day." Leon held the joint up in Taylor's direction.

Taylor hesitated, considering Leon's offer for a moment. He had given that up years ago when he'd cleaned up his act just before going to college. But he was tempted, for sure, as he thought about all that had happened during the past twenty-four hours. Getting high might help him relax, help him forget about finding Sadie Hogan's driver's license or waking up in his van on the side of the road in the middle of nowhere. Or the visit that morning from Wheeler and his FBI partner. Because right now, that was all he could think about and it felt as if his nerves were vibrating, like a bass string left to play itself out.

But Taylor knew that was a slippery slope, one he slid down when he was younger. He simply shook his head to Leon.

"Ya see?" Leon smiled. "T's on the straight and narrow now." Leon tucked the joint back into a pocket. "He's even playin' his upright again." He added as he went about stuffing his cherry sunburst Les Paul into its case.

"That reminds me," Chris said, looking to Taylor. "A friend of mine went to a jazz show last week at a new club in Acton; said she thought she saw you in the band. Was it you?"

Mick stopped what he was doing and turned to Taylor.

"You moonlighting on us, dude?"

"It was one show," Taylor said dismissively.

"You told me you picked it up again," Mick said. "You didn't say anything about playin' any jazz gig." He stared silently at Taylor for a few moments, as if trying to read his mind. "You thinkin' about bustin'?" He looked around at the others. "I mean, cuz we're booked out solid for months. We gotta know."

"Not anytime soon," Taylor said. "But eventually, yeah, I'd like to get back to NOLA at some point."

The room fell quiet for several moments before the singer, Chris, broke the silence. "Well, I think it's great you're playing the upright again and flexing your jazz muscles. Maybe we can work some of that into our gigs at some point."

An unsettling silence wrapped the room again. Mick put the case with his cymbals in it on the floor behind his drum kit and wound up a few cords up. Then he grabbed his coat and headed toward the door that led into the house.

"Oh, hey, Taylor, can I use the van Saturday?" he asked on his way by. "I need to pick up a chair I bought at Jordan's."

"Sure," Taylor said.

"Roland and I have it Saturday," Chris said, referring to his partner. "He's donating an old freezer from the restaurant to one of the shelters."

"Sunday?" Mick asked, looking to the others.

Leon raised his hand. "I'm bringing Sheila's daughter and her friends to the movies."

Mick claimed the van for Monday after work then headed out the door. And as Taylor watched him leave, his eyes skimmed past the closed overhead garage door and he saw a face in one of its windows. It was a flash, a nanosecond, but still he knew who it was. He'd recognize that straight sandy-blonde hair and those freckled cheeks anywhere. He shot to his feet.

"What the fuck?" he cried.

"What?" Leon asked, watching Taylor scramble to the garage door.

Taylor peered out each of the windows along the door's top, one after another, but the only person he saw outside was Mick getting into his new orange Dodge Challenger with its fat tires and black rally stripes. Taylor heard the rumble of its engine start as he continued to look around at the shadows.

"There was someone looking in the garage at us," he said into the glass.

His heart hammered the inside of his chest as he squinted, trying to see a dark corner of his yard by the street.

"I didn't see anyone." Chris said.

"It was probably just Mick trying to freak you out," Leon offered.

"It wasn't Mick," Taylor dismissed. "It was..." he whispered softly, as if to himself.

"Dunno," Leon said turning back to his guitar case and snapping it closed.

"Catch you guys Thursday," Chris said, grabbing his coat and heading out the door.

Leon got a garbage bag from the kitchen and began cleaning up the garage-slash-practice room and, once finished, put the garbage bag in the bin outside and rejoined Taylor.

"I'm gonna blast."

The two of them stepped from the garage into the living room and Taylor's thoughts went to talking with Wheeler and his partner in there that morning and of the missing woman they showed him a photo of.

"Hey, where'd we end up Saturday night?" he asked Leon. "When Mick was buying us all those shots."

Leon turned to him. "Man, you don't remember?"

"The end of the night's a bit fuzzy." replied Taylor, shrugging.

"No surprise. You were lit. We ended up at that new tequila joint on Merrimack. The Agore … the Agrove … the Agave. The Blue Agave. You dragged us all in there as we were walking by. You said there was this LA-MEX place in the Quarter you used to play at, Audrey's?"

"Audrey's Tequila Hut. Yeah, they had a hundred and thirty different tequilas."

"That's what you said when you pulled us in. Then Mick kept buying us shots. It was insane."

Flashes of the bar popped in Taylor's mind. The four of them doing a shot in the dark room with stripes of neon light in swirls across its ceiling. Mick inviting a few women at the bar to join them.

"Yeah, I guess I remember that. You and I walk home after?"

Leon eyed him for a second. "No, man, you were all in. I left you there around twelve thirty. I tried to get you to leave with me but you were vibing."

Taylor felt the circumspection of his friend's eyes so reached for the doorknob and opened the door. They said their goodbyes then Taylor closed and locked the front door. He stood there for a minute, trying to remember more about being at the Blue Agave with the guys on Saturday night but nothing came to him. His thoughts then turned to Wheeler and his hot, edgy partner coming to his house that morning.

He used his phone and searched *murdered women, Pawtucket Falls, Music Row*, and a breaking news story came up about the missing woman, Rachel Connors, having been found dead that morning in a field in Pelham, New Hampshire. Taylor's hands shook as he read of how her murder was believed to be committed by the same suspect as Sadie Hogan's and Michelle Townsend's. The story detailed how each woman had been strangled after being abducted from Pawtucket Falls' Music Row and that the FBI had been called in to take over the investigation.

Taylor slumped against the wall, dropping his phone onto the desk. He closed his eyes, put his face in his hands, and tried harder to remember what happened Saturday night but nothing else came to him. The alarm on his phone chimed, alerting him that it was time for his medication. He got his pills and, after staring at one in his palm for several moments, popped it in his mouth and washed it down with a drink of water from the tap. Then, looking at the medicine's label, Taylor thought of his therapist. And that was when he came up with a plan. He'd call first thing in the morning and get an emergency session with him. And he'd tell him everything; everything except the driver's license. And in the meantime, he'd carefully put down what he could in his journal and make sure to bring it with him. The guy might be a bit stiff but he was good at having Taylor think about things differently.

Feeling better, he looked around the kitchen then nervously laughed out loud. What had he been thinking? He wasn't capable of doing what he'd feared he'd done. He had become a lot of things he wasn't particularly proud of—lazy, a failure—but he was changing all that now. And he certainly wasn't a murderer. No way. He felt a weight begin to lift from his shoulders until he was shaking his head, openmouthed, in amazement at where his paranoia had led him this time. He didn't do any of this. That was why they had nothing connecting him to any of these women except talking to Sa…

Shit. Her license.

Heat exploded across his chest. He had to get rid of that license. If the FBI—or anyone—knew he had it, he'd be screwed. He scurried to the fridge and, stretching up against it like a child, pulled Teddy off its top. He then held it against his chest in the crook of his elbow while he opened its lid with the other hand.

Taylor rummaged around in the ceramic bear, feeling his way past his mother's checkbook and some assorted cash until he felt the driver's license lying on the bottom. He pinched it between his finger and thumb and pulled it out as he placed Teddy on the counter. He pulled drawer after drawer out, looking for the scissors, until he found them. He'd cut the license up into a million little pieces over a paper bag then take a drive and sprinkle the pieces out the window on some random road. It would be gone forever and so would his connection to Sadie Hogan.

He got a paper bag, opened it wide on the counter then took the scissors in his hand. And as he turned the license flat between his fingers and slid it into the mouth of the scissors, he stopped short and froze. Staring back at him from the driver's license was not Sadie Hogan.

Staring back at Taylor was the woman whose body was found dead in a field that morning, Rachel Connors.

Chapter Eighteen

G US AND VANESSA had stayed at the crime scene for several hours, hoping Rob or the CSU team would discover something pivotal to their case. After a preliminary examination and finding nothing else of significance, Rob released Rachel Connors's body to be taken to the FBI's facilities for an autopsy and closer examination.

He and Vanessa then watched the CSU team from the street as they made their way through a grid of the scene as if in slow motion, randomly picking at spots on the ground with long tweezer-like utensils. By early afternoon, Gus had checked in with the lead CSU tech so many times the young man had pleaded with Gus to be left alone then, sensing that wouldn't work, had bargained for his freedom. If Gus and Vanessa left the scene immediately, he would guarantee they'd have CSU's crime scene report that night. Gus knew a good deal when he saw it.

They then spent the better part of the afternoon and early evening interviewing friends of Sadie Hogan and Rachel Connors. Sadie's friends largely confirmed what Gus and Vanessa already knew. She was out clubbing with friends and ended up at The Mills the night she disappeared. When her friends left, she stayed behind to watch the band some more.

Vanessa had TJ run a check with Uber, Lyft, and the taxicab companies and they learned she didn't order a ride at all that night. And, thinking of the coal dust found beneath Sadie's fingernails, they asked her friends about it but none of them had any idea where that could've come from. Getting surveillance of that street the night Sadie disappeared, that the Pawtucket Falls police missed, was now the priority and TJ was on it.

Rachel Connors's friends provided a few more details than Gus and Vanessa had previously. Rachel too was out with a few friends but, unlike Sadie and her group, they had only gone to the Blue Agave so they knew her assailant very likely targeted her there. But, unlike Sadie, Rachel left her friends early yet never made it home.

It was nearly nine p.m. and exhausted Gus and V decided to grab a bite to eat at the inn then call it a day. But as Gus pulled the truck into a parking space in its lot and killed the engine, his phone lit up with a call from the pathologist, Rob, so he put it on speaker.

"We've just completed the autopsy on Rachel Connors so thought you'd want to hear what we found."

"We get anything to go on?"

"Well, we found the driver's license of the prior victim—Sadie Hogan—embedded deep in the esophagus just below the trachea. And I can confirm the time of death was around midnight so she'd been in that field for about ten hours. Cause of death was asphyxiation and she has a contusion on her neck similar to the other victims. But unlike the others, we found some type of chemical residue on her neck and cheek."

"Do you know what it is?"

"We're not sure but we'll run some tests on it. And, like the others, there's no sign of sexual assault. However, we did find a few fibers beneath the fingernails that appear to be some type of carpeting."

"There enough to get a match?" asked Gus eagerly.

"I believe so, yes. I've got one of my staff starting on it now but it may take a day or two. And, obviously we're doing a tox screen but that'll take a few days to get back as well."

"On the tox screen, Rob, can you expand the test for sedatives? The other women's tox screens came back normal but he's taking them from crowded areas. It just feels like he has to be sedating them somehow."

"Sure, we can test for a pretty long list of well-known agents."

"Rob, thanks again for rushing all of this."

"I'll let you know when we get results back."

They ended the call when Vanessa received the CSU's preliminary crime scene report as promised.

"We get anything?" Gus asked as she scrolled through it on her phone.

Vanessa read bits and pieces of the report aloud. "Recent inclement weather ... contamination to the scene ... damp and muddy conditions along with significant canine activity in close proximity of the body..."

"Ah shit." Gus groaned.

"A few miscellaneous pieces of trash—a partial candy wrapper, an old empty beer bottle—found on the periphery of the scene." She looked up at Gus. "But they were found near the road; they're not relevant."

Gus's jaw tightened in frustration. He was hoping for a break, some tangible evidence they could work with. They had Sadie Hogan's license taken from the throat of Rachel Connors but, as with the Townsend woman's license found in Hogan's throat, Gus knew there would be no fingerprints on it.

"Okay, wait a sec..." Vanessa muttered as she focused intently on her phone. She pinched its screen then looked to Gus. "Okay, so the immediate scene around the body was a hot mess. Mud, puddles, a million dog prints. Nothing of use." She held up her phone that had a photo from the report on its screen and used her finger to point out spots. "Here's the entire scene. Here's the body. You can see the flattened grass and mud and stuff all around it. But see this spot here, just outside the matted grass?"

Gus leaned closer and nodded.

Vanessa then swiped and pinched its screen again. "This is a close up of that spot. See how it's raised a bit? It's just a little higher than where the body was."

"Yeah, like a bump."

She swiped to the next photo and enlarged it then turned the phone so they both could see its screen clearly.

"Slay," she said. On her screen was a closeup photo of a footprint in a small patch of dirt between several clumps of grass. "He stood just a few feet from the body, taking it all in."

Gus studied the photo intently, having Vanessa swipe

back and forth with the photo of the entire scene.

And after a minute or so it clicked in his mind. "Or he was taking pictures of his work."

Vanessa slowly nodded. "Shit, you're right."

A call from TJ popped up on her screen so she tapped it and put him on speaker.

"V, we just finished going through the surveillance footage we got from the Blue Agave for the night the Connors woman went missing." His voice trailed off and they heard the clicking of keyboard keys before he added, "I just sent you two clips."

She played the first and they watched as Rachel Connors stepped up to the bar between two stools and raised her hand toward the bartender. One of the stools was empty so she leaned on its back as she waited. There was a man sitting on the other stool and Gus recognized him immediately.

"Is that..." Vanessa began.

"Taylor," Gus finished. "Yes, it is."

They watched Rachel for a few moments then one of the men standing beside Taylor's stool turned toward her.

"Who's that?" V asked.

"That's Leon Sampson, the guitarist," Gus said. "I recognize him from their poster." He pointed to another guy standing there. "And that's Mick Preston, the drummer," he added.

He pulled up the photo he took of the poster at The Mills and held it out for Vanessa to see. Then a few moments later a man with shoulder-length blond hair stepped into the frame and joined the others. Gus squinted at the video then referred to his phone.

"That's the other band member; Chris Houlihan, the singer."

They watched as Rachel waved repeatedly to the bartender again and they saw Taylor look her way then back to the others. And at that point, Leon stepped beside Taylor and appeared to say something. Rachel turned toward him and the two spoke for a few moments before the bartender brought her bill and she turned away. She quickly scribbled on it, put her credit card back in her wallet and turned to leave. But the drummer, Mick, had stepped into her path so, surprised, she stopped short. The two spoke while Mick waved his hand repeatedly for the bartender as he laughed and Rachel smiled, seemingly enjoying the conversation. Eventually, Mick stepped aside and swooped his arm across his body in a grand gesture for her to continue by, which she did. Then the video ended.

"Where'd she go?" asked Gus.

"That's the second clip, V," TJ said.

Vanessa played the next clip and they watched as Rachel walked into the bottom of the frame then continued down a hallway and went into the ladies' room. The hallway remained empty for about ten seconds then the drummer, Mick, stepped into the frame. He stopped at the ladies' room door and leaned his ear close to its frosted glass. He then went to the emergency exit and seemed to be inspecting its long bar that opened the door.

"He's checking if it's alarmed," Gus said.

"*That's* out of pocket," Vanessa said.

Something caught Mick's attention and his head snapped back toward the ladies' room door. He hurried back toward the entrance of the hall, turned around and began to slowly walk back down it toward the restrooms as if for the first time. The ladies' room door opened and Rachel stepped into the hallway and right into Mick. He held her from falling by her shoulders then turned sideways so as to not block her way. They watched as Mick struck up another conversation with her and the two talked for a minute or so before Mick put his outstretched hand on the wall above Rachel and leaned close to her. She immediately squirmed out from beneath his arm and stepped beside him with her back to the camera. They spoke for another few moments as she put her coat on and Mick's facial expression turned angry. He flicked his hand in the air, said something to her, then walked out of the hall and off-camera.

"Burned," Vanessa said.

Rachel paused a moment then, zippering up her jacket, went back into the ladies' room. A full minute later she stepped back into the hallway and began walking back toward the club but then stopped. She said something to someone off-camera then her face relaxed and she smiled. She then continued out of the frame and the video ended.

"Who was she talking to?" asked Gus.

"We don't know. That's a dead spot in the surveillance cameras."

"Then where'd she go?" Gus pressed.

"That's it," TJ said. "We can confirm she didn't go back into the club, but we've watched the front exit feed three times and this feed on that back entrance for the rest of the night. She never leaves the club."

Gus caught V's eye. "We gotta see that hall that she was last in. She had to go somewhere."

Gus told TJ to call the club's owner and tell him they were on their way to inspect the area where Rachel Connors was last seen then they ended the call.

"We don't know how long he kept the first vic, the Townsend woman, alive," Gus said, firing the old truck's engine up again.

"That's right," V agreed. "But we know he kept the second vic, the Hogan woman, at least seven or eight days."

"But here he has Connors just forty-eight hours before doin' her. Why so quickly?"

Vanessa was already slowly shaking her head. "Dunno. News reports spook 'im?"

"Maybe," Gus whispered skeptically as his attention was pulled toward the entrance of the inn.

An older man in a long dark winter coat was pulling a large suitcase on wheels up the entrance steps and Gus's eyes were drawn to the vacancy sign beside its door.

"Maybe he needed a vacancy."

"Fuck, you could be right."

Gus pumped the clutch several times and, revving the engine slightly, grinded the stick shift into first gear.

"Looks like it's drive-thru again," Vanessa said as the truck lurched out of the parking spot.

Chapter Nineteen

G US AND VANESSA made it to the Blue Agave in just under twenty minutes and were met at the entrance by the club's owner. Timothy Franco was a tall, thin man with a long face and bird-like nose. He wore a fashionable dark suit with a bright pink silk shirt unbuttoned at the top. He greeted them with a concerned smile.

"Hello, agents." He spoke with the precision of someone using their second language. He shook Vanessa's hand first, then Gus's. "I'm Timothy."

He escorted them into the club, past the bar, and eventually made it to a wide dark mahogany door propped open with RESTROOMS printed on its frosted glass. Once inside the short hallway, Gus used the frozen frame on Vanessa's phone to position himself exactly where Rachel had been when they last saw her on the video. He turned from the phone and looked straight at the office door about twenty feet away. On his left was the ladies' room and just past it the men's room. Opposite the men's room was the alarmed back exit door to the alley that Mick had checked on the video.

Gus then turned around and faced the opposite way down the hall. The open doorway to the club was about twenty feet straight in front of him. He knew from the surveillance footage that as soon as someone walked through that doorway the security camera in the club would pick them up. So Rachel went missing somewhere between where he was standing and that doorway. To his left was a single door with a plaque on it that read UTILITY CLOSET. To his right were two doors, one right after the other. The one closest to him had a sign on it that read NOT AN EXIT.

"What are those?" Gus asked.

Timothy stepped over to the closest one. "This leads to the basement." He pointed to the next door a few feet away. "That's a back door to the kitchen."

Gus pulled the thin, black penlight he'd taken from his truck out of his jacket pocket and, opening the utility closet, looked around. He flicked on the light switch on the inside wall and stepped inside. It had silver metal shelves lining its perimeter stuffed with supplies. He saw jugs of cleaning products, large boxes of toilet paper and paper towels, and myriad smaller boxes of straws, napkins, and other typical restaurant supplies. In one of the corners were several yellow buckets on wheels with mop handles sticking out of them. He stepped back into the hall and, flicking the light off, closed the door behind him. He looked to Timothy and gestured to the two doors on the opposite wall.

"We'll follow you."

"Let's start with the kitchen. The basement's pretty grungy, and I don't want to track that into the food areas."

Timothy paraded them into the crowded kitchen where men and women dressed in elaborate white coats scurried around feverishly, yelling back and forth at each other. It had been a lifetime since he'd taken Spanish in high school but Gus still recognized some of the more graphic insults, he and his buddies had used their newfound skills to learn.

Keeping with its name, the menu for the club was upper-scale Mexican. Gus saw large baskets filled with ears of corn and wooden crates holding fresh tomatoes in clusters of vines. He saw baskets with red, green, and purple-colored peppers and others with red onions. They passed a box holding fresh garlic cloves then one containing prickly flat green produce. Seeing Gus slow to look more closely, Timothy picked one up.

"This is a nopal. It's a cactus found in Mexico and South America, primarily. It's quite delicious and very good for you." He gestured around at all the colorful and exotic-looking food being prepared. "We're always experimenting; always looking for that great new dish or that exotic drink that sets us apart."

They walked from the area holding the fresh produce into the prep area, with its large glass-faced coolers, lines of stainless-steel counters and deep, inset sinks. Several staff members were chopping and cutting various ingredients and dropping their cuttings into silver mixing bowls. They passed through without saying a word then walked down a short hallway into the cooking area. For the first time, Gus noticed one side was open to the dining and bar area. It was lit with purple and red lighting and the counter that served as the bottom of the long window was made of thick veiny marble. If playing in bars for so many years had taught Gus anything, he could tell this place was so nice—and the food too good—they probably didn't even give the bands a discount on their meals.

Throughout their tour, Gus inspected each wall and corner but didn't find any place someone could exit the kitchen except for the door they entered and the entrance and exit the wait staff used to schlepp food to their customers. And, while the kitchen was essentially three small spaces linked together, the number of staff in that space would make it impossible for someone to enter that wasn't supposed to be there and not be noticed. Finished with the kitchen, Timothy led Gus and Vanessa to the basement.

"Watch your head," Timothy said opening the door.

Gus paused. "It's not locked?"

Timothy's lips bulged out and he shook his head. "Can't per the fire marshal. Provides access to some of the street's power lines. You'll see."

Timothy led them into the basement, bending to the side and lowering his head as he crept sideways down the winding old stone staircase. "Hold onto the railing. These stones get slippery from the moisture."

Vanessa followed close behind him mimicking his stance as she went. Gus contorted his body in ways he didn't know possible to avoid the low-hanging rafters at each step. He feared a worse situation awaited him in the old basement when Timothy stopped on the last stair. But as Gus stepped past the club owner, he was pleasantly surprised to find a cavernous space with tall brick walls and a ceiling at least twice the normal height.

"This is incredible," Gus said, looking around.

Dusty round pendant lights hung from the rafters, spaced evenly in rows from left to right. The few that still worked created small cones of light throughout the room and cast misshapen and eerie shadows onto its floors and walls. He felt the humidity on his skin and could hear the faint sound of distant flowing water.

"Yeah," Vanessa softly said, inspecting the gunk stuck to the bottom of her boots. "Incredible."

"This floor can be pretty mucky," Timothy said. "The staff have mudders upstairs in case they need to come down here." He looked to Gus's waterproof hiking boots, with their thick laces and aggressive treads. "You should be fine but I'll stay on this last step if it's okay."

The center of the room was filled with clusters of old manufacturing equipment left behind from another era and piles of random rods and straps and gears. Gus saw elaborate green metal machines with multiple levers and bars attached to wooden stitching panels and enormous spooling wheels connected to complex machines with needles and pulleys. Against the far wall was a large water wheel beside a boarded-up section of the floor.

"That's the old water wheel for the hydroelectric setup," Timothy said, seeing Gus staring at it. He pointed to the boarded-up section of floor beside the foundation. "It sat in there and beneath it is a splinter from the river. This wheel spun the generator and made electricity for the entire building."

Gus looked around for any potential exits. He stepped over behind the staircase to see a solid wall with no doors or windows. He waved his flashlight along a long silver heating duct hanging from its rafters amongst old rusted metal rods and wheels remaining from some sort of milling operation. At its top was a gap about three feet high. He pulled over an old spooling wheel and climbed atop it to look inside.

"I think that's the space that goes under the street," Timothy explained. "You'll probably see some of the electric distribution lines running through there."

Gus shined the light inside and confirmed what Timothy had said. He peered beyond the lines only to find a solid wall of dirt. After inspecting the entire crevice, he hopped back onto the floor and turned his attention to the wall to the right of the stairs. It was partially covered with broken barrels and large wooden spool wheels. But even amongst the clutter, he could see a small framed box in its center about waist high. He stepped back beside Timothy.

"What's that?" he asked.

Timothy's mouth scrunched up. "Dunno. This is only my second time down here." Seeing Gus's look of surprise he added, "We only lease the space, we don't own it." He gestured around with an arm, "And this is useless to us. We couldn't even store stuff down here it's so damp."

Gus and Vanessa walked over to the wall and together they slid a few barrels out of the way to get to the framed box. It had a small wooden door with a handle on its bottom so Gus pulled the door up to open it and shined his light inside.

"Dumbwaiter," he said to Vanessa over his shoulder.

"There's an opening upstairs in the kitchen that's been

blocked off," Timothy called from the stairs. "The owner said it didn't meet code so they had to dismantle it."

Gus looked down at its solid bottom a foot below the opening. He looked up into the dark shaft and his light hit its solid top a story above. Satisfied, he backed out and closed its door. His eyes went to the next wall, the one opposite the stairs where the giant waterwheel was. He walked along the entire wall but found no openings.

The last wall had remnants from the old mill piled high against it and it wasn't until Gus was close to it that he saw the top of a large arching doorframe behind the clutter. With Vanessa's help, he moved items until he had a clear view of an oversized, armory-style metal door cracked open a few inches. Gus leaned into it to push it open wider then stepped into the end of a room the shape of a large mailbox made entirely of brick. The walls were painted a glossy dark grey, the ceiling a bright white. There was a long, sturdy wooden table along the right wall that held dusty brown bottles of all sizes and beside it slumped an old cider press. To his left were several tarnished copper barrels with broken copper piping jutting out from their tops and bottoms. Gus walked down the center of the room and took it all in.

"Looks like an old moonshine setup," he said.

"That's cuckoo nuts bananas," Vanessa said as she inspected the equipment.

"Anything of interest?" Timothy called from the other room.

Gus scanned the small room with his light but saw no other doors or exits or even a hole a person could fit through.

He looked back to the moonshine equipment.

"Nothing for us," he yelled. "But we might've found that next exotic drink you're looking for."

Chapter Twenty

TAYLOR HAD MANICALLY paced around his house for hours, his thoughts bouncing from finding Rachel Connors's license in Teddy, to waking in his car on the side of the road just a short distance from where her body was found, to being with Sadie Hogan the night she went missing. Round and round, like a record, the entire night until he found himself both emotionally and physically exhausted.

He needed some sleep so set about doing his bedtime routine with the hopes those simple actions would help calm his mind. First, he brushed his teeth for a full two minutes at his bathroom sink and followed that up with a complete flossing. Then, after rinsing his mouth, he removed his contact lenses and put them in the compact holder with the solution for the night. Next up were the eyedrops for his dry eyes; two drops in each eye, one in the inside corner, the other inside the lid on the bottom. Then, finally, he sat on the edge of his bed and jotted down his list of things to do the next day in his small pocket-sized notepad.

He then put the latest movie Leon had brought him—*Seven* starring Morgan Freeman and Brad Pitt—in the VCR and climbed into bed. It was late and after a few minutes he felt himself begin to relax as he stared mindlessly at the old television set propped on his rickety dresser. He watched the movie with interest as characters came in and out of scenes with fuzzy trails behind them like jet planes. The screen's colors were unusually vibrant and intense as if a setting were off inside the ancient set. And, as had become the norm, Taylor laid like that for hours, staring, absorbing it all as if it were a part of him. He knew he'd been dealing with significant sleep deprivation lately but had no idea of what to do about it. The closest he got to actually sleeping was a sort of suspended-like state of being, during which he was neither asleep or awake. And it was during these periods that he had some of his most profound thoughts and feelings.

But with those feelings came erratic swings of emotion. One minute he'd be distraught that he'd ever left New Orleans and his successful jazz career in the first place. He'd become filled with hopelessness that he'd never make it back. And that feeling of anguish, of torment, would become so strong, so all-encompassing, he'd feel smothered and adrift with no way of getting back. But then the next minute he'd feel this euphoric optimism that he had a plan to get back to New Orleans and the career he'd abandoned. He was playing his upright again, finding jazz gigs and slaying them, and, with his mom now settled in a facility for the care she needed, he would soon return to New Orleans and all would be great again. And then back again to the uncontrollable sorrow. On and on this emotional rollercoaster went every night now, robbing him of sleep and chipping away, he feared, at his sanity.

Hours later, Taylor stirred to screaming, only to realize it was his own when his voice became hoarse. His sweaty legs stuck to the sheets as he rolled onto his back and his heart thrummed in his chest. He rubbed his face and brow and blinked several times to clear the fog. He stared at the ceiling and the television's light flickering on it.

Fuckin' movie.

Once his breathing calmed, he closed his eyes and inventoried the lingering snapshots from his nightmare before they faded for good. He recalled a moonlit sky and flashes of tall, swaying field grass. He watched headlights, their sphere of light silently moving left to right in the distance.

Then more gruesome, sinister images emerged at the forefront of his mind. He saw a woman's bare shoulder and neck lying against matted grass. An image of a cloudy eye snapped on, then off, like a light switch. A woman's bare knee and thigh flashed then was gone, as did a pale stomach. The image of outstretched forearms with hands clenched around a woman's taut neck appeared so real that his fingers flexed at the sensation of her cold skin on his palms. Then a woman's lower face filled the frame—her thin, petite nose, her pale shapely lips, the delicate mole above her upper lip.

Taylor's eyes snapped open in horror. That mole; he recognized that mole. He blinked hard several times as he struggled to get his bearings but the room spun around him, its walls pulsing with life. He felt a presence in the doorway but when he looked no one was there. He grabbed a bat from the milk crate beside his bed and went to the doorway.

"Who's there?" he yelled. He realized he had his phone

in his hand so unlocked its screen and shot Leon a text. *911.*

"If you're in here, you better fuckin' run," he warned, his voice angry and hard.

He clicked the ceiling light on then shut off the television so he could hear more clearly. He frantically searched his room but found he was alone. He stood still and listened intently for several moments, but it wasn't what he heard that scared him. It was what he felt. Taylor could feel the hungry eyes of a predator watching him, taking in his every movement, his every breath. He was about to call out, to scream to be left alone when he heard the creaking of the front door as it opened and Leon calling to him.

"T?"

Taylor rushed out of the room and down the hall to Leon who was standing in the middle of the living room with the light on.

"Hey, you, okay?" his friend asked.

Taylor could see the concern in Leon's eyes. "I think so." He wiped snot from his nose with the back of his wrist. "I heard someone in the house."

Leon perked up and looked around. "They still here?"

"Not sure. I was just going to check."

The two of them searched the house top to bottom before returning to the living room. Taylor plopped onto the sofa and rubbed his eyes, thoroughly exhausted and confused.

"Dude, you look like shit. You, okay?"

Taylor didn't answer but, instead, canvassed his surroundings. He took in the tiny living room with its worn carpet and smoke-stained ceiling and it was at that moment that he realized he had nowhere to go and no one to be with. He was completely alone. Except for Leon. He had known Leon his entire life and they had survived a complicated childhood in the Falls together. Leon had proven his friendship and loyalty to Taylor when they were teenagers in the most profound way. But would he do it again?

He told Leon of the dreams and visions he'd had of dead women in fields and of women being strangled. And when Leon didn't make the connection, Taylor reminded him of the women abducted from Music Row and murdered and how he feared those were the women he was seeing. He told Leon of his feelings of being watched and followed and reminded him of the face he saw looking in the garage window at them earlier that night. And he reminded Leon of them being with Sadie the night she was abducted and how, after Leon and the others left, Taylor was likely the last person to see her alive but couldn't remember a thing. He then told Leon of the visit he got from the FBI investigating the murders and of how he knew Gus, the lead agent. Taylor described finding the driver's licenses; first Sadie Hogan's in his pants pocket and of how it had been replaced in Teddy with Rachel Connors's. And, finally, he told Leon of how he woke in the van at sunrise that morning parked near the field where the Connors woman's body was found just hours later. And when he was done spewing all of that, Taylor felt relieved to have told someone, yet terrified for what he feared he might've done.

"Dude, do you really think you could've done all that?"

Taylor clenched his jaw in frustration. "Explain the nightmares and images I'm seeing of dead women." His eyes bulged and he shook his head. "I dunno … I was with both the Connors woman and Sadie Hogan the nights they went missing. That's a pretty big coincidence. And I don't remember *anything*." He paused, then tipped his head toward the door to the kitchen. "The Connors woman's license is still in Teddy right now." His eyebrows flexed upward.

Leon stood. "Show me."

Taylor led them to the kitchen, took Teddy from the top of the fridge and placed it on the small kitchen table. Removing its top, Taylor slowly emptied its contents out. He ran his hand over an old blue checkbook and spread out a wad of cash, mostly fives and tens. He fingered through the bills then turned over an orange gift card to The Home Depot.

"I don't see any license," Leon said as he helped smooth out the bills.

Taylor plunged his hand into the jar's belongings. "It was here. I saw it." His hand swiped wildly, sending the checkbook and a few bills onto the floor. He grabbed Teddy and peered inside then he jammed his arm into it up to his elbow and rooted around but when he pulled it out his hand remained empty. Plopping the jar back onto the table, he looked around wildly.

"It was in there," he said. He met and held Leon's eyes. "It was there." Taylor then put his palms on the table, locked his elbows, and lowered his head between his shoulders.

"Okay, okay," Leon repeated. "We're gonna figure this out."

"It was in there," Taylor repeated, swiping spit from his chin.

"Dude, I believe you. But right now, we need to focus on getting you some help. You've got entire *nights* you don't remember." He shook his head. "That's not okay."

Leon looked around the kitchen, with its drawn curtains and deadbolted backdoor with a dry sink pulled in front of it. "And what's with the bunker?" When Taylor didn't answer, he continued, "You have the number for that therapist? He must have an after-hours service we can call."

"We can't tell him *any* of this!" Taylor said, his voice rising. "He'll drop a dime on me in no time."

Leon held both palms up in surrender. "Dude, you won't. We don't have to tell him any of the details to get you help. We tell him you're not sleeping and that you're having nightmares but when you wake you can't really remember what about. And we tell him you're having *huge* chunks of time when you can't remember anything. All that'll be enough for him to check the meds he's got you on."

As Taylor considered Leon's plan, he remembered what his therapist kept reinforcing with him. "When you're feeling paranoid or having thoughts that the world or someone in it is plotting against you, remember what we've talked about." His therapist would say at the end of each session. "These thoughts are manufactured by your mind, symptoms of your mild psychosis and nothing more. Symptoms we are working on to correct so do not succumb to them."

Taylor relented. "Yeah, okay. But I've only got his regular office number."

"That's alright," Leon said. He looked to the greying, pre-dawn sky out the window. "It's almost morning; we'll call in an hour or two."

Taylor flicked his eyes around the room, settling on the hallway leading to the bedrooms. And he felt the weight of everything that had happened wrap his shoulders. He looked to Leon with sadness in his heart.

"I know I'm no world-beater. But I did have dreams."

Leon squeezed Taylor's shoulder and looked him in the eye. "It's all gonna be okay."

"If you say so."

Chapter Twenty-One

Wednesday

- ✓ Side effects of meds
- ✓ Erase phone GPS
- ✓ Erase phone searches
- ✓ Clean van
-   License
-   Therapist
-   New meds?
-   MA murder laws

Chapter Twenty-Two

V ANESSA HAD WOKEN Mick Preston when she phoned his home number around six a.m. that morning to make arrangements to meet. Mick was an equipment repairman and spent his days making service calls so Vanessa said they'd see him at his work around eight thirty before he got on the road for the day. In the meantime, Gus and Vanessa decided to go somewhere for breakfast so they could work through the case and everything they knew and suspected thus far.

With everything going on, Gus had lost track of what day it was. Once he realized it was Wednesday and they had a couple of hours to kill, he phoned Mel to see if she could join them for breakfast before her trip that evening. Pawtucket Falls was just twenty-five minutes from Kendalton and generally on her way back to Gus's condo in Charlestown so she jumped at the chance to see him before she left.

The three of them met at the Daybreak Diner in Pawtucket Falls, a favorite of the locals for the past forty years. Its iconic black and silver metal front was a vintage lunch car with an airstream shape, curtained windows, and signs painted in elaborate cursive writing boasting booth service.

Gus and Vanessa got there first and scored one of the five booths along the front. Gus watched short-order cooks slap bells and yell things in code to waitresses scurrying by and he marveled at the controlled chaos with which food was slid along the counter and slung onto tables. Gus had loved diners since he was a kid.

When he was in tenth grade, Gus's hippie parents left him in the care of his older brother, Jake, and went on a six-month assignment with the Peace Corps to build housing in a remote village in Namibia, a country located in Southern Africa. Two and a half years later they returned just in time for Gus's high school graduation, only to head back to Africa once he left for college. While they were away, Jake and Gus practically lived on diner food. Gus's father was a trust-fund kid so had made arrangements for their living expenses to be taken care of by a guardian of the estate. And this included a generous allowance for food and incidentals. So, living in Colorado, to Jake and Gus this meant road trips, Broncos games on Sundays and every rock concert within a hundred miles. And each of those excursions involved diners, a practice Gus carried with him into adulthood.

Gus saw Mel walk in so slid out of the booth and stood to greet her. And as she approached him, they both broke out in wide smiles, her dimples catching his eye.

"Ah, Jesus, get a room." Vanessa groaned.

Gus gave Mel a quick hug then took her coat and hung it on the hook at the side of the booth as she slid into his side. Mel met Vanessa's eyes and gestured toward V's hair.

"Love the highlights."

Mel had been around creative people for most of her adult life. The e-commerce firm she had started and sold years ago had the differentiator of combining technology experts with very artsy and creative people to enhance customer interface and usability. So Mel was very comfortable with—and had experienced—all sorts of creative expression. Her most memorable was learning of one of her designers' hobbies of welding metal sculptures in the nude.

V ran a hand over her clipped fuzz and smiled. "Thanks. It's royal orchid."

"It is a nice color," Gus remarked.

Vanessa looked at him open-mouthed. "Aw, you throwin' me some shine?"

The waitress came by and filled Gus and Mel's coffee cups, saving Gus the humiliation of having to ask Vanessa what that meant.

"How're Fred and Mr. T doing?" he asked after the waitress left.

Mel told them of Mr. T making his workshop in her basement and of him trimming out the third floor of her old saltbox house into a spare room. She then told them of how he had established a training regime for Fred who now sits, lays, stays, and comes when called.

"That's incredible," Gus said. "I was starting to think that dog was inbred." He raised an eyebrow in surprise. "Impressive."

"Oh yeah, he runs a tight ship," Mel added sarcastically with an eye roll. "Then we sit down to eat and Fred casually walks behind Mr. T's chair and I hear something rustling around. And when I look, I see Fred with his entire head inside the new bucket Mr. T made for the dog treats." Vanessa almost spit out her soda as Mel continued, "Apparently, he keeps the lid off because it sticks and he needs to sand it down a little. So until then, Fred dumpster dives for treats whenever he wants."

They all laughed hysterically as the waitress brought them their food, refilled mugs, and placed a new glass of Diet Coke on the table for V. They talked a little more about Mr. T and Kendalton in general then the subject turned to their case. Vanessa told Mel the basics—how each of the abductions occurred in Pawtucket Falls' Music Row, how completely different each of the women were, about the licenses of other victims left at each scene, and how they were puzzled as to how he could get them out of such crowded places with no one noticing.

And soon, when they had finished eating, Mel put a hand on Gus's shoulder. "I better get going so you two can talk shop."

Gus slid out and took Mel's hand while she stood. They each turned sideways to look at Vanessa before kissing goodbye. Vanessa stuck her finger down her throat and mock vomited.

Mel placed her hand on Gus's chest. "I'll go save the pet sitter from Roscoe," she said, referring to Gus's quasi-feral cat. "When d'ya think you'll be back home?"

Gus eyed Vanessa before saying, "No idea. Tell her I'll call in the next couple of days but to plan on coming until you get back."

Mel took her coat from the hook then turned to Vanessa. "You said these women had no connection to each other that you can find."

"Nothing," Vanessa said, leaning sideways in the booth and pulling a leg beneath her.

"Maybe the connection is your suspect. Not that they each knew him; but that they each *wanted* to know him. He's active in this Music Row area. He could be a band's manager or a performer; that might give him some sort of celebrity status that these women are attracted to or they're star-struck by him. They'd have a false sense of familiarity with him that might cause them to put their guard down." She raised an eyebrow. "He'd be able to get close to them and get 'em alone."

"There's one band in particular whose members keep coming up," Gus said.

Mel smirked. "Well, you can rule out the bassist." When Vanessa looked at her questioningly, Mel flicked Gus's shoulder. "You always say, no one ever knows the bass player."

Gus walked Mel to her Jeep to say goodbye and they hugged for a long time, neither wanting to let go. He made sure she had emailed him her complete itinerary so he knew her flight details and where she was staying and he verified—again—that her phone would work properly in Europe. He hugged her a final time and a loud chime rang from his phone so he pulled it out of his pocket. There was a text from Sarah Connors that she had Detective Boyd on the phone and for Gus to come join her. Above the text was a picture of the character Sarah Connors from the movie *The Terminator*. Gus and Mel both laughed then said their goodbyes, and Gus rejoined Vanessa inside.

Chapter Twenty-Three

"A MY, I'VE GOT Gus with me now," Vanessa said.

"Hey, Gus. I was just telling Vanessa that we've come up empty on that surveillance video the night Michelle Townsend went missing."

"Didn't find her?"

"No and we scoured everything; the club's footage of its exits, two traffic cams in the immediate area and footage from three neighboring businesses. Nothing."

"And you're confident your guys didn't miss anything? That's a lot of footage to go through."

"You kiddin'? All I needed to say was overtime on the feds and I had more eyeballs than I knew what to do with. Suffice to say, each tape was watched through multiple times by several people. We didn't miss anything."

They thanked her and ended the call. He and Vanessa exchanged looks of frustration then she gestured to her open laptop.

"Still nothing from Rob on the residue or carpet fibers or tox screens. But the lab's run that boot print through its usual databases and come up empty. They said it's got a unique tread and likely wasn't sold in the US. They're running it through international databases now."

"It'd be nice to get a hit on that."

"Yes. It. Would," Vanessa said slightly distracted as she focused on her screen. "There's also something interesting in the news today." Vanessa showed Gus a brief video of a breaking news report that aired last night. On the screen was the attractive blond woman that confronted them at the police station when they first got the case. She was standing by the side of a road and behind her Gus recognized the Rachel Connors crime scene in the middle of a field.

"Sources tell us that the victim found earlier today is a Rachel Connors of Billerica, first reported missing early Sunday morning when she failed to come home after being out with friends in Pawtucket Falls' Music Row. And News Center Six has learned that the death of Ms. Connors has been linked to the deaths of Sadie Hogan and Michelle Townsend by forensic evidence found at the scene. The police are calling their suspect the Talent Scout and believe he is still in the area and at large. This is Christina Collins reporting live. News Center Six."

"The Talent Scout." Gus grimaced. "Tell me she didn't just say that."

"It is on brand." Vanessa pointed out. "But wait 'til the jackals online get ahold of that." Her phone buzzed. It was TJ so she tapped the speaker button to answer it. "Hey."

"Hey, guys," TJ said, his voice smooth, his easy cadence revealing midwestern roots. "We got surveillance video for outside The Mills the night Sadie Hogan went missing."

"Nice," Gus said.

"Yeah, a traffic cam caught the front entrance and, because that building's near the corner at the end, a riverside cam caught the rear exit. Apparently, Pawtucket Falls had a problem years ago with people dumping in the river so they put up these river cams to monitor it. We got lucky. One of them caught the alley behind the club."

"We get anything?"

"Well, we see two of the guys—Mick and the singer Chris—leaving together out the front just after midnight. Then about twenty minutes later, we see the guitarist, Leon, leave. Then the club closes and the last to leave is Taylor Franklin who stumbles down the road out of view."

"No Sadie Hogan?"

"No, we don't have her leaving the club through the front or the rear."

"Damn," Gus bit. He looked to Vanessa. "Are we sure those are the only exits?"

She nodded. "Yeah, double-checked."

"Do either of those guys leave with anyone, even if she doesn't look like Sadie?"

"No," TJ said. "Mick and Chris leave together. The other two each leave alone."

Gus tried to think of other scenarios of how Sadie Hogan could've left the club without being identified on the surveillance video but, other than a disguise, came up with none. And if she wore a disguise she wouldn't have left alone.

Gus lifted his head from the phone and met Vanessa's eyes. "We have to be missing something. She was reported missing the next day and the police searched the club after that and didn't find her so we know she left within, say, thirty-six hours of going missing."

"Split it up if you have to, TJ, but we've gotta watch that tape for that night and the few days after. Maybe a worker did it and came back the next morning. I don't know. Maybe our guy isn't one of the bandmembers but someone else we're not looking for on that tape and maybe he got her out that night with a hat on or something. But she left that club."

They let TJ go then, seeing it was almost time to meet Mick, Gus mentally switched gears.

"Assuming we're not completely off-base and it is one of the bandmembers, Mick's the sketch one on the tape with Rachel Connors. Let's dig deeper into him."

"Okay, but the other three spoke with her at the bar the night she went missing." Vanessa pointed out.

"Yeah, but Mick stands out for his play by the restroom."

"Totes," she agreed. "But Taylor was the one that bartender, MJ, said was with Sadie Hogan at the end of the night she went missing. And we just saw him leave the club last and he was pretty sketch yesterday when we spoke with him. Also, don't forget, he knew that waitress, Michelle Townsend. No doubt. They're one of the house bands, for chrissakes, and she's pulling shifts there waitressing?" She let the rhetorical question hang out there.

In his mind, Gus was back in Taylor's house, with its closed curtains and smell of decay and failure, standing by the door. "Yeah, and those mud-covered boots by his door. We'll pay him another visit once we get the boot print from the Connors scene identified. See if it's the same type."

Vanessa dipped a hash brown in some ketchup and popped it into her mouth. "Could they be working it together?" she asked between chews.

"A team?" Gus asked. He rocked his head side to side then raised an eyebrow. "Could be."

Vanessa checked the time on her phone then waved down the waitress for their bill. "Let's head out so Mick doesn't leave before we get there."

Gus took the bill and left money on the table.

Then a thought came to him. "What if we come at this from the other end? Once our guy has them, he's holding them somewhere for days, weeks even. Let's dig into each of these guys, see where they each live and if they have any other properties that'd be remote enough to keep someone locked up for that period of time without anyone noticing."

"Got it," Vanessa said as she slid out of the booth and stood beside him. "And now that we're circling 'em, I'll dig into backgrounds, see what shakes loose."

Chapter Twenty-Four

MICK PRESTON WORKED at a company vaguely named Allied Equipment and Repair, located in a small office park just off Fleming Boulevard in Dracut. Gus and Vanessa got there a few minutes early so parked around back in the same lot as a row of lime green and safety-orange service vans. Vanessa had called TJ back during the ride and asked him to run backgrounds on each of the four band members, including past and present residences and any property they owned. He sent along a quick hit of Mick so Gus and Vanessa would know who they were speaking with.

"Says here, Michael Jared Preston, born in nineteen eighty-two in Pawtucket Falls, Massachusetts."

"A hometown boy, as well. But he's, what? Forty-two?" Gus asked.

"Later this month, September twenty-ninth."

"He's got a decade on Taylor. And from the photos, I'd say the same on the other two, as well."

"Has two older brothers. Parents are gone. He's been divorced twice, has a daughter from his first marriage. He went to Middlesex Community College for a year … looks like he dropped out the same year his daughter was born. Let's see … work history. He worked on the manufacturing line at a company in Bedford, then he was an auto mechanic for a few years in Burlington." She raised her chin to the long, one-story brick building out their windshield. "He's worked here the last nine years."

"Single?"

Vanessa nodded. "And he lives in a house in Tyngsboro he bought around the same time he started here. But doesn't look like he owns anything else."

Gus heard the loud rumble of a car approaching and looked up to see a bright orange Dodge Challenger round the side of the building. It had black rally stripes along its hood with two large air intakes beside them and louvers surrounding its bottom, giving it a stout, aggressive-looking stance. The driver downshifted, causing the muffler baffles to pop and snarl as the car parked diagonally across two parking spots far away from the building's entrance. They waited a moment then Mick Preston stepped from the car. He wore grey work pants with a green and orange shirt matching the company's trucks.

"Of course that's what he drives," Vanessa breathed as she and Gus stepped from the truck.

Mick stopped short when he saw them and pulled his sunglasses off in a sweeping motion like a movie star. Brad Pitt himself couldn't have done it better. He brushed the back of his pants off then leaned against his car's fender and pulled a pack of cigarettes from his shirt pocket.

"Mick Preston?" Vanessa asked as she and Gus approached.

"In the flesh." He lit his cigarette with a small Bic lighter.

"I'm Agent Lambert." Vanessa showed Mick her badge and gestured to Gus. "This is my partner, Agent Wheeler. As I said on the phone, we're investigating the recent murders of a few women abducted while at clubs in Music Row."

Mick blew smoke into the air from the corner of his mouth and nodded knowingly. "The Talent Scout. I saw the news."

Gus bristled at the mention of that god-awful nickname again and vowed to himself to hunt down the Pawtucket Falls officer that coined that name and dope slap him.

"You spoke with the latest victim, Rachel Connors, at the club Blue Agave last Saturday night," V continued. "The night she disappeared."

"Did I now?" He flicked ashes from his cigarette onto the ground. "Who told you that?"

"The security footage." Gus interrupted, taking a step closer to tighten their circle.

Vanessa held out her phone with a photo of Rachel Connors on it. "I'm sure you remember her. It was after midnight. You two spoke at the bar then again after you waited for her outside the restrooms."

Mick took another drag from his cigarette and looked at the photo. "Yeah, I remember her."

"What'd you two talk about?" asked Gus.

Mick shrugged. "I dunno. Stuff." His eyes narrowed. "We were at a bar. We hit it off so we flirted a bit."

"Didn't look much like she was flirting once you got mad and stormed off outside the restrooms," V said and, when Mick didn't reply, she added, "You looked pretty pissed."

Mick was a tall man and even leaning on his car had several inches on Vanessa. So when he turned to her, he purposely looked down.

Mick let out a long, exaggerated sigh. "That chick was a cock tease. She wasn't worth my time."

Vanessa tilted her head. "You sure 'bout that?"

Mick's mouth spread into a smile. "Besides, she wasn't really my type." His eyes took a pass over Vanessa's hair then flicked down her body, lingering a beat too long to be casual, and back up. "I like 'em a bit … wilder."

Vanessa held his eyes and blinked slowly like that now-infamous meme of a tired Boo from the movie *Monsters Inc.*

"But it's the hope that kills you, right?" he added.

"How cheery," V commented.

"When you left the club Saturday night," Gus began, interrupting the stare-off, "where'd you go?"

Mick smirked before turning his attention away from Vanessa. "I went home. Me and some guys were going riding the next morning."

"Riding?" Gus asked.

"Quads," Mick said then added, "ATVs. We went mudding the next day up by the power lines in Hudson."

"Anyone able to confirm what time you got home from the club?" Gus continued. "A roommate? A neighbor maybe?"

Again Mick shrugged, "No, no roommate."

"You stop at all on the way? Get gas or anything?"

Mick ticked his head side to side. "Nah, it's only about fifteen, twenty minutes. I went straight home."

Vanessa showed him a photo of Sadie Hogan. "We understand you spoke with her at The Mills late one night a few weeks ago."

He glanced at the photo then looked back to Vanessa and shrugged. "Don't remember."

"Bartender says you hit on her and got pissed when she blew you off. Sounds like a trend."

Mick grimaced. "MJ? How would she know? The last time that woman got hit on, Carter was president."

Vanessa referred to her phone. "Where'd you go after the club that night, August twenty-fourth?"

Mick pulled out his phone. "I think that was the night I gave Chris a ride home. Yep, he had some work thing the next day and his car was in the shop. I know because mine had just gone in that day for service." He showed them the appointment in his calendar. "After that, I just called it a night."

"Do you remember what time you left the club?"

"Probably around eleven thirty or midnight. We usually have a few drinks after our set."

After Mick immediately recognized Michelle Townsend's photo, Vanessa then asked him about the night she disappeared. "And how about May eleventh?"

Mick's thumb swiped his screen several times before he said, "I went into Boston with a friend that weekend. We hit the tables at the Encore. Why?"

"Pretty swanky," Vanessa commented, eyeing Mick. "You stay there too?"

Mick shuffled his feet, "Nah, it was a last-minute thing

so it was sold out. We stayed at some hotel nearby."

"Can he or she verify that?"

"She." Mick's lip turned up slightly. "And, yeah, I guess so."

Vanessa got the woman's name and number.

Mick pushed himself off his car. "I really gotta get to work."

Gus gestured to the building. "What *is* Allied Equipment and Repair? What does it do?"

"We sell and service office equipment. Copiers, scanners, printers."

"You service them?" Vanessa asked.

Mick nodded. "Yeah, me and about a dozen other guys."

Mick dropped his cigarette onto the pavement beside him and Gus watched as he stomped it out with a black shoe. He thought of the boot print from Rachel Connors's crime scene they'd yet to identify.

"What kinda boots you wear on those ATVs?" he asked Mick.

"You wear special riding boots. They cover your ankle and leg up to your knee and have a steel shell to protect your foot and ankle."

Gus nodded as if he were interested in getting a pair. "What kind do you have?"

"I use the Gaerne Sig Twelves," Mick said, as his lower lip hung open a bit, his head bobbing almost imperceptibly. "They're the best on the market. Why?"

Gus and Vanessa exchanged a look then turned to go. "We'll be in touch."

Chapter Twenty-Five

G US STARTED THE truck's engine as they watched Mick Preston walk toward the building. The windshield and thin side windows were frosted from cold condensation and the cabin vibrated from the old diesel's rough idle. Vanessa put a hand on the dashboard to steady herself and waited for Mick to go inside before turning toward Gus.

"Okay…" she said, stretching the word out to be sure she had Gus's attention and pausing long enough to build suspense. "Vibe check."

Gus smiled. "You don't have to be so *extra* about it."

Vanessa laughed and slapped his shoulder. The morning light caught the specks of gold in her emerald eyes and they sparkled. "Dude, ya crushed it."

Gus gave her an exaggerated nod. "Googled it." They both smiled as people began coming out of the building and climbing into service trucks.

Gus watched Mick climb into his. "He's a weak man that thinks he's a strong one," he said quietly into his window.

"That hip-musician vibe is sending me," she added softly.

He turned to her. "I wonder what type of chemicals he uses to service all that office equipment."

"Had the same thought."

He looked back to the nondescript building with its brick siding, square, black-lined windows and flat roofline. "And we need to get their customer list. See if they service any of the companies the victims worked at."

Vanessa unlocked her phone. "I'll have TJ jump on it." She called him and put it on speaker.

"Hey," TJ answered. "I just sent you the background and property checks for the other guys you asked for."

"Got it. I'll take a look. Anything jump out?"

"There's a lot in the backgrounds so I'll let you chew through those. But as for the property searches, maybe. For starters, only two of the four actually own homes. Chris Houlihan lives in an apartment building and Leon Sampson lives with his girlfriend in her house. You guys saw Taylor Franklin's house; it's in a pretty dense area. Not that he couldn't keep the women in his basement but he'd have to be careful bringing them there."

"Our guy takes them in the early pre-dawn hours," Gus said. "If there's ever a time he could get the women into his house without someone seeing, it's then."

"Absolutely," TJ agreed. "It's just not ideal. Now, Mick Preston's house? It's in the middle of nowhere. If I were looking to hold someone captive without anyone knowing, that's the sitch I'd be looking for. Close to where I was taking them from—only a fifteen, twenty-minute drive—so the risk of getting pulled over is minimized and secluded enough so I don't have to worry someone is going to see me bring them into the house or hear them scream."

"And this guy definitely has a creepy vibe," Vanessa added. "There's a few things to chase down from talking to him. He just told us one of his hobbies is riding ATVs and he wears special boots for that."

"Do you know what make? I can pass it onto the lab."

Vanessa checked her notes. "He said he wears Gaerne Sig Twelves. I'm not sure how to spell it."

"That's alright, I'll find it and get it to the lab."

"And we need the customer list for his company," Gus added. "See if they service any of the offices the vics worked at."

"Got it."

"And we need to chase down his alibis," Vanessa began. "Last Saturday when Rachel Connors was taken, he claims he went straight home. He doesn't have any roommates and he didn't stop anywhere, so can you check to see if there're any traffic cams between the club and his house?"

"Will do."

"And the weekend of May eleventh when Michelle Townsend was abducted, he claims he was in Boston with a girlfriend at the Encore Boston Casino. Can you get the security footage for that weekend, see if he's there?"

"Sure thing."

"If he is, work up a timeline of his activities to see if there's any overlap with when she was taken," she added. "We'll speak with the woman he was with but he wouldn't have given us her name and number if she wasn't going to corroborate what he told us."

"What about the night Sadie Hogan was taken?" TJ asked.

"August twenty-fourth," she specified. "We saw him on the video leaving with the singer, Chris. He said he gave him a ride home then went home himself. So the same drill on the street cams between the club and those two addresses."

"We'll talk to Chris and stop by the club and confirm they played that night," Gus clarified. "And one last thing, TJ. Mick Preston repairs office equipment; copiers, printers, scanners. Can you get a list of chemicals and cleaners they use in that process and have the lab test them against the chemical residue found on the Connors woman?"

"Sure thing. I'll get a list of their purchasing orders when I ask for their customer list."

They ended the call with TJ and Gus pumped the clutch pedal twice before grinding the truck into gear. He looked at the time on his phone. 8:53 a.m.

"You know where this Chris guy works?"

Vanessa swiped at her phone a few times. "Yeah. Head toward four ninety-five. We're going north. He works at a place called the Exeter Farnsworth Museum."

Gus looked at her in surprise. "What's he do?"

"He's a fine art restorer," she said, with a pretentious tone.

"Give 'im a call," Gus said as he pulled out of their parking space and onto the road. The truck bucked and lurched slightly as he yanked it into second gear. "Tell him we need to speak with him this morning and we'll come to him."

Chapter Twenty-Six

TAYLOR SAT IN the plush armchair biting a fingernail as he watched Dr. Cappi read over the latest entries in his journal. Being with the therapist usually had Taylor feeling better, calmer even, but not today. Something was different, he could sense it.

He stared at the sofa with its throw pillows and cream-colored linen upholstery and the burning candle on the coffee table with SWEET PEONY written across its glass in sweeping cursive. He then took in the room more broadly; the casual tidiness of it all, the lack of clutter, the soft green walls that usually made him feel lighter despite the fact he hated green. Taylor stood and went to the window and looked out over the backyard.

When Taylor promised his mother he'd see a therapist he had no idea where to find one. He'd never seen a therapist before, nor had any of his friends as far as he was aware. Then his mother suggested Dr. Cappi; one of her friends had a daughter that was seeing him and liked him. But Taylor wasn't sure how he felt about going to a doctor's home office. Taylor, as he'd come to realize, was old school in that way. Doctors did doctoring at large, sterile offices with staff and controlled environments and elaborate equipment at their fingertips in case of emergency.

Dr. Cappi cleared his throat. "These are good entries." He uncrossed then recrossed his legs, one knee tightly over the other. Dr. Cappi was a slight man with soft features and narrow, inquisitive eyes. "Very good, very detailed. There's a lot to work with here."

Taylor turned from the window and a heat rose in his chest. *Very detailed.* He had read the entries quickly on the drive over but Leon kept talking about the appointment; what they needed to tell the doctor and what questions they needed to ask. So much so, that Taylor couldn't focus and now worried he'd put too much information in his journal.

Dr. Cappi closed the journal and placed it on his lap, holding it with both hands as if it were going to jump to the floor. "You seem to be struggling again. Are you doing what we talked about each day for your accomplishments?"

During their first session, the therapist spoke with Taylor about accomplishments and how small, simple ones could provide a sense of pride and lead to other accomplishments, both small and large. He had Taylor watch a commencement speech given by Admiral William McRaven in which the admiral spoke of making your bed each morning and how that small task could lead to great things in your day and your life.

Taylor nodded. "Make my bed. Every morning."

"And your list of tasks for the day?"

Taylor teased his small, pocket-sized notebook partway out of his jacket pocket. "Every day, like you said. And I check 'em off as I go."

Dr. Cappi weighed Taylor's responses for a moment then he patted the book's cover. "Talk to me about your feelings of being watched. When did they begin?"

"A few months ago," he said, looking to the ceiling and its thousands of swirls and crevices.

"A few months," the doctor echoed with an air of surprise.

Taylor looked back out the window. "I think," he said into the glass, distracted. "I wasn't really sure at first."

"And what makes you sure now?"

Taylor turned and looked at the therapist. "I've felt eyes on me everywhere I go lately; after shows, walking back and forth to work, at the store. And the other night there was ... a face looking in my window at home."

A heat bloomed in Taylor's chest as his mind's eye saw the young woman looking in his garage door window again; sun-bleached hair tucked behind an ear, beautiful freckles atop a kind smile.

"Did you recognize them?"

Taylor's lips parted slightly, his breath creating a small fogged circle on the glass that quickly dissipated. He looked to the door, making sure it was closed tight before turning to the doctor. He gave an imperceptible nod.

"It was ... Anne Marie."

"Anne Marie," Dr. Cappi parroted, uncertainty in his voice. Then after a moment he added more confidently, "Anne Marie. Your teenage love. The one that ran away."

Taylor was nodding, faster now. "Yeah."

"Did you speak with her?"

"Nah, she was gone too fast."

"How'd she look?" the doctor asked. "She's been gone, what, fourteen, fifteen years?"

"Sixteen." Taylor corrected, his voice pensive. He met the doctor's eyes. "She looked exactly the same as the last time I saw her."

Taylor's words hung in the air like a coastal fog as he took one last look out the window then went back to his chair and sat. His eyes fell to the thick beige carpet with its light lines left from the vacuum and he could feel Dr. Cappi's eyes on him, evaluating him. Judging him.

"Your anxiety has increased," the doctor began. "Wouldn't you agree?"

Taylor's head tilted as he considered the doctor's question. "I think that's right."

"Do you think it could be related to your goal of moving back to New Orleans and that you'd be leaving your mother?"

"I don't know. Maybe."

"How did it feel to play that jazz performance you told me about?"

"It felt great."

"Do you have more scheduled?"

"I do, yeah."

"That's good. That's very good." Dr. Cappi tapped a finger on the journal again. "Talk to me about the episodes of missing time you noted."

Taylor felt his pulse quicken as fragments of memories fluttered in his thoughts. Laughing with Sadie Hogan at the bar, standing next to Rachel Connors nodding hello. He struggled to remember more but nothing came.

"There's been a few times lately where I can't seem to remember something."

"Anything significant jump out at you about those gaps in time?"

Like waking up in my van on the side of the road?

"Not really, no," he lied.

"How often has this happened?"

Taylor shrugged. "I dunno. A few times."

"And you said *lately*. When did you first notice this?"

Taylor's thoughts snapped back to learning of Sadie Hogan's disappearance while at work and of looking at his calendar to check the date weeks before.

"I dunno, probably about a month ago."

"And you've been taking your medicine regularly?"

Taylor nodded. "Yeah, but these freakin' meds. The side effects have become a real issue."

Dr. Cappi studied Taylor for a moment. "Taylor, I'm afraid the symptoms you're describing are not side effects of the medicine we have you on, but of your psychosis." He paused and the room fell quiet. "How are you sleeping?"

Taylor pushed his tongue between his upper lip and teeth. "What sleep? I find myself dozing or just zoning out for long stretches of time instead of actually sleeping." One of his eyes twitched and he rubbed it with a finger. He could feel himself getting antsy and began fidgeting in his seat.

Dr. Cappi's eyes narrowed, and he gestured to the door to the waiting room. "Taylor, your friend Leon called on your behalf this morning for an emergency session. He said he found you in distress last night and that you were having nightmares and panicking about having a lot of missing time lately. Is that correct?"

Taylor nodded once then looked back toward the window.

"Is this happening more frequently? The missing time, I mean?"

"Why does it matter?!" Taylor's voice rose angrily. He stood then looked around the room, indecisively jerking his body this way, then that. "This was wrong. I shouldn't have come here."

Dr. Cappi placed Taylor's journal on the coffee table then stood also. He stepped away from Taylor and leaned back against his desk, his hands at his sides grasping its edge. The door to the waiting room opened and Leon leaned his head in.

"Everything okay in here?"

Dr. Cappi nodded then looked to Taylor. "Everything's fine, right, Taylor? We're just trying to get to the bottom of things." He nodded a yes to Leon's gesture of staying in the room with them so Leon quietly closed the door and leaned against it.

"Taylor, it matters because this may be a manifestation of your separation anxiety. Remember, we talked about that being woven throughout your perception of events in your life. The lack of a father figure when you were young, compounded with the abandonment you felt when Anne Marie left you.

"And now, your mother has moved into an assisted living facility," Dr. Cappi continued. "You may be internalizing her departure as a form of abandonment, especially after you uprooted your life in New Orleans to move back home and care for her. Your nightmares and feelings of being watched; the missing time you're experiencing. This all may be a manifestation of all of that emotional trauma."

Taylor was shaking his head faster now, staring at the floor in front of him. "This was a mistake. I should go."

"Before you go, let's just think this through for a moment. Could someone be following you?" The doctor nodded slowly. "Sure. But you have to ask yourself why? Why would someone want to follow you?"

Taylor remained quiet, his attention dropping to the floor in front of him.

"So, Taylor, while it's possible for someone to be following you and watching you it's not very likely." The therapist's voice was calm and soothing. "Not impossible, but it does give me concern that you're feeling this way." He paused for a few moments, letting that sentiment hang in the air. "But, Taylor, you're describing significant periods of time that you don't remember and that ... that gives me grave concern. And the state of crisis your friend, Leon here, described finding you in last night only heightens my concern for your well-being."

Taylor bit down, looking to the window again.

"Taylor, I feel that we need to revisit your diagnosis. As you recall, when we began our sessions, we quickly uncovered symptoms of separation anxiety and mild psychosis.

And for a time, I feel our sessions were effective in dealing with that. But what you're describing, and your current physical state, has me reevaluating your diagnosis." He looked to Leon then back to Taylor. "Taylor, would you like Leon to step out while we discuss this?"

Taylor saw something move at the edge of the backyard. Was someone watching him? Distracted, he shook his head. "No."

"Okay. I think we're now dealing with a slightly more severe type of psychosis here that presents as delusional disorder but we'll need to confirm that with tests. Now, that may sound scary but it's not, and it's absolutely treatable. Psychotic disorders are a group of illnesses that affect the mind. They make it hard for someone to think clearly, to make sound judgments, to communicate effectively and sometimes, in more severe cases, to understand what's really happening."

Taylor's head snapped to the side as he looked at Dr. Cappi. He narrowed his eyes. "What're you saying?"

"I'm suggesting we do a full examination to determine what is happening. It's all very straightforward. We'll need to document your medical and psychiatric history, perform a very standard physical exam; maybe blood tests, an MRI. And with that as a basis we can determine the proper psychological and medicinal regimen to get you back on track."

"More drugs?" Taylor asked, his voice booming in the small room. "Is that your answer for everything? I can't think clearly with the drugs you already have me on and you want to give me more?"

"Taylor, we need to get to the bottom of this. You're describing very worrisome symptoms."

"It's the drugs you have me on!" Taylor yelled. "It has to be," he added, his voice trailing off to a near-whisper.

"Taylor, please, I'm only here to help you." Dr. Cappi pushed himself off the desk and stood, palms again open at his side. "I only want what's best for you."

And for the first time, Taylor saw his therapist in a new light, and he questioned if that was truly the case. Did his therapist really want what was best for him? He was the one that had Taylor reliving his worst memories from childhood. And he was the one that homed in on Taylor's relationship with Anne Marie early on in their sessions, picking at its every detail like a vulture with a fresh kill. And, because of that, Taylor was experiencing all of those emotions again, reliving his worst regrets and agonizing over each of his actions that led to her being gone in the first place.

Without saying a word, Taylor stepped over to the coffee table and picked up his journal, his eyes on Dr. Cappi the entire time. He then joined Leon at the door and opened it. And with one last glare at the doctor, Taylor stepped through the doorway as his friend silently followed.

Chapter Twenty-Seven

CHRIS HOULIHAN ASKED Gus and Vanessa to meet at a coffeehouse near his work and dropped Vanessa a pin with its location. They got there early which gave her time to go through the background information TJ had gotten on Chris and check out the singer's social media presence.

Gus had hoped for a diner or a small low-key place where they could chill but, instead, felt as if he'd walked into a story out of *The New Yorker*. Wanda's Caffè was decorated in a boho style and smelled of coffee, cinnamon, and pretentiousness. It had red wallpaper with sharp geometric patterns and plush couches and seats of all colors dotting its tiny space. Each of the walls were covered with brightly-colored impressionist prints and beside the door was a tall bookshelf containing small clusters of books with ancient-looking bookends, miniature statues, and various bowls and sculptures depicting different places around the globe.

After ordering, they were told by a barista working a shiny red and chrome espresso machine the size of a farm tractor that their beverages would be brought to their vignette. So, while Vanessa went to the restroom Gus chose a rectangular glass-top table that was more coffee than worktable. It had wicker chairs on one side with thick cushions and a low, rusty orange sofa along the other. At six foot four, Gus didn't think the sunken sofa was a workable option so opted for one of the chairs. He jostled his body left and right to get as comfortable as possible when a text popped up on his phone.

"This place is bussin!" It was from Clarice Starling and the photo above it was of Jodie Foster's character from *The Silence of the Lambs.*

When Vanessa joined him, he asked how she was able to keep changing her contact details on his phone without him knowing and she just smiled. She kicked off her boots, plopped on the sofa and with her legs pulled beneath her, rested her computer on her lap. "You good?"

"Um, well." He looked around, "It's a little *loud* in here. I mean, the walls, the neon sofas and chairs." He blinked. "It's a lot." A burst of music that sounded to Gus like a monkey beating on a bongo drum blurted from the speakers so he waited for it to stop before continuing. "And is this really *music*…"

Vanessa held up a palm and smiled. "Jesus, don't make a meal of it. Just answer the question."

Before he could say anything, the server brought them their beverages; an artsy ceramic mug with a sea glass-colored glaze containing Gus's coffee and a Boylan Diet Cane Soda with a glass of ice for Vanessa.

Gus settled in as best he could and the first call he made was to Rob, the pathologist, only to confirm they still hadn't gotten the expanded toxicology screen back on Rachel Connors, nor had they identified the carpet fibers beneath her fingernails or chemical residue found on her cheek and neck. He then traded texts with his pet sitter only to find out his cat, Roscoe, had bitten her but that she was fine. After that, he hounded Vanessa incessantly for anything of interest from the information she was reading about Chris until, finally, she convinced him to go through the background information on Taylor Franklin.

They were sure Taylor had lied about knowing the first victim, Michelle Townsend, they had a witness who saw him speaking with the second victim, Sadie Hogan, the night she went missing and he was on the same video as Mick and the others with Rachel Connors the night she was abducted. So, while the drummer Mick had gotten their attention, Taylor was also still in the frame for this based on what they knew.

"Jesus, this guy's had a tough run," Gus muttered as he read through Taylor's background.

Vanessa looked up from her screen, "How so?"

"Well, he wins all kinds of school and regional awards in high school for music then gets the Presidential Scholarship to Loyola; a free ride. And I told you about his experience there; he was the best bassist the moment he walked on campus. Then it looks like he stayed in New Orleans longer than I remembered—about five years—and by his reported income was far more successful than I'd thought. He was clearly hittin' it. Then he moves back home to Pawtucket Falls to live with his elderly mother who's just retired early from her secretary's job at the town hall. That was about three years ago and it looks like he's effectively been living below the poverty line ever since."

"Cray-cray."

"Then about five months ago his mother moved into an assisted living facility. So, now he's back living in his childhood home, alone, working some remedial job at a neighborhood thrift shop and playing shitty eighties music in a shitty music scene."

Gus thought about Taylor back in his rundown hometown; every day pounding its streets, working them, sucking them into his lungs.

Vanessa closed the top of her laptop. "Is he especially close to his mother?"

Gus tilted his head. "You thinkin' mommy issues?"

"He gives up his dreams and moves home to take care of her. I mean, really, who does that these days?" Not waiting for an answer she continued, "He cares for her twenty-four-seven for years, every day, gives up his life for her. Then she moves into a home, abandons him. You said that was about five months ago?"

Gus rechecked the file on his screen. "Five and a half."

Vanessa's thin eyebrow bent up, "That's right before Michelle Townsend went missing."

"So, what, he takes these women as sort of surrogates for his mother and cares for them?"

She shrugged. "He cares for them until they disappoint him like his mother did; they disobey him or don't appreciate him, something that triggers him. Then he kills them and finds another." She thought another moment. "There's no sexual assault with any of the victims."

Gus partially closed his laptop as well and leaned back in

his seat until the creaking of the wicker ceased. "Okay. Then how does Mick Preston fit for this?"

"That's easy," she dismissed. "He's a classic narcissist; may even have narcissistic personality disorder. Tomato, tomahto. With him, it's all about how important and superior he is."

"No mommy issues?" Gus questioned.

"We'd have to look into his past, but only if mommy didn't recognize how truly special Mick is. No, with him, it's all about his importance and being recognized as superior by others. You saw his reaction on that video when Rachel Connors blew him off. He was incensed. If he's our guy, we'll find that he felt dismissed, offended—insulted even— by these women somehow."

"But, again, no sign of sexual assault with the vics. How's that make sense with him?"

Vanessa was shaking her head before Gus had stopped talking. "It's not about sex with him. Don't get me wrong; he's a womanizer, for sure. But that's different; he'll think they feel lucky to be with him. With these women—if it's him—he's somehow been disappointed that they've not given him special attention or admiration that he feels he deserves. He's taking them to show them his superiority, to right the wrong they did by rebuking his attention or advances."

Gus absorbed what Vanessa said for a beat then gestured to her laptop. "Anything interesting on this Chris guy?"

She pushed the screen of her laptop back up. "Some mundane stuff. Grew up in some small town in Ohio, two sisters, a brother. Went to U-Maine for studio art and, from what I can tell, interned at this place two summers in a row before starting full-time after graduation in the art restoration department. And by looking at his socials, he's sort of a renaissance artist; he paints, draws, is into photography, and has even done sculptures. Not to mention music; singing and acoustic guitar."

"So *basic*," Gus scoffed with a smile.

She looked over her laptop to him. "More googling?"

Gus shrugged. "Just keepin' it real."

They heard the chime of the front door and Gus turned to see Chris standing just inside the threshold so held up his hand.

"Hello, sir, Chris Houlihan," he said as he got to Gus, holding out his hand. He was a thin young man with sunken cheeks and looked to Gus as though he would've been a sickly, high-need child. "I'm so sorry to keep you waiting."

Gus looked from the subtle red highlights in Chris's hair to the deep purple streaks in V's and felt strangely old. He was only thirty-five—just six years older than she was—but sometimes felt he was from a different planet. Her style, her language, the way she carried herself; it all seemed so different, so much younger. And as Gus glanced at her, then Chris's died hair, he couldn't help but feel youth slipping away, strand by strand.

Chris introduced himself to Vanessa then took a seat beside her on the sofa. "I'm so sorry," he said looking at both of them. "Normally, I'm free really anytime but we got a recently-found Homer in last week, and I've just started the restoration and some of the steps are very time-sensitive."

"A Homer?" Gus asked.

Chris nodded excitedly. "Winslow Homer. He was a famous painter in the eighteen hundreds from Boston. One of his grandchildren found a painting in their parent's attic and called us."

"Was it just old or in bad shape or both?" Gus asked with genuine interest.

"Really both. It's got the typical loose paint flecks and small cracks but it's also got a lot of caked-on dirt and some water damage. It's a real challenge."

"How do you even begin that process without ruining the original painting?"

Chris relaxed in his seat and Gus saw his enthusiasm rise as he talked more about his art. Seeing that passion in a fellow artist never got old for Gus and he never got tired of encouraging it.

"Well, every situation's different, but you follow the same general steps. First, you do a complete assessment with a high-powered microscope. See exactly what you're dealing with. Then we use an x-ray fluorescence device to determine if the paint has high lead content which was very common in the nineteenth century. Then we go about the repair. We use special glue—nanoglue—to secure the loose flecks of paint, special filler to fill in the small cracks, and special cleaners to remove the dirt and grime accumulated over—in some cases—centuries. We do this over the entire painting, inch by inch, until it's complete. Then we repaint discreet spots with special paint to bring the piece all together again, as close to its original form as possible."

"That's fascinating," Gus said.

"It really is," Chris agreed. "Painstakingly slow yet very exhilarating."

"So, Chris, thanks for meeting with us," Gus said, switching topics. He looked to Vanessa to take it from here.

"As I said on the phone," she began. "We're investigating the murders of the women who were abducted from Music Row."

Chris seemed to tense as he gave her a look to let her know he knew exactly what she was talking about.

Vanessa showed him a photo of Sadie Hogan. "The second victim, Sadie Hogan, was last seen at The Mills on August twenty-fourth. Do you recognize her?"

Chris took the photo. "Sort of." His voice cracked so he cleared it. "But I can't be sure."

"We understand Mick Preston gave you a lift home that night. Can you verify that?"

Chris pulled his phone from his back pocket. "Uh, I'm not sure. That was about a month ago..." He thumbed through his phone's calendar for what seemed like a week. "I think that's right," he said slowly. "We had an exhibition that Sunday morning that I had to be up early for..." He began nodding. "Yes, that would've been the night I needed a ride home." Certain now, he looked to Vanessa. "Yes, I can confirm that. My car was in the shop so Mick gave me a ride home after our gig."

"Do you remember what time that was?"

"It had to have been early. Like I said, I had an early

morning. So, probably around ten thirty or so, right after our set."

"And you stayed in the rest of the night?" Gus asked.

"Absolutely."

"Can anyone verify that?" Vanessa prodded.

"Um, Roland—my partner—gets home around five on weekend mornings. He can verify I was in bed asleep when he got home," Chris said, his voice rising as if it was a question. Then he clarified, "He owns a restaurant so works crazy hours on the weekends."

Vanessa took the details for Chris's partner. "We understand you had drinks with the other guys in your band last Saturday night at the Blue Agave."

"That's right."

Vanessa showed him a picture of Rachel Connors. "Do you remember seeing this woman at the bar?"

Chris studied the picture for a few moments, blinking several times as he did so. "Yes, Mick talked to her for a bit."

"Did you happen to see her leave the club that night?"

He shook his head. "No, sorry."

"And did you go straight home from the club?" Once Chris nodded, Vanessa clarified, "Roland again can confirm this but wasn't home until around five a.m.?"

"That's right."

"How'd you get home? Uber?"

"No, I drove."

Chris recognized Michelle Townsend's photo but couldn't remember where he was the night she went missing nearly four months ago so told them he'd check with Roland

and get back to them. They asked him a few more questions about the nights the women went missing and about the band then, with nothing else, Chris left them to go back to work.

"Vibe check," Vanessa said, watching Chris walk out the door.

Gus twisted his mouth. "Dunno. Something's off there."

"Agreed." She opened her laptop and began to type when Gus spoke again.

"Yeah." He nodded slowly. "We're gonna need a list of all those chemicals he just rattled off."

Without looking up, Vanessa's fingers flew across the keyboard.

"Already on it."

Chapter Twenty-Eight

VANESSA NEEDED A few hours to chase down some of the alibis they were given and the evidence in process, so they went back to the Pawtucket Falls FBI offices. After speaking with the singer Chris, Gus was more than a little intrigued at all the chemicals the Exeter Farnsworth Museum used for its restoration of artwork. Rob had said the chemical found on Rachel Connors's cheek and neck wasn't common and after hearing Chris describe all that was involved in restoring a painting, he couldn't think of a more uncommon process.

Gus parked his truck in the lot and, as they both hopped out, his hand lingered on the door's handle. He stared up at the tall glass building with its manufactured air, its floors of wall-to-wall cubicles, its muzak. Vanessa was in the middle of the parking lot before she realized she was alone and turned.

"What's up?" she asked, jutting her chin Gus's way.

Gus eased his eyes from the building to her. "I can't do it." He tipped his head toward the front door behind her. "My heads a blender," he said, using a Vanessa-ism. "I'm gonna walk a bit."

"Okay. I'll hit cha in a couple of hours so we can get

something to eat before the band's gig later," she said, referring to the Bowers Street Band's show they were going to that night.

Gus watched Vanessa slip into the building then turned and started walking. He had no destination in mind so just took random rights and lefts, lost in his own thoughts. He crossed a busy intersection and recognized where he was so turned down a narrow side street. Midway down he came upon the music store he had visited all those years ago to check out a Shen.

He paused on the sidewalk, lost in his thoughts, when his phone rang so he pulled it out of his pocket. He was getting a call from Fabio Lanzoni, the Italian model of romance book cover fame. Somewhere between getting his coffee at Wanda's Caffè and hopping out of his truck, Vanessa had managed to change her details in his contacts again.

"Hey," she said when Gus answered. "Bring me a Diet Coke when you come back. The soda machine's broken here."

"Sure thing, Fabio," Gus replied, and he heard Vanessa laughing as she ended the call. He slipped his phone back into his pocket and looked back to the music shop.

Manny's Music was tucked in between a liquor store and a frozen yogurt shop and, unlike its neighbors, had no roll-down metal garage door above its entrance. Manny was a trusting lad. Gus pushed open the wood and plexiglass door and was met with the chime of a tiny silver bell at its top. He carefully closed the door behind him and took in the vibe.

The shop was small and cluttered and smelled of glue and wood shavings. Dusty display stands were perched around the cramped space and the carpet was in need of a vacuum. To his right was a stand stuffed full of booklets containing sheet music; with a passing glance he saw the *Charlie Parker Omnibook*, the Bach Cello suites, and *Taylor Swift: for Violin*. On the wall beyond that was a large shelf filled with all sorts of bass, cello, and violin strings.

To Gus's left was a rack with clip-on and physical tuners, an assortment of cables, pickups, microphones, and small instrument stands. Short stacks of round plastic Rosin containers lined its top like little red hockey pucks. Toward the back of the room on that side was a collection of instruments on stands. A few violins, a cello, two violas, and one lone upright bass. In the center of the back wall was a single door, closed.

Gus walked over to the instruments and looked closer at the bass in its stand. It was a beaten up, light-colored plywood instrument that Gus knew was so cheap even he wasn't good enough to make that thing sound good. But he had been in his share of music stores; he knew exactly why it was out here in front. It was the cheapest bass the owner could find, one that he could rent to every kid that came in with his mommy wanting to be a musician. They'd pay the minimum six-month rental fee then three months later the bass would be returned only to be quickly rented out again. That bass had kept the lights on in this store for ages. He smiled at the few recorders placed conveniently next to the instruments to scare the parents then, hearing a muffled voice from out back, opened the door next to him and walked in.

An older man sat at a tall thin desk beside the door speaking on a corded wall phone. The shelf behind him was cluttered with broken upright bass bridges, a few wood-shaving tools, and a pile of pink paper receipts. On the floor beside the desk were several broken violin cases and a dusty fax machine with a piece of paper sticking out of it like a large white tongue. Gus wasn't surprised to see a stack of new instrument cases inside a closet door. This was the type of place that held back the free case of an instrument when sold for the opportunity to sell it elsewhere at a later time. When the man didn't look up, Gus scanned the room for what he was there for.

Violins and violas took up the far corner to his left, cellos stood on stands to his immediate right, and in the far corner beyond them stood three upright Shen basses. He could immediately tell that one was a plywood model, an SB 80, another one was a hybrid SB 150 model, and the third was also an SB 150 but the slightly larger 7/8 size. Without saying a word, Gus took the larger bass from its stand and turned into the center of the room where a short black metal stool sat for cello players on a circular ornamental rug.

He positioned his fingers on the cheap Helicore strings and began walking a blues in F. He closed his eyes as he felt his way around her through the mindless and simple changes. The neck felt heavier than the body, but she would do for now. His mind glided back to the case and he thought about how the members of the Bowers Street Band were all around these abductions, everywhere they looked. He thought of Taylor with his hardships and his troubles and of Mick and his womanizing. He considered Chris with his overly polite midwestern manners and long list of bespoke chemicals and Leon, Taylor's guitar-playing life-long friend. He knew any one of them could be their suspect, they just needed to dig deeper.

Gus's fingers were comfortable now and he noticed the action was a little too high on her but he played through it. He thought of how the victims seemed to have nothing in common except their interest in live music and of how they were each taken from different clubs and he wondered if that was significant. His mind then briefly wrestled with each woman being held for successively shorter lengths of time and wondered if he already had his next victim. Gus then walked up the G string and its nasally sound told him it was new.

After playing a while, Gus's mind settled on how they'd found none of the victims on surveillance footage leaving any of the clubs the nights they were abducted. And he wondered how that could possibly be. He moved into thumb position, finding the harmonic on the G string. And once he'd anchored himself on the bass, it soon came to him how to get anchored with the case.

Gus knew then that it was all about how the women were being taken from the clubs.

Chapter Twenty-Nine

I T WAS THURSDAY evening, and Gus wanted to experience Music Row at its busiest; see the crowds, feel the vibe, before heading to The Mills where the band was scheduled to go on at eight thirty p.m. If their suspect was hitting it during its busiest times, Gus needed to also.

They stood at the top end of Merrimack Street and Gus took in all of Music Row. The wide cobblestone street stretched out before them for several blocks, dotted with benches down its middle along with the sporadic street performer. The shop fronts lining its sides were mostly short two and three-story dwellings built of brick, converted from their original mill-related purposes a lifetime ago. Neon signs of all shapes and sizes hung over the sidewalks, some flashing while others merely glowed in the looming dusk. Gus saw signs with large golden crowns and ones with animated characters holding drink trays. He saw sweeping cursive signs and those with chunky block text. At the far end where the Merrimack River ran beneath the street, a row of old mills rose high above the others, their sides covered with billboards and arrows directing patrons this way and that.

He and Vanessa slowly walked along while Gus tried to focus on the case and the bandmembers, but the cacophony of music all around them had his mind wandering. Songs from his childhood came to him from all sides. Many were sung in drastically different keys; from Gus's experience, the result of the singer not being able to sing it in the recorded key but wanting the twenty dollars someone offered for them to play it.

They passed a small club called Charlie's and from its windows oozed a rendition of the song "Mustang Sally", and Gus immediately thought of the popular Wilson Pickett cover version. Fond memories took his thoughts away as he reminisced at how that song had introduced him to the Muscle Shoals Rhythm Section, a relatively unknown group of session musicians that had played on hundreds of the most popular songs throughout the '60s, '70s, and '80s yet gained little notoriety outside of recording circles. Something broke his train of thought, and he realized Vanessa was tapping his forearm.

"What?"

She smiled. "Have you heard anything I've said?"

He smiled back. "Sorry."

Vanessa once told Gus that she pictured his mind as a circus, a crazed, wild circus. Acrobats in tights leaping from pole to pole, swinging wildly past each other upside down on long ropes, their faces painted with all sorts of colors as monkeys rode in circles on unicycles below, screeching at the lions and elephants which roared and trumpeted in return.

She held up her phone. "I just got off with Suzie Gilford, the woman Mick Preston claimed he was in Boston with the weekend Michelle Townsend was abducted."

Gus thought of challenging whether Vanessa had really been on the phone but, instead, asked, "What'd she say?"

Over her shoulder he saw two disheveled guys leaning on a square green trash bin with handles and wheels on one side. By the skunky smell he could tell that wasn't a cigarette they were sharing.

Vanessa's face twisted. "I'm … not sure. She didn't make any sense." Gus looked at her, his narrowed eyes asking for more. "I think she was drunk," she elaborated. "First, she called Mick an asshole then asked what he said about her and if I knew if he was seeing anyone. When I pressed her again about that weekend, she said she wasn't sure she wanted to do Mick"—Vanessa did air quotes—"*a solid* if he was seeing someone else. I'll have someone go see her in person. I'm sure a badge will sharpen her focus."

Gus heard the familiar opening guitar riff of a Matchbox Twenty song spill from one of the clubs over the swelling ambient noise and a woman's high-pitched scream declaring it her song. He and Vanessa walked on and his eyes were drawn to the fading smear of pink in the indigo twilight.

"This all hinges on how he's getting them outta the clubs."

"Well, we've got nothing so far unless TJ comes up with something from the Hogan tapes."

"Let's have somebody go back through all of the footage again. There's gotta be *something* there." When she nodded, he moved on. "Oh, and hey, you get that list of chemicals from the art museum Chris Houlihan works at?"

"Not yet."

"Okay, push that. So the first vic, Townsend," Gus said, moving on. "We know she waitressed sometimes at The Mills and that Mick and Chris recognized her immediately. And we suspect—based on the look on his face—that Taylor recognized her also but lied and said he didn't."

"That's right," Vanessa confirmed. "And we'll ask the guitarist, Leon, when we talk to him later. But, as of now, we have no one we can put with her the night she went missing."

"Right. Then there's the Hogan woman. The bartender, MJ, puts Taylor, Mick, and the Leon guy with her the night she went missing. And her pissing Mick off."

"That's right, but with Taylor being the last one with her," Vanessa added.

"With Taylor being the last one with her," Gus echoed.

He watched a woman with puffed-up hair wearing a miniskirt and fishnet stockings as if she just stepped out of an issue of *Tiger Beat* magazine amble by from club to club.

"We need to hit up MJ again." He nodded to himself as he looked back to the swelling crowd in front of them. "See if anyone was with Taylor at the end of the night."

They continued walking.

"Then there's Rachel Connors," Gus said.

"And this is where it gets interesting," Vanessa interrupted. "We've got all four of 'em with her on video at the bar. Chris doesn't seem to talk to her, and Taylor and the guitarist, Leon, only speak with her briefly. It's all Mick on this one."

"Yes, it is," Gus agreed.

They passed a mime pretending to scale a building as they reached the end of Merrimack Street. Across a side street was an old bridge crossing the Merrimack River. Its pavement was dotted with potholes, and its once-ornate concrete sides were crumbling and misshapen from years of harsh New England seasons. The late autumn breeze off the water was cold and Gus noticed Vanessa crossing her arms over her midsection as he watched a small vortex of wind in an alley swirling leaves and trash in random circles.

"So, can we take anyone off the board with an alibi for any of 'em?" he asked, offering her his coat with a gesture that she declined.

"Not yet. We're still verifying Mick's. And Chris's are a little vanilla."

"Jesus. This is like trying to catch smoke," Gus griped.

His eyes were then drawn to the old mill that ran along a curve in the river, its face pocked with broken bricks like acne. He looked at a large faded arrow painted on its side. It pointed to their right and had the name of several clubs beneath it with the large words NO COVER CHARGE written atop it. He nodded for them to turn down the side street and they soon got to the corner and took a right onto Moody Street, heading back in the direction from which they'd started.

"Chris's partner vouched for him, though, right?"

Vanessa had called Chris's partner, Roland, earlier that afternoon. He confirmed Chris being asleep when he got home both the night of Rachel Connors's and Sadie Hogan's disappearances and confirmed he had worked the night months ago when Michelle Townsend went missing. And, while the details of that night were unclear, he couldn't think of a night that Chris wasn't home when he got home after a night at the restaurant during the entire twelve months they'd been living together. Vanessa had taken down all the information and thanked him for his time, but was hardly satisfied.

"Yeah, but we need some type of independent confirmation."

"Agreed."

Gus heard a few, lone bass notes and stopped in front of one of the clubs. He peered inside to see a young man playing the electric bass between several mic stands on a small lighted stage. He held the bass firm and high and plucked at the strings with confidence. Gus listened with interest as the kid played a rubato intro, and he immediately recognized the song as Victor Wooten's rearrangement of "Amazing Grace." He listened for a minute or so before they walked on.

"We haven't gotten Taylor's alibis yet." Gus pointed out. "But will once we get that boot print IDed from the Connors scene." He caught Vanessa's eye. "Push that before Taylor gets the notion to ditch 'em somewhere."

"Checking in with CSU on the daily. I think they know the urgency."

They slowly walked on, each in their own heads, until they came to an empty park bench beside a statue of the famous writer, Jack Kerouac. Vanessa sat then Gus plopped beside her. The sun had gone down but its light had been replaced by neon all around them. Vanessa hunched her shoulders and shivered.

"You find anything of interest online earlier?" Gus asked.

During munch time, Vanessa had gone online for a while, scouring the social media pages of each victim to see if there was any connection between them.

Her mouth twisted. "Nah, nothing."

"I finished going through the backgrounds TJ pulled together for each of the bandmembers. Nothing jumped out." Gus sighed. "Seems the most productive thing I've done today is paying for my pet sitter's stitches."

"Roscoe bit her again?" Vanessa smiled.

Gus averted his gaze and glanced at one of the club entrances nearby. "Scratched her with both front paws on her scalp. Wouldn't let go so…"

"For real?" When Gus didn't answer she moved on. "That guy Mick's been living rent-free inside my head ever since I saw that video of him hitting on Rachel Connors."

"I hear ya." Gus tapped his finger against his thigh to a distant melody.

Vanessa's phone rang and, seeing it was TJ Facetiming her, she answered it. TJ was close to his phone so all they could see was his round face, from his shiny forehead to his chin and jowl.

"Hey, you two in a place you can talk?"

Gus looked around at all the passersby focused on the clubs and music. He huddled next to Vanessa. "Yeah, go ahead."

TJ turned and backed away so that his face was beside a

large monitor. "We got a batch of surveillance footage in from the street cam outside the Blue Agave for the night the Connors woman went missing."

"You get her leaving?" blurted Gus.

"Think so. Check this out." TJ hit play and Gus watched as a dark sedan pulled to the curb in front of the club.

"That's the Uber she apparently called from inside the club." He fast-forwarded it until the sedan pulled away. "The driver waited the obligatory five minutes then left when she didn't show. But check this out." A few moments later Gus watched as a new dark-colored Dodge Challenger with rally stripes drove through the frame following the Uber.

"Is that Mick Preston's car?" Gus asked.

TJ paused the video then zoomed in on the front bumper of the car to show its license plate. "Asked and answered. That car's registered to a Michael Preston of Tyngsboro Mass." He then moved the screen to the windshield. They could clearly see Mick in the driver's seat, his shoulder-length hair pushed behind his ear.

There was a smaller person sitting beside him in the passenger seat but, because of the angle of the camera, their face was hidden behind the roof.

Gus leaned closer to Vanessa's phone. "Is that Rachel Connors with him?"

"The lab's working on it now," TJ answered excitedly.

Chapter Thirty

GUS AND VANESSA had planned to go to The Mills before the band went on for their set around eight thirty p.m. but now with this video wanted to get to Mick Preston as soon as possible. Gus called Jeff Cattagio as they made their way through the swelling crowd to make the case for a search warrant for Mick Preston's home and automobiles. They could interview him again and they would, but short of the man crumbling and confessing, they'd still have questions that only evidence could answer. And if that was Rachel Connors in his car that night, there could be trace evidence that tied him to her murder.

"Gus, you just don't have enough," Jeff repeated a second time after Gus kept hammering away at him.

"But this is all we're gonna get without a search. We've got him on video in the club following our latest vic, the Connors woman, then getting aggressive when she rejects his advances. Then later, after she's last seen on surveillance footage, we've got him on video driving away from the club with a woman in his car."

"But, Gus," Jeff interrupted before doing his own hammering. "What makes you think that person—because we don't even know it's a woman—is actually Rachel Connors?"

He didn't wait for Gus to answer. "You know as well as I do, that video is circumstantial at best. If we ID the Connors woman in that car then, yes, we take him. But not yet." Jeff exhaled into the phone. "It's just not enough. You know that."

"Listen." Gus cringed at how much he sounded like Jeff at that moment. "The first vic waitressed at the bar this guy Mick and his band play at every week and he admitted knowing her. And the second vic, the Hogan woman, was last seen at that same club after one of their shows and he was seen talking to her late at night."

"You check his alibis?"

Gus paused. "We're in the process of doing that but what he told us is thin, very thin."

Jeff fell quiet, and Gus could picture him running his fingers through his thinning sandy blonde hair. Gus heard a chorus of loud female voices and looked to see a group of young women stumble out of a club, arms in the air as they cheered to the sky. He thought of his friend Donny from college who would call women that did that at college parties woo-woo girls. He'd explain that they'd be the ones at parties, one drink in, shouting *woo-woo* to anything at all—a song they liked on the radio, the toasting of a new drink. Breathing.

As the women turned into the next club, Jeff's voice was back in Gus's ear. "Sorry, Gus. We need more. Any judge worth their salt is going to ask about alibis and, right now, we don't have a credible answer."

Gus ended the call and, looking to Vanessa, shook his

head. They walked around a crowd watching a young man busking beside a small statue of a bare-chested Mickey Ward with boxing shorts and gloves on. The musician wore faded jeans with holes on his knees, an unbuttoned flannel shirt over a white T-shirt and blue skater sneakers. He was strumming hard on his guitar, belting out the lyrics to R.E.M.'s "Losing My Religion", and Gus noted the large pile of cash in his open guitar case. Gus had done his fair share of busking in the Quarter during college and knew the tricks to getting more tips. First of all, just like in real estate—location, location, location. Pick the corners or sidewalks that people needed to walk by to get to the good clubs or restaurants. And, second, always—always—play songs that the wife or mother knew. They held the purse strings, regardless of what any husband or father would say.

As they made their way around the crowd, Gus saw the reporter that approached him at the police station and reported from the Rachel Connors scene. He watched as she lowered her microphone and the bright light of the camera went off. He was about to slide back into the crowd when their eyes met.

"Shit," he breathed.

Vanessa followed his stare and echoed his sentiment.

"Agent Wheeler," The reporter called as she hurried over to him, her cameraman in tow. "Christina Collins, News Center Six." She held her microphone up and without being prompted the cameraman clicked the light on and aimed it at her and Gus.

Gus stepped in close to her and used his fingers to push

the microphone down to her side.

"No interviews." He towered over the woman and used it to his advantage.

Christina donned a forced pout but when Gus didn't flinch it disappeared. She spoke to her cameraman over a shoulder, her eyes holding Gus's the entire time.

"Alright, Tommy. Why don'cha start packing up the truck. I'll be there in a minute."

Tommy lowered the camera and clicked its light off. He nodded to Gus, took the microphone from Christina and wound its cord around his arm, then turned and left.

"Okay, off the record," Christina began. "What..."

Gus opened his palm in front of her mouth. "I didn't say off the record, Ms. Collins. I said no interview."

She pushed his hand away in much the same way he moved her microphone.

"Agent Wheeler, we can help each other here."

"You're a *lifestyle* reporter?" Vanessa decried, looking at her phone.

"Not for long," Christina said, her eyes fixed on Gus.

"Your vibe ... it's giving Annie Murphy in *Schitt's Creek*," Vanessa continued.

Christina shot Vanessa a look before settling back on Gus. "The important thing is, I know the Falls. I was born and raised here. I can help you."

Gus raised an eyebrow. "I think we're good."

"With what, the summer festival schedule?" Vanessa murmured, her eyes still on her phone.

"I know Michelle Townsend's license was found on

Sadie Hogan's body." she blurted desperately. "And that Sadie's was found on Rachel Connors's."

"There's no off button with you, is there?" Gus asked.

He shot Vanessa a look then stepped past Christina and began walking on. But he'd only taken a few steps when Christina called to him, stopping him in his tracks.

"I know how he's getting them out of the clubs."

Chapter Thirty-One

G US TURNED BACK to her, his eyes narrowed. "What did you just say?"

Christina took a step closer to them. "Have you figured out how he's getting the women out of here when he takes them? I know Michelle Townsend's not on any video leaving the club the night she disappeared. And, by the looks on your faces, I can tell you don't know how the other two were taken either."

Gus exhaled in frustration then he and Vanessa walked back to Christina. "I'd ask how you know all that," he said, shaking his head, "but I don't want to know. So, enlighten us; how is our suspect getting the women out of the clubs without being seen?"

She eyed him with mock suspicion. "Quid pro quo?"

Gus remained quiet as he contemplated something he knew he'd come to regret. He glanced to his side at Vanessa who simply raised an eyebrow in return. She was thinking the same thing he was. They needed to figure out how their suspect was getting the women out, no matter the cost. If they could figure that out, they could retrace his steps. And, if they could do that, they just might catch him before he took another. Gus stepped into Christina's personal space.

"Let's hear what you have and go from there."

"I can work with that." Christina's smile lit up her entire face and Gus knew why she was in front of the camera instead of behind it. She held out her hand and waited. Gus looked down and silently stared at it.

"She wants your phone, Grandpa," Vanessa said.

Gus pulled his phone from the pocket of his faded leather jacket, unlocked it, and handed it to her. Christina tapped away at its screen for several moments then handed it back.

"There. I'm in your contacts and I sent myself a text so I have your number." Gus looked at his phone as if it'd just been violated and slid it back into his pocket. "Follow me on your socials," she added. "I'll do the same."

"I don't really do social media," he said.

Christina looked at him with the horror of a child being told there was no Santa Claus.

"What've ya got?" he pressed, his patience waning.

"Cities of the underworld," she declared with a flair.

Gus blinked and his head leaned back. "What?" he asked.

"Have you ever seen that show on the History Channel, *Cities of the Underworld?*"

Still confused, he shook his head. "No. Why?"

"Most major cities around the world were built on top of former cities. And the infrastructure of those former cities still exists today. They're like cities under cities."

Gus twitched his head side to side. "What are you talking about? How does…"

Christina interrupted him by unfolding her arms out

wide to her sides. "We have a miniature version of that here, in the Falls. This entire area surrounding the river—including Music Row—was once all textile mills that lived off of, and fed into, the river. I did a whole series of stories on it a few years back and showed how you could essentially traverse miles of distance underground and never see the light of day."

"You mean tunnels?" Gus asked, now intrigued.

She raised an eyebrow. "An entire *city* of tunnels. Most of these buildings are thought to have access points in their basements. You can go building to building, you can go out to the river and there're even some that go under the river. It's all there in the stories I did."

"We searched the basement of the Blue Agave club." Vanessa pointed out. "Where Rachel Connors went missing from. We didn't see any tunnels or ways to get into a tunnel down there."

"That's the fascinating part. See, most people think of the Falls as a former mill city, a textile city. And it is. But in 1922 there was the famous New England Textile Strike which shut down the mills over wages. That triggered many of those companies to relocate operations to the South and, as a result, the Falls—once the largest industrial complex in the country—fell on very hard times and most of its mills fell idle and vacant. But fortunately, this was during the early years of Prohibition."

Gus's mind flashed to the moonshine equipment in the basement of the Blue Agave. "And manufacturing is manu-facturing."

Christina's face lit up again with her thousand-watt smile. "Exactly. All the infrastructure was there, complete with tunnels leading right to the river, which was the perfect distribution channel. They just needed to hide some of it where they could store the illegal alcohol. So entrances to the tunnel system and storage rooms were hidden. Fake walls, trap doors, concealed rooms. One of the stories in my series focused on finding the entrances. A professor at NYU wrote a book on speakeasys and in it he documented how that illicit community of people banded together, trading ways to elude the law, and a large part of that were all the ingenious ways they created hidden rooms and passages. You just need to know where to look for the lever or other trigger to open them up."

Gus looked to the entrance of The Loft where Michelle Townsend was taken and all the women queued up to enter. His eyes wandered around the area, and at his height, he could see a good distance in either direction. It was almost eight p.m., and the entire scene was stuffed with people laughing, partying, having a good time. He wondered if their suspect was among them, watching, waiting.

"The Loft?" Christina asked, following Gus's gaze. When he didn't answer she said, "That's one of the buildings I featured in my stories. C'mon, I'll show you what I mean."

"I think we can take it from here," Gus replied, his eyes on the entrance to the club.

"What, and fumble around the basement like you did at Blue Agave only to come up with nothing?" Christina sniped. "Agent, this isn't *Scooby Doo*. You're not going to just pull down a wall light and have a hidden door slide open or lean back a book on a shelf and spin into another room. These basements were searched continuously during Prohibition by police well-versed in the capabilities of that era and, most of the time, they couldn't find even a trace of these tunnels."

Gus stole a glance at Vanessa who remained silent, yet did the raised eyebrow thing again. As always, she was thinking what he was.

Christina put her fingers on Gus's arm. "Agent, let me help. Please. I can get us in to look at the basement without anyone seeing. I've got an in with Donny, the manager. My story put his club on the map."

Chapter Thirty-Two

GUS AND VANESSA hung in the alley by the backdoor of The Loft, waiting for Christina to let them in. It was dusk, and the glow from the clubs on the other side of the building masked the starry night forming overhead with a faint haze. They could hear the sounds of the Merrimack River from where they stood and feel the cool breeze off its water. Once again, Gus offered a huddling Vanessa his coat and, once again, she declined.

"What d'ya think about all this; trap doors, hidden rooms, secret tunnels?" Gus asked.

"I don't know. Sounds a bit extra to me." Arms crossed over her stomach; she looked up to him and smiled. "But what I do know is you were giving that reporter all the feels back there."

"I don't even want to know what that means."

The back door popped open, and Christina leaned out holding the door. "C'mon," she whispered conspiratorially to them. She pressed her back against the door and motioned for Gus to squeeze past. He gestured for her to go first then held the door for Vanessa.

The three of them walked down a narrow hallway, and Gus could hear an unseen leaky faucet ringing the same note over and over somewhere nearby. They came to a plain wooden door, the area surrounding its handle rubbed lighter from years of use. Christina carefully opened it and they followed her down a narrow wooden staircase and into a small space at the foot of the stairs. Gus had expected a large, warehouse-like space similar to that of the Blue Agave. But what they found was the exact opposite.

Several commercial-size stainless steel freezers lined the wall beside them, making the space tighter than it otherwise would be. The cement floor was cracked in places and sloped slightly toward the brick wall and, overhead, the rafters of the low ceiling were stuffed with pipes and ductwork and various cords and wires. The stench of mildew hung in the air.

"This way," Christina said, leading them away from the stairs and through a winding hallway that seemed to get narrower with each step. They passed sets of empty silver shelves and stacks of empty liquor boxes before taking a left and stepping down three stone stairs into a shorter hallway that ended about ten feet in front of them. The ceiling in this hall was arched and, like the walls, made of brick painted a glossy crimson red. Christina walked to the end, motioning for the others to follow, then stood to one side.

"In the 1920s, when the mill and speakeasy here got raided, this door would automatically shut, locking the contraband behind it." She held up a long meat skewer. "Then they'd use something like this to unlock it when it was safe." She ran her palm over the smooth bricks as she crouched down in front of the wall, pressing her hand in a spot about a foot from the floor.

She motioned for Gus to take a look, so he and Vanessa knelt beside her. At the end of her finger, Gus saw a small hole in the cement the size of a pea between two bricks. Christina aimed the meat skewer toward the hole.

"You have to hold it precisely at a ninety-degree angle." She slowly inserted it into the hole and pushed, and Gus heard a faint click. They all stood, and Gus put his shoulder into the wall and it opened wide.

"That's some clean shit," Vanessa said, eyeing the latch.

"Are there lights," Gus asked, squinting into the darkness.

The smell of dirt and decay wafted around him.

"In some parts," Christina said, "But it's mostly been shut down over the years."

He took his penlight and aimed it into the space to see a tunnel of similar size to the hallway he stood in. While the glossy paint and elaborate molding were gone, the brick and arched ceiling remained for thirty or forty feet then became dirt just before the darkness closed around it.

"Has this tunnel system been mapped?" he asked, inspecting the brickwork along a wall.

"Nothing comprehensive that I'm aware of," Christina said, stepping through the doorway to stand beside him and Vanessa. "We did a rough map just to get some sense of how large it is. We estimated there's about eight or nine miles of tunnels down here, many with adjacent rooms, but no one really knows for sure just how extensive it all is."

"And you know of other buildings that have entrances?"

"Yessir. We listed several other entrances in one of my stories. I can go back and check my notes for more. But there's definitely one in The Mills where the Hogan woman was taken."

"How about Blue Agave?"

Christina's mouth twisted. "I'd have to check. It's been years."

"And you know how to open them?" pressed Gus.

"Those we found, yes. I'll have that in my notes as well."

Gus and V shared a look before Gus replied to the reporter. "Yeah, we'll need that list." Gus then grew quiet as he thought about what to do next.

This could be the break in the case they were looking for, if their suspect was actually using these tunnels. And, given none of the victims could be found on surveillance video exiting the club they were at the night they disappeared, Gus was willing to bet he was. And, if he was, there could be valuable evidence somewhere down there that helped them identify their suspect. But if there really was eight or nine miles plus rooms and other hidden surprises, the chances of them finding that evidence was slim at best. Then his mind shifted to the victims.

He was confident that Michelle Townsend was the first, but what if she wasn't? What if there were others before her, women on the fringe of society largely unnoticed and unmissed? There could be remains down there that brought closure to someone's loved ones or family. Gus couldn't take the chance that was not the case. They needed to search these tunnels, if for no other reason than to ensure there were no other remains as yet unaccounted for. He exhaled loudly and turned to Vanessa.

"We gotta search the tunnels."

She didn't flinch. "There might be others."

His jaw clenched. "There might be others," he echoed. He looked to Christina. "Get Vanessa the list of all the entrances you know of." Then, back to Vanessa, he said, "Until then, we start with this one."

He took one last look into the tunnels then turned and stepped back through the door into the basement. After Vanessa and Christina followed, he began to ease the heavy door closed until Christina stepped in front of it.

"What're you doing?" she asked. "We have to search them."

"We will." assured Gus. "But we'll do it right." He paused and his eyes settled on the dirt floor opening to the tunnels.

"We don't have time to wait," Christina pressed. "There could be other women down there."

"There are no other missing women we know of right now," Gus said.

"Who knows how long he's been doing this? There could be prior victims you've not connected to this case. Even if they're dead, we have to find them for their families."

"Oh, come off the cross," Vanessa spat, stepping toward the reporter. "You're not worried about other women being down there." She pointed to the cellphone in Christina's hand. "You just want to get some shots so you can get your story."

"That's not…"

Vanessa held up the palm of her hand and Christina's voice faded mid-sentence, as if someone had removed her batteries.

"Not gonna happen," Gus said definitively. "Not now."

Chapter Thirty-Three

G US TOOK ONE last look down the long dark tunnel and an image flickered in his mind like that of a dark horizon momentarily lit by lightning. He thought of a search and rescue he helped with the summer before college. A tourist had gotten lost in the caves of Black Canyon in the Gunnison National Park, and Gus remembered how the team from the National Park Service arrived with a comprehensive map of the entire cave network. He closed the door the rest of the way then turned to Vanessa.

"Get ahold of someone at the National Park Service," he said. "They have oversight of all the cave networks in federal land and parks. They must have a way to map 'em without having to trudge through 'em all."

Vanessa pulled out her phone and began walking back toward the stairs.

Gus turned back to Christina. "Thanks for this." He gestured toward the closed door. "You've got one in the bank."

She exhaled in defeat then squinted an eye, considering her next move.

She tipped her head toward the door. "Can I cash it in for an exclusive on what you find in there?"

Gus couldn't help but smirk at her tenacity. "Let's take

this slow. I'm new at this."

Her eyebrows flicked up and down. "Bet you say that to all the girls."

"You should leave first so no one sees us together," he said before she could continue.

Realizing that was all she was going to get, Christina left Gus standing alone beside the hidden door. He waited a few minutes then joined Vanessa back upstairs beside the back entrance they'd come in through. An old Triumph song, "Lay It on the Line," flowed from the speakers overhead, and he could hear a low undercurrent of people in the club singing along with it. He checked his phone and saw it was eight p.m.

"If we hurry, we can still get to The Mills in time to speak with Mick before their set." They began to head that way when Gus continued, "Boyd's precinct leaks like a sieve. That reporter knew everything. We gotta do something about that."

"Not my circus, not my monkeys," Vanessa replied as she squeezed between two groups of people to keep up with him.

Five minutes later, he and Vanessa arrived at The Mills slightly sweaty and out of breath. Flashing their badges, they skipped the long line, slipped inside, and made their way straight toward the stage. Across the dim room, Gus saw MJ slinging drinks behind the bar then his eyes went to Taylor who was setting up an amp on stage. As Gus and Vanessa approached, the singer Chris saw them first.

"Agents," he said, causing Taylor to snap his head up.

Another guy walked onto the stage from behind the curtain carrying a guitar and Gus recognized him as Leon Sampson.

"Hey, guys," Gus said. They all stopped what they were doing and looked over at him. "Where's Mick?"

"He won't be here tonight. He's sick," Chris said. He looked to Taylor. "Where's the sub you called? We're on in twenty."

Gus stole Chris's attention with a raise of his hand. "Gimme Mick's number."

He read it aloud and Gus called it. It rang three times then was forwarded to voicemail. Gus tried the number again with the same result.

"Jesus, I really want to talk to this guy," he said quietly to Vanessa.

"We can go knock on his door?"

Gus pictured he and Vanessa trying to find their way through the dark country roads of Tyngsboro in his truck, Vanessa reading directions from her phone as they crept along looking for driveways amongst the wood line. His eyes drifted to Leon who was sitting by himself, tuning his guitar quietly in the back corner of the stage.

"Nah. What would we say? 'Let us in or we'll speak harshly from the porch'?" He shook his head, "If we had him here, we could talk to him but without a search warrant he can just stay in his house and ignore us." He raised his chin in Leon's direction. "We've got a few minutes. Let's talk to Leon while we're here."

Gus pulled the stool by the singer's microphone over and

sat beside Leon, Vanessa standing at his side. Leon turned his guitar so it laid flat across his legs. It was a champagne white hollow body Gretsch guitar with gold fittings. He lowered his head to Vanessa then Gus.

"Agents."

"Leon, I'm Agent Wheeler, this is Agent Lambert. I'm sure the others told you we're investigating the murders of three local women."

Leon gave Gus a slight nod. "The Talent Scout. Was wondering when you'd get to me."

"The others tell you what we're looking for?"

Leon smiled shyly. "I knew Michelle Townsend from her waitressing here, but really only well enough to say hi. I met Sadie Hogan the night she was with T at the bar, but only briefly before I left and went home. And I saw the Rachel Connors woman at the bar at Blue Agave when we were all there that night but left and went home shortly after that."

Gus smiled. "Alibis?"

"We played here the night Michelle Townsend went missing from a different club entirely. Usually, we stay and have a drink before going home; not sure if we did that night but I went home after our gig. I did go straight home the night Sadie Hogan went missing. I remember because I checked with T that he was alright to get home before I left the two of 'em at the bar. And the same for the night Rachel Connors went missing. The four of us had been out and stopped into that club later in the night so I was beat. I left after one drink."

"Did you see Mick leave that night?"

Leon thought a moment then slowly shook his head. "No, sorry. But he wasn't at the bar. Nor was Chris; he left just before me. When I left, T was the last one there."

"You live with someone that can verify your alibis?"

"Yeah, but you already knew that." He smiled. "I live with my girlfriend Sheila and her daughter."

"Do you know what times you would've gotten home each of these nights?" Vanessa asked.

"I try to get home by 11:30 or so on Saturday nights. Sheila picks up cleaning gigs on Sunday mornings so has to get up early; she likes me home before locking up and going to bed. We live on the other side of the river up past the university so it's only a twenty-minute walk."

"You don't drive or Uber?"

Leon shrugged and looked around. "Uber might as well be a limo for what we make here."

Gus made a mental note to have traffic cams checked for Leon walking home on those nights.

"What do you do for work?" Gus asked. "Besides playing."

"Every musician has a day job." Leon chuckled. "Especially in this economy." His kind eyes widened a little. "Yours is cooler than most, though. T told me you play, and that he knows you from NOLA. Said you were pretty good back in the day."

Gus tipped his head. "I do alright."

Leon remained quiet for a few moments, as if sizing Gus up. "I'm a technician at a place called The Memory Garden. We restore and convert analogue audio and video to digital;

VHS, Beta, thirty-five millimeter, cassettes, all that old stuff."

"That sounds pretty cool."

Leon shrugged. "Eh, it's okay. I mean, some of the old things I see are pretty cool; photos of soldiers from way back, cars the size of this stage, stuff like that. And it pays the bills and lets me gig when I want."

"We saw your rap sheet," Vanessa interjected. "Nine years in federal prison for dealing."

Leon's face hardened. "That's right. The perfect storm. I'd been pinched twice before for selling dime bags so that was my third strike. A guy I knew came to me to move some smack for him, big payday. I thought if I did that one, I'd have enough bank to get outta here. Shit went south, dude dropped a dime on me, and I'd just turned eighteen so it was the big house for me." He exhaled with puffed out cheeks. "But that was a lifetime ago. Not into that shit anymore."

Gus heard a loud crash and looked to see Taylor angrily talking to one of the waitresses as she knelt down to pick up a spilled glass and its ice by his feet. Taylor bent over and picked up a GoPro and began reattaching it to the end of his bass's neck. Leon immediately got up and joined the two of them and Gus watched as he put a hand on Taylor's shoulder and quietly talked to him. After a few moments, Taylor shrugged Leon's hand from his shoulder and walked back stage. Leon helped the waitress pick up the ice then rejoined Gus and Vanessa.

"Sorry about that." He took his guitar but didn't sit. "We're on in five so I gotta hit it."

Gus gestured toward the waitress who had cleaned up the spilled drink and was stepping down from the stage. "Everything okay?"

"Eh." Leon grimaced. "He's been having a hard time since his mother went into a home."

"Does he have any other family around or anyone he can talk to?" asked Gus.

"The only relative he has is his sister, and she's in California and they're not really that close. He sees a therapist but…"

A man's voice called from the opposite side of the stage. "Leon, you ready?"

Gus looked to see a large overweight man standing with the other bandmembers.

Gus stood and handed Leon one of his cards. "If you think of anything else, give us a call."

He and Vanessa then hopped off the stage and found a few seats to watch the show.

Chapter Thirty-Four

TAYLOR SAT SLUMPED on the worn settee in his mother's bedroom, his arm outstretched along its back, cheek resting on his shoulder. He watched the rising sun through watery eyes as its rays lit ripples in the gunship grey Merrimack River. It was Saturday morning and he had the day off so was able to sleep in, but that had proved impossible. He had tried everything to get some sleep when he got home from their gig last night but nothing worked.

He started with his bedtime routine, religiously doing each step precisely as he did every night. He brushed his teeth for exactly two minutes then flossed completely. He removed his contact lenses—the left first, then the right—and put them in their holder with the solution for the night. He put his eye drops in each eye—one in the corner first, with one inside the bottom lid to follow—then he wrote out his list of things to do the next day in his pocket-sized notepad. And when that was all done, Taylor slid a new movie Leon brought him into the VCR—*Ghost* starring Patrick Swayze and Demi Moore—and got into bed.

But every time he began to relax and feel as if he could doze off, he'd have visions of his hands around a woman's neck, of bare arms and legs bruised and bloodied, of lifeless bodies lying in tall grass. But this time, as these images snapped on and off in his mind like a frenzied lightshow, there were glimpses of other scenes as well. He saw patches of dirt and a woman staggering away, her white, frightened face turned toward him. He saw images of total darkness with a single, small fuzzy light off in the distance. And when he was finally able to push all that aside in his quest for sleep, that was when the voices came.

He heard the whispers of women he didn't recognize pleading for him to stop, for him to have mercy. *I beg you, Taylor, please!* He heard their faint moans and cries for help and desperate gasps followed by ominous silence.

Feeling his sanity slipping from him, Taylor had sprung from bed and manically paced around the house yelling, pleading for the voices to stop. And when they didn't, he furiously yelled back unspeakable things from deep within, but still they persisted.

Desperate for all this madness to go away, he began hitting his head with closed fists over and over and over. Until finally, physically and emotionally exhausted, he collapsed on the settee in his mother's bedroom where the whispers were the faintest, but his thoughts the loudest.

Taylor knew it was him; he killed those women. And in a way, he always knew it; ever since he found Sadie Hogan's license in his jeans pocket. Sure, he tried to hide from it, tried to believe it couldn't be true. But where had that gotten him?

And as he sat on the settee watching the sunrise, he was reminded of a time back at Loyola his freshman year. The resident director had barged into his dorm room early one morning; he remembered the sunrise out his window looking a lot like the one he was staring at now. Another student claimed Taylor assaulted him at a keg party earlier that night by taking his bass and forcibly replacing him in the band that was playing. And Taylor remembered what the RD had said to him as he was leaving. *Reputations are formed in an instant, Taylor, but can take years to change. So remember. Karma never sleeps.* Taylor wondered if karma was at play now.

He had lost track of time when he heard a soft whisper calling to him. He wiped drool from his cheek as he sat up to listen more closely, swallowing hard at the metallic taste. He got up, following its calls, and was soon making his way to the kitchen at the end of the hall. The sink was filled with dirty dishes and the countertops stacked high with empty wrappers and frozen dinner boxes. The small card table was against the wall beside the refrigerator, its two chairs slid askew. The whispers were louder now but no one was in the room. He lowered his head and brought his hands to his ears but the voices only grew louder. Squeezing his eyes closed, he fell back against the cellar door, sliding down it until he was squatting on the floor.

"Fuckin' stop!" he demanded into his thighs. "Leave me alone!"

He felt a presence in the room but when he peeled his eyes open found no one there. Pushing himself up, he leaned against the counter. His hand fumbled along the front of the cabinets until he felt the handle of a drawer and yanked it open. Feeling his way over a tray, he pulled out a steak knife then scurried from the room. And as he entered the living room, he heard a knock on the front door and froze.

Fuck.

Was that Wheeler and his punk-rock partner here to take him in? He thought of Teddy on top of the refrigerator and what surprises he might cough up. He looked over his shoulder at the back door, wondering where he might go. A second knock stole his attention and he watched the door-knob slowly turn as a woman's voice screeched in his ears.

"Get the *fuck* away from me!" he yelled, bringing his hands to his ears again.

The door swung open, and Taylor opened his eyes to see Leon peering around it, concern on his face.

"Heyyyy," Leon said hesitantly, his eyes moving to the knife in Taylor's hand. "What's ... going on?" He stepped into the house and closed the door.

Taylor glared at his friend but didn't say a word. How did he tell someone he thought he was going insane and expect them not to do something about it? But before he realized it, Taylor was telling Leon of his nightmares and the images he'd been seeing again of dead women. And he told him of the voices calling to him by name, begging him to stop, and that he'd been hearing them all night long.

And when he was done, Taylor lowered his head and be-gan to sob. "I think the doc's right." He moaned. "I think this all started with Anne Marie."

"It coulda," Leon said, stepping closer. "You were differ-ent back then; drinking a lot, always stoned." He shook his head. "You weren't happy."

"But I loved her so much."

"You had a funny way of showin' it sometimes, though."

Taylor slid his hands from his face and looked at Leon. "What d'ya mean?" he asked, running his wrist beneath his nose to wipe away snot.

Leon's eyebrows scrunched together in confusion.

"You don't remember? Things weren't rosy with you and her at the end before she left." He paused a moment. "Let's just say she was wearing turtlenecks and sunglasses a lot around then. You were kind of a wreck."

The room fell quiet, the low hum of the refrigerator filling the void.

Taylor wiped tears from his eyes. "I saw her." he said, his voice cracking. "Anne Marie."

Leon tilted his head and his eyes narrowed. "When?"

"The other night, at practice. It was her I saw looking in the garage window."

But before Leon could respond, a woman's voice whispered to Taylor again to stop. He squeezed his eyes closed and tried to push it away long enough to hear what Leon was saying but couldn't. *They. Just. Won't. Stop.* Taylor felt his friend's hand remove the knife from his own then pull him close. He tried to think of what to do but it felt like tiny needles stabbing his brain. He was powerless; he gave in to the voices once more and as they begged for their lives, the images rushed back, this time flashing quicker and brighter than before. But sprinkled in amongst the posed dead women and eerie fields were now flashes of dim, cobweb-filled rooms and narrow dirt passageways.

His eyes popped open and he pushed back from Leon. He struggled for a moment, searching, scraping at long-forgotten memories like a stubborn scab. But then it all came rushing back to him. He recognized those cobweb-filled rooms and dirt passageways from a former life, a life he'd tried so desperately to forget.

Taylor not only knew he killed those women, he now knew where. He pushed away hard from Leon and turned to go, but his friend held firmly to his wrist.

"What're you doing?" Leon asked, and Taylor could hear the fear in his voice.

Taylor turned back, trying to pull his hand free but Leon grasped it firmer. "Let go of me." he demanded, shaking his arm.

"Not until you tell me where you're going."

A women's voice shrieked in Taylor's mind driving him into action. He violently shook his head side to side and began to scream. He then growled as he bull-rushed Leon back into the door, slamming his friend's head hard against it. He slipped his wrist free and stepped back out of reach.

"What the fuck're you doing?" Leon asked as he held the back of his head.

The voices in Taylor's mind were now louder than they'd ever been, and he began punching the sides of his head, chanting out loud, trying anything to make them stop.

"Leave me alone!"

"Leave me alone!"

Taylor heard Leon yell something but couldn't make out what it was as he scampered through the kitchen and out the back door.

Chapter Thirty-Five

<u>Saturday</u>

- ✓ Therapist appointment
- ✓ Delusional disorder?
- ✓ How long to choke
- ✓ MA death penalty
- Gus Wheeler
- Why hearing voices?
- Go back in tunnels
- Get rid of boots
- National park service?

Chapter Thirty-Six

G US AND VANESSA were sitting on a bench beneath a small cluster of trees in front of The Loft waiting for others to arrive. TJ had organized for a team from the National Park Service to come and map the tunnels so Gus wanted to take the opportunity to get inside them for himself and see what they were dealing with. It was around nine a.m. on a crisp September morning and the only other person they could see was a grey-haired man wearing an orange vest with PAWTUCKET FALLS PUBLIC WORKS printed across its back in bold black letters. The man held an over-sized canvas hose and was washing the walking area, directing the grime and remnants from the night before toward one of many rainwater grates in the pavilion.

Vanessa had gotten a call from TJ while he was on his drive up from Boston. They had confirmed that Mick Preston's company, Allied Equipment and Repair, did service the office equipment at each of the companies the three victims worked at. And that during the past eighteen months Mick had been among the technicians to visit each of their offices. He had also told Vanessa that the lab had finished analyzing the CCTV footage of Mick leaving Blue Agave in his car the night the Connors woman was taken but that they couldn't confirm the person in the car with him was Rachel Connors.

Gus held his paper cup of coffee by its rim with two fingers, dangling it over the arm of the bench. "I really wish we could put Rachel Connors in Mick's car that night or him alone with Sadie Hogan at some point the night she was taken."

While at the club last night, they had a chance to speak with the bartender MJ again about the night Sadie Hogan went missing. And, while Mick and Leon had met Sadie at the bar, she couldn't be sure if either of them was still at the club when she saw Taylor and Sadie at the end of the night.

"Same," Vanessa said. "But, Gus, him taking the Connors woman in his car doesn't add up. We've got none of the women leaving the clubs on video and we now know about the tunnels. So that all fits. If Mick's our guy, why's he got her in his car? And how'd he get her outta the club without us seeing her?"

"Simple. He grabs them from the clubs, uses the tunnels to get them out and to his car. We just happened to have gotten him on video with Connors. If we check footage around the other two clubs, we might find him with the other two women in his car also." When Vanessa didn't respond, he added, "We get the list of chemicals from his work yet?"

"TJ said they expect it today. But they did just get the list from Chris's work so those are in process."

"Rob shot me a text earlier," Gus said as he eyed the public works guy sweeping the stream from his hose in wide arcs along the cobblestones. "Tox screen on the Connors woman came back clean. Our guy isn't drugging 'em." He thought a moment, looking around at the rows of buildings, the overflowing garbage cans and the litter dotting the area.

"You get that list of openings to the tunnels from the reporter?" he asked as he saw a city garbage truck park at the end of the pavilion and two burly guys hop out.

Vanessa swallowed her coffee. "Yeah. She had five entrances, none in the other clubs where the vics were taken. I've got agents going to each today to verify them and they're putting motion-detector video cameras on each. So we'll know if he uses any of them."

"Good thinking."

Gus heard voices and looked to see a group of people come around a corner with TJ leading their way. TJ was a short, stocky man with broad shoulders and thick middle and while he was about Gus's age, his greying hair had him look ten years older. Listening intently to TJ were four people from the NPS, each carrying a black equipment bag, and Detective Amy Boyd. And once they were all together and introductions were made, TJ gestured to Gus.

"Alright, thanks everyone for coming on such short notice," he began. "As TJ probably told you, we believe our suspect is using these tunnels to move his victims from the clubs without being seen. He could also be keeping them down there for weeks at a time or moving them to a different location. We're not sure yet, so be on the lookout for any space that may make a suitable holding area or cell. And we're told there are eight or nine miles of tunnels down there along with open areas so be prepared."

As the group began to make their way into the club, TJ fell in beside Gus and Vanessa. "Just got word. The lab received the list of chemicals from Mick Preston's work this morning so that's underway."

"Excellent," Gus said.

The group followed Gus into the basement of The Loft. He then knelt and popped the door open using a skewer from the kitchen, just as Christina Collins had done the day before. The NPS team entered first and immediately affixed bright spotlights to the walls inside the door, aimed into the tunnels. Gus looked through the doorway at the arched ceiling running away from them when one of the NPS team members turned back his way. He was a large, stocky man with broad shoulders, and hair cut so short it looked like a scrubbing brush. Gus saw the name CHARLIE stitched on the breast of his jacket.

"This is a fairly narrow passageway, sir," Charlie said. "I'll go in first to see what's at the bottom of this slope before we have everyone enter."

Gus watched as Charlie slowly made his way down the tunnel, and they all waited in an eerie silence until the ranger came back a few minutes later.

"It opens up to a fairly wide cavern just at the bottom of that slope," the ranger said. "That'll be a good spot for us to set up."

Charlie then directed the other NPS rangers and they went about hanging plastic-encased lights at intervals along the sides of the tunnel so the rest of them could safely make their way to the open area. Once at the bottom, Gus straightened and looked around at the dirt walls and vaulted ceiling. He saw Vanessa and Detective Boyd staring up in awe so went to them.

"What d'ya say? Ready to hit the tunnels?" he asked Vanessa, stifling a smile.

Vanessa didn't even flinch. "Not my beat." Then she eyed Gus as he looked around the tunnel and her lip turned up. "Channeling your inner Arne Saknussemm?"

Gus gave her a look and seeing Detective Boyd's confusion, explained. "I was really into Jules Verne movies and books when I was a kid. Arne Saknussemm was the explorer in *Journey to the Center of the Earth* that first made it to the center." He turned toward the detective. "And, hey, I wanted to mention," Gus continued, lowering his voice. "Your precinct leaks like a sieve."

Amy smiled. "The reporter, Christina Collins."

Gus nodded and told her about Collins knowing that they had no idea how their suspect got Michelle Townsend out of a busy Music Row scene the night she was abducted and pointed out it was the Pawtucket Falls PD evaluating the surveillance footage from that night. He also alerted her to Collins's news report from late last night in which she disclosed to the public that the driver's license of Sadie Hogan was found on Rachel Connors's body."

"No surprise there. She flashes her pearly whites around the station and the men go weak in the knees. It's a wonder anything stays confidential at all."

"Well, I'll leave that longer term issue for you to figure

out. For the time being, Collins and I have a sort of arrangement. She's let in the circle a little and for the time being she keeps things to herself, but when we have something we want to go out with, she gets first dibs."

"Huh." Amy eyed Gus with interest. "So, how're your knees feeling there, agent? Little weak?"

Not for the first time, Gus wondered if the reporter had played him but, looking around at what they'd found, had no regrets. His eyes caught the NPS team unpacking their black duffel bags and watched with interest as three of them held up a handheld device that resembled a tape gun movers used to tape up boxes for shipment. He went over to one of the women who was adjusting the dials on hers. Her jacket had JACKIE sewn on its front.

He nodded a hello then asked, "Any sense how long this might take?"

Jackie tipped her chin toward their team leader, Charlie, who was tapping away at a large monitor's screen. "We'll know in a sec. Charlie," she called. "All set?"

Charlie nodded a yes back so Jackie held her device out in front of her, pointing it farther into the tunnels.

And after a few moments, Charlie called out. "Okay. We're live."

Jackie stepped next to Charlie so Gus and the others followed. He adjusted a few dials on the equipment and a fuzzy black and white image filled the screen. To Gus, it looked like the radar depiction of a large storm front or the first photo of a newly-conceived child.

"What're we looking at?" Gus asked as he leaned closer

to the image.

Charlie continued to adjust the settings and the image twisted this way and that, lengthening and shortening as it tilted side to side.

"That's a depiction of the first hundred meters of tunnel in front of us," Charlie answered. "I'm just trying to improve the clarity. And some of the data is still processing behind the image too."

As Charlie tinkered with the settings, the image settled and its resolution slowly improved until a large black and white tunnel shimmied on the screen. Its walls resembled delicate grey cloth.

"This is so cool." Gus looked up at Jackie and her device. "How's that work?"

"It uses LIDAR technology; basically, lasers paint the space around us and the sensors assemble the distances measured from reflected light into a three-dimensional image."

Vanessa rolled her eyes at Gus geeking out. She turned to walk away but beyond their small bubble of light was complete darkness in every direction. Trapped, she swung back into their conversation.

"Do you have to walk all of the tunnels to get an accurate mapping?" she asked.

"Depends on how long the tunnel is. If they're a hundred meters or less, we just have to stand in the opening to it. But we won't know until we check each of 'em out."

Charlie continued his adjustments and Gus saw the walls and floor of the tunnel begin to fill in and take on more of a solid shape. And as it did so, several bumps along each side developed, like the stub left when a branch was cut from a tree. Charlie pointed to one of the bumps. "Each of these is a tunnel off this main spine."

"My guess is we're talking a few days," Jackie said, answering Gus's earlier question as she looked up from the monitor's screen. "There's always something that slows you down; more off-shoot tunnels than you thought, steep gradation that limits your shoot, something."

"Can't you just use a drone?" Vanessa asked.

"They work okay if you have a really straight, long tunnel but these are anything but that. And the video range is usually only about a hundred meters so there's no real benefit of using them anyway."

"We've got something odd at the far end of the tunnel in that space to the side," Charlie said, attracting everyone's attention back to the monitor.

Gus squinted at the spot Charlie was pointing to. There was a thin bright line on the edge of the screen that ran along about a third of the inside wall of the space Charlie was referring to. To Gus, it looked like an x-ray of someone's hand with a nail or screw imbedded in their palm. He thought of all the discarded equipment they had seen in the basement of the Blue Agave and of how Collins spoke of Prohibition-era manufacturing having gone on down there.

"Could it be discarded junk?"

"Maybe, but it's below ground," Charlie said as he peered closer to the screen himself.

"So maybe pipes or something. There's a lot of infrastructure down here."

"It doesn't seem solid so maybe a conduit of some sort." Charlie nodded. "Or maybe it's just an air pocket or something."

"We'll get a closer shot when we get down there," Jackie said, standing straight and checking the settings on her device.

Vanessa leaned in to get a closer look. "It's tiny, though. Right?"

Charlie tapped a few keys and a scale appeared on each side of the screen. He made a few adjustments and when Gus saw the dimensions, concern sizzled and popped in his brain like water flicked into a hot frying pan. He knew exactly what it was but before his brain could get his mouth to spit it out, Vanessa poked the screen with a stiff finger.

"That's a fuckin' grave."

Chapter Thirty-Seven

I T WAS GOING to take at least an hour for the CSU team to arrive, so while they waited, Gus and Vanessa taped off the side room where the potential gravesite was so the NPS team could get started mapping the tunnels. Gus wasn't sure what they found was a grave but, if it was, they needed to preserve the scene as best as possible. They had rejoined Amy so now the three of them were back by Charlie and his equipment trying not to get in the way.

"Once the crime scene guys do their thing and we know if its male or female I can have someone start pulling missing person cases," Amy offered.

"Let's see what they find," Gus cautioned. "It might not even be a grave."

"It's a grave," Vanessa said matter-of-factly, brushing dust from the front of her pants. "Not sure what's in there," she added, standing straight and nodding. "But it's a grave."

Gus noticed the NPS ranger, Jackie, begin to head down the tunnel she had shot for the test so he left Amy and Vanessa to join her.

"Mind if I tag along?" he asked, falling in beside her.

"Not at all." She stopped and turned back toward the others. "But if you're coming, we have to get you some gear."

She led him back to Charlie who attached a small white gadget to Gus's belt the size of a man's watch. It had two pea-sized lights on it—one red, one green—and a small button in its center.

"That's a tracking device," Jackie said. "We all have one. Now we can find you if you wander off." Gus twisted it so he could see its top as Jackie continued, "Press that button if you get lost or if you need help." She handed him a compact walkie-talkie. "And keep this in your pocket. It's a low-frequency radio so we can communicate down here. It's got a range of three hundred meters."

"Wait for the CSU team," Gus said to Vanessa, Amy, and TJ who had joined them. "I'll be back in a few."

"Stay close." Jackie tapped on the small miner's light on her head. "Once we get in there this'll be the only light we have."

Gus held up his FBI-issued penlight and she nodded her approval. They made their way down the long narrow passageway, past the taped-off room, deeper into the tunnels. And as they continued on, the walls and ceiling seemed to close in around them and all noises fell away, leaving just the soundtrack of their shoes crunching on the rough soil.

Gus's senses began to bend around their environment. Sound became flatter, deadened, and defied distance. And light consumed finite space, as if told to stay by an unrelenting master. And as their steps fell into a steady cadence, he began to think and feel like their suspect as if he'd somehow slipped into his body, was walking his path. A flurry of feelings and emotions rose within him. Excitement, anger, determination, resolve. Gus absorbed these feelings, cradled them deep within him, willing them to lead him on.

They eventually came to the end and an intersection with another tunnel. Gus figured they had been walking for fifteen or twenty minutes and had gone maybe half a mile or so. They could go left or right, but when Gus looked, he found nothing but complete darkness in either direction. He looked back the way they came and found the same and he realized how easily it would be to get lost down there. His thoughts went to the victims and the fear they must've felt, the hopelessness. Even if they did somehow escape, the thought of them wandering around in the dark down there for days made his heart sink.

"Okay, step back so I don't get you in the shot," Jackie said, interrupting his thoughts.

Gus stood in the opening of the tunnel they'd come down while Jackie positioned herself beside him in the new tunnel and took a shot to their left with her device. She waited a few moments then, after checking her screen that she got the shot right, showed it to Gus. It was a grainy, greenish image that looked to Gus like what you'd see through night vision equipment. Jackie pointed to various spots on the screen.

"You can see at the far end it seems to drop down. We'll have to go to that spot and take another shot. But, look here and here." She pointed to two lighter spots along one side. "Those look like open spaces to me. Maybe rooms."

Gus looked down the tunnel into the darkness. "Yeah? Let's go check it out."

"Wait a sec," she replied. "We've got to work through these systematically. Let me shoot the other direction so Charlie has the data first."

Jackie turned and faced the other direction then, making sure Gus was behind her, aimed and took the shot. And, as before, she checked the screen, waiting for it to render its image.

"What the heck's that?" she asked and Gus heard concern in her voice. She looked down the tunnel then back at her device. He peered over her shoulder to look for himself and she pointed to a spot at the top of its screen. "See that bump there?" Her voice was now lower, close to a whisper. "On the right side of the tunnel at the end of the shoot with the white dot next to it?"

"Yeah," Gus replied, matching her hushed tone. "Is it an outcropping of rocks or ledge or something?"

"I don't think so," she said, her voice leery. "It's holding a light."

Gus's head snapped back up, and he squinted as he strained to see something, anything in the tunnel ahead. "Turn your light off," he whispered, and Jackie clicked off her headlamp and device.

They were now in complete darkness.

Gus trained his eyes that way as he whispered again, "Don't move or say anything."

They both stood perfectly still until all sounds fell away and they could only hear each other's breaths. Gus held his penlight firmly in one hand, his thumb resting on its button. He felt his Glock in its holster with the other to be sure it was firmly snapped in. And he waited. A tingling sensation spread throughout his scalp, like the scamper of a thousand tiny insects between his skull and hair.

And just when he began to think it was nothing, a small dot of light appeared on the far edge of his sightline. It was so faint that he squinted, wondering if it was an aberration of him staring into the darkness like seeing spots when looking at the sun too long. But then the dot swung sideways and he saw the side of the tunnel light up before it disappeared leaving the faintest glow where it had been. It took Gus only a second to realize what was happening.

"It's him," he whispered to Jackie. "He's turned and is walking away from us. I'm going to follow. You go back to the others and let them know which way I'm headed."

"Got it," she whispered back. "The tunnel's straight for a hundred meters but after that who knows."

Gus put his hand on one of the walls to feel his way and began walking quickly down the tunnel, hoping to get close before being seen. Every step in the rocky soil felt like an alarm bell, announcing Gus's presence to their suspect. Then about thirty yards in, his boot kicked an empty plastic bucket that was on the ground. It spun up and hit his shin before bouncing off the wall, sending a loud echoing sound out into the tunnel. Up ahead he saw the light swing his way then quickly swing back around and begin to bounce up and down as it moved farther away. Knowing he was made, Gus clicked on his light and took off in a run.

"Freeze! FBI!" he yelled, more out of habit than from any expectation it'd work.

He watched as the light swung back and forth, alternately lighting the sides and bottom of the tunnel in the distance. He saw glimpses of shadows but no form, no shape; nothing from which he could make out any details. Then the light disappeared so Gus ran faster until he came to another intersection. He quickly looked right then left and seeing the faint glow of the suspect's light in the distance dashed that way.

The light then suddenly flicked away so Gus quickened his pace and when he got to that spot found another intersection. He looked both ways but saw no light. He held his breath, closed his eyes and listened intently for anything that might tell him which way to go. He could sense danger, the way a dog knew when his human was about to the leave the house without him. Gus then heard the soft crunching of gravel beneath footsteps and realized it was coming from behind him. He spun and saw the light headed back the way they had come so turned and ran.

Gus was gaining on him now, closing the gap with each stride. His lungs burned and blood pounded in his ears as he closed in, his senses sharp from the adrenaline surge. He saw glimpses of movement in the choppy light as it turned off the tunnel. Gus soon rounded that same corner and saw the light resting in the center of the tunnel just up ahead. He sped toward it, the sound of rushing water barely registering in his mind as his lunging foot found only air and his body plunged downward. He felt sharp wood scratch along his shin and stab into his hip as he instinctively held his arms out wide, grasping for anything within reach. And as his elbows crashed onto wood one of his armpits collapsed onto a thick beam and he quickly grabbed its side with both arms.

He dangled in the air as he looked down his body into the blackness far below and he heard the deep roars of water rushing past. His eyes shot to the path he'd come down and Gus saw the edge of the dirt with pieces of rotted and broken boards hanging from it. He splayed his legs beneath him for balance and steadied his grasp of the beam, careful not to move too quickly over the slick wood. His heart was punching at his ribs as he worked out the safest way to make it back to solid ground when he heard footsteps behind him. They moved slowly, cautiously, until stopping just feet away. He struggled to turn, but his body was wedged tightly between two planks, preventing him from twisting around. Gus listened to the heavy breathing of their suspect and watched as the light rose behind him, casting his long shadow eerily onto the shards of broken boards and the tunnel beyond.

"We're gonna get you," was all Gus could think to say. "You know it and I know it."

Their suspect did not reply but the message was clear. This was not Gus's world, it was his. And he wanted Gus to know it.

Gus heard footsteps again and as they grew faint and the light began to fade, he pulled himself free from the gap in the boards and shimmied his way back to the edge. He hoisted himself up and quickly turned to see the dim light far in the distance. He had lost his penlight in the fall so took a mental image of the gap in the tunnel floor with its broken beams and missing boards while he could. It was as wide as the tunnel but only about ten feet long. Gus quickly shuffled backward then, getting a running start, leaped from the edge just as the distant light flickered out.

Time seemed to slow as Gus became airborne in the dark, rotating his arms and legs as if riding a bicycle to propel himself over the broken bridge and river below. Not able to see, he mis-timed his pumping legs with his landing and crashed onto his knees and his body slammed hard into the dirt. He quickly got to his feet and, with a hand against the wall, raced to the end of the tunnel where it came to an open cavern similar to the one that the NPS team had set up in.

The sound of rushing water was much louder now so Gus took his phone from his pocket and shined its light around. He saw a small vein of the Merrimack River running across one corner of the open space, its flow fast and heavy. On the opposite wall he saw the openings of four tunnels so dashed that way and peered down each but saw nothing. Along the wall next to him were several more openings so he raced to look down those but, again, no one was there. Gus stood still and listened but the noise of the rushing water was simply too loud for him to hear the sounds of faint footfalls in the distance.

Frustrated, he stepped to the center of the cavern and bent over to catch his breath when he realized he had no idea how to get back to the team. He'd simply followed the dot in the distance with no regard for remembering lefts or rights. He tried his walkie-talkie but after getting no response knew he was out of its range. Gus then straightened and pressed the button on the tracking device attached to his belt and the green light flashed, letting him know it was working.

And as he replayed the pursuit over and over in his mind like a mistake during a gig—trying to find that one detail that would make him better at it the next time—he heard the sound of a piano beginning to play somewhere far off in the distance. A vocalist began singing a melody Gus recognized but couldn't place. In between breaths, his mind dug through his memory for the answer then, as if the volume was suddenly raised, Gus looked up, realizing what he was hearing.

He lowered his head, shaking it side to side as he did so, and in a whisper began to sing along with Ol' Blue Eyes echoing off the cavernous walls.

"The best is yet to come and, babe ... won't it be fine?"

Chapter Thirty-Eight

B Y THE TIME the NPS team found Gus and got him back to the others, the crime scene techs had arrived and were processing the potential grave. Vanessa had gone back outside to make some calls so, needing some fresh air, Gus soon joined her. Amy got them coffees from a nearby shop so the three of them gathered outside the club beneath a small decorative tree. The early morning drizzle had burned off and the air was thick and steamy, feeling more like an August dog-day than the mid-September morning it was. Gus repeatedly pulled his damp shirt from his lower back to no relief.

"So, you didn't see him at all?" Vanessa asked. "His height or maybe his build?"

Gus shook his head in frustration. "No. He was just a dot of light in the distance."

"You okay?" Amy asked, pointing to the spots of blood on the bottom of his shirt and side of his pantleg.

"Yeah, I'll survive." He thought of their suspect's taunting song at the end when he'd clearly gotten away, having had enough fun toying with Gus for one day. "Nothing damaged but my ego."

"I thought you'd be used to that by now," Vanessa

quipped.

"Hey, V. F-Y-I. Words hurt."

They both smiled and, as Gus rubbed the torn hole in his pantleg, he said, "But there's no doubt he knows those tunnels. He toyed with me the entire time. At one point he doubled-backed on me—I have no idea how—and began going back the way we came. By the time I fell into that old rotting bridge I had no idea where I was but he certainly did."

"Did he say anything or make any sound that stood out?" Amy asked.

"Nothing. But I don't think he was expecting us down there. I think we surprised him."

"Why d'ya say that?"

"Just a feeling. When Jackie first saw a figure on her screen, we went dark and listened. And it was a couple of minutes before he put his light back on and we saw him again. I just think we stumbled on him by chance and he took a beat to decide what to do."

Gus replayed his pursuit in his mind again but came up with nothing new. "But now he knows we know about the tunnels." He took a last gulp of his coffee and tossed his paper cup into the trash. "Wonder what he's gonna do with that?"

Over Boyd's shoulder, Gus saw TJ walk out of the club with his ear pressed to his phone. Seeing Gus and the others, he said a few things then ended the call and headed over to join them.

"Jesus, heated up out here," TJ said, wiping his brow

with the back of his hand. The bottom of his pantlegs and shoes were covered with dust. "It's nice and cool in those tunnels."

"Any news?" Gus prompted, tipping his head toward the club's door.

TJ wiped his hand on the back of his shirt. "They're human remains; saw the front of a skull myself." Gus felt Vanessa physically turn toward him but ignored her as TJ continued. "The crime scene guys are processing it now so it should be fully uncovered in an hour or so. Called Rob; he's on his way." TJ added, referring to the pathologist, Rob Pappas. He caught Vanessa's eye. "He always bitch at you?" Without waiting for an answer, TJ continued, "'Cause every time I call him for something, all he does is bitch at me."

Gus and Vanessa smiled until they realized TJ hadn't.

"Ah, don't worry, TJ. That's how you know he likes you," Gus offered.

TJ looked at Gus like a lost puppy. "He calls me donkey."

"That's just his way," Gus said, stifling a laugh.

"I guess," TJ said feebly before perking up. "Anyway, that was Tony on the phone just now," he said, referring to his partner, Tony Blackford. "The lab's identified the footprint at the Connors scene. It's from a privately-owned company in Montana called Black Dog Boots. This particular boot was a limited release in Europe—Frankfurt to be specific—in the 1990s and never made here in the US so that's why its tread wasn't in the standard databases. The sole's very worn but apparently it has a crack or cut in it on the outside of the toe area so we find the boots we can match it pretty easily."

Gus and Vanessa exchanged a look. They'd now go for those boots at Taylor's house as soon as they could. Gus thought a moment about the other moving pieces of the case.

"Lab test the chemicals from Chris Houlihan's work yet?"

"Still in process. They did identify the residue found on the Connors woman though." TJ tapped at his phone. "I had Tony text me the name of it. It's called octyl ... phenoxy ... polyethoxy ethanol," he stammered then looked up. "That's all one word. Anyway, it's some kind of cleaning agent or more precisely a chemical component of a cleaning agent. But the lab guy said now that they know what it is it'll be easy to test for."

"They done analyzing the list from Mick's work yet?"

"Didn't say, but I'll check. But we heard back from the agent from the Pawtucket Falls office that interviewed the woman he said he was in Boston with at the casino. V, it seems you were right; that woman is anything but believable. First, she mixed up the dates they were there; it wasn't even the right month. She was confused on which casino they had gone to; she kept telling the agent the name of the motel they stayed at which has no casino. I guess she really struggled with getting any details correct. The agent got the distinct impression she was trying to say things she'd been told to say."

"Okay, stay on his alibis," Gus said. "We need to find

something if we're gonna get a search warrant for his house and car. And find out where he was this morning."

"Will do," TJ said.

Gus took out his phone and saw he had a voice message from an unknown number left over an hour ago. He stood, making heavy work of it, then stepped from the group and listened to a brief message from Leon Sampson so called him back immediately.

"Leon, it's Gus Wheeler. What's goin' on?"

"Hey, thanks for calling. I wasn't sure who else to call," he stammered, his voice carried by uncertainty. "Remember last night when we talked I told you Taylor's been struggling?"

"I do." Gus stopped pacing. "Why?"

"Well, he's been seeing that therapist I mentioned for a while now but the last few months have been pretty intense and he seems to only be getting worse."

"Go on."

"Well, the other night I found him at home in the middle of a manic episode. He was convinced someone was in the house with him but the house was empty. I searched it myself. And he's become really paranoid. He's convinced he's being watched and followed and that someone's out to get him."

"Is he dangerous?"

"Well, I guess that's why I'm calling. I didn't think so but now I'm not so sure. He's been seeing things, pretty disturbing things."

"Like what?"

"Like murdered women and stuff. And when I came here this morning to check on him, he was having another episode and this time he was also hearing voices. And … he was holding a knife."

"Leon, what'd he do?"

"No, no, nothing. He gave it right to me," Leon interrupted. "But I'm calling because he broke down and told me everything he's been going through the past few months. Things I didn't know." Leon paused before continuing. "Agent, he thinks he might've killed those women. And he said he found a few of their driver's licenses in his house."

Gus straightened then turned toward Vanessa with wide eyes. Seeing his reaction, she left the others to stand beside Gus and hear his side of the conversation.

"Leon, did you see them?" Gus asked.

"No, he told me about them the other night but when he went to get 'em there was nothing there. It was super strange. I called his therapist first thing this morning, so we have another emergency appointment at four p.m. today but I don't think he's gonna go."

"Why d'ya say that?"

"Well, I called and brought him to an emergency appointment yesterday, and it didn't go well, at all. He stormed out."

"Do you know what he's being treated for?"

"I don't know exactly. The psychiatrist called it delusional disorder or something like that. He also said that Taylor has deep-rooted separation anxieties and some kind of psychosis."

"Is he dangerous? Does the therapist think he's a danger to himself or others?"

"Well, that's the other reason I called. He became violent earlier; slammed me against the wall when I tried to help him."

"Where are you? Are you still at his house?"

"No, I'm home now but he's not there. He ran out after he attacked me, and I haven't been able to get ahold of him since."

"How long ago was that?" asked Gus, catching Vanessa's eye.

"A few hours ago now. I tried to get ahold of him for about an hour before I called and left you that message."

"Leon, give me the name and number for that therapist."

Gus repeated the therapist's name and phone number aloud so Vanessa could jot it down in her pad then told Leon he'd done the right thing and ended the call. Gus filled Vanessa in on the entire conversation and her eyes bulged.

"That boy's got *all* the goods."

"Sounds like it. Let's put a BOLO out on him, see if we can find where he is." Gus tipped his head toward Vanessa's pad. "And in the meantime, we've gotta get to that therapist to see what we're dealing with here."

Chapter Thirty-Nine

TAYLOR'S THERAPIST, DR. Cappi, had an opening before his four p.m. appointment with Taylor, so Gus and Vanessa hustled over to his office to meet with him. The three of them sat in chairs around the oval coffee table in the doctor's office, a stout purple candle lit in its center.

"As I explained on the phone," Gus began. "Taylor Franklin's name has come up in our investigation, and we understand he's a patient of yours."

"That's correct," the doctor confirmed.

"His friend Leon suggested you'd diagnosed Taylor with a form of psychosis, is that correct?"

"I'm afraid I'm not at liberty to discuss the details of Mr. Franklin's care," the doctor replied. "Doctor-patient confidentiality."

Gus leaned forward and rested his elbows on his knees. "Doctor, we're investigating a string of murders, horrific crimes, and we have reason to believe Taylor is involved in them in some way."

"Agent, I want to help. I really do. But I'm afraid, legally, my hands are tied. Unless he's confessed to a crime or I feel he's a danger to others, I can't break confidentiality. Now, if you had a warrant, I'd be compelled to speak with you. But without one…"

Gus's jaw tightened. "Doctor, we believe Taylor's become violent and we're concerned for the safety of others."

Dr. Cappi eyed Gus for several moments before responding. "Agent, I'm afraid that's not sufficient for me to violate my confidentiality. I need to either evaluate him and see this behavior for myself or be served with a warrant for that information. Again, I'm sorry, but my hands are tied."

Gus leaned back in his seat and looked to Vanessa. She had *that* look; the look she got when she had a devilish idea. She lifted the tiny notepad off her lap an inch or so and flicked her eyebrow up and down, reminding Gus that she'd written down the key points of his conversation with Leon a short while before.

She turned her attention to the psychiatrist. "Doctor," she began. "Suppose we describe the symptoms and *hypothetical* diagnosis of a suspect. Would you be able to comment on the situation, hypothetically, and suggest a possible course of action? In the interest of public safety, that is."

Gus watched the doctor's face relax slightly as he caught on to what she was getting at.

"Why, yes." The doctor nodded slowly. "I can share my views freely on a hypothetical situation. For the public's safety, of course."

"Excellent." Vanessa spun her pen across her fingers in a sort of victory lap. "So, suppose a person had been diagnosed with"—she referred to the notepad—"delusional disorder."

"A very severe psychotic disorder, indeed," the psychiatrist interrupted. "But be careful, agent. I would venture a guess that this person's symptoms *present* like delusional disorder. A formal diagnosis requires very detailed physical and psychological evaluations."

Vanessa nodded. "Noted. And this person also had deep-seeded separation anxieties to compound things."

"Yes, I could see that. Anxiety does not directly cause psychosis; however, the two conditions do have some similar symptoms. And a person that has had severe anxiety for an extended time may experience a psychotic episode."

"Got it," Vanessa said, the intensity in her eyes trained on the psychiatrist. "Can you…"

Dr. Cappi held up a finger in that professorial way. "Another causal factor I'd note, agent, that isn't a popular view these days, but facts are facts, is the use of marijuana. Contrary to what the lobbyists and politicians want you to believe, cannabis is a known risk factor for the onset of schizophrenia. In fact, studies have found that cannabis use is involved in fifty percent of schizophrenia, psychosis, and schizophreniform psychosis cases. *Fifty* percent." He paused and collected himself before continuing, "So, say hypothetically that your suspect had been a habitual user of marijuana at an age when his body and psyche were going through significant development. Even if they no longer use it, it could most certainly contribute to a psychosis or a psychotic episode and likely worse, longer-term mental health issues as well."

Vanessa nodded. "Understood." She referred back to her notes before continuing. "Can you give us an example of how a person could develop a deep-seeded separation anxiety? Could, say, their mother—a single parent—being placed into an assisted care facility trigger that type of anxiety?"

"Oh, it's much more systemic than that. Suppose"—Dr. Cappi raised an eyebrow of concern toward her— "hypothetically, this person lost their father figure as a young child. That would seed this separation anxiety during a very vulnerable stage of emotional development. Then suppose this person's first true love left them at another pivotal developmental age of sixteen or seventeen, when a young person's hormones are heightened for long periods of time making them extremely vulnerable emotionally. Well, that ... that abandonment could scar this person significantly. They would carry that with them through other relationships, plutonic or otherwise. So, then, say this person uprooted their entire life to care for a loved-one; left the career they had dreamed of since being a child, moved back into their childhood home, back into the environment in which this early trauma had occurred. That alone could cause severe anxieties. But then their loved-one that they uprooted their entire life for moves away, leaving them alone. Abandoning them, again. It wouldn't matter that their loved-one needed specialized care; that rational thinking wouldn't enter at all into their subconsciousness. As far as their emotional subconscious knows, they were abandoned."

"That would be damaging," Gus observed.

"Agent, that's the type of emotional trauma that leads to psychosis and a psychotic break. I'm telling you this to provide you with some context. If this person had really done what they feared, it was not spontaneous and it was not without root cause. And if they have, in fact, suffered a psychotic breakdown, there's a very strong likelihood they may not even remember the specific acts in their conscious memory."

"Okay, okay," Vanessa said, referring to her notepad once more. "So, suppose this person began exhibiting odd behavior and symptoms."

"Such as paranoia and feeling followed or watched?" Dr. Cappi interrupted, nodding knowingly. "Yes…"

"And … hearing voices and thinking there was a woman in their house calling to them, threatening them," Vanessa interrupted, referring to the notepad. "And seeing images of murdered women and finding key pieces of evidence from these murders in their home that, when sought by others, were not there."

Dr. Cappi arched his eyebrows. "Images of murdered women?"

Vanessa nodded. "That's correct. And suppose this person confided in a close friend that he believed he was responsible for these murders."

The doctor's eyes bulged. "If that were true, that person would need specialized care immediately."

"So, doctor, if you had a patient that exhibited these symptoms and shared them with you, wouldn't you be required to report it to law enforcement?"

"Of course, especially the images you describe and the acts of violence they believe they've committed. But, agent, I'd have to hear those directly from that person. It wouldn't be enough, say, to simply be told that they've heard voices." The doctor paused momentarily before continuing, "I'd have to be very careful, legally. Like you, I need evidence or direct knowledge of these acts before being able to act on them."

"And is that something you believe you could get?" Gus asked. "You know, hypothetically, if you were to have a session with this person?"

The doctor glanced at the clock and, seeing it was three forty-five p.m., uncrossed his legs and crouched to stand. "I do. And speaking of which, my next patient will be arriving any minute so I suggest you and your partner leave before they do."

Gus and Vanessa stood also and thanked Dr. Cappi for his time.

Chapter Forty

G US AND VANESSA anxiously awaited the call from Dr.
Cappi after his session with Taylor, hoping the psychiatrist had heard the more menacing details of Taylor's symptoms directly from his patient and could act on them. Gus expected the hour session to likely go long, given both the severity of Taylor's condition and the fact that it was the doctor's last appointment of the day. But Gus had been wrong.

At four twenty p.m.—twenty minutes after the session was due to begin—Gus got a call from the psychiatrist telling him that Taylor hadn't shown for their appointment. The doctor had tried Taylor several times on his cellphone but had yet to reach him. Gus and Vanessa immediately drove to Taylor's house but this time their knocks on his front door went unanswered. Vanessa pulled up the background information TJ had pulled together on Taylor and found he worked at the nearby thrift shop, Nifty Thrifty, so that was their next stop.

They found the busy shop tended by a harried, impolite young woman with hair so strikingly black it seemed sprayed on. Her matching eyeliner and swarm of piercings throughout her face and ears gave her the look of a character from a

John Carpenter movie. She curtly told Gus and Vanessa that Taylor had not shown up for work and Gus couldn't tell if her clipped answers were due to her sour attitude or limited facial mobility.

Next, Gus called Leon but the guitarist hadn't heard from Taylor either. He told Gus, however, that it wouldn't surprise him if Taylor showed up for their gig that night; he'd gotten used to the free meal they got when they played and Taylor definitely needed the money.

By the time they spoke with Leon, it was almost six thirty p.m. so Vanessa checked on the BOLO put out on Taylor but he hadn't been seen. They had an hour or so before they needed to be at The Mills so used the time to chase down a few things still in motion. Their first call was to TJ who answered on the first ring.

"Hey, V, I was just going to call you. The lab just got back to us. None of the chemicals on the list provided by Mick's company—Allied Equipment and Repair—were a match for the residue found on the Connors woman."

"So he's cleared." she said.

"Well, his alibis are still shit but this is a check in that column. And speaking of alibis," TJ continued. "We found the guitarist, Leon Sampson, on CCTV walking home just after eleven p.m. the night Sadie Hogan was taken just like he said."

TJ then updated Gus and Vanessa on other activities while he had them. He told them that the NPS was now estimating they'd be done mapping the tunnels around end of day tomorrow and that they'd not yet identified any other spots that looked like potential graves. He also told them the pathologist, Rob, had been to the scene and saw the remains but had been called away before TJ could speak with him.

"Thanks, TJ," Gus said. "Let us know if you hear back from Rob."

Their next call was to Tony Blackford at the Boston office. Gus had Tony call off the analysis of the casino footage. They could use the manpower elsewhere.

"Damn, guys were gunnin' for the overtime."

Tony then told them they had finished going through the traffic cam footage outside The Loft for the night Michelle Townsend was last seen. They found no sign of Mick Preston's beefed-up Dodge Challenger but did see a minivan that resembled the one registered in Taylor's mother's name. It was a cloudy, dark night and the van passed in the distance so they couldn't be sure but were getting the footage cleaned and enhanced. And, finally, an agent from the Pawtucket Falls office had spoken with Leon's girlfriend and she confirmed what Leon had given them for alibis. He was home around eleven thirty p.m. or midnight each night.

After chasing all that down, Gus called Jeff Cattagio and updated him on recent events. After talking it all through, they agreed they likely had enough for a warrant to search Taylor Franklin's home. But Jeff wanted Gus to speak with Taylor himself to assess his state of mind and see if he could get the musician to divulge anything they'd heard from Leon or the therapist directly to Gus.

It was getting late so Gus and Vanessa got a large pizza

from Papa Gino's—Hawaiian with jalapeños for Vanessa—and were having a late dinner in his truck. Gus looked out his window toward Music Row.

"Ya think Taylor'll be here tonight?" he asked into the cool glass.

"Dunno," she said, her words thick and sluggish around the food in her mouth. She slowly chewed and looked with Gus toward Music Row then swallowing asked, "If he is, how d'ya wanna handle him?"

"Carefully. If he is as distressed as Leon described, we need to get him off the streets." He turned back to her. "Maybe I speak with him one on one, musician to musician."

Vanessa nodded her agreement and as Gus looked back out his side window, he caught sight of Taylor entering The Mills. He dropped his half-eaten slice into the pizza box and brushed his hands off over it. "He just went in. Let's go."

The two of them hustled out of the truck and quickly made their way across the street and into Music Row. As they neared the club's entrance, Vanessa took a last heaping bite of her pizza and dropped the crust into a nearby barrel. They flashed their badges to the doorman and once inside immediately saw the singer, Chris, at the front of the stage. He was adjusting the monitor near his mic stand and, behind him, was Taylor kneeling by an amp at the back. Gus hopped up onto the stage and went straight to Taylor while Vanessa hung back and watched from the bar.

"Hey, Taylor, got a minute?" Gus asked.

Taylor continued uncoiling a wire. "Hey," he replied, his

eyes trained on the amp.

Gus pulled over a stool and sat so he could see him better. "I understand you and Leon went at it this morning."

Taylor turned his head to the side, barely glancing at Gus. "Nothin' for you to worry about." he said dismissively.

Gus heard the arrogance in his reply, and it brought him back to their years at Loyola. Taylor was always the one looking to be on the pedestal, always in desperate need of praise. But as Gus looked around the shitty bar with its chipped tables, drunk crowd, and tacky, beer-stained floors it dawned on him. He had been so in awe of Taylor's playing abilities that he never realized how those same abilities were actually holding him back. While Taylor was desperately seeking admiration, always jumping and falling, Gus had been thrilled to just be learning and practicing his music day in and day out and able to play the next gig. Taylor was the hare, and he the tortoise. And at that moment Gus realized all his childhood hang-ups were gone. He had won the race he never knew he was in.

"Hey," Gus said, catching Taylor's eye. "I'm worried about you, brother."

"Don't fuckin' *brother* me, Wheeler." Taylor scowled, leaning away. "Get the fuck outta my face."

"C'mon, man, we've got history. Seems like you're going through some stuff. We can help."

"*You* help *me*?" Taylor scowled. "Says the guy who was beggin' me—a freshman—for tips on how to swing in college." He recoiled away from Gus. "And look atcha now. You got a long way to go ... *brother*." Finished with the cord, Taylor pushed past him and went to the others, so Gus hopped off the stage and joined Vanessa.

"You guys were choppin' it up. What'd he say?"

Gus watched as Taylor stepped close to Leon. His head tilted and the two began angrily talking. Gus was watching someone convinced the world was against him. But he also knew they'd never get Taylor to admit to hearing voices or seeing images of dead women, let alone to killing them. Gus knew he'd lost him, probably for good.

"We've got enough for a warrant," Gus said calmly.

"What'd he say?"

Gus's eyes lingered on Taylor for another beat before turning to Vanessa.

He blinked once, slowly. "We know he assaulted his friend in his home with a knife, and I believe he's a danger to others."

Vanessa slowly leaned her head back, and her mouth twisted. "So, *that's* how you wanna play this?"

Gus probed a molar with his tongue. "We need to get into that house, and now. He's spiraling, no doubt. He'll never admit to us what's going on. We need to take 'im."

"Okay," Vanessa said, her voice rising with doubt. "I'll get it going tonight. I'm sure we can find *some* judge to sign it. We'll have it in the morning."

Gus replayed the conversation with Taylor in his head, checking himself. He'd heard the arrogance and the defensiveness. And the denial and the fear. And he'd seen the anger and rage in his eyes. But, amongst it all, somewhere in there a lie was hiding.

Chapter Forty-One

G US AND VANESSA stayed at The Mills through the band's first set, sitting at a table back by the bar so the band couldn't see them through the bright lights. Vanessa had several appetizers and a few diet cokes while Gus stuck to iced water. He had watched Taylor and listened to his awful, sometimes erratic, playing that only got worse as the night went on. The singer, Chris, told the audience the band was taking a short break and Gus heard soft music start playing from the speakers overhead.

Vanessa tossed her crumpled paper napkin onto an empty plate and her phone rang with a call from TJ. She pressed her phone tightly against an ear and cupped her hand over the other one as he told her that they had positively identified Taylor Franklin's van as the one in the surveillance footage outside The Loft the night Michelle Townsend was abducted. And since Taylor's band had not played at The Loft that night there was no reason for that van to be driving by at that late hour. Vanessa thanked him then ended the call and told Gus.

Gus's eyes widened. "That make ya feel better?"

"Well, at least now we'll have the okay to search for the right stuff."

Gus felt someone looking at him so turned toward the side of the room closest to the stage. Leaning back in a chair was a large man with thick, curly hair and an overgrown beard. Gus recognized him immediately and slid his seat back.

"Hey, there's a guy over there I met on the tour a few weeks back. I'm gonna go say hi."

"I'm gonna pop off," Vanessa said, standing. "I'll grab an Uber. And I'll let you know when we get the warrant."

Gus headed for the guy in the corner while Vanessa turned and slipped into the crowd. She bumped and poked her way to the far side of the large room before being spit out by the door for the restrooms. She leaned against a column and took a minute to text TJ and have him get the warrant going to search Taylor's home and car.

"Hey," a male voice said a little too loudly.

Vanessa looked up to see a young man standing beside her holding two drinks. He had a baseball cap on backward, and she noted his glassy eyes as he held one out to her. "You look like a vodka tonic girl." He slurred and swayed slightly to the side.

"Not happenin'," she said dismissively, looking back to her phone.

"Aw, c'mon, loosen up. You don't know what you're missin'." His voice rose at the end as he swished the drink he was offering her through the air between them.

Vanessa noticed a group of young guys with the same frat-boy vibe huddled in the crowd behind him looking their way. The young man swayed into her line of sight and she nodded toward the glass he was taking a drink from.

"You sure you want that?" She slowly waved an open palm in a circle in front of him. "Looks like you're going through something."

"C'mon, honey," he said after swallowing, again holding up the other drink for her.

"You even old enough to be in here?" she asked, her full attention on him now.

The guy's head rocked back as he asked through a burp, "What's it to you?"

Vanessa slid her hand in her pocket and pulled out her wallet, flipping it open to show him her badge.

"Oh, ah, sorry, officer. Ahhh…" he stammered.

Vanessa tipped her chin to his friends who were all now painfully trying to look disinterested in their conversation.

"I think it's time you and your buddies call it a night, don't you?"

"Totally, for sure." His head swayed side to side. "I think, I think we were just going anyway."

The man wobbled around then shuffled away as she opened her Uber app and ordered a car to take her back to the inn. Seeing it would be ten minutes until it arrived, she decided to hit the ladies' room before the drive. As she opened the hallway door to the restrooms, Vanessa noticed Taylor leaning on the bar between two stools just a few feet away. His hair was snarled and disheveled, and she noticed holes in his jeans and canvas sneakers. She watched as MJ brought him two shots and a tall draft beer. He downed one of the shots then poured the other into his beer and took a long drink. Vanessa thought about approaching him but before she could, he turned and caught her eye. The two of them stared at each other for several moments before Vanessa turned and entered the short hall to the restrooms.

As the door closed behind her, the overwhelming noise of the crowd fizzled to a low murmur. She took a few steps toward the ladies' room when her phone rang and, seeing it was the reporter Christina Collins, answered it.

"Ms. Collins."

"I just wanted to be sure you got the list of entrances I sent over earlier."

"We did. Thank you for that."

"And I just checked my notes from that piece and found a sixth entrance in the club The Mills. Where the Hogan woman was taken? I thought you'd want that right away."

"Absolutely. I'm actually there right now." Vanessa looked to her left at a door to the kitchen, then to her right at two other doors. One had a sign that read UTILITY CLOSET and the other had one that read EMPLOYEES ONLY. "Can you talk me through finding it?"

"Absolutely." she said, enthusiasm now in her voice. Vanessa heard the clicking of a keyboard. "I've got it right here."

Vanessa opened the door with the sign EMPLOYEES ON-LY on it and flicked the light switch just inside the door. There was a small landing about five feet long that led to a set of stairs.

"Okay, you'll want to get to the basement," Christina said.

Vanessa propped the door open with a doorstop she found on the landing then walked to the top of the stairs. She was about to start down them when the cell reception got weak and the reporter's voice began to break up.

"Small chim … side … bri…"

Vanessa walked back to the door. "Ms. Collins, I'm losing you when I head into the basement, so why don't you walk me through it and I'll call you back if I can't find it."

"Okay. Once you're in the basement, you'll see a small chimney made of red bricks. At the base of that chimney, you'll find one of the bricks loose. Remove it and inside you'll find a small metal handle. Pull that handle and to your left you'll see a section of the stone wall click open. It's about four or five feet wide so you can't miss it."

Vanessa thanked the reporter then ended the call. She turned back toward the staircase and began to walk that way when an arm wrapped around her neck from behind and a hand pushed her head forward. She registered the door closing behind her as her chin was pressed firmly into her chest and the arm began to tighten on the sides of her neck. Vanessa knew immediately she was in a chokehold and only had twelve, maybe fifteen seconds before she'd black out. She held firmly to her cellphone and punched around her side, hitting his hip and his thigh repeatedly but his arm only tightened. She was becoming lightheaded and had to act fast. She ran her feet up one of the walls then thrust backward, sending them both hard against the wall behind them.

"Fuckin' bitch." He grunted into her ear, and she could smell the alcohol on his breath.

His arm tightened further as he bull-rushed her forward and slammed her face against the wall. Vanessa's world exploded with white light and blood gushed over an eye and beneath her nose. Her head swam with confusion as she clawed at him over a shoulder, his shirt collar slipping between her fingers. And, as they both slumped onto the floor, Vanessa swiped once more but felt only air.

Seconds later, her hand flopped off her shoulder, her body went slack, and her eyes fell closed.

Chapter Forty-Two

I T WAS TWO thirty a.m. and Taylor was sitting on his couch, jamming on Leon's glossy white guitar to a Megadeth song stuck in his head. The amp he had dragged in from the garage sat on the floor in front of him, aimed in his direction with its volume on the highest setting. He had finally found a way to drown out the voices in his head so played as fast and as loud as he could. All the doors and windows were locked and the shades drawn so the entire house was dark except for the light pulsing into the room from the television. After his bedtime routine hadn't settled his mind, Taylor had stuffed the first VHS he saw into the player, *Shutter Island*. His twisted brain registered the insanity vibe of the movie but soon moved onto something else before he could swap it out.

A duffle bag laid at his feet, stuffed fat with clothes and all the money and gift cards he had in Teddy. Taylor was shaken after speaking with Gus earlier before their gig and knew it was only a matter of time now before they came for him. He had to run. But before he could finish getting all his stuff together, the voices became too much so he grabbed the loudest instrument he had and drowned them out.

His hand began to cramp up so he stopped playing to

stretch his palm and fingers. After his last session with the therapist, Taylor had tried to remember when he first started hearing the voices and realized it was sometime after the most recent victim, Rachel Connors, was taken. It was then that the idea to kill again had taken root. It stood to reason because he wasn't hearing the voices during the periods the women were abducted, held, and killed. So maybe, Taylor thought, that was the only way to make them stop. He heard another faint whisper so held the guitar up again and smothered her pleas in its chords.

Taylor quickly became lost in the music, his eyes squeezed closed, his head slamming up and down. His forearm burned and his wrist ached but he had no thoughts of stopping again. He couldn't listen to the women moaning and pleading for their lives any longer; it was all too much. He had to make it stop.

His head settled into a quick up and down twitching that followed the movements of his wrist. The music absorbed him in its melody, filling his every sense, until he was lost in its waves. He stayed this way for a long, long time, wrapped in the notes until suddenly the music drained away. And the electricity that stung his hands, arms, and face gradually faded.

"Dude, what're ya doin'?" a voice yelled in his head.

When it called again, Taylor opened his eyes to see Leon and Mick standing in front of him, frightened looks on their faces. He simply stared at them until Leon turned off the amp.

Mick turned to Leon, gesturing toward Taylor. "He

looks fuckin' rabid."

Taylor stood and looked to Mick. "Fuck you."

Mick went into the kitchen as Leon took his guitar from Taylor. "What's with this?"

"The fuckin' voices. I had to drown 'em out."

"You're still hearing 'em?"

Taylor nodded, once. "Louder than ever."

"Dude, we need to go back to Dr. Cappi. Get you some help."

Taylor's nostrils flared. "We're not telling anyone," he bit. "Got it? They'll fuckin' lock me up and throw away the key."

"What're you gonna do?"

Distracted by a noise in the kitchen, Taylor looked that way. "Mick, what the fuck you doin' in there?"

A moment later Mick came back into the room with three beers and handed each of them one. Taylor took his and, eyeing Mick with suspicion, switched beers with Leon before taking a swig.

"What're you guys doing here anyway?"

"I called and texted about a dozen times but you didn't reply," Leon answered. "I just wanted to check on you before I went home."

"And I bumped into him outside Delaney's just before last call," Mick said, referring to a bar in Music Row, before taking a pull on his beer. "Thought I'd tag along, see for myself." His eyes bulged. "But, dude." He nodded slowly. "You need some serious help."

Taylor ran his fingers through tangled hair and looked

around the room. "Yeah, been dealing with some shit."

"Where'd you go after our set?" Leon asked, leaning the guitar against the couch. "One minute you were getting a drink at the bar, the next you were gone."

Taylor looked around, trying to figure out what Leon was talking about. He heard a woman's voice whisper. *Please stop*. And an image of walking along a dark path came to him.

"I think I walked home," he said hesitantly.

"But your van's in the driveway," Leon said.

"You drove?" Mick laughed, staring at Taylor. "Classic." He then noticed the duffel bag on the floor. "Going somewhere?"

Taylor's eyes flicked to the bag then back. "You guys just need to go."

"What's going on?" Leon asked. "What're you doing?"

"I gotta get off this rock." he said, feeling like he'd heard that somewhere before. "Whatever the hell's going on here, it's bad."

Leon's face twisted in confusion. "What ... what're you talking about?" he stammered.

Taylor shook his head quickly side to side. "Just go. It's not safe being around me now."

"I'm starting to get that vibe," Mick said, eyeing Taylor with suspicion. "But stop with the riddles. What the fuck's going on?"

"Wheeler knows I did it. He's coming for me," Taylor said angrily. He looked at Leon, "And like I told you." He shook his head. "I'm not going down for this."

"Going down for what?" Mick asked, looking from Taylor to Leon for answers.

Taylor heard the soft cries of a woman's voice and shook his head again side to side. His chest was getting hot and his eyes flicked around the room. He had to get out of there. He leaned over and grabbed his duffel bag and, as he turned to go, Leon stopped him with a hand to the chest. Taylor snapped his shoulder away.

"Get the fuck away from me!"

Leon stepped closer and grabbed Taylor's arm. "Stop!"

A woman's voice echoed Leon in Taylor's mind. *Stop!* Taylor squeezed his eyes closed and the duffel bag slipped from his fingers and fell to the floor. He pulled his arm free and lunged at Leon, throwing punches wildly at his head and shoulders. Mick scurried next to them and wrestled Taylor off then pushed him away.

Taylor groaned and brought his hands to his ears. "Fuckin' shut up!"

Leon wiped blood from his lip. "Jesus, T. What the fuck?"

When Taylor didn't answer, Leon stepped closer causing Taylor to raise his hands up in front of him.

Leon said to Mick over his shoulder, "Dude ... a hand?"

Taylor began slapping the sides of his head. Long stringy drool dangled onto his chest.

"Mick, a little help here!" Leon said louder.

"Fuck that," Mick said, taking a step backward, rubbing scratches on his forearm. He slid his beer onto the desk. "I did *not* sign up for this shit. He needs serious help."

"That's right, he does," Leon replied. "And we're gonna get it for him."

"Don't you dare fuckin' call anyone!" Taylor yelled, a hand on the back of his head. "No one! I gotta get outta here."

Leon held his hands up in front of him in surrender. "Hey, I hear ya. But you won't get out of the Falls in the shape you're in right now. You gotta get your shit together first."

Taylor's eyes dropped to the floor as he thought about what Leon was saying.

"And you can't take the van," Leon continued. "Once they know you're gone they'll put an APB out on it and you'll be cooked."

Fuck.

"I ... I can walk to the bus station. Grab a bus."

"They got cameras all over that place." Mick pointed out. "They'll know exactly where you're headed and when you're gonna get there."

"The buses aren't even running this late anyway," Leon added.

Taylor began to pace, twitching his head side to side to keep the voices at bay.

"And the airport's out, for sure," Mick said.

"I gotta go. I gotta go," Taylor mumbled, his eyes on the floor.

And in between his chants, the desperate cries of women filled his head again. "Shut up!" he yelled angrily. "Shut the fuck up!"

Leon took out his phone and, stepping into the kitchen, called the after-hours number Dr. Cappi gave him. A woman answered after a few rings and Leon gave her his name, Taylor's full name, and described the situation just as Dr. Cappi had told him to do. He heard the *click-clacking* of a computer keyboard through the phone for several moments before the woman spoke again.

"Is Mr. Franklin a danger to himself or others?"

"I don't believe so, no."

"Is he in a safe location?"

"Yes, he's at home."

"Okay, I'll pass this message on to Dr. Cappi. What number can the doctor reach you on?"

Leon gave her his cell number and thanked her before ending the call. He walked back into the living room to a wide-eyed Mick standing beside Taylor who was lying on the sofa in a fetal position, his hands over his face. Leon stepped next to Mick.

"What happened?"

Mick held out a woman's locket hanging on a thin gold chain. "He just saw this hanging from one of the tuning pegs of his upright and began to cry and mumble shit."

Leon took the necklace and pried open the locket. On one side was a black and white picture of an older man with a military-style haircut. On the other was a photo of a young woman with light blonde hair pulled into a ponytail. She was smiling wide and Leon's eyes were immediately drawn to the freckles covering her cheeks and nose."

"This is his old girlfriend's locket, Anne Marie. That's

her grandfather; he died when she was a kid. She *never* took this necklace off." Leon's eyes settled on Taylor who was sobbing into the couch.

"What the fuck?" he whispered in disbelief.

Chapter Forty-Three

GUS WOKE TO the snappy opening verse of Taylor Swift's "Shake It Off" and his head physically twitched on the pillow. His arm swung in a wide arc over the side of the bed and slapped around the nightstand. He peeled his eyes open and moved his cheek off a small spot of drool as his hand clutched his phone. There was a time when Gus would get annoyed at these pranks Vanessa played, when he'd bitch at her to stop, tell her they weren't funny. But not anymore.

Gus was raised by a pair of hippies whose fundamental vocabulary centered around phrases like cool and hang loose. These were the parents that believed a child should have freedom from boundaries, emotional space to discover who they were as an individual. These were also the parents that left Gus and his brother Jake—while both were still in high school—to go build homes for the needy in Namibia.

But despite this freedom from a young age—and many former girlfriends would contend because of it—Gus had an inner anxiety lurking beneath his cool, calm musician vibe that compelled him to succeed at anything he did. And that drive would often manifest itself as a compulsion, a manic tendency that draped Gus in a seriousness he sometimes couldn't hide and was not proud of.

Fortunately for Gus, Vanessa would take none of it. The childhood she endured made laughter and finding the funny in almost anything a survival instinct. So she kept up her pranks, despite Gus's protests and griping, and continued her funny sayings and takes on situations. Soon, Gus found himself looking forward to her pranks and comical take on life and knew he was better off because of them, because of her. And it didn't take long for Vanessa to become truly special to Gus; not in a partner or sexual way, but as a best friend and the younger sister he never had. And, over time, Gus realized that as different as they were from each other they had formed a unique bond—an invisible connection, like the moon to the tides.

Gus felt Mel roll over as her hand fell onto his side. She had texted him late last night when she'd landed at Logan—back from her trip early as a surprise—and met him at the inn after he left the club.

"Vanessa?" she whispered. He could almost hear her smile.

"Who else?" he grumbled as he answered his phone. "Wheeler."

"Gus, it's TJ. I just got the search warrant for Taylor Franklin's home and car."

"Okay, great." Gus's throat was dry, his voice hoarse.

He rubbed his eyes with a finger and thumb then pinched the bridge of his nose.

"But I can't get ahold of Vanessa," TJ continued. "She texted me late last night to chase down the warrant but now isn't answering her phone or texts."

Gus cleared his throat. "What time is it?" He held the phone away from his head and swiped to clear several texts out of the way so he could see the time. It was 6:34 a.m. "Jesus, TJ, it's only 6:30."

"I know, but she said she wanted it early so you guys could get there before the guy went to work."

Gus propped himself up on an elbow and put TJ on speaker so he could check his texts. He had one received at 1:27 a.m. from Mommy. Its photo was a black square with the name printed in its center in bright white lettering. He opened it and immediately confirmed it was Vanessa.

Sick as a dog. Shitty bar food. Going dark to sleep in.

"Ah, shit, she texted during the night. She's sick with food poisoning or something. Can you run the warrant up here? Meet me at the address?"

"Sure thing. I can be there in about an hour."

Gus laid back onto the pillow and ran his fingers through his hair as Mel slid beside him beneath the covers and rested her hand on his chest.

"But, hey, Gus, before you drop. Looks like you guys crushed it on this one. I picked up a message from the lab this morning. They went through Rachel Connors's cell phone and found Taylor Franklin in her contacts."

"Don't tell V." Gus croaked before clearing his throat again. "She was on him from the start." He swallowed. "I'll never hear the end of it."

"Good luck with that."

"Any news on the tunnel mapping?" Gus asked, now creeping awake.

"Nothing since yesterday. I'll give 'em a call on the way up. I'll see ya in about an hour."

Gus ended the call and put his arm around Mel who was now resting her head on his shoulder.

"Sounds like you've got someone in your sights," she said into his chest.

"Yeah, the bassist I told you about."

"The one you went to Loyola with?"

"Yeah. There's some mental health issues going on there we need to figure out."

"Isn't there really mental health issues going on with anyone that murders women?"

"Well, when you put it that way." Gus kissed the top of her head. "But this is different. He's on meds and stuff. It's just a horrible situation."

Mel rolled her head up a little and their eyes met. Gus had fallen in love with Mel so quickly it made his head spin and it hadn't stopped since.

"You really think it's him?"

"I do." He exhaled. "From what we can tell, he was the last one to see the second victim alive; the bartender saw them together at the end of the night. And we've got him on video with the last victim the night she was taken and the first woman picked up shifts waitressing at the same bar he and his band play at several nights a week. And we've got his van on surveillance tape outside the club the night she was taken."

"Couldn't be a coincidence? That Music Row area strikes me as a place that's fairly insular when it comes to its bands and crowds."

"I wish it were. But he's also been having a lot of psychological issues the past few months; hearing voices, hallucinations, that sort of thing. And he told his friend that he's been seeing images of the murdered women and thinks he might've done it."

"There ya go."

"And you heard TJ just now. The last victim had Taylor's number in her contacts."

They each fell quiet for a few moments before Mel broke the silence.

"You'll do the right thing," she said softly, touching his scruffy cheek with her fingers. "If it is him, no one's going to show him more compassion than you." Her hand cupped the side of his face and her eyes grew serious. "You know that, right?"

Gus smiled. "Yeah. Yeah." He caressed her cheek, running his finger over a dimple and her face softened at his touch.

Gus knew one of Mel's few insecurities was that her pronounced dimples could make her look young or worse, cute. And that wasn't the persona she was going for at her board of directors' meetings. When she'd first told him this, he'd said she was perfect, to which she countered that their very existence proved him wrong. So he had compromised.

"Perfectly imperfect," he whispered to his love.

She smiled, widening the dimple and prompting both to laugh. He kissed her and the world around them melted away. He wished for nothing more at that moment than to be able to stay in bed with Mel all day.

Her hand moved from his cheek to around the back of his neck as she pulled him into her. And after a minute or so she stopped kissing him and pushed her head back into her pillow.

"Don't you have to shower and get going?" she asked.

Gus pulled the sheet from between them and slid next to her beneath the covers. Her body was firm, her skin warm against his.

"TJ's coming up from Boston so I've got about an hour or so to kill."

Mel smiled as their lips met again.

"Challenge accepted."

Chapter Forty-Four

> <u>Sunday</u>
>
> ✓ National park service?
> ✓ Go back in tunnels
> ✓ What does FBI need
>   for arrest?
> ✓ Pack clothes
>   Get rid of boots
>   Get cash
>   Fill van tank
>   Old plates in garage
>   Wipes
>   Gauze
>   Water
>   Protein bars
>   Charge GoPro
>   Add minutes to phone

Chapter Forty-Five

G US WAS A few minutes late meeting TJ and team at Taylor Franklin's house, but a happier man for it. TJ and the four agents he brought with him met Gus on a street just around the corner from the house as two techs from the CSU team arrived.

"Hey, Gus." TJ said to Gus as he hopped out of his truck. "Ready?"

Gus nodded a single, stiff nod. "Yeah." He looked to the others. "You brief everyone?"

TJ introduced Gus to the team then said, "They got the basics."

"Okay," Gus began looking at the other agents. "Two things you're specifically looking for." He held up a finger. "One, Taylor told his friend he found the driver's licenses of the second and third vics, Sadie Hogan and Rachel Connors, in his house but when he tried to show his friend they were gone. We found Hogan's on the body of Connors. But Connors's license is still missing and could be in that house." He held up a second finger. "We have special interest in a pair of boots. Last time I was there they were covered in mud beside the front door. We need to get those to see if they're a match for the print found at the Connors scene. Our suspect wears an odd boot, a specific model of a brand called Black Dog Supersole boots, size eleven, and the tread has a large slice in it on one side."

Seeing no questions, Gus then turned to the CSU team. "And two things you're specifically looking for. Carpet fibers were found beneath the fingernails of the Connors woman and an unusual residue found on the body." He looked to the agents. "And, sorry, guys, but we'll need to bag any cleaners or chemicals we find for testing against that residue."

Gus then said to TJ, "I'll stay with Taylor when we enter. You five start the search while I interview him. It might be a volatile environment in there so let's keep the tension down. Just go about your business; no chatter, no comments. He doesn't have much but get all the devices you find. I know he's a big gamer so make sure to get his console and gaming gear. If he's been communicating with someone through that we'll want to know. I'll get his phone when I sit with him." He paused and looked around the group. "We good?"

With each confirming, they got in their cars, drove around the corner and parked in front of Taylor's house. Gus was the first to the door so, once TJ joined him with a copy of the search warrant in his hand, Gus knocked a few times. After waiting and hearing nothing inside, he knocked again, this time harder and faster.

"Taylor, it's Gus. Open the door."

A few moments later, Leon opened the door, squinting at the morning light. His eyes were puffy and red and his hair greasy and knotted.

"Leon," Gus said, surprised. "Everything okay?"

Leon's jaw tightened and, as he opened the door wider, he cleared his throat. "Yeah ... yeah, seems to be now. Mick and I came to check on Taylor late last night and he was full-on crazy; hallucinating, hearing voices, freaking out." He took a deep breath and shook his head. "He was a mess."

"How's he now?"

Leon rubbed the sleep from his eyes. "Eh." He shrugged. "I pumped him full of his meds until he calmed down. And he finally slept a little earlier but he's still pretty fucked-up." He pushed the hair out of his eyes and lowered his voice. "He's still hearing voices. He doesn't want me to know but I can tell. His eyes will flick to a different spot when he hears 'em, almost like they're poking him from inside."

"We need to speak with him."

"Good luck." Leon's eyes drifted to TJ and the other agents. "What's going on?"

Gus turned to TJ who held up the search warrant. "We've got a warrant to search the premises and his van," Gus said.

Leon pushed the door fully open and looked over a shoulder. Gus followed his eyes to Taylor sitting on the couch drinking something from a mug he held carefully with both hands like a child. Beside the front of the couch was a large amp with an electric guitar resting against it.

Gus directed the CSU team to the minivan parked in the driveway then he and TJ entered the house followed closely by the other agents. Gus glanced down at the mat beside the door but the muddy boots were gone. TJ and the others walked past Taylor; TJ went into the kitchen, while the others proceeded down the hall toward the bedrooms. Gus sat on the couch beside Taylor and held out the search warrant he'd taken from TJ.

"This is a search warrant giving us the right to search your house and van."

Taylor nodded, taking another sip from his mug as he stared out the front door Gus had left open.

An agent Gus thought was named Neil walked into the living room carrying a large sealed evidence bag. He was a young man with a five o'clock shadow and thin rectangular eyeglasses. As he headed toward the front door, Gus stopped him and took an empty bag.

"Phone," he said to Taylor, waiting for him to look Gus's way. When he didn't, Gus pressed. "We need your cellphone." Gus held out the opened bag and, after Taylor didn't move, picked up the phone from the sofa with a gloved hand and dropped it inside. Gus sealed it and handed it to Neil who took it with him out the front door and Gus watched as the agent loaded the evidence bags into the belly of a brown windowless van.

"Taylor, I need to ask you a few questions," Gus began.

Taylor nodded and Gus watched as his eyes flicked from the front door to several spots around the floor in front of him. Gus side-eyed Leon who raised both eyebrows and slowly nodded in answer to Gus's unasked question.

"Taylor, we've identified your minivan on traffic footage driving by The Loft the night Michelle Townsend was abducted," Gus said. "Do you remember being there that night?"

Taylor shook his head almost imperceptibly. Gus noticed his breathing had become more erratic, and he saw a string of drool forming on the other side of his chin.

Taylor squeezed his eyes closed. He lowered his head and Gus saw his shoulders tense. Then Taylor began to slowly rock back and forth, and Gus heard him begin to make a low growling sound as his hands tightened until there were streaks of white on his fingers. A female agent named Bridget walked through the room with an armful of sealed evidence bags and Gus watched her go out the front door before continuing.

"Taylor…" Gus began again, "We know you found Sadie Hogan's and Rachel Connors's drivers licenses here in your house. Do you remember that?"

Taylor's rocking quickened but he remained quiet. Gus looked to Leon who was leaning forward, his elbows on his knees. Leon raised his head toward the kitchen doorway, speaking softly. "In Teddy. The cookie jar on top of the fridge."

Gus looked back to Taylor. "Taylor, do you remember putting those licenses in Teddy or taking them out?"

Taylor slapped his palms on the sides of his head several times, mumbling to himself over and over, his voice strained and gravelly.

Neil stepped back into the room holding up a large clear evidence bag with a pair of muddy boots inside. "Black Dog Supersole boots, size eleven," he said softly to Gus with a nod. "Tread has a large slice in it on one side."

Gus leaned closer to Taylor, looking at Neil as he spoke. "Taylor, you're going to come with us so we can talk some more in private." He then read Taylor his Miranda rights and stood. "I'll help you get him in the car," he said to Neil.

Leon stood also. "I'm gonna head out if you don't need me."

"Maybe just help us get him in the back of the car before you go?"

Leon nodded then paused as Bridget walked through the room again, this time with an evidence box filled with VHS tapes, a large videorecorder the size of a news cameraman's and a bag of toiletries containing deodorant, toothpaste, a contact lens case and a bottle of its solution, and several brown bottles of medication. They let her walk through then Gus placed a hand beneath Taylor's arm to help him stand.

Taylor let out a raging growl and before Gus knew it, he had his arms around Gus's waist and was driving him backward. Gus fell over the amp, landing hard on the floor with Taylor on top of him. Taylor began furiously punching Gus.

"I'm not fuckin' going anywhere!"

Neil and Leon pulled Taylor away and wrestled him to the floor.

"Ahhhhh!" Taylor screamed into the carpet, his eyes wild, rabid.

Gus stood and brushed hair from his face then wiped a line of blood from beneath his nose. He watched Neil press his knee firmly into Taylor's back and put handcuffs on him.

Then he and another agent that had rushed into the room pulled Taylor to his feet as the musician thrashed around wildly like a trapped animal. Taylor craned his neck, his muscles and tendons bulging, and looked to the ceiling as he let out a monstrous scream. Drool spilled down his chin.

Gus felt the cut on his swelling lip as he looked to Neil and gestured toward the front door.

"Get 'im outta here."

Gus watched the two agents struggle to get a rabid-looking Taylor out the front door when TJ called from the kitchen.

"Gus." His voice rose with urgency. "You need to see this."

Gus made sure they got Taylor into the back of one of the sedans then turned and headed to the kitchen. TJ was standing at the kitchen table and on it sat a large ceramic bear jar, its head on the table beside it. Gus saw the concern on TJ's face as he approached and, confused, gestured with his chin.

"What is it?"

TJ flipped open a black leather wallet in his gloved hand and Gus immediately recognized the shiny silver FBI badge on one side. His eyes narrowed as he leaned over, only to see a young and smiling Vanessa in the photo next to it looking back.

"He's got Vanessa," TJ said as a shadow touched his face.

The room tightened around Gus, his anger filling every crevice, every porous space, as his vision narrowed, the darkness at its edges as if a dimmer switch had been pressed.

"I'm gonna blow up his entire fuckin' world."

Chapter Forty-Six

VANESSA ENDED ANOTHER coughing fit, her eyes filled with reluctant tears, and forced a dry swallow. She still had the copper taste of blood in her mouth and her bottom lip was heavy and fat. She tried to breathe through her nose but it was clogged with dried blood; she was sure it was broken. And her throat was scratchy and sore; she hadn't had anything to drink since the club and that was hours ago. How many hours, she didn't know, but too many, she was sure. She couldn't tell if her raging headache was from dehydration, the beating her head took, or both. But she knew it wasn't good.

The weeping fieldstone walls kept the room cold and damp and the air felt polluted and secondhand, making breathing difficult. She blinked, pushing tears down her cheeks, and her vision slowly cleared but she again looked to her lap. Vanessa did anything to not watch the old television propped in front of her but with her hands bound to the arms of an old chair she had no way of blocking out its sound.

She had swung in and out of sleep, fluttering around it like a moth to a flame. And once she woke, she tried yelling but quickly realized it was futile. If she was within earshot of anyone, of anything, they'd have heard her. That was when she realized how deep into the tunnels, he must've taken her. At one point, she heard a faint shuffling by the doorway behind her and craned her neck around to see a pack of mangy rats eating something in the corner. That was probably the most she'd panicked since being taken.

Vanessa had a thing for rats, and it wasn't a good thing. Gus knew this stemmed from her childhood in the projects and had challenged her on it one time, saying that every place had its nuisances. He told her of dealing with chiggers growing up in Colorado, small microscopic bugs that gave you rashes or worse from feeding on your skin. And of living with cockroaches at every apartment he'd had in New Orleans, regardless of how nice or expensive it was, and of how they preferred to nest in mattresses. And he reminded her of the black flies that came out in New England in May—mayflies—and how annoying it could be to just walk outside. Vanessa then told him a story from her childhood of a friend in the apartment next to hers watching a new kitten dragged by rats through a hole in their baseboard one night. "Such a nuisance," she had said.

Gus hadn't raised the topic since.

She looked around the small cellar room and had the feeling somehow that it was morning but had no way to confirm it. There were no windows so no natural light of any kind; just a single lightbulb dangling from the rafters with its tattered string and grungy coating of grime. The wall to her left was wet in spots and she thought she could hear running water somewhere around her but the acoustics were so odd and distorted she couldn't be sure. A jarring scream from the television had her squeeze her eyes closed and clench her jaw, waiting for it to end. And when it finally did, she took a beat, willing her heart rate to slow.

Vanessa was still pissed he got the drop on her, but the ensuing hours of being bound to that chair caused her rage to morph into determination. She was determined to outsmart him, determined to break free and escape, and determined to catch and punish that sociopathic fuck.

She strained again to lift her hands from the chair, but the plastic zip ties were unforgiving. She did the same with her legs, to the same result. Her boots and socks had been removed and her feet were numb from the cold. She licked her lips and slowly looked around the room for about the thousandth time, looking for anything she could use to get out of there.

Beside the television was a small video camera on a tripod with a cord connecting to the back of the TV. Behind that was a wooden dresser and, unlike everything else she could see, it was clean and relatively dust-free. On its top was an empty VHS sleeve, two GoPro video cameras with head straps, a box cutter, and a near-empty bag of plastic zip ties. Beside the dresser was a set of makeshift shelves constructed with cinder blocks and rough boards that spanned the entire wall. It was filled with rows of VHS tapes, stacks of small camcorder cassettes and DVDs. Towering stacks of additional VHS tapes filled the floor in front of the shelves. Vanessa counted 232 VHS tapes and there seemed to be just as many camcorder cassettes and DVDs. She had tried to shimmy her chair that way—her eyes trained on the boxcutter—before realizing its legs were chained to each wall, fixing her in place.

To her right were a few gallon jugs of store-brand spring water against the far wall that she could only dream of getting and to her left was nothing but dirt leading to the wall. She knew the doorway behind her had a pile of pipes and a large cardboard box beside it, but the chains prevented her from getting anywhere near them.

Above her were dark rafters filled with cobwebs and spider nests and she could see several black metal pipes running through the room from left to right between some of them. When she was done surveying her surroundings, she arrived at the same conclusion—*if* she could somehow move her chair, the boxcutter would be her first destination with the water being a very close second. But then she looked again at the thick, shiny silver chains running from each wall to the legs of her chair like spokes to a hub and knew that wasn't going to happen. She'd have to focus on how to convince him to untie her.

The VCR atop the television made its loud clicking sound so she knew the tape had ended and was being rewound. Vanessa had estimated that the tape was about an hour from beginning to end and that was, as far as she could remember, its eighth playing. But she had passed out at least twice so really couldn't be sure. Another few clicks and the television screen blinked several times and that was when she knew to look away and brace herself.

A woman's shrieking scream filled the room, and

Vanessa held her eyes closed until it stopped. She had watched most of the video once through, as disturbing as it was, looking away only during the most heinous parts. She learned a lot about him through both his actions and his interactions with his victims. Now she just needed her chance to use it.

The scream began to fade but Vanessa remained tense, her shoulders hunched, until it finally stopped. There was a shuffling sound, like wind over a microphone.

"How do you feel?" he whispered with care in his voice.

"Um…" the woman cried.

Her voice was shaky. Vanessa could hear her strain.

"I, ah…"

"Shh, shh … there, there," the man comforted. "Can I get you anything?"

But before the woman could reply, there was a loud muffled gagging. Then, through heavy breathing, Vanessa heard him whisper.

"It's the hope that kills you."

Then all was silent.

Chapter Forty-Seven

ABDUCTING AN FBI agent has a similar effect as yelling *code blue* in an emergency room. Gus's first call was to Jeff Cattagio, and he caught his friend in a director's budget meeting. The yelling and arguments in the background on Jeff's end were so loud that Gus found his voice muted out. But not his torment.

He told Jeff of Vanessa's abduction and that she had called an Uber from the club but never showed so they knew she was in the tunnels. Jeff promised Gus any resources he needed to find Vanessa, which was exactly what Gus expected. Gus then told Jeff of Taylor's current mental state, updating him with the behavior he'd witnessed at Taylor's house. Jeff said he wanted to run the situation by the attorney general to be sure what they did next was by the book then abruptly ended the call.

Gus's second call was to Charlie, the NPS lead in charge of mapping the tunnels. He told Charlie about Vanessa's abduction and asked the ranger to get his best search and rescue team to the tunnels immediately. He'd meet them there as soon as he was done interrogating their suspect. Those tunnels were a city unto themselves and that the straightest line to finding V's exact location was to get it directly from her abductor. So with all of that in motion, he left Taylor's house and went straight to the Pawtucket Falls FBI offices where he had the young agent, Neil, bring Taylor for questioning.

Before Gus could make it in to speak with Taylor, Jeff called back with specific instructions for the interview. Upon hearing of Taylor's psychological issues, the AG advised Jeff to make sure there was a forensic psychologist present when Gus spoke with him. If the case ever went to trial, the prosecution would need an expert to attest to Taylor's state of mind and mental capacity during questioning and that all procedures had been followed. So Gus now paced back and forth in a viewing room and in his mind was everything except silence. He could feel the encroaching darkness of dread deep inside him.

He watched Taylor through a one-way glass and wondered how all this could've happened. Gus's protective instincts had spiked when he began dating Mel and the thought of her being hurt again tormented his dreams and haunted his quiet times. But he had never thought to worry about Vanessa.

His phone buzzed with a call from TJ. As part of the scramble after finding Vanessa's badge, TJ had a runner rush the evidence from Taylor's van to the lab for analysis while they began to process his house. He also had a team in Boston immediately try to track Vanessa's cellphone and pull its data records to see if they could at least find the last spot it had been. It hadn't been long since they found her badge, but information was starting to trickle in.

"You talk to Taylor yet?"

"Not yet," Gus answered. "I'm waiting for a forensic psychologist to get here to sit in."

"I'm glad I caught you; things are starting to hit. In the highlight category, the lab matched the carpet fibers found beneath Rachel Connors's fingernails to the carpeting in Taylor's minivan."

"Great," Gus said, feeling the pieces begin to slide into place. "Was the team able to get any chemicals from his house to test against the residue found on the body?"

"Were they ever. There was an old workbench in the basement with all kinds of cleaners and glues and other stuff on it. They found paints and antifreeze and motor oil but also more exotic stuff like paint thinner and turpentine and linseed oil. I mean, they even found creosote and that was banned by the FDA in the seventies as a carcinogen."

"Jesus."

"Yeah, and they found a stash of stuff in the spare bedroom too with his instruments: mineral oils, something called Fast Fret string lube and a bunch of cans of Mohawk finishing products."

"Yeah, that's all stuff for his instruments."

"But there was a lot more, Gus. It's gonna take the lab a minute to test it all."

"I hear ya."

"That said, I'm not sure we're gonna need it. They matched the tread of the boots taken from his house to the print found at the Connors scene."

"You may be right. Anything new on V?"

"Yeah, they found blood on the inside of the basement door of the club and a trail down its steps," TJ said.

"We knew there was an entrance down there somewhere with Hogan being taken but now we're gonna have to find it. It might be the quickest way to V."

Gus's eyes returned to Taylor, and it took everything in him to not charge into that room and beat Vanessa's location out of him.

"Gus," TJ said, interrupting his thoughts. "There was a *lot* of blood."

The regret Gus felt of not watching over Vanessa, not protecting her, had been weighing heavily on him. The guilt of the good inevitably made room for the deeds of others.

"I hear ya, TJ. We're gonna find her."

TJ didn't answer and Gus heard him speaking to someone else through the phone.

A few moments later he was back. "Gus, they found video footage of Vanessa on Taylor's phone."

Gus heard a ping in his ear.

"I just sent it to you."

Gus and TJ watched the video simultaneously, commenting to each other on speaker as they did so. Gus watched as the footage showed a beaten and bloody Vanessa in what looked to be a cellar room bound to a chair by her wrists and ankles. Fear gripped him until he saw her raise her head and growl at the camera.

"She's in worse shape than I thought," TJ said.

"Yeah, but we just confirmed she's in those tunnels. Look at the stone wall and the dirt floor. She's down there somewhere."

"You're right, but we gotta get to her soon though."

TJ's words triggered another fear in Gus's mind. Given her physical condition, how long could she really survive down there? He thought of tramping around in those tunnels with the ranger, Jackie, and of how cold and damp it was and how difficult those conditions made it to breathe. And he remembered getting turned around and lost while chasing their suspect and how the terrain was so deceivingly difficult to traverse. Even if Vanessa did escape—and by looking at her on the video that was a very big *if*—there was a strong likelihood she'd never find her way out.

Gus had TJ send the video to Rob, the pathologist, and less than a minute later, TJ had Rob patched into their call. The two of them listened as Rob watched the video from a medical point of view.

"Okay, I've paused it at the thirty-two second mark and zoomed in a bit as her head is facing our way," the pathologist began in his typical clinical tone. "You'll note the swollen eye, the contusions on her temples and beside each eye. That, coupled with the vomit on the front of her shirt, suggest she's likely got a concussion. The blood on her cheeks and chin and neck and the swelling of her nose suggest a broken nose. There's a significant amount of blood loss, Gus." Rob grew quiet and Gus was about to speak up when he continued, "Note her lips and cheeks have a bluish tint to them. Gus, I'd say we're dealing with the onset of hypothermia here."

"Makes sense, Rob. I've been in those tunnels. It's cold with a jacket on."

"And she has no jacket—just a shirt—and notice her shoes and socks have been removed. She's covered with goosebumps too." Rob fell silent for a long time before he continued, "Gus, if you play the video all the way through, you'll notice water jugs on the floor along one of the walls. Which begs the question. With our suspect in custody, when's the last time Vanessa's had any water?"

"She had a few diet cokes last night when we were together but no water."

"Unfortunately, that's worse. Diet Coke is a diuretic so would lead to increased urine production. Looking at her lips more closely, you can see they're cracked and split in spots." Rob paused. "Gus, I'm afraid it doesn't look good."

"Do you have a sense of timing; how long she might have before..." The question hung in the air with no one able to put an end to it.

"It's difficult. It seems that we're dealing with both dehydration *and* hypothermia which is a very dangerous combination. We know that the body can only survive three to five days without water. When was she taken?"

"Last night around ten p.m."

"And you said she didn't have any water earlier?"

"No, just Diet Cokes."

"Okay, so it's been fourteen hours since ten last night. Let's say she didn't have water for four hours before that?"

"At least," Gus replied.

"Okay, six hours. So let's call it twenty hours without water. She's in a terrible state, so I'd say in her condition we're looking at the lower end of that range. Three days or seventy-two hours minus the twenty."

"So, fifty-two hours."

"Fifty-two hours," Rob echoed. "But, Gus, we've only discussed her physical state. Victims in her physical condition undergoing that type of distress often have highly damaged psychological states. And that dynamic alone could cut that time in half."

"Not with Vanessa," Gus said with conviction. "The survival instinct is strong with that one."

Chapter Forty-Eight

G US THANKED ROB then TJ dropped the pathologist from the call. Gus opened the clock app on his phone and tapped the timers tab. He set a timer for fifty-two hours and labeled it VANESSA. The digital numbers began to count down.

51:59:59 … 51:59:58 … 51:59:57…

He then turned his attention to Taylor through the viewing window and watched as their suspect slumped back in his chair, bent his head back and began talking to the ceiling. TJ's voice in Gus's ear stole his attention back.

"Hey, Gus. A few other things before you jump. They dusted Vanessa's badge but there were no prints on it, not even hers. It was clearly wiped. But they did ID that body found in the tunnels. I just sent you a pic of the gravesite to get a sense of what else might be down there."

Gus put TJ on speaker and pulled up the photo. It was a shallow grave in the dirt with several numbered yellow cones and a measuring stick beside it.

"They're the remains of a girl that went missing about twelve years ago, an Anne Marie Tompkins," TJ continued. "She was sixteen and in the system as a runaway."

"Sixteen," Gus murmured, as he looked over the petite

skeleton of a girl too young to carry her own story. He chewed on the name but didn't recognize it. "Name doesn't ring a bell."

"You sure?"

"Yeah, why?"

"Well, it'll ring a bell for Taylor. He was questioned about her disappearance; there's an interview with him in the file."

Gus thought of the assessment his therapist had given he and Vanessa; the anxieties and psychosis taking root in Taylor from such a young age. And Gus recalled the therapist saying Taylor's first love had run away when they were in high school. The hairs on the back of his neck bristled.

"She was his girlfriend," he breathed.

"She was his girlfriend," TJ echoed.

"How'd she die?"

"Strangulation. The hyoid bone was fractured."

They talked about it for another few moments then ended the call. Gus knew both Leon and Mick also grew up in Pawtucket Falls, but that Leon was closer to Taylor's age so thought he'd give him a call about this Anne Marie Tompkins.

"Leon, what can you tell me about Anne Tompkins from high school?"

"Anne Marie? She was Taylor's girlfriend. Why? Is he mumbling about her again?"

"What ... no. What're you talking about?"

"Last night, when he was in the middle of it, Mick found a necklace of Anne Marie's hanging on Taylor's upright. And when he asked Taylor what it was, Taylor just broke down."

"What'd he say exactly?"

"I dunno, I wasn't in the room. I was in the kitchen calling the doc. But I can call Mick and find out."

Gus thought of how Mick had successfully dodged them for days when Gus was trying to get ahold of him.

"Yeah, do that. But, before you do, what can you tell me about her?"

"Well, she was toxic, that one."

"How d'ya mean?"

"Agent, I'm sure you saw how good a musician T was when you met him."

"I did."

"Yeah, well, he got full rides to the Manhattan School, Julliard, Berkeley, NYU, all the top music schools. But Anne Marie was really pressuring him to stay local so they could be together. She was holding that boy back."

"Is that how Taylor saw it?"

"Privately, yeah, and he became really resentful. His home life wasn't great either, and he knew music was his ticket out. Now, don't get me wrong; he loved her, for sure, so he went along with it. He was planning to go to UMass and they were talking about getting an apartment once they graduated to get her out of that house. But it changed him, man. It was like he was giving up or something."

"How so?"

"He just pulled back from everything. Started listening to metal instead of his jazz, would stay home a lot. Stopped hanging out with friends. He just became ... different. Sorta dark in a way."

Gus thought about what the therapist had said of Anne Marie's leaving being a significant emotional trauma in Taylor's life and now wondered if it was more *how* she left that had its impact on him.

"Then she left?" Gus nudged.

"Yeah. When she ran away it definitely hit him and stuff. But soon he got back to the guy he used to be. He ditched the metal crap and was listening to jazz again. And he was playing his upright like never before and loving it. He just seemed like the old T again. And I swear he chose Loyola because it was the farthest school away from here."

"I did wonder why he went there of all schools," Gus said, his eyes on Taylor.

There was a short pause before Leon spoke again. "Yeah. Really, if ya think about it, Anne Marie leaving was the best thing that ever happened to that boy."

Chapter Forty-Nine

THE FBI FORENSIC psychologist arrived from Boston a few minutes after Gus ended his call with Leon. Dr. Rebecca Morgan was a young woman with a long, narrow nose, stern gaze, and straight brown hair that cupped the bottom of her jaw. Gus gave her an overview of their case and described the behavior he'd seen from Taylor. He then told her of Taylor's behavior that Leon witnessed and how Taylor had confessed to Leon of hearing women's voices and of seeing images of the dead women. And, finally, Gus described his and Vanessa's meeting with Taylor's therapist, Dr. Cappi, and the events from Taylor's past that Dr. Cappi identified as the likely basis for his psychosis. Dr. Morgan's eyes narrowed slightly as she looked past Gus and through the viewing window to Taylor.

"Agent Wheeler, the symptoms you describe are very worrisome from a competency perspective." She eyed Taylor for several moments before looking back to Gus.

"We believe he's taken my partner, so it's imperative I speak with him. And we know she's badly injured so time is of the essence here, doctor."

"Yes, Director Cattagio stressed that as well, and I sympathize with your situation, I really do. But my professional responsibility here is to the psychological well-being of Mr. Franklin and to ensure that any information or confession we get from him will stand up in court." She paused and her eyes went back to Taylor as she continued, "Do you have any other way to locate your partner?"

"We believe she's being held in a network of tunnels beneath the city. But they're vast and endless. We simply don't have the time to search them all."

A yell came from the interview room and they both looked to see Taylor with his elbows on the table, his head down and his hands cupped over his ears as he rocked back and forth.

Dr. Morgan turned to Gus, her head slowly shaking, and he knew what she was thinking.

"Five minutes," he blurted. "That's all I need. He and I have a history. I can get him to tell me where my partner is. All I need is five minutes."

Dr. Morgan's lips parted a little, allowing her to lick her upper lip. "I'll need to give him a cognitive test first; establish he's not having a psychotic episode and understands where he is and the situation." Her eyes widened and her head tick-tocked side to side. "But I'm not optimistic."

"How long will that take?" Gus asked.

"We use a standard test for psychosis and schizophrenia. It has fifty yes or no questions."

"Fifty?" Gus asked. He pointed to Taylor through the window. "Look at him. You know how long it'll take to get him to respond to *fifty* questions?"

Dr. Morgan watched Taylor for a few moments more.

Gus knew she had been pressured hard by Jeff—and likely her own boss—to cooperate with them to find Vanessa at all costs. But Gus could tell she wasn't the type that responded well to pressure or influence. He just hoped she didn't have an oppositional reflex to it.

"Please, doctor," he said with a sensitivity in his voice. "He's our best shot at finding my partner alive." And as Gus said those words aloud the gravity of the situation washed over him.

His chest grew hot, his mouth turned dry. He cleared his throat and collected himself, waiting for the doctor to respond.

"Agent, we have to be sure he's mentally stable before we introduce questions or topics to him that may be disturbing or triggering." He could see her thinking as she then offered, "How about this? I can ask him the first batch of questions; it's only a few gating ones. If after those I believe he's in a coherent mental state, you can interview him. But if he's not or he relapses into another psychotic episode the interview terminates immediately." She squared up to him and looked him in the eyes. When Gus hesitated, she continued. "Agent, that's the best you're gonna get. I suggest you take it because looking at him rocking back and forth has me wondering if we don't just admit him to a psych facility now for testing."

Gus believed her; this was the best he was going to get, so he relented and the two of them joined Taylor in the interview room. Hearing them enter, Taylor slowly looked up and removed his hands from his ears.

"Hey, Taylor," Gus said quietly as he sat across the table

from him.

Taylor's eyes were wide and glassy and had dark, puffy circles beneath them. Dr. Morgan sat beside Gus.

"Taylor, this is Dr. Morgan. She's a clinical psychologist, a doctor that specializes in what you're dealing with."

Dr. Morgan leaned over the table, sure to catch Taylor's eye. "Hi, Taylor." Her voice was tender and caring, nothing like the sterile, clinical tone Gus had just endured in the viewing room. "Gus tells me you've been struggling lately. I'm here to help you determine exactly what is happening and to figure out how we fix it, okay?" Taylor's eyes roamed her face before he looked back to the table. "Is it okay if I ask you a few questions?"

A nod.

She pulled a thin folder from her bag, placed it carefully on the table and opened it. "So, Taylor, I just need a yes or no answer to these. Do familiar surroundings sometimes seem strange or confusing or unreal to you?"

A long silence ensued before Taylor gave her a quick nod. "Sometimes," he whispered.

"Do you know where you are now?"

"The FBI. In the Falls."

"Okay, good. Taylor, you're doing great. And sometimes do things that you see appear different from the way they usually do?" Taylor remained quiet for a long time so Dr. Morgan leaned a little closer. "Taylor, did you understand my question?"

"My house," he answered. "Sometimes it looks weird, like I'm in a dream or something."

"Okay, good. Taylor, this is very good. I only have a couple more. Have you heard unusual sounds like banging, clicking, hissing, clapping, or ringing in your ears?"

"Sometimes," he whispered. "Clicking and hissing ... ringing sometimes."

"Do you hear any of those now?"

Taylor shook his head swiftly.

"And Gus tells me that you've been hearing voices. Is that true?"

He nodded and moved his hands back loosely over his ears. "Sometimes that's all I hear."

Dr. Morgan side-eyed Gus with a raised eyebrow. "And what do these voices say? Do they tell you to do something or are they just talking to you?"

Gus could see Taylor's shoulders begin to twitch and feared they were losing him.

"They tell me to stop hurting them. They scream and cry and beg me to stop."

"Who tells you to stop?" Dr. Morgan asked.

When Taylor didn't answer, Gus leaned low to the table to look at Taylor's face. His eyes were flicking around the tabletop; Gus knew he was almost gone.

"Taylor," Gus said, trying to get his attention. "Please, Taylor, I need your help." He slowed his cadence. "I need you to concentrate and tell me where you took my friend Vanessa."

Gus watched as Taylor's hands began to tighten around his ears and he started slowly rocking back and forth again. He then felt the firm grasp of Dr. Morgan's hand on his elbow.

"Taylor," she said. "Are you hearing those voices now?"

Taylor's rocking quickened but he remained silent. Gus pulled his elbow from the doctor's grasp and reached out and pulled one of Taylor's hands from his ear.

"Taylor, it's me, your friend, Gus."

Taylor raised his head and looked at Gus with red, pleading eyes. His scruffy chin was quivering and when he went to speak, drool spilled from his lower lip, dangling over the table.

Dr. Morgan's words came to Gus from behind. "Agent, we're done here. Taylor…"

Gus reached across the table with his other hand so that he now held both of Taylor's wrists. He knew he had one last shot to get Taylor's attention, to get him back.

"Taylor," he said sternly, weaving his head right and left close to the table to make eye contact. "Look at me. We found Anne Marie. We found Anne Marie Tompkins."

Taylor blinked and his head twitched as if he'd gotten a shock.

He tilted his head and looked at Gus with fear in his eyes. "Anne Marie?" His voice was a raspy whisper.

Gus nodded, leaning closer so their faces were inches apart. Gus heard an objection from the doctor but ignored her.

"That's right. We found Anne Marie in those tunnels, right where you left her."

Taylor's eyes widened and filled with tears, and Gus noticed his lips begin to move as if he were speaking, but no sound came out. Gus shook Taylor's wrists, trying to keep him present.

"I know you loved Anne Marie and how much she meant to you. Vanessa's my Anne Marie, Taylor. Please don't let me lose her like you lost Anne Marie. Where is she? Where did you take Vanessa?"

Taylor stared at Gus without blinking or saying a word as tears spilled onto his cheeks. Gus heard the doctor's chair slide back and could tell she had stood but he continued to hold Taylor's attention.

"Tell me!" Gus stressed, trying to break Taylor from his gaze. He squeezed tightly around Taylor's wrists. "Where's Vanessa?!"

"Agent!" Dr. Morgan commanded from behind, matching Gus's tone and demeanor. "That's enough. This interview is over."

After a few seconds, when Gus didn't answer or acknowledge her, he heard the doctor slap the red emergency call button beside the door and alarms began to sound outside in the hall. Agents came rushing into the room and Dr. Morgan directed them to remove Gus immediately. He squeezed Taylor's wrists a final time as he began to get tugged away.

"Where did you take Vanessa?!" he yelled into Taylor's vacant eyes.

It took three agents grabbing Gus by his arms and shoulders to get him out of his chair, then they forcibly pulled him from the room. Outside in the hall, once the interview room was locked and secure, Dr. Morgan pushed her way through the agents and stepped in close to Gus.

She pointed a finger up at his face. "Agent, your actions

in there were reckless and reprehensible!" she scolded. "Do you realize how damaging that likely was for Mr. Franklin's psychological well-being?" But before Gus could answer, she added. "I hope your conscience never lets you forget what you've done here today."

Gus shook the last agent's hands from his arms and stared the young man down until he stepped back. He looked at Dr. Morgan with disgust then pushed his way past her and the others.

"I hope you can live with *your* conscience," he said over a shoulder, as he headed for the exit. "If my partner ends up on a fuckin' slab."

Chapter Fifty

VANESSA'S MOUTH FILLED with the metallic taste of blood as she flopped her tongue onto her lower lip. Her eyes widened and she looked to the ground.

"Fthuck." Her tongue throbbed, but at least she now had something, she thought, to swallow and soothe her raspy throat.

She had surveyed her surroundings for hours looking for the weak spot, the one potential vulnerability she could use to get free. She needed to channel her energy and frustration into something productive. So, in the end, she had settled on the chair. The wooden chair.

After a few concentrated breaths to dull the pain, she went back to tussling with its arms and legs. She simultaneously kicked her legs out and yanked her arms up, envisioning herself behind closed eyes as doing a vaudeville dance to an upbeat tune. But neither arm or leg moved more than the slight shift the plastic ties would allow. Not to be deterred, she tried again and again, her mind picturing herself dancing wildly across a lighted stage.

Exhausted from another fit of struggling, Vanessa slumped in the chair to rest a minute. The lack of food and water combined with the hours of being tied down, unable to really move, had sapped her of strength. And the pulsing of her bruised, swollen ankles and wrists had morphed to sharp pains with each thrust. And that was nothing compared to her pounding head and fuzzy vision.

Her mind raked back over her attacker and how she completely misjudged his narcissism and deviant ways. She had screwed up, she knew it. She found him shy and approachable and his willingness to speak with them had masked just how dangerous he was. And as much as she despised admitting it to herself, she had been lulled by his musician vibe. She now had an appreciation for how the other women had fallen prey and it made the bile rise in her throat.

The tape in the VCR machine clicked and began its rewinding process. Vanessa thought she was going to lose her mind if she had to listen to that tape one more time and lashed out in a burst of rage, flexing her arms and legs from the chair and screaming at the television screen. She felt a trickle of blood run down her bare ankle and foot as she slammed back and screamed to the rafters, trying to purge her anger, her frustrations. Her fear.

"Aaaahhhhh!!!!"

The tape began again so she continued her mottled moan-scream so as not to hear its beginning, but her raspy voice quickly turned quiet. She shook her head violently side to side and rocked her shoulders with it until her chair legs lifted from the floor with her movements.

And that was when she heard it. The faintest of sounds.

She stopped and listened with renewed acuity. She flexed

each leg in succession, but heard nothing. She pulled up on her left arm but it was firmly affixed to the chair, then her right and found the same. She then pulled her right arm in toward her body and that's when she heard it again.

Craaaaack.

She moved her right wrist side to side and the arm of the chair wiggled noticeably with it. And Vanessa's split lips turned upward into a smile.

Chapter Fifty-One

G US SAT IN his truck, its engine rumbling at an angry idle. The sky outside his windshield was the color of fire and ash, as if the world around him were burning to the ground. He thought of calling Jeff, calling in a chit with his long-time friend to work his magic and get Gus five minutes alone with Taylor in the box. No video recording, no audience behind the one-way glass, no psychologist telling him what he could and could not ask. Just him and Taylor; he knew he'd get Vanessa's location. And he also knew Jeff could lose his job for arranging such an off-the-books session.

He tapped TJ's number on his phone and the agent answered on the second ring.

"Hey, I've been waiting for your call." Gus could hear people talking and shouting in the background. "How'd it go with Taylor?"

"It didn't," Gus said flatly. "We're gonna need to find V the hard way."

"Okay, what d'ya need?"

"Charlie's getting his best search and rescue team to the tunnels now. Check with him if he needs extra bodies and, if so, round up everyone you can find and get 'em to The

Mills."

"Will do. But, Gus, shouldn't we meet outside The Loft? Where the NPS team is based?"

"It feels like it'd take too long to work our way through those tunnels to get close to The Mills. That's a good distance, even in a straight line."

"True, but I've got the map, remember?" TJ reminded.

"I know, but follow my logic. V put up a fight but he still got her. Which means he had to have subdued her somehow."

"Right, but we've found no drugs in any of the other victims," TJ pointed out.

"It doesn't matter *how* he did it," Gus corrected. "Just that he did it. There's no way Taylor could carry her very far, not in that terrain down there."

"V's pretty thin, right?" TJ countered.

"Thin or not, subdued she's dead weight. And that'd be tough for anyone. Which means, even though there are eleven plus miles of tunnels down there, V has to be within a pretty tight perimeter of the entrance to those tunnels beneath The Mills."

"Great logic but, Gus, like we said earlier, we don't know how to get into the tunnels from there."

"Leave that to me."

Gus and TJ ended their call then Gus immediately phoned Jeff. He wanted his boss and friend to hear about the interview with Taylor from him. Jeff answered his cell after putting the director of the behavioral analysis unit—Dr. Morgan's boss—on hold. Once he berated Gus about his actions in the interview with Taylor, Gus told him about the NPS search and rescue team and that he might need more agents for the search.

"Gus, of course, I'll get every agent I have to Pawtucket Falls. Just say the word. But that stunt you pulled with the Franklin guy?"

"I know, I know. I got you in the shit."

"Gus, it's not that. I can take care of myself. It's you … you know there's only so much air cover I can give you, right? But the way you're goin', you're gonna run outta road someday."

Gus was taken aback at Jeff's sincerity and thanked him for his concern. They spoke for another minute or so and left it that Gus would let Jeff know if he needed more agents then they ended the call. Gus knew he'd gone too far in the interview with Taylor and, as a result, had gotten Jeff in the crosshairs with the brass. He also knew Jeff was right. He could take care of himself. But Gus would still make sure he took the bullets for that instead of Jeff when the time came.

Gus then made the phone call he'd been dreading for days. The reporter, Christina Collins, answered on the first ring.

"I was just going to call you," she said as she answered his call. "I left Vanessa a message earlier but haven't heard back. Did she find the entrance last night?"

Gus stiffened. "What entrance?"

Christina told Gus about finding the location of the tunnel entrance in the basement of The Mills in her story notes and calling Vanessa late last night, then talking her through finding it.

"What time was that?"

"Ten fifty-two," she said after checking the recent calls on her phone. "Why?" Her voice rose, carried by concern. "What's happened?"

"Meet me at The Mills immediately," he said. Then he paused, uncomfortable with what he needed to say next. "And bring your boots."

Chapter Fifty-Two

G US WAS STANDING with TJ and Charlie and his search and rescue team in front of The Mills when he saw Christina briskly walking their way so went to her.

"You got the instructions to find the entrance?" he asked eagerly.

He noticed Tommy—Christina's cameraman—come around a corner lugging their broadcasting equipment as Christina held up before they made it to the others.

"I do … but, Gus … I know this is shitty timing but my editor just climbed all over me about this story. He wants a broadcast. Now. Something exclusive." She grimaced. "I'm so sorry to have to ask; he's just getting a ton of pressure to stay ahead of the bloggers on this one."

Gus could feel the rage rising inside him and taste the regret of having made a bargain with her as the phantom ticking from Vanessa's timer on his phone hammered inside his head.

"Now?" he asked slowly, his voice a deep rumble as he struggled to keep his emotions in check.

Christina shook her head apologetically several times. "I'm so sorry." Her eyes left his and she looked to the ground. Then after a moment she looked back up to him.

"Never mind. The guy's an ass anyway." She turned to Tommy who had stepped beside her.

"We'll do a quick update piece here, in front of the club. Call Janet and have her get pictures of Agent Lambert and the guy in custody, Taylor Franklin. And the FBI's set up a hotline so have her get that and run it on the banner. Tell her when the studio does the piece to have a split screen to the photos. I'll reference them."

She turned back to Gus and pointed away from the club. "Step over there so you're not in the shot. I need one minute then I'm all yours."

Gus tipped his head. "Thank you." he said softly. Then he held her eyes. "You'll get your exclusive. I give you my word."

Gus watched as Christina took her position in front of the club and, as she did, something caught his eye in the distance behind her. Slowly creeping left to right along the street at the end of Music Row was a small service van, its lime green and safety-orange colors standing out like the woman in red in *The Matrix*. Gus squinted to read the large writing along its side. ALLIED EQUIPMENT AND REPAIR and knew it was from the drummer Mick's company. He thought of sending someone after it but by the time the thought crossed his mind the van was gone and his attention was pulled back to Christina as she tossed Tommy her microphone and walked his way.

Gus and she then quickly made their way over to TJ and the group of agents. Charlie had told TJ earlier that it was best to leave this phase of the search to the search and rescue team. Having others in the narrow—and at spots, danger-ous—tunnels would only serve as a distraction for the experts.

Once they gathered as a group Charlie briefed everyone on the search. He then distributed fresh, fully-charged portable tracking devices and walkie-talkies to each of the rangers and made sure they all had the latest copy of the map of the tunnels they created. They weren't done with the mapping, so he pointed out the areas where they believed more tunnels existed. With the team set for the search, Christina led them into the club.

The basement of The Mills was a large, rectangular un-finished space, its four walls constructed of fieldstone. Gus stepped off the last stair behind Christina and TJ and looked around. The long wall behind the stairs had three large arched indentations that reminded Gus of the doors along the front of an old carriage house. They were solid stone and were either former doorways filled in or some sort of decora-tive feature; he assumed the former given they were on a basement wall. And as he oriented himself, he was fairly certain that side of the building ran along the street in front of the club. The wall to his right was an ordinary stone wall with a few boxes and some old equipment stacked against it. The wall to his left had a square brick chimney in its center and to the right of it was a small garage-sized room created by a three-quarter height stone wall running parallel to it from the other side. The opening of the room faced the chimney so Gus took a step toward it before noticing Christina looking at her phone.

"No service down here," he said.

Christina side-eyed him and held it out. "Notes from my story with the entrance location."

Gus followed her as she headed straight for the open end of the stone box in the corner beside the chimney. Its floor was the same stone as the rest of the basement but stained varying shades of black throughout, as were the lower parts of the three walls. There was a large rusty metal door on the wall in the corner opened a crack, the walls immediately beside it a solid black. Christina kneeled by the chimney as Gus stepped inside the enclosure and ran his fingers along the black soot on one of its walls and looked at his fingers. He rubbed his thumb over his fingertips then brought them to his nose. The black substance smelled musky and woody and, oddly, somewhat fruity. And that was when it hit him. He held up his fingertips and gestured to the walls around him.

"This is coal dust. This must be some sort of coal chute."

"The Hogan woman," TJ said.

Christina looked up at them from the floor. "I don't follow."

"Sadie Hogan had traces of coal dust beneath her fingernails." Gus opened his palms to the ceiling and looked around him. "She touched one of these walls."

"Makes sense," Christina replied as she quickly shimmied one of the red bricks at the base of the chimney loose and dropped it onto the floor. She reached her hand into the small space and they all heard a loud click. Gus turned toward the sound and saw a line of mortar weaving around stones exposing a gap now in the wall. He pushed on the seam and a section of the stone wall about four feet wide swung inward.

Gus used his penlight and, seeing it opened into a long tunnel, stepped aside so Charlie could take a look. Charlie then oriented the other rangers to their location on the hardcopy map and they split into three groups of two with each group taking a tunnel. Gus stepped past Charlie and joined the other rangers.

"Agent," Charlie said to Gus. "Let them take it from here." He nodded once. "They're pros. We'll set up here in the basement and monitor their every move."

Gus arched an eyebrow. "There's no way I'm not going in."

Charlie paused then relented with a nod and out of his peripheral vision Gus saw one of the rangers look to the ceiling in exasperation.

"Stick with the group," Charlie said.

He handed Gus his walkie-talkie and the tracking device from his belt.

Then he looked at the group of them. "Okay, guys, let's get at it. Clock's ticking."

Chapter Fifty-Three

G US SAT ON a bench outside The Mills, his stinging, watery eyes zoning at the bitter white numbers on his phone counting down the Vanessa timer.

31:08:23 … 31:08:22 … 31:08:21…

The morning sun hung low in the sky over the Merrimack River, taunting Gus with a new day. The NPS search and rescue team were huddled around a table by the entrance of the club with a few large boxes of coffee on it, courtesy of the Dunks just down the street. It had been a very long physically and psychologically exhausting night, one not without its missteps. There were several injuries throughout the night, mostly twisted ankles and banged-up knees but one of the rangers did need medical attention for a cut suffered when he fell down a small shaft he was inspecting. Then, later into the night, two of the searchers got lost as they ventured deep into the tunnels and had to be rescued. The real danger occurred, however, when one of the rangers decided to follow a tunnel not on the provided map only to get trapped when its ceiling partially collapsed on him. And through all that, they had managed to search all of the tunnels mapped thus far, yet found no sign of Vanessa.

TJ emerged from the group of rangers with two coffees

in hand and walked over, handing one to Gus before sitting on the bench beside him. He brushed dust off his arms and pantlegs and for the first time Gus noticed he too was covered in dirt. When TJ was finished, he looked to Gus.

"What d'ya think?"

Gus saw the defeat on TJ's face. He ran a hand over his face before replying. "We had to have missed something," Gus declared. "Miles of tunnels down there … we had to have missed *something*."

"Maybe," TJ said. He took a large gulp of his coffee then added, "Or she's in one of the tunnels not mapped yet." He turned to Gus. "Charlie told me earlier they think they've mapped all the tunnels that are safe to be in." His eyes wandered back to the search and rescue team by the table. "They were talking about that tunnel collapsing earlier; seemed pretty freaked about it."

"I don't give a shit if someone thinks they're unsafe," Gus said. "If V's in one of 'em then it was safe enough to get her there. It'll be safe enough to get her out."

Gus took a drink of his coffee and leaned forward. Holding his paper cup between outstretched fingers, he rested his elbows on his knees. He stared at the ground, willing his tired mind to think of something, anything, to find Vanessa. He would gladly go into those unmapped tunnels to get her out but he had no way of navigating around down there and, by the sounds of it, he'd likely be going in alone. He pinched the bridge of his nose and rubbed his eyes then, hearing footsteps, looked up to see Charlie standing beside them.

"Hey," Gus said, sitting back against the bench. He

looked over a shoulder toward the other rangers. "Everyone okay over there?"

Charlie nodded, "Yeah, they'll be fine."

"TJ said you thought you've mapped all the tunnels that are safe."

"That's right and Jackie just confirmed it. What's not mapped doesn't look structurally sound. And, I think, from what happened earlier more collapses are a very real possibility."

"We have to go in, though," Gus said standing. "If she's in one of 'em we've gotta get her out."

"Gus, I hear you. I really do. But even if I thought those tunnels were safe to go into…" He poked a thumb over his shoulder at the other rangers. "Those guys are fried. I can't send 'em back in there, not without some rest. That'd be reckless."

There it is again, Gus thought, *reckless*. Was it reckless to want to find Vanessa? Was it reckless to do whatever it took to bring her back alive? *Fuck reckless*. But before Gus could say any of that, TJ spoke up.

"Charlie's right, Gus. Everyone's exhausted. And even if they weren't, where would we send them? We have no idea where V might be down there."

"*Fuck!*" Gus yelled to the sky, his arms flexed by his sides, his back arched.

The group of agents went silent and turned and stared at him. He had to figure out how to find Vanessa, reason out a path forward in his mind for the search. He could get fresh bodies, he was sure. One call to Jeff and the phone tree would light up again. That wasn't the issue; the issue was they had no idea where to look for her. And without more mapping of the tunnels, they wouldn't even have an educated guess as to where to begin.

Charlie looked to his team and, over his shoulder, said, "I'll be right back." He walked over to the other NPS rangers and Gus watched as the group of them got into a heated discussion.

Gus knew he needed to come at this differently. How could he narrow down the area where Vanessa likely was? They had searched Taylor's house and van and, other than finding Vanessa's badge and the muddy boots, they'd found nothing that spoke to her location. They had nothing that would lead them to Vanessa. Only Taylor could do that. He alone knew where she was.

He knew he'd never be let back in to speak with Taylor, not after what happened during his interview yesterday. His eyes were drawn to the reporter, Christina, who was doing a live broadcast from in front of The Mills when his phone rang with a call from Jeff. He hesitated, wondering if he should answer it, but he'd need to take Jeff's call eventually so tapped the green button.

"Any word on Vanessa?"

Gus filled him in on the night's activities and its result.

"Anything I can do?" Jeff asked, his voice clipped and tight.

"Get me another few minutes with Taylor?"

"Gus, that door's closed," Jeff interrupted.

"But if I could just—"

"Gus, you don't understand. Even if I *could* make that happen, we've lost him."

"What d'ya mean lost him?"

"Apparently, Taylor had some sort of breakdown after the interview yesterday; became violent to himself and others, screaming, yelling at people not there. They committed him to a psychiatric facility under suicide watch; he's been sedated and restrained until they can get his medication sorted."

Gus thought a moment, taking a beat, then told Jeff he'd let him know if they needed anything before ending the call. He twisted his belt so he could see the face of the remote tracking device and pressed the test button; green, plenty of battery.

There were a lot of things Gus didn't know. Would Taylor ever become lucid enough again to tell them where Vanessa was? And if he did, would it be in time? How long could Vanessa really survive down there?

But Gus knew one thing for sure. Regardless of the answers to any of those questions—and the thousands more rattling around in his circus-filled mind—he'd be in the tunnels looking for her when they were answered. He met TJ's eyes but before either one could say anything Charlie rejoined them.

"Well, I might get fired for this," Charlie said as he got to them. "But we've got a second team coming. They'll be here in a couple of hours." His eyes widened. "They're contractors, not NPS. These guys are the ones you call when no one else will go in; they don't need maps."

Gus tipped his head in a thank-you then TJ's phone rang.

Looking at the caller ID the agent said, "Boston office." He answered the call and stepped a few feet away from Gus and Charlie.

Gus felt the tracking device on his belt to be sure it was secure.

"I'd ask if you're going back in, but I'll save my breath," Charlie said. "I'll get you a new tracker so we both have fresh batteries."

"You coming?" Gus asked.

"Someone's gotta get you outta there alive."

"What the fuck?" TJ said loudly into his phone.

Gus and Charlie both turned to see him walking briskly in their direction with his hand over the bottom of his phone.

"This is Tony," he said to Gus, his voice high and rushed. "A guy called into the hotline he saw in that reporter's story earlier. Says he recognized the hot punky-looking agent that went missing from the bar. And he saw the guy that followed her into the hall where the restrooms are."

Gus's hope deflated and he glared at TJ. But before he could tell him to stop wasting his time, that they already knew who that was, TJ spoke again. This time louder than before.

"Says it wasn't the guy in the photo. It wasn't Taylor!"

Chapter Fifty-Four

Monday

✓ Frame Taylor

Chapter Fifty-Five

VANESSA SHOOK HER arm rapidly side-to-side, as if shaking a dog's teeth from her sleeve. And with one loud crackle, the arm of the chair broke free and her shoulder dropped down. She quickly brought her freed hand to the other and the chair's other arm was broken off in seconds. Moments later the splintered wood was on the floor beside her and she had removed the zip tie from each wrist. She tried to pry her ankles free but the chair's legs were strong and unforgiving. Staring at the boxcutter on the dresser just feet away, she considered how she could get to it. Then finally deciding on a plan, she pushed herself up off the seat and, holding the back of the chair, carefully stood.

Her ass and lower back were numb from sitting so long and her legs were shaky and weak; she gripped the chair's back tighter as she struggled to stay on her feet. Vanessa stood for several minutes until finally the tingling had stopped and feeling came back to her legs. Her jeans were bunched up and slightly askew so, hooking a thumb through one of her belt loops, she twisted them straight and that was when she felt something odd. She slid her hand inside the front of her jeans and realized her underwear had been removed while she was unconscious. Panic rose within her as she gingerly felt around, but was quickly relieved to feel nothing was sensitive. She then thought of the prior victims—none of whom were raped—and calmed herself further.

Once stable on her feet, Vanessa removed her long sleeve shirt and her skin seemed to tighten on her, wrapping her from the cold, rank air. She took her belt off as quickly as her numb fingers would allow and tied the end of one sleeve through its loop, pulling on it several times to be sure it was secure. Then, aiming for the boxcutter, Vanessa tossed her belt underhanded as if playing cornhole and held onto the end of her other sleeve. The belt floated through the air, coming down to slap against the side of the dresser, short of her target.

She thought of using her pants but the zip ties around her ankles wouldn't allow them to be fully removed. So Vanessa took off her bra and fastened it to the other end of the belt. She then went about tossing her makeshift rope at the dresser several more times until, finally, her bra rested squarely on the boxcutter. She yanked hard, sending the boxcutter onto the floor just a few feet from her. Then, scooching it over, she cut the ties from her ankles and stood free.

Her muscles were tight and achy so she quickly got dressed then grabbed one of the unopened gallon jugs of water and drank in long gulps. She splashed her face and neck to wash off the blood then carefully rinsed her swollen nose. Next up was the television. She yanked the plug from the power strip attached to a line of car batteries behind it and the room darkened, just the low wattage, single light bulb hanging from the rafters remained to light her way. Groping around the room, she found a large rock and proceeded to smash the TV screen and pummel the VCR. No one would be using those again. She closed her eyes and rubbed them hard with a finger and thumb, trying to scrub the images away.

Now, she had to get out of there. She knew she had to act fast; she had no idea when her assailant would return, but had seen what he would do when he did. She first looked for her boots, her socks and her jacket but found none of them so turned her attention to getting supplies. She took the remaining nutrition bars from the plastic bag he had left behind and stuffed them into her pockets and did the same with the boxcutter. She grabbed a long power cord from the dresser and looped it diagonally around her shoulder and chest like the strap of bullets on a gunner then eyed the stack of heavy water jugs with indecision. In her weakened state she both desperately needed that water, but also dreaded lugging it around. She impulsively grabbed two and dropped them by the door.

Vanessa stepped over to the shelves stacked tightly with VHS tapes on their sides. She tilted her head, reading the childish handwriting on a few of the labels. BRIGET 11/2006 ... NADALY 2/2007 ... STEFFENY 5/2007. She leaned back, scanning the hundreds of video tapes and realized they spanned over a decade. But before she could comprehend all that she had found, the scurrying of rats outside the room snapped her back to her search.

She turned her attention to the dresser but the top drawer wouldn't fully open. Realizing it was caught on something inside, she slid her hand in and pushed soft fabric down. She then eased the drawer open and found it jammed full of women's underwear. She held up a pair and, realizing they were soiled, rummaged through the rest. She did the same for the other two drawers, then opening the bottom one found what she'd hoped for—her underwear. She'd be damned if he had a trophy of her. She quickly put them on then stepped to the door.

Vanessa's sluggish brain did a quick inventory—food, water, boxcutter, electrical cord in place of a rope. But she knew from before that the tunnels were both dark and treacherous. She needed to be able to navigate them somehow and make sure she wasn't walking in circles. She hadn't found any compass or flashlight and, knowing she had to improvise, got an idea. She hurried back to the dresser and held one of the GoPro video cameras. Its screen was cracked so when she held the on button for several moments and it didn't turn on, she tossed it aside. She quickly grabbed the other one and, clicking it on, a bright light shone onto her sleeve. The battery was low but it would have to do, so she fastened its strap to her head and the light shined in front of her like a miner. She clicked it off to save the battery then grabbed a black magic marker lying next to the videotape sleeve and returned to the doorway. She took a few seconds and did all she could do. It would have to be enough.

Standing in the doorway, she looked left, then right, but each way was complete darkness. She knelt to grab hold of the water jugs when she heard a low mechanical whirring sound and the ground in front of her glowed in a dim, yellowish light. Vanessa slowly looked to her right and saw the shadowy front of a man's body standing in the middle of the tunnel. As her eyes scraped upward, she saw the light from a GoPro she knew was strapped to his head like hers. And dangling in the darkness where his face should have been were two green circles that she immediately recognized as night vision goggles. Vanessa's sluggish mind took a beat to register what she was looking at.

And in that moment, in that silence, dragons dwelled.

Then her tormentor said one simple word.

"Run."

Chapter Fifty-Six

G US KNEW THIS could be his last chance to find Vanessa's location in the tunnels and he wasn't going to miss it. There would be time for reflection afterward; time to figure out what he'd done wrong, what he'd missed, what he hadn't picked up on or dismissed too quickly. Why he focused on Taylor and fucked up because of it. But right now, he had to push those questions aside, stuff them away somewhere deep in the bowels of his subconsciousness to fester alongside his other anxieties. Right now, it was all about finding Vanessa—whatever it took—and finding her quickly. And the one person who knew her location was now very much within reach.

He and TJ left Charlie and the others outside The Mills to go to the FBI's Pawtucket Falls offices and interview the witness. Gus knew he had about two hours before the mercenary search and rescue team Charlie had called arrived. Gus and TJ pulled into the parking lot as TJ's partner, Tony, was parking his car. Tony had driven up from Boston to join them in the interview. The three of them climbed the steps and, as they reached the door, Tony handed each of them a sheet of paper.

"Here's the transcript from the kid's call into the hotline." TJ held the door open. "The agents that picked him up called me on the way. Apparently, he's got a video of him and Vanessa talking."

Gus looked over his shoulder at Tony as they rushed down the hall toward the interview rooms. "A video? What the hell'd he have; a bodycam?"

"I don't know; didn't see it. But they said it was dark and choppy so I had them get it to the lab then I called them from the car; told them the situation and that we needed it processed now. They're on it."

The three of them streamed into the interview room together, one after the other. The young man was sitting at the grey metal table in its middle and looked up as they entered. He wore a white baseball cap backward on his head and a wrinkled T-shirt with a large green Boston Celtics logo on it. Gus nodded to the agent standing beside the door for him to leave then the three of them sat. Tony turned on the recording device in the middle of the table and stated the date and time before gesturing to Gus.

"Kyle Doomers?" Gus asked, referring to the piece of paper.

"Yes, sir," Kyle answered, his voice hesitant, timid.

"Kyle, I'm Agent Wheeler, and this is Agent Jefferson and Blackford."

Kyle picked at one of his fingernails as he looked to each of the agents in turn.

Gus leaned forward and rested his forearms on the table to keep Kyle's attention. "We're with the FBI. Kyle, you're not in any trouble here. We just want to ask you some questions about what you saw at the club the night before last."

Kyle swallowed and licked his lips. "The missing agent, yeah."

"I understand you have a video of you and Agent Lambert speaking. Can you tell us how you got that?"

Kyle cleared his throat and nodded. "Yeah, I'm rushing a frat on campus. That's why I was at the club. The frat guys brought all us pledges there. One of the upperclassmen used his phone to record me talking to her."

"Did you know she was an FBI agent before speaking with her?"

Kyle's eyebrows squeezed together. "No. We were there for a pledge challenge. I was talking to her for that."

"You were talking to Agent Lambert as part of a frat pledge?" Gus asked.

Kyle nodded quickly as TJ interrupted with another question.

"What was the pledge? To pick up a girl?"

Kyle turned to TJ. "Not just any girl, the *hottest* girl. Whoever picked up the hottest one got a pass on the rest of the rush and was in."

"So, you hit on Agent Lambert." prodded Gus.

Kyle's eyes narrowed. "Yeah," he scoffed. "She's smokin'. I'd have won for sure."

"What'd you two talk about?"

"We didn't really talk. She just blew me off."

"What'd she say?" TJ interrupted. "Exactly."

The young man paused a moment. "First, all she said

was *not happening*. Didn't even look up from her phone."

That sounded like V to Gus. "Then what?" he asked.

"When I didn't leave, she showed me her badge and asked me how old I was. The frat guys know the bouncer so got all us freshman in without IDs so I kinda freaked. That's when she told me to go home and get some sleep."

"Is that all she said?"

Kyle nodded. "Yeah, so I started to leave then I saw her go in the door to the restrooms. And that's when I saw a guy follow her in."

"Did you get a good look at him? Can you describe him?"

Kyle's mouth scrunched up. "I didn't. When I talked to her, she was leaning against one of the posts so when she walked away toward the restrooms she was on the other side of it, and it kinda blocked some of my view. And the bar was dark and really crowded. By the time she hit the door there were already a couple people between me and her. And..." Kyle's eyes flicked to the table then back to Gus. "I was pretty drunk and ... well, I wasn't really staring at the back of her head when she walked away. But I did see the back of a guy go into the hall after her."

TJ pulled up a photo of Taylor on his phone. "And you're sure it wasn't this guy; the guy on the news."

Kyle perked up. "Hundred percent."

"But how can you be so sure?" Gus challenged. "You just said it was dark and crowded and there were people in your way."

"Because when the agent walked away, I still had two

drinks; mine and the one I bought for her. But I was scared if we were still there when she came back, she'd have us busted. So I ditched my drinks and we all got outta there."

"Kyle," Gus interrupted. "I don't follow."

Kyle stabbed his finger to the image of Taylor on TJ's phone. "*That's* the guy I gave the drinks to. He was sitting at the end of the bar by the restroom door."

Chapter Fifty-Seven

VANESSA WAS CROUCHED over, her head hunched down between her shoulders, one knee on the dirt like a track sprinter settling into their starting blocks. Her mind spun with thoughts about what to do but if watching that video for two days straight taught her anything it was that no one escaped doing what he told them to do.

"I said run," he whispered louder.

Vanessa felt her leg trembling beneath her and knew she didn't have the strength to fight him, to end this right now. But she had to do something; the only thing running would do was guarantee her a starring role in his next home movie. She took a silent inventory of what she had—electrical cord, water jugs, GoPro strapped to her head, boxcutter, energy bars, magic marker. The boxcutter was clearly her best bet, but how to get close enough to use it was the question. He stood about ten feet away, purposely out of reach. And he was too far for her to lunge at without some sort of distraction.

She replayed scenes from the videos in her mind and recalled how he asked one of the women if she was okay, if she needed anything; giving her false hope right before strangling her. He needed to dominate his victims. He needed them to be weak, for them to need him, to rely on him. To obey him. She needed to play to his ego, not hers.

With the fragments of a plan floating in her mind, Vanessa slid her left hand up the side of one of the water jugs and removed its cap. She took a deep breath and tightened her fingers on its handle, holding it by her side out of view. Then she began to slowly stand and, as she did so, she slipped her right hand into her pants pocket and flicked the blade out of the boxcutter. Steadying herself, Vanessa stood in the doorway, head down, eyes on the wall in front of her.

"Please," she whispered in the weakest tone she could muster. "I'm injured. I can't run." *You sick fuck*, she wanted to add.

"You can stand; you can run."

She heard the whir of his night vision goggles and out of the corner of her eye saw the green dots of light surrounding each lens rotate as he focused them on her.

"Okay, okay. I can do it … give me a sec."

She heard the low rumble of an exhale escape his lips.

"It's the hope that kills you," he whispered softly, as if to himself.

She staggered slightly to the side, bending over as she leaned against the doorframe closest to him and she saw him take a small step closer. Vanessa then began to slowly slide down the doorframe and he took two steps toward her, his hand outstretched to keep her from falling.

And that was when she went for it.

She snapped her head up to face him and flicked on the bright white light from the GoPro, blinding him through his night vision lenses. She then swung the open water jug in a wide arc with her left arm and heaved it his way. Water sprayed from it as it spun in the air and crashed down on his GoPro, knocking it askew on his head. Pulling the boxcutter from her pocket, she lunged toward him as he staggered backward and into the side of the tunnel.

Vanessa swung the blade wildly, hitting his lunging fists, his forearms, his meaty shoulders until he grabbed her throat and thrust her back against the wall. Stars filled her vision as her head bobbed with confusion and his grip tightened around her neck. His head was turned from the bright light so she took one last swing of the blade and landed it firmly into the back of his shoulder.

He craned his neck, turning his face upward in pain and groaned into the air as his hand slipped from her throat and he dropped to his knees. Vanessa staggered away from him and shuffled out of reach. Gasping for air, she looked back to the doorway of the room she'd been held in, then to her captor who was clawing his way to his feet. She had no idea where she was or how she'd make it out of these tunnels alive. But Vanessa knew one thing for certain. She would never do what he asked.

She turned from the doorway and the tunnel he'd told her to run down and, flicking the light from her GoPro off, slipped into the darkness in the opposite direction.

Chapter Fifty-Eight

G US AND TJ stood in the interview room, each processing what they'd just heard in silence, while Tony
sat at the table pulling up the case files from the system.
After showing the frat boy, Kyle, several other photographs
of Taylor and hearing the kid give the same response to
each—Taylor was the guy at the bar, not the guy that
followed Vanessa into the hall to the restrooms—they
concluded the interview and let him go.

"Gus, what the fuck?" TJ asked.

Gus didn't answer as he chewed through things in his
mind but it quickly became too much. He needed to talk it
through. These were the times he appreciated having Vanessa
as his partner the most. She was able to take the disparate,
seemingly random thoughts his dyslexic mind churned out
and turn them into coherent, actionable items. His eyes went
from the open door to TJ, then flicked around the agent's
doughy face as Gus tried to organize what he was going to
say.

"It's gotta be one of the bandmembers," Gus said at last.
"They're all over this. We have to figure out what we missed.
Anything that's not airtight needs to be chased down." Gus's
thoughts immediately went to Mick and of the Allied

Equipment and Repair service van creeping by the scene yesterday. He then thought of Rachel Connors by the restrooms caught on video and of how angry he got when she rejected him. Vanessa's words rang fiercely in his mind.

If he's our guy, we'll find that he felt dismissed, offended—insulted even—by these women somehow.

"Let's start with the drummer, Mick. We ruled him out because the residue found on the Connors woman didn't match anything on the list of chemicals provided by his company."

"That's right," TJ confirmed.

"But what if that chemical wasn't from his work? What if it's something he has in his basement or something that's where he holds the women? Like the coal dust under Hogan's fingernails."

TJ was nodding slowly. "Yeah, shit."

"And what about his alibis? Did we ever find him on the footage from the casino?"

"No," said Tony from his seat. "But we stopped reviewing it when we didn't get a hit on the chemicals."

"Get someone back on that now," Gus said to Tony. "We need to know if he was there." Gus thought a moment, "And get a BOLO out on him," he added.

Tony turned back to his computer with a nod.

"Now, what about the guitarist, Leon?" Gus continued.

"His girlfriend confirmed he was home with her and her daughter after his gig each of those nights," Tony said to his screen. "And we've got him on CCTV walking home alone the night Sadie Hogan was taken like he said."

"And the singer, Chris?" Gus pressed.

"Gimme a sec," Tony said as his fingers flew across the keyboard. "We took our eyes off him after we tagged Taylor for this so…" A few more key taps and Tony began to scroll a document across his screen before finishing his thought. "Lab found no match to the list of chemicals the museum provided."

"But, again, those chemicals could be where he's keeping 'em."

"And his partner verified what Chris told us," TJ added. "Chris was in bed each of those nights when his partner got home but, remember, that wasn't until about five a.m."

"So, basically, we've got no alibi for Chris."

"Well, both he and Mick told us that Mick gave him a ride home the night the Hogan woman was abducted," TJ pointed out.

"What time was that?" Gus asked.

Tony tapped a few keys on his computer. "Mick said it was around … eleven thirty or midnight. And Chris said…" Tony scrolled up a few pages. "Chris said they left early, around ten thirty."

"And we've got no one that puts Mick at home after that."

"That's right," TJ said.

"So, they both left somewhere between ten thirty and midnight but no one can put them at their houses after that." When neither answered, Gus continued, "The bartender, MJ, told us Taylor showed the Hogan woman the green room just before last call which is two a.m. So, we've got no eyes on either Mick or Chris for at least two hours—maybe more—before that time."

The room fell quiet as that realization hung in the air.

Gus's jaw clenched. "Fuck," he whispered. He looked to the others who were waiting for his direction. "Either one of 'em would have enough time to make it back to the club by then," he said. He then looked to Tony. "Get a BOLO out on Chris too. We need eyes on both these guys."

"But, Gus, Chris had no car," TJ said.

"I'll check with taxis and car ride services," Tony said, turning back to his computer.

"Mick did," Gus said, his confidence rising.

"But what about the physical evidence?" TJ asked. "The carpet fibers matching Taylor's van and the muddy boots we found at his place? If Mick or Chris is our guy then how..."

"Not sure," Gus interrupted, seeing where TJ was going. "But Taylor's been hosting band practices at his house for months and the band uses his van to haul their equipment. They've both had plenty of access to both those boots and the van for a very long time." His eyebrow flicked up, "Well, and hell, either one of 'em could've planted the vics' driver's licenses there too."

"But wouldn't we have seen either of them on CCTV footage going back into the club?" Tony asked as he tapped away at his keyboard.

Gus turned his way. "Not if they used the tunnels we wouldn't."

Chapter Fifty-Nine

V ANESSA HAD STUMBLED to the end of the tunnel, her hand on a wall the entire way for support. She didn't dare turn her GoPro back on as she tried to get some distance between her and her attacker. And, besides, she needed to use it sparingly anyway. After all, an old, broken GoPro likely bought used was an act of faith to begin with.

She had looked over a shoulder in his direction about fifty yards back before taking a turn in the tunnel and the height of the glow from his GoPro suggested he was standing where she'd left him, preparing to follow her.

She felt an opening in the wall to her right and, groping her way around in the dark, discovered she was at a three-way intersection where she could only go left or right. Her head throbbed, her body was sore from the fight, and her bare feet moved clumsily from the cold. She rubbed her hands together to try and get some feeling back into her fingers and felt the stickiness of fresh blood. She needed to see which way to go so crouched down low and flicked on the GoPro.

To her right was a long, straight tunnel for as far as she could see. But she knew she couldn't outrun him, not in her weakened state.

She looked to her left and discovered that tunnel had partially collapsed at some point, one side of its ceiling now stacked in rubble on its floor. There was a small opening on the other side but as Vanessa peered into it, she saw the tunnel had also collapsed farther in. Passage seemed possible but it would require time and care to make it through safely.

She stood, leaned against the wall to rest a moment and flicked off her GoPro. And as her battered mind started to assemble what to do next, she heard a shuffling noise coming from the tunnel she'd come down. She crept to its opening and saw a faint glow far in the distance like that of a looming sunrise.

Vanessa needed to act fast if her half-baked plan had any chance of working. She pulled an energy bar from her pocket and carefully tore the top of its wrapper off to expose just the edge of the bar. She then walked several feet into the other side of the new tunnel and dropped the piece of white foil wrapper onto the floor. Careful to step where she had previously, she backed out of that tunnel and headed for the debris in the other side. She took the electrical cord from around her torso and, crouching, swept it side to side to wipe away her footprints as she backed up to the rubble. She then squeezed her slight frame through the narrow opening she'd looked in before and slid into an air pocket in the pile of debris the size of a small doghouse. And she waited.

The stones and packed dirt encasing Vanessa acted as a cooler, sealing her in the dampness and bitter cold of the tunnels. She wrapped her arms around her torso and crouched into a fetal position as best she could in the cramped space, trying desperately to conserve much needed body heat and energy. Her feet and hands had gone numb long ago and she could feel the coldness slowly making its way up her extremities.

Vanessa clenched her jaw to keep her teeth from chattering as her body began to shake uncontrollably. She pulled her arms tighter around her midsection and kept her eyes trained on the opening in the rocks. She thought she heard shuffling from outside in the tunnel and was about to lean over and take a look when the pocket she was in lit up with white artificial light. She pushed herself back as far away from the opening as the tight space would allow.

The light became brighter, more intense as shadows from the rocks and rubble were cast onto the ceiling of her space. She heard the crunch of approaching footsteps and the sound of labored breathing so close she saw tiny plumes of dust pulse off the rocks of the opening.

Vanessa held her breath as the fear of being found shredded her insides. Her mind raced for ideas of what to do, how to fight him off from that tiny space but she knew it was impossible. She could punch at his groping hands and swing at him with her box cutter but eventually she would lose her energy and her will. And he would have her. She eyed the smaller opening at the back of her space and tried to size it up but her blurred vision and exhaustion made it difficult. She might be able to fit through it, get deeper into the rubble, but there was no way she could do so before he could grab her legs and drag her to him. And even if she could beat his lunging arms, she had no idea what she'd be sliding into.

There could be an unencumbered tunnel beyond the narrow opening or an even tighter space in which she would be trapped for good. But to Vanessa, even that fate was better than succumbing to him.

Her eyes locked on the hole leading farther into the rubble, Vanessa steeled herself to act. And just when she was about to uncoil her arms and legs, the light flicked away and she was left in darkness. She cautiously leaned forward and peered out to see her attacker slumber his way toward the other side of the tunnel, guided by the bubble of white light in front of him. She watched as he paused then knelt and picked up the corner of the shiny white foil wrapper from the energy bar she'd left on the ground. He held it up to the light then, after inspecting it for several seconds, turned off the video camera and the tunnel once again went dark.

Vanessa held her breath, praying he would take the bait and continue down that way. And after several moments, her prayers were answered when she heard the whir of his night vision goggles click on followed by the sound of his fading footsteps.

Chapter Sixty

THE ENERGY LEVEL in the interview room spiked as TJ and Tony began talking over each other, listing out all that had to be chased down. Charlie called to let Gus know the special search and rescue team had arrived and was ready to head into the tunnels. Gus thought about how the case had shifted on him and of how Mick and Chris were back in the frame so he told Charlie to send the team into the tunnels without him. With his frustration rising, he looked to the Vanessa timer on his phone.

27:12:11 … 27:12:10 … 27:12:09…

With TJ and Tony squawking at each other, then to others on the phone, the circus in Gus's head was in full-on chaos—monkeys screeching, elephants trumpeting, acrobats spinning in midair. He needed to find someplace quieter so he could think things through. So he left the interview room and, with nowhere specific to go, began to walk the halls. He couldn't get the thought of Mick and Rachel Connors's interaction at the Blue Agave out of his mind and of how the bartender MJ had said that he hit on any woman with a pulse. And Gus knew it was Mick in the van yesterday checking out the scene. He knew, technically, that both Mick and Chris were still suspects, but his focus was squarely on the drummer. He still didn't think the singer Chris had it in him to abduct and murder women but the question was: did Mick? There was no doubt in Gus's mind that he was a womanizer and Vanessa's voice in his head calling him a narcissist with sociopathic tendencies had him now believing he was capable of murder as well.

Gus had been walking for several minutes and found himself passing a small room with an agent sitting in front of a large flat screen television with what looked like a movie being fast-forwarded on it. The television was muted and the agent had tiny wireless earbuds in his ears as he stared at the screen. Gus stepped into the room and the agent looked up and nodded a hello then looked back to the screen. After a few moments, the agent stopped the video, ejected a bulky VHS tape from the player beneath the screen, then inserted another one and began the process all over. Gus looked at the stacks of identical black tapes piled on the table, each with the name of a movie handwritten in black Sharpie on the white label along its spine.

"Are these the tapes from the Taylor Franklin search?"

"Yessir," the agent answered, taking an earbud from his ear.

Gus motioned to the screen with the scenes flickering by. "You're not watching them at regular speed or listening?"

"No sir. Fast-forwarding them for the first thirty minutes or so to make sure they are what's written on them." He held up his earbud. "Latest playlist to pass the time."

Gus's phone buzzed with a call from TJ so he tapped the speaker button to answer it.

"What do we got?" he asked anxiously.

"Lab's still working on the video the frat kid took so I asked them to send it to both of us when they were done. I also had 'em hold off for now on testing all the chemicals we got from Taylor's house."

Thinking of chemicals, Gus asked, "What's the name of that chemical again? The one found on Connors?"

"Let's see…"

While TJ was getting the name of the chemical, Gus's eyes went to the television screen and he flinched at what he saw.

"What the fuck was that?"

Seeing his reaction, the agent turned from Gus and his conversation with TJ back to the screen and paused the tape.

Frozen on the screen was a scene with Morgan Freeman sitting in the reception area of a police station staring at the large round clock on the wall.

The agent turned the cardboard VHS slipcase toward him and read the writing on its label. "This is the movie *Kiss the Girls*. That's Morgan Freeman and…" He looked to the face of the VCR. "That's forty-one minutes into the movie, sir. I was a little distracted so it's gone a little longer than the others."

"Can you rewind this slowly, frame by frame?"

"Sure thing," the agent replied.

He placed his hand on a large dial beside the keyboard and began turning it counterclockwise and Gus saw the tape rewind in a jerky slow-motion on the screen.

"Okay," TJ's voice came from Gus's phone. "I'm going

to have to quote this so I don't get something wrong. Says here, quote, they ran the residue found on the victim's body through their gas chromatograph and found an odd peak that resolved as p-tert-octylphenoxypolyethoxyethyl alcohol, unquote."

Gus waited for more and when it didn't come, he grimaced. "TJ, what the fuck *is* that?" he asked, exasperated.

"Let's see what Google has to say," TJ replied.

Gus leaned over beside the agent.

"You see what you wanted, sir?"

"Not yet. Can you go a little quicker. I saw something when it was fast-forwarding so I don't think we're going to miss it if you go faster."

The agent did as Gus asked and quickened his pace a second time at Gus's further urging. The tape was rewinding at close to regular speed and after nearly a minute Gus saw the close-up of a woman's bluish face, her jawline and bruised neck filling most of the screen.

"There," he said, and the agent stopped rewinding it on that frame.

Gus leaned closer and looked at the grainy screen for a moment. He had seen *Kiss the Girls* dozens of times and knew it didn't have any scene this gruesome in it. "Rewind it back until you get to a different scene then play it with sound at regular speed from there."

"Okay, here we go." TJ's voice rang from Gus's phone. "Says it's an active agent in a product called Photo-Flo."

"Never heard of it," Gus said. "What's it used for?"

"Hold on."

"Here we are," the agent beside Gus said.

Gus turned back to the screen as it began to play. He and the agent watched as Morgan Freeman arrived at a police station then the scene flickered and jumped to Michelle Townsend getting strangled in a dark tunnel. They heard the throaty gasps and Gus's eyes narrowed, bewildered when she called Taylor's name, begging for it to stop. Then the scene cut back to Morgan Freeman entering the station.

"Okay, you can buy it on Amazon," TJ said from Gus's phone. "Let's see ... product description ... product information..."

Gus leaned over and picked up the cardboard sleeve for this VHS tape and looked at its cover. It was a Maxell brand tape and, as the agent had said before, the label on its front read *Kiss the Girls*.

"Says here," TJ continued, "that Photo-Flo is used to remove water stains from old photographic film."

Gus turned over the cardboard case and printed in large lettering on its back was the name THE MEMORY GARDEN.

Gus's head spun as he recalled talking to the confident, helpful Leon Sampson sitting on the stage just a few nights before.

Every musician has a day job ... I'm a technician at a place called The Memory Garden ... We restore and convert analogue audio and video to digital; VHS, Beta...

Gus held his phone close to his mouth, alarm rising with his voice.

"TJ, it's Leon! Leon's our guy!"

Chapter Sixty-One

G US HUSTLED BACK down the hallway and when he got
to the interview room both TJ and Tony were standing
beside the table, waiting for instructions.

Gus looked to TJ first. "Get an arrest warrant going for
him." Gus told both of them about the murder scenes
spliced into the video he and the other agent discovered and
of how the VHS tapes were from The Memory Garden,
Leon's place of work.

TJ stabbed at his phone and stepped to the corner of the
room to make a call. Gus looked to Tony.

"I'll get an APB out on him," Tony said. "From
memory, he doesn't have a car, but I'll put one out on his
girlfriend's, just in case."

"And I told that kid looking at the videos to start over,"
Gus said. "He's to watch every second of each of those videos
and document anything unusual he sees or hears. Bang on
him to get it done right."

Tony nodded then pulled out his phone. "I'll go sit with
him after I get the APB going."

Gus's mind was spinning with what else they could do to
get to Vanessa quicker.

TJ ended his call and turned back to him. "We should

have the arrest warrant within the hour."

"You hear back from the search team at all?" Gus asked.

TJ simply shook his head.

Gus looked at the time on his phone. "Okay, it's quarter to one. Leon keeps pretty rigid hours at work so he's probably there. Get me that number."

Three minutes later, there was an APB out for Leon and his girlfriend Sheila's 2017 Honda Civic, and Gus had spoken with Leon's boss. Leon was due back from lunch soon. So, Gus and TJ left Tony to bang on the agent with the videos, chase down a search warrant for Leon's place of residence, and to push the lab on the video the frat kid took. Gus knew he had Leon with what they already had, but also knew there was nothing like watching someone in the act on video. Gus called Jeff during the drive to let him know they had the arrest warrant in process and brought him through all they had learned to get them there.

"Jesus, Gus, this feels like Lucy with the football," Jeff bitched. "How'd we not lock in on this guy from the start?"

"He's got alibis for each night, for chrissakes." Gus looked to TJ who was nodding. "And we have him on CCTV footage walking home the night the Hogan woman was taken."

"Well, and remember," TJ added, "everything lined up for Taylor; the boots, his van in the CCTV footage, he was with two of the three vics the nights they were taken, and he had *no* alibis."

"Don't forget the visions of the murdered women and their voices in his head," Gus added.

"Yeah, well, there's that," TJ confirmed.

"And I think we know how those images got into his head," Gus added.

He told Jeff of the spliced-in scenes they'd seen in one of the VHS tapes confiscated from Taylor's house and why they believed it was made by Leon.

"You know where he is?" Jeff asked.

"Yeah, he's at work. His supervisor said he left to run an errand but should be back within the hour," Gus answered. "Headed there now."

"Expect any trouble?"

"Not taking any chances," Gus said matter-of-factly. "We've got three cars meeting us there. He's not going to take on eight of us."

"He might go for suicide by cop," Jeff retorted.

"Not gonna happen." Gus shot back. "We're almost there. Call you when it's done." Gus jabbed the red circle on his phone's screen with irritation.

He knew Jeff was frustrated and getting heat with how this case had gone, but Jeff was especially skilled at covering his own ass in situations like this. And if this all went tits up, he'd be reading those same words from Jeff in the official inquiry.

Gus then called Detective Amy Boyd as a courtesy and caught her as she was heading out of the precinct for lunch. He told her of them confirming Leon Sampson as their suspect and that they were on their way to his work to make the arrest. She told Gus she'd have a few cruisers patrolling the area for additional back up and that she was on her way to join them.

Gus arrived at Leon's work ten minutes later but, before parking, circled the block slowly. He scoped-out alleys and other potential exit routes in case Leon were to make a run for it and passed two cruisers as he did so. He parked at the end of a row of cars on the side street and had a clear line of sight to the building's entrance.

There were two exits to the parking lot on opposite corners, one on University Avenue and the other in front of his truck on Gershom Avenue. Gus had one car of agents park in the parking lot opposite the door to the business, with the other two cars positioned along the streets just outside the entrances to the lot. This would allow them to spot Leon when he approached, while also allowing them to surround him for the arrest as he tried to enter his work. Once that was done, Gus turned to TJ to say something but before he could the back door to his truck opened and in hopped Amy.

"That was fast," he said. He met her eyes in the rearview mirror.

"Didn't wanna miss all the action."

Gus heard a helicopter fly overhead so craned his neck to look up through the windshield. Seeing it was a Pawtucket Falls Police Department copter; he raised an eyebrow in the mirror to the detective.

"They were already out and over Methuen." She shrugged, holding up a black portable radio. "I just had them take a spin by in case we needed them."

"I got eyes on the suspect," one of the agent's voice squawked from Gus's radio. "He's walking west on University toward the building, just passing the Dunks. He's wearing jeans, a gray sweatshirt and has a plastic shopping bag in each hand. He just crossed the street, approaching the café." There was a short pause. "He's coming up on the edge of the parking lot now."

"All agents, this is Wheeler. I'll approach on foot. When I give the signal, close off all exit points and surround the suspect. But I want no fire. Repeat, no fire."

The three of them hopped out of his truck and stood by its hood. "You two get positioned in that corner over there." Gus said, pointing to his right toward the back corner of the lot. "If he somehow makes it between me and the agents in the car, he'll head for that low spot in the fence."

Gus waited for TJ and Detective Boyd to get in position behind parked vehicles then casually entered the parking lot and, as he did so, he saw Leon walking in the far entrance. Leon was staring at the ground in front of him as he headed toward the front door of the business. After five or six strides he pulled up and looked around, as if feeling eyes on him. And he looked right at Gus.

Gus watched him carefully for several seconds, wondering what was going through the guitarist's mind. When Leon made no move—to run or otherwise—Gus raised his arm high in the air and rotated his finger round and round. The agents parked in the lot sprang from their car; their guns aimed directly at Leon. The two sedans came rushing into the parking lot from the streets, sirens blaring, and parked diagonally across the entrances. Agents spilled from each and, leaning on open doors, trained their weapons on Leon.

TJ and Amy came striding into the lot side by side with weapons drawn, stopping between Gus and the other agents to form a semicircle around their suspect. And, as if on cue, the Pawtucket Falls PD helicopter swooped in and hovered overhead, the whooping of its blades and engines drowning out the noise of the city around them.

Gus lowered his arm then followed Leon's glance up at the building. The windows along that side were filled with faces glaring down at the FBI agents and the commotion and the guns, while others looked in surprise to the helicopter above. Leon turned his attention back to Gus and as the flashing red lights washed over them both, dropped his bags to the ground as the agents surrounding him cautiously closed in.

"On your knees!" one yelled.

"Hands behind your head!" another called.

Leon slowly raised his arms and laced his fingers behind his head before dropping onto his knees. One of the agents holstered his weapon then pushed Leon's head down as he twisted one of his arms around and behind his back. And as the agent slapped the handcuffs on, Leon raised his head and looked over to Gus once more.

And Gus saw a wide smile spread across his face.

Chapter Sixty-Two

VANESSA LET AN entire year pass, or just a minute; it was impossible to tell in the tunnels. Then her world began to speed up and she could feel her emotions clambering at the gate before getting the best of her. She began to cry; sadness and despair overtaking rage and determination, if only for an instant. She felt as if all was ending, certain the world outside these tunnels was ablaze in a fiery hell. Laughter, joy, happiness, hope; all consumed with only ashes left behind. Life became insignificant; a flicker between two worlds of eternal darkness.

After some time, she scorned herself then dragged her ragged body through the narrow entrance of the hole and slithered over the rubble like a seal sliding into water. The tunnel floor was hard and cold and the dirt pressed against her cheek like an icepack. She rolled onto her back and bent a leg up to her chest. Then, releasing it, did the same with the other one. She needed to get the blood flowing in her arms and legs, but the longer she stayed on the dirt floor the stiffer she felt. She rolled onto her stomach and, pushing herself up onto all fours, stared into the dark tunnel ahead. She knew a monster was there, lying in wait for her. A ravenous monster, hungry for her, slithering in the shadows.

She felt him all around her.

She used one of the walls for leverage and slowly got to her feet. Her body was shivering and she could tell her breathing had become slow and shallow. She tried doing squats to improve her blood flow but as she began to crouch down one of her legs gave out and she fell clumsily against the wall. She got herself back to a standing position and settled for bending each leg at the knee.

Vanessa felt drowsy still and the lack of energy frightened her. She knew the shivering and numbness in her arms and legs were the early signs of hypothermia and that drowsiness and low energy were alarming signs that it was progressing quickly. She needed to move, primarily to get the blood flowing in her extremities but also to get as much distance as possible between her and her attacker while she could still walk. If she was overtaken by hypothermia, Vanessa knew she was in for bouts of confusion, a significant deterioration in her energy level, and coordination and, ultimately, loss of consciousness leading to death. And if she was going to die down there, it wasn't going to be where he could find her.

She felt her way along the wall until she came to the opening of the tunnel she had come down. She thought of the room she'd been held in and did a quick inventory of its contents but came up with nothing she could use to cover herself or get warm with. She then considered which way to go and realized there was only one choice and it was not a great one. She didn't have the energy to get through the rubble behind her, even if that second hole did lead to an open tunnel and not just more crawl space. And she couldn't risk going the way her assailant went; if she collapsed in the tunnel, he'd easily find her. She would have to go back the way she came.

Vanessa knew going back past the room would be going the way her attacker wanted her to go to begin with, which meant she'd likely be headed deeper into the tunnels. But then Gus entered her mind and two thoughts rose to the hazy surface. The first was that, knowing Gus, he'd have bugged the shit out of those NPS rangers until they got their entire roster in these tunnels looking for her. So, she would head that way—the way that sick fuck wanted her to—and she would pray she found either an NPS ranger or a private place to die before he came for her.

Then her cracked lips parted in what would barely pass for a smile as she played with the second thought she had about Gus. If by some miracle she did make it out of these tunnels alive, she'd set about changing her contact photo in his phone to popular final girls.

Having settled all that, Vanessa began to shuffle down the tunnel only to realize the tight space all around her conspiring to give her away. The dirt crunched beneath her feet; the walls amplified her heavy breathing. Everything she did, every movement she made, a betrayal.

Cautiously pushing on, Vanessa's misfiring mind went to the last change she'd made to her contact in Gus's phone, and the opening verse of Taylor Swift's "Shake It Off" began to play in her head. Vanessa was not only decidedly not a Swiftie, she'd openly scorn the artist's music if it came on the radio in Gus's truck. But as she kept plodding forward, her steps fell into a cadence along with the song and she realized that its upbeat melody was helping her continue to keep moving forward.

Once she made it around the bend in the tunnel, Vanessa saw the faint light of the lightbulb spilling into the tunnel from the room straight ahead. Then, once at the door she peered inside to make sure she hadn't forgotten anything she could use as a blanket or to put on her feet but she had not. Her eyes went to the marking she'd made beside the door on the inside of the room and her hand fell on the marker still in her pants pocket.

Vanessa then pushed herself straight and, steeling herself once more, turned into the dark tunnel. And as she slid her bare foot forward along the dirt, taking her first step, she began to sing along with the song in her head.

I stay out too late. Got nothing in my brain ... ooh, ooh, ooh, ooh.

Chapter Sixty-Three

T J HANDED GUS a manila folder. "Here's the deep dive you asked for on Leon Sampson."

The arrest and processing of Leon had taken over two hours, each second passing in Gus's head like the gong of Big Ben. The Vanessa timer was now just below twenty-one hours.

Gus flipped it open. "Anything of note."

"Unfortunately, a sad but familiar story. Single mom, multiple jobs, Leon being the oldest of four forced to take on the role of father." TJ tipped his head toward the papers in Gus's hand. "Mommy dearest has several drug arrests and one for prostitution." Gus looked to TJ for more. "There's a note in the file; vice guys said she wasn't a pro. Then Leon got nabbed for dealing and did nine up at Berlin." TJ finished, referring to the federal prison in Berlin, New Hampshire.

Gus flipped a few pages in and came to a glossy eight and half by eleven photograph of a dark brown leather belt coiled on top of an evidence baggie. It had an ornamental metal buckle so Gus rotated the folder to get a closer look and realized it was an exact replica of an old Maxell cassette tape. His eyes were drawn to the oversized *X* in its name.

"We think that X in Maxell is what left those odd marks on the victims' necks," TJ offered. "If you turn the belt around and run it back through the loop there, you can easily slide it tighter and looser without the holes catching on the prong. We'll have the lab confirm it."

Gus studied the photo for another few moments then closed the folder.

"There's more." TJ handed Gus another folder, identical to the first. "The lab results of the evidence taken from Taylor Franklin's house." TJ poked his chin toward the papers in Gus's hand, urging him to take a look for himself.

Gus flipped it open and scanned a toxicology report, and he raised an eyebrow. "LSD?"

TJ nodded. "Looks that way."

Gus looked through the one-way viewing window at Leon who was sitting alone in the interview room. His legs were shackled together and his hands were handcuffed to a metal ring on the table. Gus had kept him alone to stew in his own fear and anxieties but, unlike most others, Gus sensed Leon had neither of these.

"What're ya thinking?" TJ asked.

Gus took a deep breath and exhaled. "He knows we need V's location. And he knows he's the only one that can give it to us." Gus thought a moment. "But he'll wanna talk, lead the conversation—all narcissists do." Gus turned back to TJ. "I think I'll just let 'im."

Gus joined Leon in the interview room and, once settled with his folders in front of him, leaned back in his chair. He let the clock on the wall tick off the seconds for nearly a minute—a minute he knew he didn't have—before speaking.

"How old were you when this all began for you?" Gus asked, breaking the silence.

Leon relaxed yet remained silent.

Gus tapped a finger on one of the folders. "You had to grow up early."

Leon gave Gus the ghost of a nod. "Every kid in the Falls grows up early." His face became remorseful, repentant even, or a nearly perfect imitation of these emotions, as if rehearsed before a mirror.

But his eyes said it all. He had vacant, lifeless eyes that swallowed the light like a black hole.

"Did it begin with Anne Marie Tompkins?" Gus asked, referring to the teenaged girl's remains found in the tunnels. "Or are there other victims that we don't know about?"

Leon's face relaxed and his demeanor shifted. "Anne Marie was the first."

Something in his voice told Gus there was more.

"Nine," Leon added, interrupting Gus's thoughts. "I was nine when I started watching them."

"You watched them through their windows at night, fantasizing," Gus said with confidence. "The daughters or the mothers?"

"Both. But I had my favorites."

"Were all your fantasies sexual?"

"Aren't most young boys'?"

"What happened with Anne Marie? Why was the sexual fantasy no longer enough?"

Leon smiled. "Careful, agent, you're punching above

your weight class now. You're trying to understand things that are profoundly beyond your comprehension."

Gus leaned back and draped an arm over the back of his chair. "Try me."

Leon leaned forward, his face hardening as if irritated that Gus had asked. "What I experience is far beyond anything that could be described as fantasy. You simply wouldn't understand. My body absorbs the universe around me. It's as if my bones are the conduit for electricity, igniting my nerves to experience things on an existential level. My vision becomes sharper, heightened; sounds and colors more vibrant. The physical world becomes irrelevant. Satiating my needs is *all* that matters. Once you cross that metaphysical line, nothing can hold you back. Not our misguided laws or social norms, risk of punishment or retribution, fear of death, or even damnation. Those constructs are as meaningless as the life you're about to take."

Gus maintained eye contact as the room fell quiet, the hum of the fluorescent lights filling the void.

"Why did it become violent with Anne Marie?" he asked finally. "Why was she different?"

"She was mine." Leon's tone was dismissive.

"But why not take others? By your logic, they were *all* yours. Was it because she chose Taylor over you?"

When Leon remained quiet, Gus took a different tact. "You admit to sexual fantasies from the age of nine, yet you killed Anne Marie when you were, what? Sixteen? Seventeen? Do you remember when your fantasies became steeped in violence?"

Silence.

"It had to have been sometime during that period. How did you satisfy those violent tendencies if Anne Marie was your first?"

"I had my toys."

"You broke into their homes," said Gus matter-of-factly.

"Yes."

"What did you take?"

"Underwear." Leon's lip bent upward slightly. "I'd go through the hamper."

"Did you assault them? Rape them?"

Leon's eyes narrowed. "Agent, you don't *taste* the flesh."

"Where did you keep the underwear?" Gus asked. He tapped the folder again. "I've seen the file; your childhood home was very small. Weren't you worried your mother or brothers would find them?"

Leon's face flushed into a sinister smile. "Everyone needs a nook."

Gus tilted his head slightly but when Leon didn't explain he moved on. "What was it like, the first time? How did you feel?"

"It made me ill. The sounds, the smell. I was in a fog for days; couldn't sleep, couldn't eat. You're in a state of constant freefall. You've abandoned all morality and find yourself in an existential crisis you can't begin to comprehend. You've done something forever, something permanent. There's no going back. But as you come out of the fog you realize how freeing it is. You're no longer constrained by morals or societal norms. So you think—why not again? But this time, you'll do it right."

"Michelle Townsend."

"Yes."

Gus nodded slowly, as if just realizing something. "Your drug conviction. Nine years in federal prison. That explains the time gap between Anne Marie and Michelle Townsend." Leon didn't respond so Gus continued. "Tell me about Michelle."

"She reminded me of Anne Marie if she'd been allowed to grow older. Her cheekbones, her mannerisms. Her neck. She awakened me. I spent *a lot* of time with that one."

"And the others. Sadie Hogan, Rachel Connors?"

"What's there to tell? I wanted them."

"Do you speak with them?"

"Only at the end." Leon looked at Gus as if just now having a thought. "They seem to need that."

"They die slowly," Gus stated.

Leon's eyes closed partially as he offered Gus a single nod.

"Loosening and tightening your belt around their neck. Keeping them between life and death."

"Yes."

"How do you feel when it's done?"

"Rejuvenated. You could never understand how you feel when you see that light finally go out."

"No remorse or guilt. Or regret?" Gus prodded, his voice a whisper. Leon remained silent so he continued, "Where did these feelings you have toward women come from? The malice, the disgust."

"We are disgusted by that which we desire."

Gus saw the boredom growing in Leon's eyes and knew he needed to get to Vanessa's location.

"We saw your tapes," Gus said, changing topics. "The videos you made for Taylor."

Leon smiled.

"You spliced in scenes from the murders, and you had them call to Taylor, beg Taylor. And you laced his eye drops with LSD so he'd hallucinate and believe he was responsible for murdering those women." Gus paused contemplatively. "Why? Was it because of Anne Marie? Because he took her from you?"

"No," Leon dismissed. "I had Anne Marie when it counted. When her entire *world* was me."

Gus tilted his head. "Then why, why Taylor?"

"Do you know who was with me that night I got arrested dealing smack?"

There it was, thought Gus. "Taylor," he breathed.

"Taylor. But did I nark on 'im? No, 'cause my boy had plans. He'd scored himself a full ride to any music school he wanted. He was gettin' out. He wrote me every week while I was in. Dude was crushin' it. So, I do my time, thinkin' I too got plans. I'm gonna get outta this hell hole too, join 'im in NOLA. But then, what's the fool do? He comes back. He said it was just to get his mother in a home but three years later she's still with him. That's when I knew he was never leavin'. I did all that time inside for nothin'."

"So you set him up for the murders. To do *his* time," Gus said, now understanding it all.

"Everyone pays their tab eventually." They both fell quiet for several moments before Leon continued, "Ya know that boy actually thought he saw her the other night?"

"Anne Marie?"

A nod. "Looking in the garage window at our practice."

"You have anything to do with that?"

Leon's head recoiled slightly. "No, that boy's crazy-ass mind worked that up all on its own." His stare then became sinister again. "But I used it. She had a special locket with photos of her and her grandpa. It was special; never took it off. So, of course, I took it that night. And after T said he'd seen her I left that necklace in his house for him to find." The outsides of his lips eased upward. "Shoulda seen that boy crumble; straw that broke the camel's back."

Gus knew they were running out of time to find Vanessa; he could feel it. He glanced at the clock on the wall. It was coming up on six p.m. He instantly did the mental math; twenty hours left to find Vanessa.

He leaned forward, resting his forearms on the table. "Leon, where's Agent Lambert?" When he got no answer Gus continued, "You've punished Taylor. They don't think he'll *ever* recover, and if he does, he certainly won't be the same. His sentence will be the rest of his life. You've done it, Leon, you've won. It's not too late to do the right thing." He slowed his cadence, "Where's Agent Lambert?"

Leon also rested his forearms on the table, sliding his arms as far forward as the chains would allow. Gus saw bandages running up each forearm and knew they had to be from Vanessa. But as he was about to ask Leon about them,

Gus looked him in the eyes and knew he'd lost him.

"We're done here," Leon said, pulling his arms back until the sleeves of his sweatshirt covered them completely. "You've gotten everything you need from me."

Chapter Sixty-Four

THE LATEST NPS search-and-rescue team had worked through the night and into the better part of the morning yet had found no trace of Vanessa. Gus didn't need to look at the Vanessa timer to know he was running out of time but he did anyway.

3:11:43 … 3:11:42 … 3:11:41…

For Gus, however, time was no longer a tangible, linear concept. It had been engulfed in the raging flames of desperation.

He and TJ were outside The Mills beside the same bench as before, Gus pacing as he anxiously tried to decide what to do next. There are many types of silence, but what Gus felt at that moment was thickly marbled with apprehension and fear. His over-tired brain whirred with ideas and thoughts, each slamming into the next with brutal intensity. Gus had never truly considered that he wouldn't find Vanessa in time, never let his mind or psyche go there. So as he watched the timer tick off critical second after critical second a panic rose within him he'd never experienced before.

"We could squeeze Leon again," TJ suggested, interrupting Gus's anxieties, if only for a nanosecond. "Or maybe cut him a deal for her location."

"It's not about a reduced sentence for him." Gus snapped. He wiped his mouth with his shirt sleeve, searching the row of buildings for an answer, an idea—a clue even—for what to do next. "He's psychotic. It's about winning, about being smarter than we are."

A bright light popped on to Gus's side, washing the entire front of the club in a white light. He turned and watched as Christina Collins positioned herself in its center and gave her morning report on the story. He listened as she recounted the identification and apprehension of Leon Sampson as the Talent Scout. She spoke of the residue found on one of the victims being linked to him and of how the FBI had evidence he had been with each of the victims the nights they were taken. And while she got some of the finer details wrong, Gus was yet again impressed—and dismayed—with all she knew of their investigation. She gestured to the NPS team behind her and told her audience of the ongoing search for the abducted FBI agent being conducted in the tunnels beneath parts of downtown Pawtucket Falls. She concluded her report by referring interested viewers to her prior series on those very same tunnels then signed off.

Without saying a word, Gus headed over to speak with her. She and her cameraman Tommy were packing up their gear and, as Gus approached, he caught Tommy whisper something to her. She turned; arms folded across her midsection.

"Agent. I would've liked a heads-up to Mr. Sampson's arrest. I thought we had a deal."

"We do," he said. "It just all came together so fast." He

mentally moved on. "But time's running out to find Vanessa." Gus felt her eyes boring into him but not waiting for her to answer, he added. "I need your help." He unfolded the paper map of the tunnels the NPS lead, Charlie, had given everyone for their search. Gus laid the oversized paper on the ground and the three of them knelt down beside it.

"This is the map of the tunnels we've been using. It's not complete, but it's the best we have." He pointed to one of its sides. "This is beneath this line of buildings we're in front of here." He then pointed to the other side. "This is the river, here." Christina and Tommy leaned in over it as he continued, "The series you did on the tunnels a couple of years ago. Can you get the map that professor helped you make for it?"

"Sure." Christina used her phone and pulled up an archived story on her network's page then called up the map she and the professor had constructed for the story. She put the phone down in the center of Gus's paper so the three of them could see it.

"It's nowhere near as detailed as yours," she began. "Remember, we didn't do this to create a mapping of the tunnels per se. We were simply trying to estimate the scope of them."

"Doesn't matter," he interrupted. "I'm just trying to figure out what we could've missed."

"Well, for starters…" She pinched the phone's screen larger and moved it to the right. "You're missing the tunnel under the river and on the other side."

"I know. The NPS guys said the tunnel under the river's collapsed in spots so's not safe to enter."

"Well, and even if your partner is in there, it's going to

be tough to find her. We estimated that side to be about twenty, thirty percent of the overall tunnel system down there. That's about three, maybe four miles. But that is where a lot of the rooms are. We figured out that's where a lot of the moonshine was stored during Prohibition before being shipped out on the river."

"Your interview with the Sampson guy," Tommy said. "He say anything about a location or any hints at where she might be?"

Gus swiftly shook his head. "Nah." He then replayed his conversation with Leon as best he could in his tired mind. Leon's childhood, Anne Marie Tompkins being his first victim, his Peeping Tom activities, the underwear he took for his souvenirs. He leaned back onto his legs and looked at the other two, trying to replay that part of the conversation in his head.

"What?" Christina prompted.

Gus squinted at her as he tried to recall potentially critical details. "When he was a kid, he began watching women and girls a lot. When that was no longer enough, he started breaking into their homes and stealing their underwear."

"Souvenirs," Christina said.

"That's right. But he was just a kid and the house he and his three brothers and mother lived in was tiny. So I asked him why he wasn't worried about his mother or brothers finding the underwear he'd stolen and his answer sounded weird to me. He said *everyone needs a nook.* Maybe he meant a crawl space or his childhood home's near…"

Christina grabbed Gus's forearm and their eyes met.

She leaned closer. "Those were his exact words? *Everyone needs a nook.* You're sure?"

"Yeah," Gus said. "I remember because he said it in this sort of subtle singsong way."

Christina turned her phone so she could see its screen then pinched at it several times before turning it back around for the others to see. "Growing up, we had this small family-owned grocery store in our neighborhood owned by the Chronopolous's called The Nook. Its slogan was *Everyone Needs a Nook.* It went out of business years ago but"—she pointed to a small box on the map—"the building sits right on top of where that tunnel comes out on the other side of the river."

Chapter Sixty-Five

CHRISTINA TOOK HOLD of Gus's arm, quickly leading him through Music Row, over the crumbling cement bridge he and Vanessa had seen a few nights before, and straight into a densely populated street in Pawtucket Falls' East End neighborhood. The wind had picked up; its bitterness whispers of the coming winter.

They passed small, ramshackle houses, tightly packed together, until finally she slowed at a cross street and stopped in front of a small building on the corner. Gus saw missing clapboards, a broken window and a faded, tilted sign above its door.

"The Nook," he read aloud.

The front door was boarded up, and its cement steps had cracks weaving throughout like the map of a dense city.

"C'mon," Christina instructed. She briskly walked along one side of the building, navigating the broken and uneven sidewalk as if by muscle memory, until she came to a small alley at the back. "The back door's just around here."

They stepped over some garbage, around a small wooden box attached to the building broken on two sides, and past a toppled over pile of wooden pallets. The backdoor was boarded up like the front but Gus could tell someone had been entering the building by the gap in two of the boards. He pulled one to the side and realized it was attached with a single nail at the top which acted as a makeshift hinge.

Gus pulled out his penlight. "I'll lead from here."

He twisted through the narrow hole then held it open for Christina to do the same. The area they stepped into was dark, gloomy, and had the musty smell of mold and rotting wood. Shining his light around in a slow, wide arc he took in their surroundings. They were in some sort of storage or utility room. Along two walls were floor to ceiling metal shelving, its chrome coating rusty and flaked off in spots. The wall to their right had cabinets along its top and a countertop running its length with two deep sinks in the middle. Gus turned his attention to the far end of the room and its partially-opened door and moved that way.

"Careful where you step." Christina cautioned from behind. "A lot of these abandoned buildings are drug dens. Watch out for company or needles on the floor."

He carefully pulled open the door, and they stepped into a large space that had been the store. To their left was a row of silver coolers with faded stickers on their glass doors advertising sale prices of beer and soda. In the center were five aisles that ran from where they stood to the front of the store and beyond them was the checkout counter beside the front door. The face of the counter and wall behind it had papers with turned up corners taped to them advertising cigarettes, lottery tickets, and a variety of energy drinks and chewing tobacco.

Gus saw a doorway to their right on the back wall so

headed over to it, shining his light down each aisle as they went to be sure they were alone. He found a hall that ran to the back of the building, parallel to the room they'd entered through. It had a restroom door on the left that was held open by an empty liquor bottle and next to it was another, identical door with a plaque on it that read EMPLOYEES ONLY.

"That has to be it, right?" Christina asked.

Gus waved his light over the door and the sparkle of a shiny silver Master padlock caught his attention. It was looped through a latch at eye level locking the door closed. Five minutes later—after ransacking the store and finding a large screwdriver—Gus was back at the door frantically prying at the latch on its molding. The deeply-lagged screws took him several minutes but he managed to loosen it just enough. He then put his shoulder into the door several times until it finally splintered and swung inward.

Gus and Christina quickly made their way down the swaying stairs and into the basement. There were several unplugged, dingy-white freezers beside them, their moldy doors propped open, each empty. A line of shelving matching that in the storeroom held several rusty cans and empty jars and a stack of cardboard boxes were piled high in one of the corners. But Gus barely gave any of that a glance.

His attention was focused on the section of foundation held open by a large board, its open edge defined by the uneven line of stones. Upon closer inspection, he confirmed this door would blend completely into the wall around it when closed; someone had found a hidden door to the tunnels. He pulled the heavy door open wider and, using his light, peered inside. Gus then turned back toward Christina and nodded as he flicked the switch mounted just inside the door.

And they both looked down a seemingly endless dirt tunnel with large construction lights strung along its ceiling.

Chapter Sixty-Six

V ANESSA HAD BEEN slogging through the tunnels for hours and was physically and emotionally exhausted. She'd taken another water jug with her when leaving the room a second time but quickly realized she wasn't strong enough to carry it, let alone her battered body, for any real distance. So she ended up drinking as much of it as she could then dumping out the rest and hiding the squashed-up container beneath a pile of rocks she'd come upon. She had seen the fury on Leon's face when she knocked him back in the tunnel, the wrath. She had no idea when he would come back this way but knew he would. And, when he did, she certainly wasn't going to leave a trail of garbage in her wake for him to follow.

She got into the practice of turning the GoPro off to conserve its battery when she believed she was in a long, straight portion of the tunnels. But given the limited coverage of its light and her increasing disorientation, her assessment hadn't always been correct and she'd fallen hard several times and had the welts on her legs and forearms to prove it. The fatigue had become almost crippling and the constant nausea and blurred vision convinced her that in addition to everything else she was also battling a concussion.

Vanessa came to the end of a tunnel and the sight of it splitting into two caused her to sag against the wall in despair. Wandering around these tunnels aimlessly finding no one and no way out had decimated any confidence she'd had leaving that room. She shined the light from the GoPro into the opening of each and discovered she had been here before. Meager tears tiptoed onto her cheeks. Vanessa was not an emotional person; her early years in the inner city of Detroit had taught her what a liability that could be. But this had all become too much.

Any remaining energy she had drained from her as she realized she had been walking in circles; for how long, she couldn't be sure. Being immersed in the darkness in her weakened physical and mental state made Vanessa feel as if she'd entered a sensory deprivation chamber. Time had become a very elusive concept. But she had to keep going because she knew Gus would never stop looking for her. And that thought, that comfort, pushed her on.

Having gone right last time, she went left but after a few determined steps the tunnel dropped out from beneath her like a trapdoor. Vanessa collapsed in a heap, tumbling downhill for a good distance before slamming into a large rock with her head and shoulder. The darkness around her filled with sparkles of white light and she spasmed as she lay dazed on the cold dirt. The GoPro had fallen off so she groped around beside her with ragdoll-like hands until she eventually felt its hard plastic and picked it up.

She pushed herself into a slumped sitting position and a sharp pain exploded up her leg. Letting out a feral cry,

Vanessa fumbled with the GoPro but couldn't get it to turn on. Tears spilled onto her cheeks as she frantically slapped its side until finally the dim light blinked once, then twice, and stayed on. She hesitantly looked down at her leg to find the jagged end of a bone sticking out from her ripped jeans just below her knee. She gagged and lurched away, vomiting onto the ground beside to her.

Once finished, Vanessa gingerly wiped her mouth and leaned her head back against the cold stone. Her vision was blurry, and her head spun with pain and confusion. But she knew the pain was secondary, something to be squeezed into a box and shoved aside. The pain, the seemingly unsurmountable effort to keep going, was life. To give into it now was death.

She waved the camera's light around but only saw darkness beyond its narrow, fading halo. She had fallen into some sort of hole or cavern and had no idea what surrounded her. Her frantic mind turned to her injury.

She needed a tourniquet to stop the bleeding but couldn't focus long enough to figure out what to use. She gripped her leg tightly at the knee, trying to control the pain through gritted teeth but it only grew worse. Then, after a minute, the light on the GoPro flickered one last time and went out.

Alone and freezing in the dark, Vanessa felt a fear she'd never experienced before. She'd come too far, overcome too much, to die here; like a swimmer who swam across a raging sea only to die lying on the shore. She dreamed of walking out of these tunnels into a bright sunny day, of staring up into the hot sun—a sun that warmed her to her bones—like a child dreamed of becoming an astronaut.

Vanessa sat like that for many minutes before her fantasies were interrupted by a sound far off in the distance. She knew that hearing was the first of the senses to register in a brain when a person woke and the last to close down, so she would use that. She listened more intently until she heard the faint scampering of rats growing louder. She knew they could smell blood from miles away and the thought of them all over her drove her into hysterics. And in that moment, Vanessa truly understood what insanity felt like. She squeezed her eyes closed and her entire body tensed with terror.

But eventually the panic faded, as did the pulsing pain in her leg. And her heart rate slowed. And gradually, second by second, minute by minute, Vanessa felt herself slipping away. Until finally a calmness, a serenity, enveloped her.

And so too did the darkness.

Chapter Sixty-Seven

G US CALLED TJ to tell him about the entrance to the tunnels they'd found and sent him a pin with their exact location so the NPS team and EMTs could find them. He and Christina then quickly made their way down the long tunnel as it gradually brought them deeper and deeper underground. The last light hung at the bottom where the tunnel leveled out and opened into a small, tight space. The air was thick with humidity and the temperature had dropped considerably from that above ground.

The small area had stone walls and a dirt floor and, aside from some garbage, was mostly empty. There was an opening to another tunnel in the opposite corner so Gus went straight to it but, unlike the one they'd come from, it was completely dark. He peered over a shoulder at a wary-looking Christina.

"Not too late to head back up. Wait for the NPS guys," he said, nodding his chin back toward the lighted tunnel.

She held up her phone and Gus saw she was videotaping their trek. "Not a chance."

The two of them headed into the tunnel with the cone of white light from Gus's penlight leading their way. The height of its ceiling gradually lowered until Gus found himself bent over, shuffle-walking sideways like the Hunch-back of Notre Dame. Eventually, it spilled them onto a small stone landing with the entrance of another tunnel on the opposite wall. They could hear the rushing water of the river nearby and noticed the walls were no longer dirt but moss-covered fieldstone.

"We're definitely at the edge of the river," Christina said, stepping beside him.

He entered the new tunnel and after a few feet found that it turned hard to the left. They hurried for several minutes until they came to the opening of another tunnel on their left. Gus shined his light straight ahead, past the opening, and saw a pile of rubble.

"Looks like that way's collapsed." He stepped over to it and found a small hole in the pile of debris. Shining his light into it, he discovered a small open pocket with another hole at its back. He leaned in and aimed his light through the back hole but saw only more debris.

"Not sure this is passable." He stood and walked back to Christina. He gestured down the new tunnel. "Looks like it's this way."

They walked about a hundred feet or so when the tunnel bent to the right and, as soon as it did, Gus saw something far off in the distance. He squinted to get a better look then tapped his light off. And as his eyes adjusted to the darkness, he realized it was the dim glow of a light in the distance.

"Is that a light?" Christina asked, her words echoing off the old stone.

Gus tapped his light back on and began to quickly shuffle-run toward it. As they got closer, he realized it was coming from an opening in the side of the tunnel and stepped into the doorway to a small room. His eyes were drawn to shelves filled with VHS and smaller video tapes and tilting stacks of tapes on the floor beside them. He inspected the bulky, old television with its cracked screen and the smashed VCR on the ground beside it then his eyes fell on the armless chair positioned in front of them both. He picked over miscellaneous items on top of a dresser: a compact GoPro camera with a cracked screen, a bag of plastic zip ties, a roll of duct tape. He then opened the top drawer and discovered dozens of women's underwear and, opening the other drawers, found more of the same.

"What the..." Christina whispered as she slowly waved her phone over the entire room, getting it all on video. "Is this his kill room?" she asked.

Ignoring her question, Gus stepped to the chair and picked up a dirty cloth rag lying on its seat. It was wet with blood. He then knelt down and inspected a print in the soft dirt left by a small bare foot.

"Vanessa's?" Christina asked.

"Can't tell." He pointed to the broken arms of the chair on the ground and the cut zip ties beside them then held up the wet rag. "But I'm guessing, yeah. This blood's fresh." His eyes scoured the scene, hungry for anything to go on. "She broke out," he said, catching Christina's eye and nodding. "She's alive."

Gus took one last look around the room. Seeing no other exit, he went back to the doorway.

"But that means she's in these tunnels somewhere," he said as he looked left then right.

He pulled his phone out and tapped on the Vanessa timer.

1:41:37

He stared at his phone as the seconds ticked away and he realized his timer was an alien instrument down there. Time was fungible, porous even, in that environment, whereas his timer was a slave to precision, to order; foreign concepts in the tunnels' vast maze of chaos.

Gus quickly shoved his phone back into his pocket as Christina brushed up against his back, trying to see what he saw. "Which way do you think she went?"

"Not sure." He tossed the rag onto the floor then shined his light back the way they came. "We didn't see any other tunnels except the one we came down."

He swung his light around toward the left and, as he did, something caught his eye on the wall inside the room next to the door. He leaned over with the light to take a closer look and there on one of the stones written in harried, squiggly writing were the initials A.S.

Gus smiled and stood straight.

The wall lit up with light from the video on Christina's phone as she stepped beside him and, seeing Gus's smile, she asked, "What is it?"

"A-S. Arne Saknussemm." He turned to her and seeing her confusion elaborated. "Vanessa knows one of my favorite stories growing up was *Journey to the Center of The Earth* by Jules Verne. In the story, the first explorer believed to make it to the center was Arne Saknussemm and he wrote his initials in the dirt and elsewhere along the way so others could follow his path."

"She knew the killer wouldn't get that, only you would," Christina said, nodded slowly. "Genius."

"Yes, she is," Gus breathed, again taking a closer look at the initials. "They're written on the left side of the doorway." He gestured with his light to that side of the tunnel outside the door. "She went that way."

He and Christina went left and picked up their pace, driven by a renewed sense of urgency. They hiked through tunnel after tunnel, continually directed by Vanessa's sloppy and sometimes barely-legible writing. And as they ventured deeper into the tunnels, their world closed in around them, defined by the small circle of light by which they were led. Gus felt the shadows seething, as if alive, waiting for them to falter. And, step by step, time dissolved and he was left with an untethered feeling as if detached from the world around them.

Exhausted, they pulled up at a fork of two tunnels and Gus recognized where they were. He bent over and leaned against a wall to catch his breath.

"What is it?" asked Christina as she leaned next to him. The bright white light of her phone blinded him but he could hear the exhaustion in her voice.

"We've been here before," he said.

"How do you know?" She slowly waved her phone around in a wide arc to take in their entire location.

He pointed to the threshold of the tunnel on their right.

"That A-S is larger than the others. She went over it several times with the marker. I recognize it."

"Shit. We've been going in circles?"

Gus nodded—just once—as his confidence began to dissolve in an acid bath of fear and dread. He straightened his back and stood as upright as the tunnel would allow, his head remaining hunched over.

He was about to call TJ on his shortwave radio to check in with him when a buzzer echoed off the walls around them. He removed his phone from his pocket and read the message on its screen.

VANESSA TIMER COMPLETE.

His heart hammered in his chest and his vision narrowed. He grabbed the radio again to call TJ when it dawned on him—if he just realized they'd been walking in circles, there was a good chance Vanessa realized it here also.

"But if *we* know that..." he whispered, as if to himself. He looked into the other tunnel—the one on the left—and aimed his light into its opening but saw nothing noteworthy. He then took several steps in and, as he did so, saw a flat circular plastic strap on the dirt floor. He picked it up and turned it in his hands to see bright yellow lettering.

GOPRO.

His mind skipped back to the contents on top of the dresser in Leon's room—a bag of plastic zip ties, a roll of duct tape. A compact GoPro camera. He was holding a head strap to a GoPro camera.

Gus rushed deeper into the tunnel then held up as it fell away in a steep decline. Gripping a rock in the wall, he leaned over and waved his light into the darkness below and the first thing he saw was a bluish white bare foot protruding into the space from behind some rocks.

"Down here!" he yelled to Christina.

He turned and, hunching onto all fours, his hiking boots bit into the loose soil as he began to back down the slope.

"Wait! A rope," she said, stepping to the edge.

She aimed her light to the other wall and Gus saw a thick rope knotted around an iron ring near its bottom. The rope ran along the ground down the entire slope so Gus grabbed hold of it and repelled to the bottom in seconds.

He shined his light over Vanessa to see what he was dealing with. He noted the blood-soaked pantleg and her broken leg, cuts around her wrists and along her forearms, and smears of dried blood around her nose and mouth and in her hair. Light shined from behind him as Christina joined him, holding her light steady for him to see.

Dropping his phone, Gus gently slid his hand beneath her head and his palm became cold and wet. His heart pounded with fear as he felt for a pulse with his two middle fingers.

"She's alive," he said, his voice cracking. He leaned closer and whispered in Vannessa's ear. "Hey, V. Hey, can you hear me?"

Her head twitched but her eyes remained closed. Gus took the shortwave radio from his belt and called for help to anyone that was listening on the channel. TJ immediately responded and Gus told him how to follow Vanessa's initials on the rocks and walls and that Christina would be waiting for them. Christina climbed back up the tunnel using the rope and Gus could hear her speaking into her camera as he slid Vanessa partially onto his lap.

Gus unzipped his jacket and, wrapping it around her, held his best friend close to his body for heat. He spoke softly to her while he brushed hair from her eyes and dirt from her cheeks. And eventually, her eyelids partially opened but her eyes bounced left and right as they struggled to focus.

"Hey," he whispered with relief. "You scared me."

Vanessa blinked slowly once, then twice, then he heard her whisper.

"Boo."

She strained to swallow and her lips moved, but Gus couldn't hear what she was trying to say.

"Shhhh," he said. "Save your energy. EMTs are on the way."

But Vanessa's lips continued to move. Fearing she was trying to tell him something about Leon or maybe another victim, Gus leaned closer only to watch her eyes roll back in her head.

Epilogue

I T WAS A sunny Halloween afternoon, and Gus was in his truck having just come from spending the morning with Vanessa at Mass General Hospital where she'd been airlifted to after being rescued. He had helped the EMTs carry her stretcher out of the tunnels and had gone with her in the chopper to Boston. Gus then stayed at the hospital for several days afterward as she underwent surgery to repair the compound fracture in her leg and the doctors pumped her full of medicine to reduce the swelling in her brain. Then, when she'd finally come to, Gus made sure he was at her bedside and the first face she saw. Once the doctors had gotten her stabilized and she was lucid and speaking, she told Gus about powering on in the tunnels to Taylor Swift's "Shake It Off" in her head. So the next day, Gus went about decorating her room with bright pink Taylor Swift paraphernalia. She was bedridden and he was not going to miss this opportunity.

The news of the FBI catching the Talent Scout became an instant national story and, being a man of his word, Gus had given Christina Collins the exclusive she'd been promised. So when the video she'd taken of her and Gus's trek through the tunnels in search of Vanessa became the basis for a true crime miniseries dropped on Netflix, Christina's series on the hunt and capture of the Talent Scout was nominated for multiple journalism awards. Christina Collins had filed her last lifestyle piece for the foreseeable future.

But, despite the flattering press, all was not rosy inside the FBI. Dr. Morgan had filed a formal complaint detailing what she felt was an abusive, callous interview of Taylor Franklin by Gus. Her complaint and accusations had triggered the formation of a committee to investigate the matter. And having sanctioned Gus's interview with Taylor, Jeff Cattagio quickly became a target for those envious of his position and desirous of his office. But, in the end, Gus testified before the committee and took complete responsibility for both organizing and conducting the interview as he—and he alone—saw fit; hence, taking Jeff out of the crossfire. There was talk of suspension and even formal charges against Gus, but he and Vanessa had been hailed for their cunning abilities in apprehending the Talent Scout so no one on the committee could see their way to suspending—or worse, charging—its new-found face of FBI excellence. So, like so many other controversies at the FBI, this too got snared in bureaucracy and the news cycle inevitably churned onto the next story.

As with every investigation, Gus continued to tie up each loose end well past the apprehension of their offender to make sure their case was as tight as possible. He pushed the lab to reevaluate the surveillance footage they'd gotten outside The Loft the night Michelle Townsend went missing; the footage on which they believed they saw Taylor's van drive by. And, eventually, using facial recognition software they were able to confirm Leon was driving the van that night. Gus also went to see Leon's girlfriend, Sheila, and when pressed about the alibis she'd given Leon, she confessed that she had lied. Leon had told her those late nights were the only times he could safely sell pot to make the extra money they needed so she had trusted him.

Gus also visited Leon at the psychiatric hospital where he'd been committed for a ninety-day evaluation period to determine his competency to stand trial. Gus wasn't sure why he went; maybe to see if Leon felt remorse for all he'd done, or maybe just to get another peek inside the mind of a psychopath. But while the two of them met for nearly an hour—during which Leon did most of the talking—Gus took away just one interesting piece of information. Leon proudly described to Gus how he walked home from The Mills the night Sadie Hogan was taken, purposely taking streets that he knew had CCTV cameras to establish an alibi for himself. And of how he then used the tunnels to go back to the club and abduct the young woman, having slipped roofies into Taylor's drink beforehand so he'd not remember a thing. The rest of what Leon said amounted to nothing more than hyperbole and self-indulgence from a severely disturbed mind.

Gus parked his truck and hopped out into a cool autumn breeze. He looked up at the imposing brick buildings of the Sinclair Psychiatric Hospital where Taylor had been taken for care. But, unlike his visit to Leon, Gus wasn't there to take but to give; understanding, comfort, compassion, he wasn't sure. But he would give, nonetheless.

Gus had been headed up to Mel's to help her and Mr. T hand out candy to the trick-or-treaters that night when he impulsively took the exit off the highway to stop and see Taylor. So as he headed toward the building's entrance, his thoughts drifted to the next few days off with Mel and his hand fell to the outside of his jeans pocket and the ring box inside.

Entering the building, Gus checked in at reception and was quickly escorted by an older male orderly to Ward D where the incapacitated and restrained patients were held. Gus and his escort turned into the opening of a long, sterile white corridor with rooms on both sides and the orderly held up.

"He's in room four thirty-six." The man pointed. "Near the end on the right. They're still sorting out his meds," he added with an air of warning, then left Gus to his visit.

Each door had a large opening in its upper half and as Gus slowly made his way down the corridor he peered in at other patients along the way. He saw both men and women, some old, some tragically young. There were patients strapped to beds, while others sat in chairs mindlessly staring out windows. And as Gus approached Taylor's room, he heard angry whispers so held up and leaned beside the door.

"That's right, keep begging you fuckin' bitch. It. Felt. Gooood to kill you."

Gus peered into the room and saw Taylor sitting on the floor in the corner, panting as he picked at something on the tile beside him. He watched as Taylor slapped the side of his head then shook it uncontrollably side-to-side, drool flicking onto his shoulders. Gus leaned back away from the door and, lifting his face toward the ceiling, exhaled in sorrow. He couldn't bring himself to visit with Taylor, not while he was in that condition.

He pushed off the wall and as he began to walk back down the hall, he heard a low grumble come from inside Taylor's room.

"Die you fuckin' whore. Die."

Gus's jaw clenched and he forced his thoughts to Mel, and his hand slid back over the ring in his pocket. And just when he thought he'd made it out of earshot, an angry, sinister whisper crept along the hallway behind him.

"It's the hope that kills you."

The End

Acknowledgment

Writing this second book was an important goal for me to accomplish and, as with the prior novel, I certainly didn't achieve it alone. A huge thanks, as always, to my wife Lisa. Your wit and humor carried me through the challenging times, while your ideas and unique take on everything helped make this novel what it is. You are truly an idea machine. I'd also like to thank our son Sam, for your brutal honesty when something just wasn't working and for all your help to make the music scenes and Gus authentic and true to life.

To our daughter Mac, thanks for your daily encouragement and for making me look good (as good as possible) across my social media platforms—wonders never cease. To our son Gabe, your encouragement seemed to come at all the right moments and your humor hit all the right spots. Thank you. And to Avery Scripter, member of The Squad, the same. Our talks about writing, and mutual encouragement, are a blast.

To Jack Schafer, thanks for all the help with the technology aspects of this story and for helping me keep those details authentic. Of course, your positivity and faith in my ability to transmogrify the "techie stuff" onto the page helps a lot!

A special thanks goes out to two friends: Tony Harrington, for all your help in my search for the perfect title. You are my AI guru. And to Olaf Karstens. Who knew that doctorate degree in chemistry would one day lead you to the acknowledgements section of a fiction novel? Your help with chemicals and the testing processes used to identify them was invaluable.

A heartfelt thanks to my agent, Kathy Green. I am forever grateful to have you in my corner. And thanks to the team at Tule Publishing—Jaiden, Mia, Lee, Meghan, Kelly, Monti, and Heidi—for all of your support along the way. Finally, an enormous thanks to my editor, Sinclair. Thanks for all of your guidance, advice, and mostly, your unrivaled patience as I grinded this story into shape. You are a rock star.

If you enjoyed *Wings of Madness*,
you'll love the other books in...

Gus Wheeler FBI Thriller series

Book 1: *Karma Never Sleeps*

Book 2: *Wings of Madness*

Available now at your favorite online retailer!

About the Author

R. John Dingle was born and raised in New England. In fact, despite extensive travel, a move to Australia represents his only bragging right for actually residing outside the six-state area. John and his wife currently call a small island in Mid-Coast Maine 'home', both living, writing and boating from their restored 200-year old house (which they continually assure their three adult children is not haunted). The psychological thriller, Karma Never Sleeps, is John's first novel.

Thank you for reading

Wings of Madness

If you enjoyed this book, you can find more from all our great authors at TulePublishing.com, or from your favorite online retailer.

TULE
PUBLISHING